BLACKSPARROW

THOMAS ALAN EBELT

ISBN: 978-1-4834-1172-9 (sc)
ISBN: 978-1-4834-1174-3 (hc)
ISBN: 978-1-4834-1173-6 (e)

Library of Congress Control Number: 2014907962

Lulu Publishing Services rev. date: 6/9/2014

I dedicate this book to my wife Judith, whose wisdom and faith sustained me through the completion of this book. Thank you for your encouragement, insight, and patience.

Though there are references in this story to real things, places, and events, the facts are shamelessly twisted and stretched to suit my wayward imagination.

This book is a work of pure fiction, and nothing else.

PROLOGUE

April 1933
Lakehurst Naval Station, New Jersey

The giant dirigible *Akron* prepared to leave the ground with a crew of seventy-six at 7:30 p.m. in a thick and chilly April fog. With her astounding 785-foot length completely hidden from view in the gloom, her eight German-built Maybach engines fired one by one and soon purred smoothly, awaiting the commander's orders for liftoff. The powerful motors changed pitch, and like a moaning ghost, 240,000 pounds of Duralumin superstructure, miles of silvery cotton skin, and 6,500,000 cubic feet of helium took to the air.

Built in 1931 and christened the ZR-4, She was the largest aircraft in the world. Longer than two and a half football fields, her sleek cigar-shaped hull blotted out the sun when she passed overhead. She was truly a "ship of the air," and rightly called the "Queen of the Skies."

Because she used non-flammable helium for lift, the engines were mounted inboard, four to a side, adding to her sleek profile. The propellers swiveled 180 degrees to assist maneuverability. She was also equipped to carry five Curtiss F9C-2 Sparrowhawk fighters in her belly, launched and retrieved by a retractable trapeze.

In two years, the *Akron* had completed nearly five dozen flights, many of them cross-country. Tonight she was on a trip to Philadelphia, across Delaware, and then back north along the coast to her landing site. A distant storm lay low over the southeastern horizon. Her seasoned commander kept a wary eye on the weather. He was not concerned, however, believing that this short flight would come to no harm from it.

Safely in the air at a comfortable cruising speed, the skipper reviewed chart positions. He was Lt. Comdr. John A. MacAllen—just Mac to his junior officers. He recently turned fifty, and with a slight mustache, and gray at the temples, he looked every bit the seasoned naval officer he was. With his feet solidly planted on the slowly rolling deck, his pale eyes squinted watchfully into the darkness ahead.

"Would the captain like some coffee?" a quiet voice asked.

He gratefully accepted a steaming mug from the attendant making his way through the control car. He sipped the brew and shivered involuntarily. His uniform was made of heavy cloth, but tonight it barely kept away the damp evening chill.

His shoulders ached, and he absently pondered how he had recently made the mistake of complaining about it to his wife. He had endured days of her fussing and ministering, until he longed to escape to the skies again.

Ah, sweet Judith, he mused. She had stood beside him, uncomplaining, for twenty-four years, and what did she get for it? A grumpy husband and a big house that was too large since their son, Thomas, had gone away to college.

A sharp pain jabbed at his neck and shoulders, and he rolled his head in an effort to find relief from his flaring nerves. Later tonight, he would come home to a small light burning on the porch. His wife would be upstairs asleep. He thought of her warm body under the down blankets and flannel sheets. He would undress quickly and climb into bed. She would mumble something endearing, but unintelligible, as his cold skin touched hers. Then, they would nestle together like spoons, soon falling asleep, breathing slowly in unison.

Mac's grey eyes squinted from habit, peering into the distant horizon, ever watchful for any danger. His manner was calm, but the men knew, that beneath his relaxed confidence lay vast reserves of energy. He ran a tight ship, and rightly enjoyed the admiration and respect of his crew, most of who were handpicked and seasoned.

An hour later, they were drifting slowly over the lights of Philadelphia. The fog had cleared, and glowing dots formed patterns and designs beneath them in the darkness.

After another hour of randomly lit countryside, the skipper's shoulders became a throbbing irritation that no stretching could relieve. He took two aspirin with his third cup of coffee, noting his eyes were beginning to feel grainy, probably from the lack of a good night's sleep. He tried to shake it off, and thought of the warmth and comfort of his own bed waiting for him after a few more hours of flight.

The *Akron* responded smoothly to the powerful Maybachs as they brought the airship to a new heading. Soon the Atlantic coast came into view. They continued a short distance beyond it out to sea before changing course to follow the shoreline home.

Mac struggled to shake off his fatigue and shoulder pain, which was slowly enveloping him. He noted, with concern that the wind had picked up, and was brisk enough to cause the huge airship to roll lazily from side to side. His mind seemed to battle through a fog.

Realizing that they had encountered the edge of the approaching storm, he hoped they could outdistance its fury, and reach a safe mooring at Lakehurst. Then he fell unconscious to the deck, joining the others who had already succumbed to the drugged coffee.

In the galley, a dozen grim crewmembers exchanged furtive glances. One smugly checked his watch, and then nodded to the others to put down their serving trays. They did not look or act like newly assigned crew now, they behaved like a well-seasoned combat team. For over an hour, they had served gallons of drugged coffee to the crew, making note of any who refused the drink. Now they sought them out and disabled them with forced injections. A few fought back, but were quickly subdued. With the last of the crew drugged or unconscious, a small contingent of men entered the control car and took over command of the *Akron*.

The new skipper took the controls and ordered a course change. If any of the dispatched crew could have heard his voice, they would not have understood the German dialect.

The *Akron* sailed farther out to sea, buffeted by the winds of the approaching storm. Small teams removed the bodies of the unconscious men, and stacked them near an access hatch.

It was now past 11:30 p.m., and the storm finally caught up with the airship. Strong bursts of wind buffeted the *Akron*, and she skewed around in different directions, dipping alarmingly from side to side and end to end. Sweat beads covered the cold faces of the crew as they struggled to maintain course. Finally, they reached their destination and caught sight of a lighted signal from below.

"There, the ship is just ahead to starboard!"

Inside the aircraft hangar bay, a determined group of men prepared for the gruesome task of dumping the unconscious bodies into the sea. The leader of these men seemed unusually cheerful. He was a big man with a ruddy complexion, and known for his brutal nature. He walked among the bodies, kicking them and uttering vulgar words of profanity. He stopped abruptly near one prone man and yelled over his shoulder.

"Hey, Franz, look at this one. I think he's playing possum."

Franz walked over. "How can you tell?"

Nicholas pointed with the toe of his boot. "I saw his eyelids move after I kicked him."

"Leave him be, Nicholas. He'll be dead soon."

"No, look, I'll show you he's still awake."

Nicholas stooped down and lifted the limp hand, as if to check for a pulse. "Watch this." He bit the man's finger, and the sailor jerked his arm back, bellowing in pain. Nicholas mashed a heavy fist into his face, and the man slumped back to the deck.

"See, I told you."

He lifted the arm, and bit down on the finger again. With a crunch, he completely bit through flesh and bone, and spat the bloody digit onto the unconscious man's chest.

"He's out now!" he said, standing up, wiping blood from his chin.

"Ach, you crazy fool." Franz turned away in disgust. "No wonder they call you 'Nick the biter.'"

The men completed their unsavory task of dumping the bodies into the sea. In all, sixty-four men fell unknowingly to their final doom.

Through the storm, the men could make out the lights of a specially modified freighter. The great dirigible lurched drunkenly in the wind, as the dark ship rose and fell in pounding seas. Lightning stabbed all around them, and nervous glances were exchanged as they realized how impossibly difficult their next task would be.

Long ropes snaked down from the airship. The Maybachs strained as they pushed and jockeyed the dancing airframe into position over the freighter. Rain and spray made the decks and the dangling ropes slippery, and the slicker-clad crew struggled to grasp the mooring lines and make them fast. Within thirty minutes, however, they secured the dirigible to a tower on the tossing freighter, and secured a rope ladder to allow for the exit of the crew of saboteurs.

Soon, a second ship, the German tanker *Phoebus*, moved in and launched a lifeboat in the lee of the freighter to bring back passengers. Three of the *Akron* assault crew jumped from the freighter deck into the frothing water near the lifeboat and then men quickly hauled them aboard. Their damp clothing would ultimately show evidence of someone plucking them from the sea. As they rowed back to the *Phoebus*, they came across an *Akron* sailor's body, and they hauled it aboard. It would be useful as a prop for the ruse they intended to play when they reached shore.

The *Phoebus* sailed away from the freighter and its extraordinary tethered cargo. The freighter crew busied itself with the final task of dumping tons of aluminum alloy framework and lacquered cotton fabric into the sea. They knew that the United States Navy would spare no expense to locate the site where the *Akron* had supposedly gone down. Divers would identify the twisted and scattered remains lying beneath the waves.

With the storm abating, the freighter and its trophy steamed away to a location far from normal shipping lanes. The three who transferred to the *Phoebus*, rehearsed the story they would tell to the American Naval authorities when they reached shore. The master of the *Phoebus* would describe seeing the navigation lights of the *Akron* near the water, thinking they belonged to a plane. He would speak of the heavy seas and forty-five knot winds, and of finding five men clinging to a large fuel tank; one to slip into the sea before they could reach him, and another unconscious when rescued and soon passing away.

The three so-called survivors knew their stories well, and were eventually transferred to the Coast Guard destroyer *Tucker*, and taken to the Naval Hospital in Brooklyn for treatment and debriefing.

Three nights later over a calm and empty sea, the *Akron* left its mooring above the freighter. The identifying insignia blacked out, the airship was refueled and restocked for a long flight, and its crew augmented by trained men from the freighter. The *Akron's* diesels fired as the new crew hauled up the rope ladders.

The airship lifted regally and disappeared into the star-speckled night. It climbed to an altitude of five-thousand feet before heading on a southerly course toward Cuba, and then westerly to Mexico.

CHAPTER 1

July 21, 1935
Northwestern New Mexico

Old man Atcitty was so out of breath that his vision was starting to blur. Stars flashed in his head, and his chest ached from the stress of running in the ninety-degree desert heat. He stumbled desperately on weak legs. His dry tongue rolled across spittle-flecked lips.

He feared the pain in his chest meant that his heart would stop, and he would die just as the young white doctor at the Indian hospital had told him. "You have a sick heart. Your arteries are hard and clogged with too much fat." The doctor knew that Atcitty would never consent to an operation, so he had warned him not to exert himself. He had given him some nitroglycerine pills—pills that were sitting on the top of the dresser in the log hogan a hundred feet in front of him.

Atcitty gasped noisily as he lost his balance and twisted his foot on a loose slab of shale. He fell, gouging his knee on a sharp rock, and tumbled to the bottom of a shallow wash. His heart beat like a jumping animal in his chest, fighting to free itself from the bone and flesh that held it captive. He could smell the high desert dust that stuck to the sweat on his face, and he sobbed in pain as he struggled to get up. His grandson was due to come home in a few more days...if only he were here now.

In his mind, he could still see his great-granddaughter; the young girl lying like a bloody rag doll next to the partially eaten carcasses of the sheep she tended. A haze of bluebottle flies pulsed around her in the afternoon heat; it almost looked as if the air was alive above her torn body.

He had scarcely a chance to react to the grisly sight when he saw... the abomination! His skin had tingled in an odd way. His body felt loose inside, and his hair stood up on the back of his neck. He realized that the large creature, still busy feeding on a sheep carcass, had not noticed him yet.

Atcitty had crouched in the low brush and backed away from the carnage, mentally cursing himself for not bringing along his rifle when he had left the hogan looking for young Sara. Easing behind a rocky outcrop, his heart had suddenly throbbed with pain. Clutching at his chest, he bent over trying to stifle a moan he was sure the beast had heard. Then he had run as fast as he could back toward his hogan over the low hill ahead of him.

The old Navajo grunted as he spit dirt from his mouth and rose to his hands and knees from the sandy wash. He could hear the eerie bark of the creature closing the gap behind him. Atcitty hissed in pain and regained his feet, and he loped and staggered the remaining distance to his door.

He felt the beast nearly upon him, and fearing to look back, he quickly pulled himself inside and threw the door shut. He spun around and fumbled for the wooden plank. It dropped to secure the opening just as a heavy body crashed against the wood.

Atcitty jumped back. The door held! He broke from his frozen stance and rushed for his carbine. He knew that it was loaded, and he quickly levered a shell into the firing chamber. Remembering the nitroglycerine pills, he reached with his left hand to the top of the narrow chest of drawers behind him. He grabbed for the pill bottle, knocking a handful of other items to the dirt floor. Clawing at the lid, he finally spilled a capsule into his mouth. Soon his breathing came easier, and the throbbing pain in his chest began to fade.

He listened to the creature moving outside the walls. He heard it pant as it circled the small, six-sided cabin. Then silence. He looked around the dusty room until his eyes stopped at the small window. Was it large enough for the monster to gain entry? Maybe! He hurriedly set the rifle down and grabbed for the mattress on his bed. He threw it against the window. Then, spilling the remaining articles from the chest of drawers, he quickly dragged it up against the mattress. In the quiet gloom, he sat down on an old kitchen chair with his rifle across his knees.

He turned his head left and right as he strained to hear any movement from the beast. Still silence. Atcitty let out his breath. He slowly rose and stepped across the room, only to stumble on a tin kettle that had fallen to the floor in his earlier frenzy. The kettle clattered noisily off the cast iron stove in the center of the room, and in response, the creature shrieked outside.

Suddenly the roof heaved, displacing rivulets of dust and dirt that sifted through the wattle of branches crisscrossing the ceiling. The dirt roof! Could the beast get through the roof? Digging noises sent a chilling shiver down the old man's back. Strange panting and barking sounds came from the creature as its efforts bore fruit, causing it to become even more agitated.

In the cloying darkness, a wave of calm slowly washed over the old Navajo. His courage and strength began to return, and he realized at last, who the creature really was. He remembered the story passed on from generation to generation; from his grandfather, from his grandfather's grandfather, and back to the very beginning of "The People." Back to when the ancients crawled up to the surface of the Earth from the underground, and were set upon by a "Monster."

The beast of the ancient creation legends had come back! Atcitty would die, of course. No mortal man could stand against a god.

The digging above had become more frantic. Time was running out. Atcitty reached to a low shelf, and he found a writing pad and a small box of pencils. He must warn someone. He knew in a few days, neighbors might stop by. Perhaps his grandson would finally return. He wrote one word in large, double-stroked letters, and he left the page in the dust on the kitchen table. Retrieving his rifle, he began to sing a warrior's chant. He would not die in this hogan. His ghost spirit would be free, rather than trapped inside these walls.

The roof shook as branches snapped, and large chunks of dirt fell to the floor. Already the old man could see dusty beams of light shining through the ceiling. It would be only a moment or two before the beast dug its way through. Atcitty reached inside his shirt for the old medicine bundle hanging from a leather thong around his neck. He held the greasy pouch in his hand and thought of the small items it held; corn pollen, a small bone, an animal tooth, and a feather. He then thought of his lovely great-granddaughter and spoke in a loud, determined voice.

"It is not a bad thing to die well."

Gritting his teeth, he lifted the latch and quickly stepped out of the door, away from the hogan. He turned and fired, and levered and fired again, and again at the horrible fiend on the roof.

A loud scream of pain and rage burst from the creature, and it quickly leapt from the roof upon the old man. It drove him to the ground, raking its scimitar-like claws across his belly and throat.

Atcitty yelled his defiance, and blood sprayed from his lips in a last gush of air as the creature's jaws bit down and crushed his chest.

CHAPTER 2

Sam Begay drove into the dirt parking lot of the Thoreau Trading Post at ten minutes to noon. A small cloud of dust blew lazily across the lot to the east, and he watched it dissipate into the desert. Directly overhead, the bright sun caused the air to shimmer in the distance and create small shadow-pools under the trees.

He had driven east on the gravel road from Gallup for almost an hour, and already the heat made his uniform shirt stick to his skin.

A twisted pinon tree afforded the only shade in the lot, and Sam edged his grey Plymouth truck underneath it before he shut off the engine. The old adobe trading post squatted in disrepair across the small parking area. Pushing his tan Stetson back from his forehead, Sam wiped away the sweat with his wrist. His neck hurt. He twisted his head left and right, feeling the tendons pop as he tried to loosen his muscles. He took a deep breath, savoring the tang of pinon, and listened to the wind and the ticking of the truck engine as it cooled.

Sam had just turned forty, and he knew he carried more weight than he should. His big frame was typical Navajo in shape, thick and muscular in the torso, and narrow in the hips. His hair was jet black and straight, and cut short in the white-man's way. He adjusted his hat again, pursed his full lips, and stepped out of the dusty truck. As senior Federal Indian Officer, he took great pains to look the part. His uniform was clean and pressed, his black boots shined like polished obsidian; or at least they did when he started the day. The heat and dust of the Reservation inevitably took its toll on appearances.

The Greyhound bus from Albuquerque would arrive soon, and for the hundredth time, Sam thought of where he and the passenger he would meet would be going today. His growling stomach suddenly reminded him that it was nearly time for lunch. Frowning, he gazed to the east where the bus would be coming from. His eyes turned slowly south, then west, following the uneven line of tree-covered hills of the Continental Divide. His stomach growled again, and he turned and walked toward the low adobe building. A hot blast of wind and dust gusted across the parking lot just as he entered the relative cool of the trading post. Sam removed his sunglasses and waited for his eyes to adjust to the dim light.

"Ya-hah-tee officer," croaked a hoarse voice across the room to his right.

Sam walked toward the rumpled, bent over shape behind the counter. "Ya-hah-tee Jake. Not very busy today?"

"Pfft," the old man answered. "We got rush hour right now." Then he added quickly, "But I'm never too busy to help my best customer. New truck?" he inquired knowingly.

Old Jake, the trading post owner, was a large, stooped, and gnarled man over seventy years old. Big shoulders hinted at the imposing figure he must have been as a younger man, but now his faded shirt hung over his bones like loose canvas over a tent frame. There was no roundness of fat or muscle, just angles and edges of tendon and bone. His big right hand clutched claw-like to the handle of a stout cane supporting his body.

Sam had known Jake ever since he had joined Federal law enforcement twenty years ago. They didn't get along very well in the beginning, but once the white man got past his suspicious nature toward the "Indian Lawman," the two had found each other to be a welcome and useful source of news and gossip.

"Being your best customer then," Sam said, "I'll have one of your very expensive grape sodas." He added reluctantly, "Yeah, it's a new truck."

Jake would tell of how he'd butted horns with the "thick-headed Indian" until the two realized they weren't going to crack the other's skull, so they decided to be friends. The storekeeper's eyes rolled upward as he turned and lifted the lid of the battered Coca-Cola cooler behind him. He pulled a bottle from the lukewarm water and levered the cap off. He set the dripping bottle on the scarred wooden counter and wiped it with a towel as Sam reached into his pocket for change.

"I hear there was some bad goings on north of here," he said, pumping the officer for information.

Sam looked at the coins in his hand and picked out a nickel. He placed it on the counter. "Jake, with the speed and scope of the local gossip network, I suspect that you know just about all there is to know about anything that goes on in this corner of the Res."

"Humph!" the old man snorted as he snatched the coin and dropped it in the till. He adjusted the position of his cane. "You don't have to step around the question with me. Witches, skinwalkers, coyotes, superstition, and rumors are all I hear about...and nobody knows anything else, or wants to talk about it. Fewer people around lately, too. A lot of 'em moved away I guess, but it sure don't make any sense; and it ain't good for business either!"

Sam's jaw clamped tightly as he considered the superstitions that went along with talking about witches and such. "It's a bad thing Jake, real bad! Old man Atcitty and his great granddaughter were killed by some kind of animal. I can't tell you any more about it right now, but I will later if I can."

An awkward silence followed, broken by the unmistakable, mechanical huffing of a large vehicle as it grunted into the parking lot. Both heads turned to the flyspecked front window to see a blue and grey, slab-sided bus materializing from a cloud of caliche dust.

"Looks like you're going have to get me another one of those grape sodas, Jake. I think my passenger is going to be thirsty when he gets off the bus."

Old Jake retrieved another bottle from the cooler and scooped up another nickel from the counter. He hobbled to the window and watched as Sam shouldered the screen door open with a soda bottle in each hand. The Indian walked across the parking lot to the Plymouth, and then leaned against a dusty fender, taking a long pull from his drink while he waited.

The bus door opened, and soon a tall Indian male stepped down carrying a duffel bag. He stood for a moment blinking in the sun. When he noticed Sam, he put his head down and walked toward the truck.

Sam watched the familiar pigeon toed walk and saw that the young man appeared tired. He wore his shirt sleeves rolled above his elbows, baring his arms strongly corded with tendon and muscle. The old dungarees seemed to be too short for the long legs sticking out of them, his old boots were shapeless, and the same color as the dirt in the parking lot. An old baseball hat cast a shadow across his face, but it couldn't hide his large nose.

From the trading post window, Jake watched the tall man walking, stiffly like a water bird, up to the police officer.

"Lordy," he muttered, rubbing his whiskered chin, "it's Dan Yazzie."

Sam stuck out his arm, offering the bottle of soda. Neither man spoke. The young Indian dropped his duffel and took the bottle, tipping it straight up and downing half of its contents. His skin was dark, giving evidence to the last three years spent on a prison work gang in the hot, New Mexico sun.

Dan wiped his mouth with the back of his hand, and eyed the lawman's dark sunglasses. "Hi Sam, long time eh?"

Sam removed his glasses and extended his hand. Dan looked at it for a moment, and then reached out with his own. Both men's eyes were solemn. Dan picked up his bag and stepped into the shade. He leaned against the truck, and they both finished their drinks in silence.

Sam fidgeted, looking at the ground. He could still remember the horribly torn bodies he had seen at the hogan. He finally found some words.

"Dan, I'm afraid I have some bad news for you." He looked at the other man, searching for an easy way to tell him.

Dan stared straight ahead, and spoke in a soft voice. "I figured you did."

Sam swallowed hard. "It's about your grandfather...and your daughter, Sara."

Dan Yazzie dropped his head, and turned to the lawman. "Take me out there Sam, I already know about it."

"But...how...who told you?"

"Warden. Somebody told him, and he took special pleasure in telling me. He said that my last few days in a cell should be an experience to reflect upon."

"Jacobs and Donaldson," Sam said through clenched teeth. He pictured the two FBI agents from Albuquerque who took charge of the crime scene, and dismissed him for being too close to the deceased. It had to be them. This was just one more frustrating incident in his not so happy career as a Federal Indian Officer. He could stand the subtle lack of respect, and the veiled taunting from some of the FBI people he reported to, but this deliberate act of meanness...Sam felt his face growing hot with anger. Both men had agreed to let Sam be the one to break the news to Dan.

Sam's jaw was tightly set. "Toss your bag in the back and let's go."

CHAPTER 3

The dusty Plymouth bounced on the dirt road past the settlement of Thoreau, headed north into the canyons of the high desert plateau. Sam downshifted frequently as they climbed. They drove through a few dry washes, grateful that the low gear of the truck easily took them through the soft sand. A hawk could be seen occasionally riding the rising thermals; wings outstretched, watching for a jackrabbit to jump from cover.

They traveled in silence, each man lost in his thoughts. Sam could hardly stand it any longer. He was searching for something to say when Dan spoke up.

"New truck?"

"With a raised eyebrow, the lawman glanced at his passenger, trying to form an appropriate answer. He smiled when he saw Dan's half hidden smirk.

"Yeah, after twenty years of being an overpaid Federal Police Officer, it turns out they saw fit to throw in a new vehicle too. White men—go figure 'em."

Dan Yazzie couldn't help grinning at Sam's response.

The awkward silence broken, Sam Begay's features softened.

"Dan, I can't tell you how sorry I am for you to go through all this right now. Here you've just gotten out and…" Sam couldn't seem to find the words to finish his sentence.

"It's okay Sam; you don't have to worry about me."

He noticed that the ex-con's jaw was tightly set, betraying his inner turmoil; conflicting with his words.

Sam unconsciously let out a great sigh. Dan seemed to understand.

"I appreciate you checking in on me and my family over the past three years."

"Huh? Oh...well, that's okay." Sam was uncomfortable that his passenger had read his mind.

They continued to climb. The truck gears whined, and the engine hooted and howled as they wound up through the rocks. Soon, Sam pulled off the road on a wide curve overlooking a dry riverbed, and he shut off the engine.

"I brought some lunch,"

He reached behind the seat for a paper bag. They ate bologna sandwiches and a small jar of sweet pickles, while stretching their legs out the opened doors.

"I used to ride a horse through here when I was younger." Dan said. "See that ridge over there? I found a stream back in one of the canyons and caught some small trout. I used to camp out here a lot. I never liked to be around home much when my old man was alive."

"He froze to death out by Gallup, didn't he?"

"Yeah. When I was twelve. We went to live with my mom's dad after that. She disappeared a year later. Hosteen Atcitty was good to me. He taught me how to be a man. He taught me about the desert."

Sam started the Plymouth again, and they continued on the last leg of their drive. Dan looked out the window deep in his own thoughts.

"Tell me how it happened Sam."

Startled by Dan's straightforward words, Sam looked at his passenger and gathered his thoughts. He knew that the time would come for him to tell what he had seen at the Atcitty hogan. He began slowly, replaying the events of that day like a movie in his mind, speaking to his passenger in a clear and concise fashion like his training had taught him to do.

"Some of your neighbors got in touch with me, and I drove to the place about 11:30 Monday morning. I could see buzzards circling the area. I found your grandfather on the ground, about fifteen feet in front of the hogan. He'd been chewed on pretty bad."

Dan's eyes widened at Sam's words.

"I figure he'd been out there a day or two. At first, I couldn't find your daughter, so I began calling out for her. Then I noticed another bunch of birds over a hill, south of the hogan. I hiked about a quarter of a mile, and then I saw half a dozen sheep carcasses in the open. When I got closer, I found out that one of them was…Sara."

Sam took a deep breath and let it out slowly. Dan stared straight ahead, showing no emotion.

"There was nothing I could do, so I drove to Crownpoint and called the Feds in Albuquerque. They sent out a couple of guys, and we met up in Thoreau. They followed me back to your grandfather's place. It turned out the two guys were a couple of idiots. They walked around and looked at the bodies, and they didn't even look for tracks. They looked inside the hogan for a few minutes, and then they said they would file a report. One said it looked like an animal attack, maybe a cougar or a bear. They told me to contact the relatives and have the bodies taken care of."

"FBI sonsofbitches!" Sam said with feeling, "They must have called the Warden in Santa Fe when they got back to the office."

Dan was shocked to hear Sam use such strong words. He noticed the man's face was red with emotion.

"You don't think it was an animal attack?"

Sam looked over with narrowed eyes and slowly bit off his answer. "It was an animal alright, and I'm going to show you some tracks you're not going to believe."

They drove between two low mesas, and came up to a small two-track on the right. Sam braked and downshifted, and then he edged off the main road. A cloying cloud of dust caught up to the truck and enveloped the cab. Moving ahead in low gear, they bounced and crawled for another three miles over a dirt trail. The vegetation was low, sparse, and brown. The twisting track eventually took them over a rise, and beyond it, they saw the family compound.

Dan Yazzie knew the bodies would be gone; taken care of quickly according to tradition, but his heart still pounded as they drove up to the hogan. They both stepped out of the truck and stretched, and then walked toward the small cabin. Something didn't look right to Dan, and his eyes widened as he noticed how the hard-packed, dirt roof had been torn up.

"Ho-lee…" He said under his breath.

Sam called Dan over to where he had found the old man's body.

"Your grandfather was lying here on his back." He motioned with his hands. "His Henry rifle was about five feet to the right, over here. He had fired it four times; I found the casings. His clothing was ripped, and his throat and torso were torn open."

Sam looked down as he pointed out what he described. He raised his eyes to Dan and spoke ominously.

"His chest was crushed."

"Crushed? Like by a vehicle?"

Sam shook he head. "By some big, powerful jaws!" He stooped down, and with a piece of stick, drew an elongated 'U' in the dirt, about eighteen inches long and ten inches wide.

"It had a bite pattern something like this and teeth around an inch in diameter."

Dan's forehead wrinkled in thought as he connected the crude drawing to the description Sam gave. When he spoke, it was with hesitation.

"I don't know of any bear or cougar that could do that."

"Nope," Sam said. After a short pause, he added, "But I do know what could."

"What?" Dan was very bewildered.

"Crocodile," said Sam. He stood up and scanned the horizon. "I saw one attack a deer once in the Everglades in Florida. Hard to forget what it looked like; it didn't crush the deer's chest though."

Dan looked at Sam as if he had not heard him correctly.

"Crazy, huh?" Sam provided the words his friend was searching for. "The FBI guys didn't believe it either. C'mon, let's take a walk up the ridge."

Sam led the way along a path to the top. In the flat clearing beyond, two buzzards leapt, croaking their annoyance at having their meal interrupted. As they clawed for the sky, their long, black wings beat small tornadoes in the dust.

"That's what's left of the sheep." Sam said pointing. "I found little Sara out there. I'm not going to tell you anything more, but I picked this up, and thought you'd want it."

Sam pulled a thin chain and pendant from his shirt pocket, and he put it in the other man's hand.

Dan looked at the small silver and turquoise necklace. It had belonged to his wife, and he had given it to his daughter on her birthday, before he went to prison.

Dan's legs seemed to grow numb, and he sank to his knees. Sam reached to help, but then slowly turned and walked away. Dan clutched the piece of jewelry to his chest, and he didn't notice the other man leave.

Ten minutes later, Dan returned to the hogan and found Sam leaning against the truck. He started to say something, but Sam interrupted.

"You don't have to say anything to me Dan." Sam swallowed a lump in his throat. "Follow me, I'll show you what else I found."

He led the way past the house. They walked a hundred feet into a patch of dry grass, and then beyond it to a narrow dried-up watershed. Sam stepped down the low bank and walked a few yards, stopping in front of a scrap of old tarp. A rock at each corner held down the frayed piece of canvas. He removed them to reveal what was underneath.

Dan stooped down to see. There, in the soft soil, were animal prints like none he had ever seen before. They were large, about fourteen inches long and seven inches wide; three long toes with wide pads and claws. The impressions were deep. Dan turned to Sam with a strange look on his face.

"Is it...was it made by a bird?"

Sam looked down at the large tracks. "Yeah, a four-legged, five hundred pound bird."

Sam replaced the tarp, and they walked back to the hogan. Dan Yazzie was too stunned to speak. He considered, and then dismissed Sam's flip remark about a big, impossible bird, yet he felt the man really believed what he had said.

Back at the hogan, Dan suppressed an involuntary shiver as he stepped inside. He saw dirt-covered chaos. The roof was partially gone. Dan looked around and slowly started to sort through some of the personal belongings. He found comfort when he touched some small thing that reminded him of his daughter or his grandfather. Dan dusted off a few pieces of old furniture, and then began to feel as if he were moving in a dream.

It was like being back inside a mental shell, like the one he crawled into three years ago when he went to prison.

Dan saw the small kitchen table covered with broken sticks and dirt from the shredded roof. He scooped up handfuls of debris and tossed it out the door, and then brushed off the remaining layer of dust. He picked up a piece of notepaper, and in the dust-mottled light, he read the bold pencil strokes. Dan felt his hair stand up; his hands shook, and his eyes blurred.

He didn't know how long he stood there, but clarity suddenly came to him. He had prayed for a path; a new road to take for the rest of his life's journey, and now he knew what that road was. Dan took a deep breath, and walked out of the hogan.

"Sam, look at this!" He approached the truck and spread the paper on the hood. "Monster." Dan read the word, as Sam looked on. "Do you think this has something to do with the killing and the footprints?"

Sam's face was like stone. "I'm afraid to even think about what I think." He looked at his friend. "I think there was a definite reason that your grandfather wrote the word 'monster.' He didn't write 'bear,' or 'cougar,' or 'robbers,' or anything else on the note; he wrote 'monster.' It's not a word someone would use to describe something of this world." Sam took a deep breath. "I think he used that word because he wanted it to mean something else; something from the spirit world perhaps."

Dan stood in silence as Sam spoke.

"Just think of those tracks. I've never seen anything like them—nor have you, and we've both tracked everything in this desert since we could walk. If they were made by the creature that caused the massacre—and I don't think anything else could have done it—then we are facing something that you and I can't even imagine."

Dan clenched his teeth with resolve. His mind made up.

"Sam, I'm going to track this animal; this monster, and I'm going to kill it! I don't care how long it takes me. I don't even care what happens to me. I am going to kill it, and then I'm going to tell it that my daughter and my grandfather have been avenged."

"I know Dan; I won't try to stop you. I'll help you."

"I don't need any help!"

"Stop!" The officer said, and then his emotion quickly faded. Embarrassed, he spoke in a soft voice.

"You need more help than I, or anyone else, can ever give you. Now I will speak some words that you need to hear and understand." Sam licked his dry lips and chose his words carefully. "I think this creature, whatever it is, will not be killed easily, if at all. I know of your need to go out and find it, and to avenge your loved ones. I also know that you will need my help to prepare for what you are about to do."

Sam paused as he gathered courage to say what he feared even to think.

"I think your grandfather wrote that name because he believed the creature to be the monster Ye'iitsoh."

Disbelief, and then comprehension, struggled for control of Dan's face.

"Do you mean the monster that the shamans speak of—the one from the beginning of creation when the People came up from the underground— The Hero Twins; Monster Slayer?"

Dan looked straight into the stony face of his friend. "You're serious about this?"

CHAPTER 4

Mathews Airfield, North of Albuquerque

"Dammit!" Kip Combs said, barking his knuckles for the third time, trying to tighten the last bolt on an engine brace. He gripped his hand and sucked air through his clenched teeth while he waited for the pain to subside.

"What?" his sidekick, Doo, asked peering from the other side of the biplane through his round spectacles. The boy's cheeky grin showed faked innocence.

"Oh, this piece of crap airplane..." Kip attacked the bolt again with teeth clenched, finally managing to snug down the brace. "Piece of crap," he said again with satisfaction.

Kip's outburst revealed volumes about the shortcomings of the old Curtis JN-4H, "Jenny," mail plane. Doo noted that it also revealed volumes about Kip Comb's shortcomings—impatient and hard to please, and running hot and cold depending on the day or the job at hand.

This year had been tough for their aviation business. The country couldn't seem to climb out of the depression, and they'd found little work flying the odd bit of cargo, and the occasional passenger. They barely made enough money to keep the old bucket up in the air...and to eat. Doo's stomach growled in acknowledgement.

The aircraft was old, and held together by faith more than by structural integrity. They both agreed the best thing to do would be to find a museum or a junk yard that would take it off their hands.

Kip and the plane, were both tightly strung; and Doo loved them both. He skittered to the other side of the Jenny to finish his work, and to hide the knowing look on his face.

Kip stepped away, kneading the small of his back to relieve the ache from working under the engine cowling. He was an impulsive, brooding twenty-four year old, and his grey eyes could burn with fire if he were provoked. There was an unconscious confidence in the way he moved. A small, white scar stood out on his tanned skin over his right eye. His nose followed a slightly crooked path down his face.

Kip walked slowly to the front of the hanger into the bright morning sunlight, wiping the grease from his hands, and carefully avoiding the scraped knuckles.

He eyed the pink ridges of the Sandia Mountains, and noted the fringe of white clouds that framed them. The city of Albuquerque lay to the south, sunlight reflecting off the windows of the taller buildings as they simmered in the heat.

Kip immediately noticed the sour look on Captain Jack Abbot's face as the man walked purposefully toward him. The Captain owned the airfield. He was a big man; well over six feet tall and probably weighed near 230 pounds. It must have been all muscle when he was younger. Now, in his fifty's, the muscle sagged and created a paunch, but the captain was still not the kind of man you would want to pick a fight with. A retired military engineer, he owned the small airfield and did some tinkering in his workshop behind the office, where his niece, Lisa Ann Abbot, worked.

Something in his determined walk told Kip that Captain Jack was agitated about something. It couldn't be the rent on the hanger; Doo just paid it last week. There were only two things that ever got under Jack's skin; Lisa Ann, and Kip's rent.

"Kip, have you seen Lisa Ann?"

The pilot shook his head. "I haven't seen her since yesterday Captain." Kip wondered what she had done now. "Why, is something wrong?"

The heavy man was sweating profusely. "I don't know, darn it. She took off early this morning with a young man who wanted to show off his new car: a shiny green job with an open top. I told her to be back in an hour because I needed her to finish some paperwork. Well, it has been over two hours and still no Lisa. When I get ahold of her, I'm tempted to…oh; I don't know what I'll do."

Jack Abbot produced a handkerchief and mopped his face in a quick circular motion before he tucked it away.

"Now Cap'n." Kip said with a drawl.

He knew exactly how the big man felt, driven to the same state of mind many times by the same girl.

"I'm sure Lisa Ann just got carried away with that shiny car and all…"

Kip stopped in mid-sentence as he thought of the Captain's independent-minded niece. She was in her early twenties, shapely and blonde; with big green eyes, a husky voice, and an edge to her personality that was sharp enough to flay the skin off a sailor. Nevertheless, she could be sweet too…sometimes.

Doo walked up with a piece of canvas patch in his hand. "I saw her, Captain. I just opened up the shop when she and that guy took off raising dust. She was all giggly, and they drove into the desert over there towards the Sandias. Maybe they had some car trouble."

Doo and Kip exchanged a quick knowing glance.

"Or maybe some other kind of trouble," Captain Jack said, frowning.

Kip looked around and then spoke up. He hoped to put her uncle at ease.

"Okay, I'll take the Harley and see if I can find her. They're probably just stuck somewhere, buried up to the axles in soft sand. Don't worry, I'll bring her back."

"Well, I hope so." Jack produced the handkerchief again. "I've got work to be done here, and she's out acting like she's on vacation."

He turned and walked briskly back to the office, chin stuck out like the prow of a battleship, the ends of his white mustache flowing like flags from the fantail.

Kip and Doo exchanged worried glances.

"Go ahead Kip. I'm just about through putting the patch on the wing. I'll have it all done by the time you get back."

"Thanks, Doo."

Kip handed the grease rag to his friend, and then walked to the side of the hanger and jumped on his Harley. A low rumble and blue smoke came from the exhaust as he started it up.

Doo pointed and yelled that their tracks should be somewhere to the left of the trees beyond the airstrip.

Kip sighted the trees, nodded, and took off kicking up a rooster tail of dust that feathered away to the northeast. He found the tire tracks just where Doo had indicated, and he followed them into the low rolling hills leading up to the Sandias.

Kip gritted his teeth. That silly little twit, he fumed. Was he angry? Why? She wasn't his girl; not really. He didn't love her, did he? Well, maybe a little. Kip's anger simmered, and it slowly morphed into concern.

"Ah, heck," he said aloud, and gave more gas to the powerful motor. Paths, trails, and dried up watercourses, crisscrossed the desert, but the tire tracks of the car were easy to follow. Soft sand grabbed at his own tires, threatening to dump him from time to time, but the sidecar kept the machine upright. Kip watched constantly for sharp rocks that could puncture a tube.

After about twenty minutes, he stopped, shut off the engine, and reached for his binoculars. He saw nothing moving. The desert was quiet except for the lisping wind. He fired up the Harley again. No main roads came out this far, so he knew they couldn't cut into town. In another twenty minutes, he stopped again and killed the engine. He still only heard the wind. He peered through the binoculars, east to west. Wait, he saw a flash of color a half-mile ahead. Kip tossed the glasses into the sidecar and fired up the engine.

Cutting off the trail to shorten the distance, he nearly drove the bike off a sharp cliff. He hit the throttle again, heedless of the danger from rocks and drifting sand.

He finally saw a blonde head, and arms flailing beyond the top of a hill. A man's head soon came into view; then disappeared. The Harley powered ahead until it caromed off a large rock and threw Kip over the handlebars. He landed in some brush twenty yards from the struggling couple. He staggered to his knees spitting twigs and sand, and then took in the scene.

Lisa Ann, a bit disheveled from her ordeal, was struggling with a stocky young man who attempted to drag her back to his car. He turned and saw Kip crawl from the brush. Lisa took advantage of the distraction to swing a roundhouse punch that connected with his jaw. She broke free from his grip, and sat down hard as the young man fell backwards and rolled downhill. She saw him get up and run to the car. He jumped behind the wheel and ground away at the starter. He mashed the pedal down in desperation, but the car sat buried hopelessly to its axles.

Kip was on his feet. He loped downhill, glancing quickly at Lisa Ann, noting that she seemed to be all right. He reached the car; engine roaring, transmission grinding, tires spinning, and dust flying. The boy behind the wheel was mewling as he desperately tried to extricate the vehicle from the soft sand.

As Kip approached the driver's door, the radiator suddenly let go, and in a moment, the engine seized in a cloud of steam and oily blue smoke. The boy slumped back in the seat. He stared at his hands on the wheel and tried to control his breathing.

Kip said, "Friend, let's be reasonable. This car is not going anywhere. That means, you're not going anywhere that I can't lay my hands on you if I want. Now, open the door and come around to the front of the car."

Kip barely got his last word out. The boy flung the door open and rushed him with such speed, that it caught him unprepared. Kip fell, and landed on his back. He saw his attacker ready to deliver a kick to his head. Some instinct took over; and as his opponent's foot came at him, Kip rolled, gripped the foot, and quickly stood up. He lifted the leg in an ark that dumped the boy on his head.

The boy was quick to get up. He ran back to the car and reached into the back to pull out a tire iron. He held it like a club and swung at Kip as he advanced.

Kip backed away to avoid the blows. He was steered toward a loose, rocky slope, and as he stepped back, he lost his footing again and fell.

The boy rushed up and stood over him.

"Asshole, I'll teach you to mind your own business."

Kip saw the raised arm and the heavy bar of metal. Just then, the sole of a boot materialized between the boy's legs, and Kip heard the sound of a solid *wumph*. The boy dropped the tire iron and crumpled on his side in a fetal position, moaning in a weak voice.

Lisa Ann leaned over to Kip and offered her hand. As she helped him up, Kip saw she had dusted off her slacks and straightened her torn blouse. He also noted that she wore a pair of sturdy riding boots.

"Don't ever think that I can't take care of myself," she said.

She glanced triumphantly at the boy writhing on the ground.

"Don't feel bad Clark, I wasn't going to give you a chance to use 'em anyway."

Kip scowled as Lisa stepped closer with a concerned look. She caressed his cheek with her hand.

"There you go again," he said, "overrating yourself."

He grabbed her wrist just as he felt the touch of her nails. He held on tightly, and they both glared at each other. She finally relaxed her arm and looked dubiously over at the Harley.

"You might as well take me home now."

They walked up the hill to the motorcycle, and Lisa arranged herself in the sidecar. Kip glanced back at the automobile. Clark was on his hands and knees throwing up. Kip put on his helmet and goggles, and then he glanced at Lisa as she stared off in the distance.

"What, no thank-you?" he said and kicked the starter.

Lisa jerked around. "You bast...," was all he heard before the engine caught.

Kip made sure that the ride back was rough and jarring. Lisa didn't say a word. By the time they drove up to the airfield, Kip was feeling cranky. He didn't know if he should be relieved that she was safe, or angry because she did such a stupid thing in the first place, or both.

Did he love her, or not? Maybe both, he decided. He still couldn't keep his eyes off her when she wasn't looking, and why did he feel so protective of her? What was it he felt when he saw her with her torn blouse? Oh hell, if only she would stop harping at me to quit flying and get a real job, he thought.

Back at the airfield, Kip stepped off the bike and helped Lisa Ann from the sidecar. She stood stiffly in front of him, and he took her gently in his arms. She clung to him, forehead on his chest.

"By the way," she said lifting her head, "don't' forget I was the one who saved you."

With that, she turned and briskly walked to the house. Kip stood slack-jawed, watching her until she disappeared inside the door.

Lisa Ann Abbot had a singularly, unique ability to drive Kip to the very brink of insanity. When they had first met, they were both smitten, and had an intense, but short, affair. Her desire for him cooled when he told her he wanted to fly airplanes for the rest of his life. She wouldn't talk about it after that, and whenever he insisted that she explain why she didn't like him being a pilot, she would start a heated argument, or simply walk away.

Kip eventually gave up, and tried to ignore her, but ignoring Lisa was impossible. She was constantly showing up at the hanger. She would dress provocatively and bring him a sandwich or some cookies. Sometimes she would just stop to ask a question about the plane, or to discuss the day's news or weather.

Why did she keep coming around? What does she want from me? "Damn!" he said under his breath and then kicked the Harley back to life.

CHAPTER 5

Kip pulled up to the office. He told Capt. Jack that he had found Lisa Ann, and had taken her back to the house. She was fine; they just got the car stuck in some sand. She would be back to work after she cleaned up.

"Good thing," Jack said. "Thanks Kip, I guess I owe you one."

Kip suspected that Jack knew there was more to the story. Well that was Lisa's problem. She could explain it. There was a time when Kip would have gladly spent his days trying to make her happy—but not anymore. Boy, she could be a royal pain in the ass!

Thinking about Lisa usually soured Kip's mood, and now was no exception. He parked his Harley next to the hanger and barged into the small office ready to argue with Doo about something. His partner looked up and instantly took in Kip's state of mind.

Before Kip could speak, Doo said, "Kip, we have a customer!"

Kip stared at him for a moment, his brain shifting gears; then he noticed someone sitting in the chair next to the file cabinet.

"And I'm in a hurry!" a low female voice said.

She stood up, and Kip saw she was tall and lean, and had a bold smirk on her face. Her outfit was a tailored skirt, a short jacket, and a beige blouse and hat.

She held her purse in front of her and repeated in a no-nonsense manner, "I said I was in a hurry!"

She was all business. Kip felt his face warming as his temper rose. Doo jumped in before Kip could form a sarcastic retort, and he took over the conversation.

"Kip, this is Diana Witherspoon, uh…, from the university. She's an archeologist, and she wants to rent our plane. Miss Witherspoon, this is Kip Combs, our pilot."

"My pilot, I presume?" the brassy young woman inquired.

She looked at him up and down, and glanced around the small dusty office. Then with one raised eyebrow, she boldly fixed her stare back on Kip.

"So, you can fly me to Chaco Canyon?"

Kips face was red as he stared back at her.

"The question is not, if I *can*, but if I *will*. Not today honey, I'm busy!" He quickly walked past her into the depths of the hanger.

Doo gave the girl a nervous, apologetic smile and then darted after his friend.

"But Kip," he said as he caught up to him, "we need the money!"

He pulled himself around to face him, and grabbed two handfuls of his shirt.

"I said we need the m-o-n-e-y; the rent, gas for the Jenny, food to *EAT!*"

Doo was not going to be ignored. They stared nose to nose for a moment, and then Kip relented with a sheepish grin. Doo released his grip, and Kip's eyes rolled for Doo's benefit. Kip slowly walked back into the office.

"So, Chaco Canyon eh?"

"Yes '*honey*,' you do know where that is, don't you?"

"I do." He smiled.

"Good. How much will it cost? And how quickly can we leave?"

Kip sized her up. He was starting to warm up to her frank, forward manner. Green eyes, he noted. Black hair cut a little short for his taste though. No lipstick.

Kip smiled easily and answered, "Forty dollars and one hour! Can you be ready, Miss. Witherspoon?"

Her answer came with her own smile that lit the drab room.

"Why yes, Mr. Combs, I can."

In fifty minutes, she returned with her luggage. Her change of clothing was a pair of rugged looking khaki shorts, and a shirt with pockets. She wore sturdy hiking boots with white socks rolled over the tops.

"Is there some sort of a landing strip out there?" Kip asked, admiring her dimpled knees.

"Yes, of sorts," she said, squinting in the sunlight, the warm wind blowing her hair. "There's a relatively straight road leading to the site from the south. I think it will be more than adequate for this kind of plane to land and take off."

Later, with their passenger secured in the front cockpit, Kip told his partner that he would be back in a little over two hours. Doo nodded and handed Kip his gear. He stowed it and strapped himself into the rear cockpit.

The engine caught with a smoky belch that soon settled into a noisy, clattering idle. Kip tested the foot controls. Satisfied that all was in order, he taxied out, turned west into the wind, and opened the throttle to the stops. The craft leapt nimbly into the air, and Kip quickly banked to the northwest.

Kip always enjoyed being off the ground again, but the thrill of flying was not what made his heart beat a little quicker just now. An image of Lisa Ann slipped through his mind, and he pushed it away to allow a new picture to form of his female passenger.

Off the ground, the rickety, canvas-covered biplane was a graceful and nimble bird. Affectionately known as a 'Jenny,' this one was postal service modified, with the standard 90-horse engine replaced by a 150-horse, Hispano-Suizo, power plant. In addition, two regular gas tanks were hooked up together to double the fuel capacity and increase her range. She was noisy, and she vibrated like a shivering dog, but she was fast and nimble.

Kip's Aunt Vicki had given him the biplane when she got married and retired from the barnstorming circuits. She had flown the aircraft since the late twenties. It was still in fair shape, but it had seen many years of use in her daredevil days, and in the mail service before that. She had given him the plane for his twenty-third birthday, and Kip knew he would have to spend a good amount of his time repairing one thing or another. If it wasn't an engine part, or some control cable, it was a weakened frame component, or some fabric that needed patching.

Fix it, fly it, and fix it again, he always said to Doo. However, today the old crate flew like a dream.

The sky was clear, he had money to pay the rent, and he had an interesting young woman in his plane. Diana Witherspoon; he rolled each syllable over in his mind. Who was she? What was she really like? One thing for sure, she wasn't anything like Lisa. Lisa was flighty, unpredictable, and alternately hot and cold. From what Kip could tell, Miss W. was just the opposite; she had a take-charge attitude, and she appeared to be used to giving orders and getting her own way. One thing he knew for sure, the girl in the front cockpit intrigued him. He needed to get to know her better.

They quickly passed over the Rio Grande, and then over the black, eroded cones of the three small, extinct volcanoes along the west mesa. A much larger extinct volcano, Mount Taylor, floated like a ghostly, blue island sixty miles to the west. Kip felt good, and he loved the way the 'Jenny' responded to the controls.

He leaned forward and tapped his passenger's shoulder, yelling over the engine noise.

"Would you like to see some fancy flying?"

The girl cocked her head questioningly, and he made a swooping motion with his hand to explain. She nodded vigorously, and smiled.

He gave her a 'thumbs up' and said to himself, okay; let's see how she likes a loop.

A normal, ninety-horse 'Jenny' did not have the power to perform such a maneuver with a passenger in front, but the extra sixty horses made aerobatics and other fancy flying easy. Kip thumbed the throttle forward and climbed until the plane nosed over the top. They quickly gained speed as they plunged toward the ground. Completing the loop, he heard his passenger "*whoop*" with glee.

Tapping her shoulder again, he signaled a barrel roll with his hand. The girl nodded and clutched the padded edges of the cockpit. Kip moved the stick, and the plane cartwheeled around the tips of its wings and leveled off again. A "*whoo-hoo*" came from the girl this time. Kip smiled; maybe this Diana Witherspoon wasn't so stuck on herself after all.

Scanning the horizon, and then checking his compass, Kip made a small course correction and found the landmark he was seeking. They flew past Cabazon Peak, a lonely eroded pillar of basalt that protruded from the desert floor. This was roughly the halfway point. Below, the rock and sand lay carved in flat erratic waves, giving evidence to ancient beaches and dunes. Seasonal watercourses wound through them, looking as if a giant palate knife sculpted them. The eroded hills lay freckled with small clumps of vegetation.

Soon, the mesas and the broken village walls of the Chaco Valley came into view. They circled the area, and Kip noticed a tower of white, cottony clouds forming to the west, threatening rain. Diana turned to get his attention, and pointed to the thin road below. This was to be their impromptu landing strip.

The rough roadway made the plane vibrate and lurch as it touched down, and when they finally slowed and stopped, thick dust billowed around them. Kip kept the engine idling and helped Diana from the cockpit. As he retrieved her luggage, he noticed a car speeding toward them.

"That's my ride," she said, nodding at the vehicle as it kicked up an impossibly large plume of dust. She shook Kip's hand. "Thank you for an interesting flight." Her eyes captured his, and her smile warmed him like the sun.

"Look me up the next time you need a lift," he said. Kip felt light-headed as he searched for more words. "Wait, what kind of work do you do out here? I'd like to know more about it…and about you."

Diana's smile slowly faded and turned vague. "Well, we're just doing some digging and site identification. The students…" Her voice trailed off as a beat-up Model 'A' Ford arrived; fenders flapping like wings, and the brakes squealing like an off-key saxophone. The impossible dust cloud enveloped everything.

They both coughed, as Kip watched the driver step from the car to greet them. Diana introduced her assistant, Carl Walker. He was a friendly enough fellow with a firm handshake. He quickly stowed Diana's gear in the car while Kip struggled to find something else to say.

Diana looked at Kip and thanked him again for bringing her out. As she walked to the car, Kip's heart sank like a punctured tire.

Carl pushed the starter and brought the old Ford clattering back to life. He circled around, and then headed back to the dig site.

Obviously, she had no interest in him, Kip thought; as he watched the impossible dust cloud follow the car down the road. She had her work… and she had Carl. Kip got back inside the Jenny and fed gas to the engine; in a moment, he was in the air headed for home.

Carl dodged the ruts and potholes as he drove. He looked tentatively at Diana as she stared absently ahead, deep in thought.

"Well?" he asked.

She turned quickly and gathered her thoughts. "Oh, I checked, and we can't get permission to explore the small mesa; it's owned by the mine."

"No, I meant you; your father's funeral. Are you alright?"

Diana looked at her hands in her lap, and then back to Carl. Her teeth clenched in determination.

"No, I'm not alright. I won't be alright until I find out how he died."

CHAPTER 6

Carl Walker stopped the Ford in front of Diana's tent. She stepped out and shaded her eyes with her hand; she could just see the plane, a small speck in the distance. Funny guy, she thought, arrogant, but kind of fun and charming when he got over himself. He could sure fly a plane though. She smiled to herself as she remembered his words about wanting to know more about her. It was a shame she had no time for such things right now.

Carl handed out her bags and saw her interest in the plane. "Have a fun flight?"

"Oh, it was okay." She took the luggage. "We've got some planning to do. Can you meet me in the main tent in about thirty minutes?"

Carl was studying a topographical map when Diana arrived. "Some sandwiches in the cooler if you're hungry," he said, chewing on a ham-on-white.

Choosing a wedge of sandwich, she joined Carl at the map table.

"Here's the small mesa," he pointed with a corner of his sandwich. "It's just to the north of the larger one where the mining operation is. I found your father right about here. You can see the steepness of the cliffs. It was pretty clear that he died from a long fall." He looked at Diana, studying her reaction.

"You see, that's just what I don't get. My father couldn't stand heights. He couldn't even get up on a ladder without feeling dizzy. He always stood back a good distance from steep drops—they made him sick. I want to go out there today and see the place where it happened."

Carl stood up. "Look Diana, I know you want to go out there to set your mind at ease, but it can wait until tomorrow. You have been away from your work for two weeks. Your students need you. They're finished with their current site, and they want to ask you about where to start next. They want to show you some things they've found, too. They're pretty excited about them."

Diana struggled with her emotions, and finally gave in to Carl's good advice.

"Of course, I keep forgetting that you're the site manager. I guess I need to rely on you more."

Carl could see that Diana was near tears, thinking about her father. He reached over and put an arm around her shoulders. She lowered her head and shook with a brief silent sob before pulling away.

"You're right, I need to see the students and let them know they can count on me to keep this project on track."

Kip Combs lost his moody funk as soon as he was in the air. "To hell with women!" His words were lost in the noisy hammering of his engine.

He abruptly decided to take a southerly course home, and he set the plane's nose toward the cone shape of Mount Taylor. It would take a little longer getting back to the airfield, but that was fine; he needed time to clear his head.

He and Doo barely made enough money to pay the bills, which was another way of saying, 'broke.' He wanted more than that. His sidekick was eighteen years old now, and as far as Kip was concerned, he was already a man.

Kip remembered how they had met. Doo had found him unconscious in his old plane after he had crashed in the desert north of Albuquerque. The engine had stalled, and Kip had aimed at the thin track of the Santa Fe road to attempt a landing. He had managed to line up with the roadway, but a strong gust of wind blew the plane over sideways, and he had crashed a hundred yards off the road.

As Doo dragged him from the wreckage, he fell backwards, breaking his ankle. Kip had suffered a couple of broken ribs, and a broken nose and collarbone. They had both ended up in the hospital together and became fast friends. Doo told him he had been hitching from St. Louis when he saw Kip's plane gliding overhead. He told Kip that his family was poor, and his mother had passed away, leaving him with no other kin. So, he'd decided to hitchhike west to find his fortune.

Some fortune, Kip thought. Doo stuck around and turned out to be a good mechanic and a darn good friend. Every time Kip saw Doo limping, however, he felt a sharp pang of guilt. He owed Doo. He owed him more than he could give him.

"What the HELL!" Kip's mind returned to his noisy cockpit as a loud engine screamed over the snorting of his own. A burst of wind buffeted his plane, and he saw a light colored shape with red trim rocket past. Kip struggled to control the biplane in the strong turbulence, and he strained to get a good look at the other aircraft.

"Where is that reckless maniac?" he said, and then he saw the plane climbing from below on the right. It was another biplane! Wow, was it fast! It was at his three o'clock now, and it stood on a wing tip as it passed in front of him. The high-pitched engine and a wall of buffeting air assailed Kip again, as he struggled with the controls. They were over a high, sandstone mesa, and Kip noticed some buildings tucked in a circular canyon below. Anger boiled in him as he gritted his teeth. He looked right and left for the other aircraft, but it was gone. The nerve of that asshole!

In a few moments, his heart rate came down, and the heat dissipated from his neck and face. He decided to change course directly toward Albuquerque. Just then, the fast biplane appeared again, thirty feet off his left side. It throttled back and kept pace with the Jenny. Kip got a good look at the other aircraft this time. He noticed an unusual set of bars attached to the top of the upper wing. The other pilot waved with his hand.

What the heck does he want? It finally came to him with a shock; the plane was a Curtis Sparrowhawk! It was a plane built to land in mid-air on the Navy dirigibles, the *Akron* and the *Macon*; but both airships were on the bottom of the oceans now; one in the Atlantic, and the other in the Pacific.

"What do you want?" Kip yelled. He made a rude hand gesture at the other pilot, and the Sparrowhawk put on a burst of speed and peeled away. It swiftly returned, however, closing at a ninety-degree angle, and Kip saw the flash of its twin guns. He heard the noisy whiz and smack of the bullets hitting the fuselage, and he reacted immediately. He slammed his feet at the controls, doing his best to dodge as he dove toward the desert floor. He continued maneuvering for several minutes, and then with panic subsiding and anger smoldering, Kip searched the sky for the armed fighter. He couldn't find it. The Sparrowhawk had vanished.

Later, with the pink crest of the Sandia Mountains filling the horizon, Kip flew over the Rio Grande toward Mathews Airfield. He was still angry, and he mulled over the details of the one-sided dogfight. It was just crazy! That maniac shot live rounds at him, for crying out loud! Those were real bullet holes in the canvas!

In spite of the encounter, there was no vital damage. The 'Jenny' still handled well enough, though Kip was sure he and Doo would have some serious patching to do. The more he thought about it, the angrier he got, and by the time he touched down at the airfield, he was in a very foul mood.

Doo saw the damage immediately. "What happened to the plane? Are those bullet holes?"

"I'll tell you in a minute." Kip dragged himself inside the hanger and sat down with a Coca Cola while Doo jumped around in frenzy.

"What about the damage to the Jenny?" Doo said for the fifth time. His impatience was becoming unbearable. "I know you took the girl to Chaco Canyon, but what about the holes in the plane?"

Kip took a big slug of soda, and then belched loudly to announce his readiness to tell his story.

"Okay, okay." Kip knew he had pushed Doo to his limit. "I was on my way back, and I decided to fly south towards Mt. Taylor. I figured I would check out the lava fields before heading home. I guess I was daydreaming, when a loud, screaming rocket dove down across my nose! I nearly crapped my pants! It was one of those Navy, Sparrowhawk fighters!"

"Was it really fast?" Doo asked eagerly, wanting to hear all about it.

"Yes it was. They are 700 pounds heavier than the Jenny, but they have about three-times the horsepower; and the wingspan is half of what the old girl's is. I ought to know, because I was a Navy pilot, and I flew one of the early models when they were being tested on the new aircraft carriers. I even flew one from the *Akron* for a short time." Kip's face suddenly took on a perplexed frown.

"Doo, with the dirigibles gone now, why would one of these airplanes be flying around here—in the desert?"

"Who knows, just tell me about the bullet holes."

"Well, he came around and flew straight at me. He passed me close! Next thing I knew he was alongside, waving." Kip stopped abruptly and scowled, remembering something. "No," he said slowly, "he wasn't waving at me; he was trying to wave me *away!* That's why he shot at me, because I didn't change course."

"Do you know where you were when you saw him?"

Kip tried to remember as much as he could about the area. "I didn't see him when I flew to Chaco from the southeast, but when I flew south towards Mt. Taylor, he showed up like a bat out of bejezus! Hey, get me a map!"

Kip bent over the unrolled paper and pushed a finger along his flight path. "It was just about here…desert, rocks, washes, mesas…hey, I did fly over part of a mesa, and I saw some buildings tucked away in a round canyon. What would be out there to be worth shooting at someone about? What kind of government operation would use a Sparrowhawk in the middle of the desert?"

"We're going to find out, aren't we?" Doo asked, already knowing the answer.

"Yeah, but I can't very well call the Navy and ask them."

"What about showing them the bullet holes in the Jenny?"

"Aw, they'd probably just say it was some moth damage, or dry rot, or something. I wonder what's going on out there that they want to keep a secret."

"Secret? Who's keeping a secret?" a female voice said from the doorway. "What about bullet holes?" Lisa Ann sauntered over to the desk, and bent over to look at the map.

Kip nearly fell off his chair trying to stand up, and Doo reached over, and jerked the map off the desk. Lisa's face was flushed with interest

Kip said, "Oh, uh, Lisa Ann, I'm glad you're here. I wanted to see you…I, uh, wanted to ask if you were all right after the…the thing with the guy in the car this morning. Say, would you like to go see a movie tonight? There's a new feature in town, lots of gunplay. Kind of a G-man thing, I guess." Kip swallowed noisily, and hoped he could sidetrack her from his conversation with Doo.

Lisa glared at Kip, and then at Doo. Both men smiled innocently. Finally, she said, "No, not tonight." She took a deep breath, and dropped the bomb she had planned.

"I have another date tonight."

CHAPTER 7

The Blacksparrow Mine south of Chaco Canyon

The grim-faced Sparrowhawk pilot cursed as he flew toward the mining complex. "That damn idiot! He almost flew right over the place before I caught up with him. Curse the fool for not having enough sense to fly off when I buzzed him the first time. He deserved to be shot at, the bastard!"

Lt. Nicholas Ells was not happy. He mentally roasted the other pilot over hot coals, and then he had another thought that chilled him to the bone: he let the fool get away! He remembered the standing orders now. Pilots were not to use their guns unless there was a significant danger or a security breach. Then, the orders were to, quickly, and with lethal force, neutralize the target and obliterate any evidence.

The blood drained from his face, and his guts began to churn with anxiety as he realized the magnitude of his error. He would receive severe punishment if the Commandant were aware of this. His mind squirmed as he considered the possibility of covering up his actions. Would the mechanics notice that he had fired the guns? Of course they would—but at what? How would they know? Could anyone have heard the staccato sound of the .30's hammering away in the sky? Possibly; but maybe not.

The exhaust headers of the radial engine screamed and echoed back from the rocks as the Sparrowhawk swooped low over the mesa. The landscape was bare, except for a few stunted junipers struggling to survive. The echo of the reflected engine noise muted, briefly, each time he overflew one of the dark canyons. He cleared the lip of the plateau and banked sharply west. He saw the buildings and the airstrip tucked inside the small valley.

Massive arms of ancient sandstone encircled the mine, broken only by a narrow gap to the east, allowing for road and rail access. As he brought the speedy biplane down to the runway, he felt the lift effect from the ground, and then the tires yelped as he touched down. Nicholas taxied the small fighter to the hanger, and his crew came out to service the plane.

When he cut the engine and stepped down from the cockpit, he told one of the workers that he had test fired the guns on his way back to the field, and that one of the guns had appeared to jam.

Nicholas then headed for the bunkhouse. He ignored the other men, his mind busy with his own predicament. His face bore an evil look; a fact noted by those he passed.

Evening came fast as the sun sank behind the mesa walls. Inside, in the cool darkness of a sprawling log house, a thin man sat behind a desk; his back straight in his leather chair. A few papers lay before him. His delicate and bony hands rested on the edge of the desktop like two large, fleshy spiders.

He was Commandant Thomas Bloundt. A small light illuminated the papers on the desk, but his angular face and icy blue eyes remained hidden in shadow. He wore a checkered western shirt with pearl buttons, but his German features and stern demeanor were pure military.

In a chair facing him across the desk, sat an uneasy, Lt. Nicholas Ells. He held his hat in his lap with both hands, as if to keep it from running away, leaving him alone to face the man before him. The air seemed cloying, and Lt. Ells desperately willed his heartbeat to slow down. His eyes darted left to right, never lingering on the stiff form behind the desk.

The Commandant had already read the memo several times. However, it served as a good prop to hold his attention while his visitor waited and squirmed. This one is a greasy worm on a hook, he noted with distaste. Slowly, he lifted his cold eyes and leaned forward. Ells would not meet his stare, confirming the Commandant's assessment. He absently set the paper aside.

"Lieutenant," he began pleasantly, with a thin smile, "how long have you been with us on this mission? Two years, is it?"

Ells looked up quickly. "Since the taking of the *Akron* sir." His beady, pig-like eyes lowered again.

"Come Nicholas, we don't have to be so formal here. I understand there is a funny nickname that your fellow junior officers call you. What is it... oh yes, 'Nick the biter.' Isn't that it?"

"Yes...yes it is." The stocky Ells shifted uneasily.

"Nick the biter," the Commandant repeated. "Would you tell me just what kind of circumstances could have spawned such an unlikely name as that?"

Of course, Commandant Bloundt knew exactly what had spawned such a name. He knew the family history and background of every man under his command. He knew their strengths and their weaknesses, their dreams, their fears, and he knew when they would speak truthfully, and when they would lie.

Bloundt's voice was friendly, but Nicholas could sense the presence of the lash just underneath it. He cleared his throat.

"Well sir, I was in a fight once..." His voice trailed off.

"Go on, go on," prompted Bloundt.

"Well, I was in a fight, and...well, this guy insulted me. He called me a fat toad or something like that. He said he didn't like the way I treated his sister." The stocky man's lips pursed, and then formed a small, lurid grin as he recalled the girl. "And then he jumped me. We were fighting and rolling around, and he was getting the best of me, so I grabbed his head, and bit off his ear." The grin widened on his face.

Bloundt appeared to consider the man's story for a moment.

"Did you eat it?"

Nicholas stared at his superior's face, appearing not to understand the question.

"Did you eat the ear Lieutenant? Did you ingest the prize?"

"Well no," Nicholas said, his confusion was obvious.

The man behind the desk speared his unfortunate victim with an evil glare and leaned further forward.

"Had I taken such a prize from someone, perhaps someone like you Nicholas, I would have taken your heart instead. I would have cut it out with my knife, and eaten it in front of your disbelieving eyes while it was STILL BEATING!"

In the silence that followed the shouted words, Nicholas felt his bowels growing numb. His face was sweating, and he fought a sudden urge to urinate. His mouth was dry, but his hands were wet and clammy, still clutching desperately at his hat.

"But that's just the problem with you Nicholas," Bloundt said offhandedly, slowly relaxing back in his chair. "You don't finish what you start."

"But Sir…," Nicholas knew he was about to be skewered.

"STOP!" his superior shouted, leaping to his feet. "If you lie to me now, I will kill you before you can stand. You fired your guns at another aircraft, and then you let the fool fly away to report it!"

The unfortunate Lt. Ells began to shiver.

"We barely have a month to finish our work here, before we execute the last phase of our mission and return home. For over three years, we have avoided the scrutiny of the Americans with guile and finesse. But now, with a twitch of your stubby finger, brought on by some feeble electrical impulse from that putrid mass of greasy meat you call a brain, you have put us all in jeopardy!"

Now the unfortunate man's limbs were numb beyond any feeling.

"Lieutenant Ells, in the past I have used your rough skills to take care of the odd problems that have come up. Now, I find that I no longer need, nor desire, those services. As of this moment, I am stripping you of your rank. Tomorrow, you will move into the enlisted men's quarters and begin serving the remainder of your time performing janitorial duties. Is that clear?"

Nicholas' lips moved, but he could not speak.

"You are dismissed!"

As the man stood shakily, to leave, the Commandant said, "Cheer up Nicholas. Who knows, if you perform your new duties with distinction, you may be allowed to leave this place with the rest of us."

Bloundt paused for his words to sink in, and then he hissed, "Now get out of my sight!"

CHAPTER 8

Diana woke up the next morning thinking of Kip Combs and her plane ride. The canvas walls of her tent rippled softly in the wind. Above her head, the material was dappled with sunlight shining through the dancing shadow of a juniper bough.

She laid on her cot, listening to the chirping of a robin, her hand reaching across her ribs to squeeze a firm breast. Her fingers moved down her flat stomach to the thin tangle of hair, and when she felt her body respond to her vagrant touch, she gasped and sat upright. She had work to do and there was no time for thinking such things.

Throwing the blankets aside, she quickly swung her legs off the cot, and pulled on her jeans. I am twenty-six years old, she told herself, much too mature to have a crush on a wild, reckless, young pilot. She chased the thought from her head and ran a brush through her dark hair. She glanced into a small mirror and made a face at what she saw.

Archeology was not the glamorous career she had thought, when her father first described his exploits. She was a precocious, eight-year-old tomboy, and she had grown up reading books and looking at pictures of ancient cities; no imaginary tea parties or dolls for her. After college, she had learned that real archeology was time-weary research and months of hard work outdoors. The sanitary facilities, she grimaced, were not for the squeamish or bashful.

With the sudden death of her father Professor Witherspoon, the university asked her to take his old position as expedition leader on the summer dig at Chaco Canyon.

Diana ducked past the tent flap and stood in the bright sunlight. She squinted at the massive layers of reds and browns in the surrounding cliffs, and then at the contrasting greens of the low trees. She gazed over the tall, stone-chinked walls of the Pueblo Bonito ruin and marveled at the ingenious master plan that guided the Anasazi to build this three acre, 'D' shaped city a thousand years ago. Nearby, the Chaco wash cut through the sheltered valley—dry at this time of year. Small clumps of patient dogwoods lined the low banks, waiting for the life-giving, seasonal floods.

Ragged applause greeted here when she entered the mess tent, for being the last one up. She joined her students at the long table. They were beginning the excavation of a small site to the east of Pueblo Bonito today, and the diggers eagerly debated the potential importance of the low, broken mound.

Diana thought of the strange artifact found near the new dig site. It was a pottery shard with some odd designs that didn't match the familiar ones of the Anasazi. She sensed that they were from an earlier time. Diana smiled; a mystery always intrigued her.

With breakfast over, and the students busy at work, Carl walked with her along the path through the ruins. He was a reliable site manager, and he had an organized mind, and an uncanny knowledge of machinery.

He had been an associate of her father's, though she had only met him in recent months. She was attracted to him at first, but though he had been charming, he had shown no real interest in her. He kept his thoughts to himself, and she finally decided it was enough that he was a competent site manager.

Carl spoke as they walked. "Diana, I want to tell you something about your father…about when we found his body."

She stopped abruptly, and Carl appeared to struggle for a way to explain. "I found him first, and I had a chance to inspect his body before the others got there. I found marks on him that couldn't be explained by the fall that killed him."

Diana searched Carl's eyes for more information. "What do you mean?" A knot of anxiety began to form in her stomach.

"I think it would be best if we did our exploring very quickly today. We may be watched, and I want to be out of there before anyone has a chance to react to our presence."

Diana and Carl took the old Ford south on the rutted road to the place they wanted to explore. He drove carefully to avoid raising too much dust.

He cut off on some trails to the north of the mesa, away from the mining site. The day was already hot, with noon still an hour away. They parked and hefted their packs, and began to hike around the perimeter. Neither spoke until Carl motioned to a section of the steep talus slope.

"We can climb here. A narrow trail leads up to the top. Hopefully, we can find the spot where your father stood before he fell."

Diana nodded grimly and followed. They climbed, stopping often to rest and take sips of water. Animals probably made the path over the years. The last section was more difficult, because it involved crawling over an area of fallen rock, but soon they were on the top of the mesa. Carl motioned to stop, and he pulled out a pair of binoculars to survey the rocks ahead. Diana sat down, wiping at her face and neck with a piece of cloth moistened from the water in her canteen.

"From the position of the big mesa, I'd say the place we want is just to the left of that square boulder over there." He pointed for Diana to see. "Let's stay behind cover as much as possible."

Diana crouched and followed Carl.

"It's got to be somewhere around here," He said. "See that cleft over there? That was above where your father was found."

"Exactly what are we looking for Carl, footprints? It's all rock up here."

"Yes, footprints, or maybe just scuff marks. It's not all rock, but even rock can sometimes show evidence of a struggle. Maybe we can find a scrap of cloth or a spot of blood. Let's stay six feet apart, and keep our eyes on the ground."

She nodded, and they both paced back and forth along a hundred foot swath near the cliff, working closer to the edge on each pass.

A half-mile away, a sentry on the larger mesa noticed movement and brought his glasses up. He studied the two forms. It looked as if they were searching for something. With a low curse, he put the binoculars away and rode rapidly down the trail toward the mine.

Commandant Bloundt was in a foul mood when he stepped outdoors from his quarters. He had taken reports from his heads of staff while eating breakfast, and they assured him of the completion of the mining operations within a month. They needed another dozen workers, however. Bloundt did not like the risk of drawing more attention by creating a new group of missing persons, but staying here at the mine any longer than another month would create an even bigger risk.

Their clandestine operation had begun over three years ago. The first of their group had arrived by twos and threes, put ashore by submarine, to disperse into the coastal countryside and make their way west. They met at a safe house in Albuquerque and drove to this location.

It took over two years to construct the mine, all the surrounding buildings, and airstrip. The rail spur took a little longer to finish. Theirs was a well-funded mission, and they had secret assistance from a key State official. The taking of the dirigible was a bold, but necessary, step. It brought in the last of the men and supplies, as well as a means for escaping. That time was rapidly approaching.

Bloundt felt the weight and stress of command, and he was relieved when his headache began to dissipate as he walked across the compound. He approached the large building that housed the mine hoist and crushing equipment, first. The Americans would be surprised to find that the small coalmine operating on the property was in reality, a uranium mine.

They worked a convenient seam of coal as a cover to hide the real ore that was collected: rich yellowcake, dangerous to mine because of the radiation, but vital for the dreams and ambitions of the Fuhrer.

Discretely, over time, local indigenous families had been kidnapped to toil in the mine, and ultimately, to give their lives for the glory of the Third Reich. Due to the remote location of the abductions, their captors knew that few of the people would be reported missing. Kept in cages below ground in the mine, most captives sickened within several months, and developed horrible running sores. They rarely lived much longer. A few of the German hands wore mining gear and leisurely worked a coal seam to keep up a front, and to disguise the secret operation.

Two men nodded when Bloundt entered the building—he ignored them. It was important for everyone to act the part of civilians to keep up their deception to any outside straying eyes, but Bloundt's pride was beginning to wear thin from the lack of receiving a proper salute. He longed for the sound of brusque German speech, instead of the foul American English used to disguise their mission. He also missed the women back home, drawn to him because of his money and his rank.

The captive females here may be satisfactory for his men, but Bloundt considered them to be beneath his station. Influenced for too long by his father and by the fascist movement in his native country, he would not consort with an inferior race.

He left the building after a short inspection and walked toward a section of the tall cliff wall that all but encircled the compound. He smiled as he stopped before the cliff, marveling at the disguised hanger door. He was within six feet of it, before it became apparent that the section was a three-dimensional mural of painted metal and concrete. It disguised the massive sliding doors: 150 feet tall and 200 feet wide. He strode to an access door at the side, and entered a small reception area.

"I'll have your report now Gerald."

"Here, sir." The man stood and handed him a thin file of typed pages. "The airship will be ready to fly tonight at your orders."

"Good. We have another acquisition to make before they head to the supply site in Mexico. When the ship returns, your team can start making ready for the last stage of the mission and our final extraction."

Bloundt allowed himself a brief, self-serving vision of receiving the credit for shipping a supply of uranium ore to Germany, and for delivering personally, the captured American dirigible. This was good, but it was the third gift he would bring, that gave him the biggest thrill. He sighed as he reviewed the checklist in the file. He made a few notes and handed it back to the attendant.

"Yes Gerald, all is in order, as I've come to expect from you. It's a shame that the dirigible was seen by the old professor on our last flight for captives."

"Yes Sir, but our lookouts did observe the man, and he was taken care of."

"Tut-tut my boy, I'm not placing blame on anyone. It's just that, right now, I don't want any more mishaps to compromise the mission."

Bloundt's eyes turned to the nervous man. He did not need to say any more; Gerald's face and armpits were damp with sweat.

Bloundt smiled with satisfaction. He had ordered his man at Chaco Canyon to take care of the old professor, and to make his death look like the result of an accident.

He pursed his lips as he thought of the efficient killing machine the agent was: an arrogant mission partner, but still, a very useful and necessary tool. His position with the students was a fortunate one. It allowed him to keep watch over their activities, and to make sure none of them got too close to the mining operation.

"I'll just take a quick look at the ship, Gerald, and then be on my way. I don't wish to slow down the preparations your team must make in these last weeks."

The young man was visually relieved as the Commandant walked through the interior doorway into the hidden hanger.

Bloundt felt a twinge of awe every time he looked upon the dirigible. He admired the huge shape of the *Akron*—now renamed the *Nighthawk*, with black paint covering the original silver color. It nearly filled the cavernous space, roofed over with steel beams, over 150 feet high and 800 feet deep. The dirigible was only slightly smaller than the Fuhrer's *Hindenburg* was.

The taking of the *Akron* was one of Blount's proudest moments. The men and equipment it brought, including the planes, and all of its other capabilities, had been a vital step. Using it as their escape vehicle would be a final thumb in the eye of the Americans. The theft would be a thing that would spawn legends: legends that Thomas Bloundt would wear like the medals of a hero returning to the Fatherland. He left the building whistling a marshal tune.

Bloundt squinted as he stepped into the sunlight. He strode over to the last stop on his daily tour: the aircraft hangar at the end of the runway. When he entered the building and walked past the parked Sparrowhawks, he felt the same kind of giddiness he had felt as a young man, the first time he unbuttoned the blouse of a full-busted girl. Bloundt strode purposefully toward the back of the building. He held his breath as his eyes followed the lines and curves of the brightly lit machine before him. It was obviously an advanced aircraft, and his mind boggled to imagine it buried in the rock nearby for such a very long time.

He knew that scientists and engineers in Germany were developing a flying wing at this very moment. Admiring the angular shape before him, he knew that the Horton brothers' best designs back home would look like flying bricks by comparison.

Thomas Bloundt reverently reached out to touch the pitted surface of the craft. He stroked its wing edge and marveled that a thing buried in the earth for thousands of years could still look so fresh and alive. Of course, it could not fly in its condition; perhaps scientists would never figure out what powered it in the first place, but oh, what a magnificent prize for the Fuhrer to display to the world.

"Commandant," a voice spoke from behind him. It was one of his junior officers.

"Yes Richard, what is it?"

"Our scout on the north rim just reported that there are two people on the small mesa; a man, and a woman. They are searching near the area where the old professor was disposed of."

Bloundt froze. "Damn!" he said loudly, startling the young officer. "Send out riders right now to identify them; and put two men on the north rim from now on, so one can stay while the other reports any future activity. The visitors must find nothing to implicate us. Now go!"

Bloundt took a deep breath and turned his attention back to the sleek craft. It resembled nothing ever made by man.

Walking back to his quarters, Bloundt thought of the mission, and of the heavy odds they had beaten to come this far. They were so close now. His headache returned, and he imagined all the mistakes and missteps that could occur before it became time to leave. He cursed luck, for the fickle bitch she was.

CHAPTER 9

"Here," said Carl Walker pointing at the ground, "and here. See the small stones and the light scuffmarks on the rock where someone stepped on them. There's some more over here."

Diana studied the areas Carl pointed out. "Over here too," she said, "and here's a part of a boot print."

"That dark spot over there," Carl said, "I think its blood."

Diana felt cold, and then anger grew, and her face turned red. Tears burst from her eyes. "Those dirty bastards."

Carl spoke over his shoulder. "Here's what I was looking for." He lifted a stout branch about six feet long. "See how the end is broken off and forms a half-moon. I found marks just like this on your father's body. Someone killed him."

Diana stared at the long stick through tears, not wanting to believe what she heard.

Carl's voice became soft. "He was beaten and pushed over the edge."

"Who... could do such a thing?" she said.

"Maybe a drifter or someone from the mine, we'll probably never know."

They left the mesa a short while later and headed back to Chaco Canyon. As the old Ford motored away, three riders watched from a distance. A blonde man hidden in the rocks nearby stayed until the riders left.

Carl and Diana did not speak on the way back. The rough ride jostled her to numbness. She bit back her sobs but she could not stop the tears.

When they reached the Chaco camp, she muttered a soft "thank you" and ran quickly to her tent.

Carl drove away. He had seen a flash of sunlight off the field glasses of the riders. A brief smile formed on his face. He knew the professor had been interested in the small mesa, and he had kept notes about his explorations in his journal, but the book wasn't on him when Carl searched the body. He needed to find it.

A short while later, he stopped to talk to Diana on his way to the mess tent, "I'm sorry you had to see those things today."

"No, it's alright. I asked you to take me there. Carl, I feel I've got to do something, but I just don't know what."

He saw the resolve on her face. "I'll go back again tomorrow and have a better look around."

"I'll go too. I want to..."

Carl cut her words off. "No. I didn't tell you, but I saw riders when we left the mesa today. They must have lookouts posted."

"But I have to do something." Her teeth clenched.

"Be patient, I'll be gone a day or so, and as soon as I get back, I'll fill you in on anything I've found. Your students need you now. You've been away for too long, and they need your help and guidance. Don't forget, you promised the University you'd take over your father's work."

Diana sighed. "You're right Carl. I need to focus on my work right now."

The man gauged his next words to sound off-the-cuff.

"Your father kept a journal someplace, have you seen it?"

"No, why do you ask?"

"Well, I thought there might be information in it that would shed some light on why he was up there in the first place."

"Do you think so? I'll look around for it. Carl, be careful. As soon as you get back, I want to know everything you've found out. Agreed?" Diana stared at Carl and repeated her question. "Agreed?"

"Agreed," he said.

Diana finished cleaning up and went to the mess tent to eat. She sifted through the accumulated piles of notes and correspondence in her makeshift office, and then met with her students to lay out plans for a new dig. After supper, she went to bed, and slept fitfully.

Morning found her tired, but eager to begin the new excavation. She took her coffee to the small mound where the students were gathered.

The boys and girls were in good spirits, and they asked a barrage of questions when she walked up. She couldn't help but catch their contagious excitement.

Who can tell me the name of the person known for the early, landmark work here?"

Four hands went up, and one tall boy spoke. "That's easy, Miss Witherspoon, Neil M. Judd in the early twenties."

"Right, Charles. And who can tell me when the Chaco culture began to change from basket weaving and part-time farming, to a more successful civilization, resulting in a rapid population growth; anyone?"

This time a Hispanic girl spoke up. "It was around 500 A.D., I think."

"Yes Tessa. Sometime after that, the early Anasazi began to use pottery; probably brought in by trade with their southern neighbors in Mexico. They also began using more sophisticated tools and weapons; like the handled axe, and the bow and arrow."

"What did they use before that, Miss. Witherspoon? I mean, for hunting and defending themselves."

"Good question Jeremy. Can anyone answer that? Donna?"

"They used rocks and slings, and spears, and maybe an arrow thrower."

"That's right, and they eventually became so successful at farming, that their population grew by leaps and bounds. They used irrigation to protect themselves from the droughts that hindered the other tribes further south But by 1300 A.D. they were all gone."

"Why?" asked Donna.

"No one knows." Diana beamed a triumphant smile. "That's why we're here. Now, I want you all to begin with this new mound. We have questions to answer and theories to confirm or disprove. By the way, did someone say they found some unusual designs on some rocks nearby?"

"I did," said a boy considered a heartthrob among the girls in camp. "Donna and I found them when we were…exploring."

"Oh?" Diana said with a sly smile. "And what kind of exploring were you two doing?"

Hoots of glee and good-natured teasing erupted, but the boy and girl deftly shrugged them off. They did however; share a small secret smile that Diana noted.

"Let's go see them," she said. "The rest of you begin setting up your equipment and your site map, and then get started on the digging. When I get back, I want to see what you've found just below the surface."

Diana and the two students walked southeast along the dry wash meandering through the ruins. When it turned south at the mouth of the canyon, they continued east a short distance to Fajada Butte.

The rocky sentinel stood alone, its many tiers, skirted by a rugged talus slope. They climbed a section of tumbled slabs and found a narrow cleft. Shuffling single file between the pressing rocks, they soon found themselves in the semi-darkness of a small cave.

The boy lit a kerosene lantern left from their previous visit, and said, "Over here." He led Diana around a corner to a small hidden room at the bottom of a ledge. He climbed down and showed Diana what they'd found.

She could hardly believe her eyes. The shapes and figures were different from anything she had ever seen before. They were exquisitely drawn and resembled a blend of early Egyptian and Olmec designs; but with something different added, almost alien. They were elegant in their simplicity. There were colors too—blue, white, yellow, and a rusty red.

"Oh my," she said, lightly touching one of the painted swirls with trembling fingertips. "We need to get a camera, and more light."

CHAPTER 10

Sam Begay arrived at the Thoreau Trading Post around mid-morning. It was windy and hot, and two days since he left Dan Yazzie at his grandfather's hogan with supplies, two horses, and a rifle.

His mind kept going back to something…it was about what Jake had said. The old man had been unusually talkative about witches and other Indian superstitions. It wasn't that Jake was above spreading rumors if it would bring customers to the store, but it was certainly odd of him to blurt it all out like that. Jake was not subtle, but he did know proper Reservation etiquette. One did not talk about ghosts and witches in polite conversation. No, the old fox knew something, and he wanted to draw Sam out to see if he knew more than he had told him.

Sam pondered the complexities of the white man's mind as he entered the building. The warped screen door brushed a small bell, and the old man stood up behind the counter, smiling.

"We-ha, I can hardly believe it. I get a visit from Sam Begay, twice in the same week. Could it be he's here to greet another bus? Naw, too early for that. Maybe he's got a craving for another grape soda."

"You know damn well why I'm here Jake. I want to talk to you about what's been going on around here lately."

Jake fixed him with steely eyes, his thick, unruly eyebrows added to the effect.

"I thought that would get the old wheels turnin' in your mind. Ain't no cop ever born, especially an Indian one, who can ignore a mystery."

Sam stepped to the counter, frowning. "You might as well get me one of those damn grape sodas. If I gotta listen to some old man rattling on for a couple of hours, I'm sure going to get thirsty."

Jake set a cold bottle on the counter and toweled the water off.

"I guess you want me to start at the beginning." After a suitable pause, the old man said, "Talk of witches and coyotes and such, has been going on here on the Res. since the First People crawled up from the underground. Funny thing though, the talk got more frequent two or three years ago. Shirley Hostie got everything started. She got everybody riled up when she swore her cousin and his family went missing...just like that."

Jake snapped a gnarled finger and thumb to punctuate his statement.

"She said she left them one afternoon, and when she came back the next day, they were all gone. The house was vacant. Now, Shirley was known to take to the bottle pretty good, so everyone just took it as an alcohol addled dream."

"So what happened?" Sam let his interest show.

"Nothing," Jake said offhandedly. "Oh, she talked on for a couple of months, insisting that someone had committed a crime. Then she just quit."

"Quit?"

"Yeah, she disappeared too. No one's heard from her since."

Sam's eyes were wide. "I don't recall this being reported."

"It wasn't. Shirley was—well, not very reliable, and everyone figured she was crazy. So the talk stopped."

"Was there any talk about a large animal killing livestock or people?"

"You mean like a cougar or a bear?"

"Maybe."

"No, nothing like that, but I have been hearing more and more stories about skinwalkers and witches. Also, there is an unusual story that comes up now and then. It's about a growling cloud."

Old Jake timed his last revelation at the very moment Sam tipped up his bottle of grape soda and took a big swig. Sam swallowed desperately and coughed.

Jake smiled with satisfaction. "Yep, a growling cloud. Couldn't be thunder; they would have said it was thunder, but growling, now that's a different thing. My older brother, Bob, used to fart, and tell me and my sister that it was the clouds growling." He giggled, and then he became dead serious. "But this growling cloud has white men in it who climb down ropes and take people away."

Sam was in a thoughtful mood when he walked outside. He could not rely on the stories of superstitious people. Skinwalkers; spirits wearing the skin of animals, and witches and ghosts, were blamed for almost everything bad that happened on the Reservation. However, he also knew that superstitions usually had an inner core of reality, like a nut hidden inside its shell. His traditional upbringing made him shiver at such thoughts.

He brought in a map from his truck and laid it across the counter. Old Jake pointed out places, and Sam made notes where he indicated people lived, and where certain odd occurrences had happened.

When Sam drove away, he was certain of two things: he would find the clues he needed somewhere on this map; and it would take at least a week to cover the entire area.

CHAPTER 11

Carl Walker, on foot, took a direct route from Chaco Canyon to the small mesa. His well-muscled frame moved like a jungle cat, and he exhibited the endurance of a trained athlete. Shaded by his Stetson, his dark eyes squinted across the heat-rippled horizon. He looked competent and in total control of his environment.

Carl arrived at the north face with plenty of daylight left. The area was sheltered from any prying eyes on the larger mesa to the south. He had explored sections of this edifice before, but not much on the north side. He drank sparingly of the tepid water in his canteen, knowing the heat of the day wouldn't diminish for many hours.

He walked along the base of the mesa and saw where a large section of the cliff had fallen away in recent years. He found a few petroglyphs nearby, but they showed nothing that interested him. After an hour, he set his pack down. He was stretching his back when another slab of rock broke off the cliff with a loud *crack*. The ground shook as the rock slid down and shattered into smaller pieces.

The dust had settled by the time Carl reached the spot. He looked about for anything of interest, but found nothing. He eventually backtracked to the game trail leading up the slope, and he followed the dim path to a sheltered spot near the top where he planned to bed down for the evening. He would explore more in the early morning hours, and then head back to Chaco Canyon while his water lasted. He ate a cold meal and nodded off as darkness came.

Across the reservation, the sun dipped below the western hills as two Navajo boys ended their game of catch. It was becoming too dark to see the dirty rubber ball they were playing with. They both said goodnight to their grandmother, who was watching them from her old wooden rocker outside the doorway of her hogan.

She lived alone. Her two sons and daughter each had their own houses across the yard, and they had their own families. A broken down Ford truck, without doors and wheels, lay off to the side of one of the buildings. Kerosene lamps burned in the three houses, but not in grandmas. She sat in the growing darkness, contentedly looking at the bright pinpoints of the stars.

After a while, the lights went out in the houses. Grandma was asleep in her rocker, snoring. The soft wind began to moan. The moaning became louder, then quiet again. The stars abruptly disappeared above the houses, and grandma woke with a start. She looked up to see dark shapes dropping from a large black space above her. A shadowy rope materialized and dragged slowly across the yard. Abruptly, a black shape detached itself from the rope and flew at her. She thought to cry out, but a club exploded against her head before she could speak. Other ropes appeared in front of the houses, and silent shapes dropped, and then spread out toward the buildings. At a clipped signal, they kicked the doors in and their bright lights flooded the interiors. There were screams and sounds of struggling, and then it all stopped.

Lights lit up the yard and more ropes fell with harnesses attached. Dark-clad men strapped the unconscious bodies into the harnesses and men above pulled them upwards to disappear in the darkness.

The moaning became louder again; like the howling of a host of banshees. Soon the noise drifted away and left the yard, houses, and the surrounding desert, as silent and still as a grave.

CHAPTER 12

A hundred miles away, Lisa Ann Abbot held her sweater tightly around herself to fend off the night's chill. A few lights glowed softly from the airstrip a hundred yards behind her. She stood on the fringe of the desert, facing a sky lit with a million stars. It was after midnight, and dozens of critters peeped and skittered unseen in the darkness.

She never did have a date planned for tonight; she had no idea why she told Kip that she did. Lisa sobbed as her throat tightened with emotion. She took a quick drag from her cigarette, flicking the ash with her thumbnail while she exhaled.

"Damn," she said through cold lips—another sob. She blinked back tears and talked to the night as she relived her old nightmares.

"So what if I spent a year living on the streets? I didn't have a choice did I? Damn right I didn't. Oh, I could have stayed in Chicago and let my stepdad have his way with me every Saturday night; and then let my mom slap me around on Sunday. No, I had to run away to try to make it on my own. I did it too." She stood straight. "Maybe it meant I had to be with some men who were worse to me than the one I ran away from, but there were others who were nicer...a hell of a lot nicer...nice...like Kip."

She took a big gulp of air and yelled. "And I'm not going to apologize to anybody!"

As the echo faded she thought of the events of the past two years; starting when her Uncle Jack found her and brought her to New Mexico. She met Kip and his Aunt Vicki when they still had their aerobatic thrill show. Lisa convinced Vicki to let her do the wing walking routines, and in a short while, with her looks and a tight bathing suit, they begun to draw the crowds in.

She fell in love with Kip, and they had an intense, but short-lived, affair. Barnstorming was on its way out, and Vicki retired from the show and moved away to get married. Kip began to haul passengers and cargo, and the stunt flying was over. For some reason, so was their love affair. She told Kip all about her past, but he said it didn't matter to him—or did it?

Lisa Ann wiped her eyes. "I'll never be good enough for Kip or anybody else. Why can't I just stay away and leave him alone? All I do is act like an idiot when he's around!"

She looked up, and held her breath when a corner of the sky flashed and a bright light shot away from it, speeding westward. It faded quickly, but Lisa and the creatures in the night, all held their breath for a moment in awe of the spectacle.

"Someone heard me huh?" she whispered. She watched the stars for a while longer. "Maybe someone did."

CHAPTER 13

The Blacksparrow Mine sat behind two patrolled gates that connected the encircling arms of the mesa. A dirt road from the mine ran to the east, and connected to another leading north to Chaco Canyon and south toward the small village of Crownpoint. A small guard shack stood at the intersection.

The guard sat finishing his sandwich as he peered through a narrow window into the night. There was just enough room inside for a chair and a small table. It was cold, and the wind blew against the crude wooden shelter, hissing and howling like a live animal. The man jumped when a lost tangle of brush thudded against the side, and then scraped its stick-fingers along the wall before whisking past. As he shivered in the darkness, his mind imagined unseen desert ghosts.

The guard was thin and displayed poor hygiene. His breath and his body smelled of spiced food and sweat. This, and his unfortunate habit of complaining, made him a target for disciplinary action, and ultimately, earned him this lonely assignment.

The desert was driving him crazy. He longed for the forests and rivers of his homeland. He imagined how happy he would be when the next month was over, and they could leave this barren place and go back to Germany. He longed for the taste of good sausage and beer and for the sight of plump young barmaids with their ample breasts spilling from their bodices.

He was envisioning this and other anatomical wonders, when a loud thump against the wall startled him. He snorted to himself for being so jumpy, and then realized that the wind had stopped. He reached slowly for his rifle, senses alert. There came a scratching along the wall. The guard hardly dared to breathe as adrenalin coursed through his body. He rose from his chair and glanced through the window into the gloom, straining to hear any other noises.

A burst of wind hit the shack and howled away, but no thumping or scratching came with it. He waited, still holding his breath. Another minute passed. Suddenly, an animal's scream pierced the night, sounding almost human, and the guard's heart began to beat fiercely.

As blood pounded in his ears, he forced himself to take slow, shaky, breaths of air. A rabbit, he thought; and then a nervous smile spread across his face. It was a rabbit, he assured himself. They screamed like human babies when caught by a predator. A wolf or a coyote had found a meal tonight, that's all it was.

He breathed easier and sat down in his chair. The wind blew again, and this time the building creaked. Odd, he thought, he didn't hear any howling from the creature that caught the rabbit.

He was pondering this, when the door burst open and a large, hissing, beast leapt upon him, upsetting the table and chair, and driving him to the floor. A foul stench filled his nostrils in the darkness. He gasped and tried to scream, but large, snapping teeth quickly found his face and throat and shook him violently, as strong, sharp claws shredded his torso.

A large, shadowy shape dragged the torn body from the shack. The guard was dead, but his body still quivered as the creature ripped the first mouthful of gore from his heaving chest. In the chilly air, steam rose from the bloody mess as the beast ate its meal under the cold, silent stars.

CHAPTER 14

In the desert not far from Chaco Canyon, Dan Yazzie sat with a blanket wrapped around his shoulders. He leaned against his worn saddle with a rifle across his knees and stared at the starry vault of the sky. He was drowsy, and imagined himself as a traveler sitting on this celestial rock called Earth as it rolled through time and space.

Startled by a brilliant flash of light, he saw something glowing shoot across the sky. Dan shivered, and he realized that he had been holding his breath.

He had been on horseback for two days weaving a zigzag trail across the uneven desert. Dan had come across three abandoned hogans, but they showed no sign of roof damage similar to what he had seen at his grandfather's place.

Tonight he camped near the side of a sandstone cliff. The small campfire was cheery, but as it began to die, Dan's thoughts turned morose, and he crawled through the memories of his three years in prison.

Confined to a small concrete box most of the time, barely large enough for a cot and a dented bucket for a toilet, the experience had scarred him. Growing up in the wide, open desert, he had trouble catching his breath in the small confines of his cell. He often thought he would die and was surprised he didn't. Now free, Dan breathed the fragrance of the cool, night air, and he fell asleep and dreamed.

He dreamed of lying in his cell, watching the dark ceiling break away as he floated out of the prison. He dreamed this many times over the past years, and though his body stayed in the cell, he believed his spirit floated free with the night wind. It would always return to his body before morning, but this time it was different. This time his spirit and his body left the cell together. He looked back and saw the prison walls crumble to dust.

Now he dreamed he was standing in his grandfather's hogan. There was no damage to the roof, and everything was the way he remembered it. He wondered where his daughter and grandfather were. Suddenly, there was a noise and the roof shook as if a heavy weight landed on it. He heard a scratching sound, and then the sound of frantic digging came to him from above.

Clumps of dirt fell from the ceiling and landed at his feet. The sound of heavy panting grew louder. Then the entire roof shook as a large clump of sod fell to the floor. It left a gaping hole above him, and in the darkness, two red eyes glowed at him, and then the howling scream of a demon spoke his name.

Dan awoke kicking his legs and flailing his arms. He managed to grasp his rifle, and he rolled to his knees. He was sweating, and he gasped for breath as he frantically looked around him in the darkness.

The hogan was a dream, but his ears still echoed with the howling scream he had heard. The sound had been real!

Dan Yazzie was spooked, and he stayed awake for the rest of the night. He sat in the darkness, wrapped in his blanket, gripping his rifle in both hands. As he shivered in the cold, his mind stirred through the memories of stories told by the elders about the First People: the stories of zigzag lightning, and flint armor, and the Monster Slayer. He wished his grandfather were here to help make sense of his dream, and of the bright light that had flashed in the sky.

Dan quickly pushed away the thought. Thinking of the dead was bad luck. Eventually he fell asleep, but he awoke hours before dawn to the nickering and stomping of the horses. He gripped his rifle tightly and listened in the darkness.

A noise like a lisping moan came to him on the wind. The moaning seemed to come from nowhere and everywhere. The volume kept changing. Now he could barely hear it over the whistling of the wind. He looked about, but could not locate the source, then he glanced skyward and his blood froze.

He saw the stars eaten by the sky itself! A huge, dark mouth moved slowly above him ingesting thousands of bright lights. As it passed, it excreted the stars behind it. Dan had no explanation for this. He watched the phenomenon until it disappeared beyond a distant mesa. The moaning was gone, leaving only the soft whispering wind.

Dan's hands shook, and he quickly added sticks to the glowing embers of his campfire. He built the blaze higher and sat close to the warming flames, fighting the turmoil in his mind. There would be no more sleep for him tonight.

CHAPTER 15

The sound came softly like the wind; a whispering moaning that gradually became louder. Carl Walker sat up abruptly from his sleep and tried to determine what direction it was coming from. Then he saw it: a huge, dark shape passing overhead, headed south toward the mine. Carl scrambled to put on his boots, and he hefted his pack and followed as the dark thing drifted over the next mesa.

A few miles away, as the dirigible hovered above the compound, a grid of lights came on to guide it downward. Its black skin dully reflected the glow as mooring lines dropped to the ground crews. They removed the human cargo, and hauled the airship inside its hidden lair.

Commandant Bloundt watched as the crew took the captives past where he stood. He counted twelve, one an old woman that they carried. They took the natives into the mineshaft to the waiting cages. Not many, he mused, but enough for now.

Carl Walker made his way down the side of the mesa while the light of the stars guided his footsteps. He crossed the desert, moving confidently toward the larger mesa. He followed the eastern face until he came to the gates, and he began whistling a random tune so as not to startle any gun-happy guards. Carl stepped into the lights, and a guard challenged him immediately.

"It's just me boys; lonesome Carl coming to pay a visit to the Commandant."

The compound was still lit up as he walked through the gates, but the dirigible was nowhere in sight. He went directly to Bloundt's quarters

"Ah Carl," Bloundt acknowledged his visitor and stood to greet him. "What brings you here so early in the morning?"

Carl fixed the man with icy eyes. "What's the big idea of taking the airship out this close to the end of our mission?" Carl was not happy.

Bloundt wrinkled his nose as if he had detected an unpleasant smell. "Don't snap at me," he said. "You may have scouted out, and set up this site, but I'm the one that makes the decisions and overseas it all. That goes for everything, from the dirigible, to the Indian rug you're standing on."

Carl looked down and dropped a dribble of spit between his boots. He ground it in with his toe while gazing steadily at the other man.

Bloundt snarled, "We can take up our quarrel with the Fuhrer himself, if you wish, when we get back to Germany, but for now, I will not allow you to usurp or undermine my authority. You brought the Witherspoon girl to the small mesa. Why?"

Carl smirked, "She wanted to know where her father was killed. I thought it was better to take her there, rather than let her go off by herself. You forget; I am part of the University crowd because I cultivated the professor's confidence beforehand. It gives me a plausible reason for being there, so I can watch their activities, and keep them out of your hair."

"But you did let the old man get into my hair."

"Yeah, and now he's not!" Carl snapped back.

Both men glared at each other. Bloundt eventually shrugged his shoulders and sat down.

"Would you like some coffee? We need to finish our plans to leave this flea-infested desert."

Outside the gates, a man hid where he could see the entrance. He had followed Carl from Chaco Canyon earlier in the day, now he lay behind some brush watching the guards pace under the lights. After an hour, when Carl didn't come out, he crawled away and hiked west around the mesa. An hour later, he appeared on the top of the edifice amid the dark, twisted junipers. He was alert for any sentries, as he searched for a vantage point to view the compound below. He reached the inner edge and lay down to peer into the grounds. Searchlights moved slowly across the shadows.

He was surprised not to see the dirigible. Where did it go? He could make out the lines of an airstrip, and he knew some of the buildings were hangers, but he saw none large enough to shelter the huge craft he had seen earlier. He saw the dark hole of the mine, and the steel rails that led up to it, but the opening was too small to conceal the airship. Could it have taken to the air again? He didn't think so. He would have seen it; but it wasn't here now.

He crawled back from the precipice and found a place of concealment where he could rest and still observe the complex. He settled back to nap for a few hours until daylight.

The Commandant looked up from his plate of scrambled eggs, and he set his fork down as he heard the sound of boots on the wooden stairs outside his quarters. A frantic rapping came on the door.

"Yes?" He said loudly, and a wild looking guard, nearly out of breath from running, opened the door.

"Commandant SIR!"

"Yes, yes." Bloundt said, annoyed to have his breakfast interrupted. "What is it?"

"It's the outer guard sir—from the road station. He's…been killed."

Bloundt stood up so quickly, his plate danced across the table, and his chair bounced noisily against the wall.

"Killed? What are you saying?"

Still trying to catch his breath, the guard gasped his reply. "He's been… eaten sir!"

"What? Make some sense man! Where is he?"

"He's outside by the gate. They just brought him in."

Bloundt rushed out the door and ran to the gate. A group of men stood around the back of a pickup truck. The end of a blanket hung out from the open tailgate. He pushed the men aside to see what was in the truck, and he stared in shock at the mangled, bloody chunks of meat and bone. Bloundt was no stranger to death and gore, but the condition of the guard's body made his stomach contract ominously.

Carl was there, and said, "If it wasn't for the shredded clothing and a few identifiable parts, it would be almost impossible to tell what kind of creature this used to be."

Bloundt glared at him fiercely. "Where did you find him?" He choked back his breakfast and waited for someone to reply.

"Jerry and I went out to relieve Shultzie, and we found what was left of him on the ground outside the guard shack, sir. The door was off the hinges, and everything inside was all broken up and splattered with blood.

We gathered up the…biggest pieces, and I left Jerry there to stand guard while I came back with the body."

"You two get this blanket off the truck and take it to the infirmary. Carl, get in the truck and come to the guard shack with me. The rest of you men, jump in the back. We're going to scour every inch of desert around the station and find out what did this."

An hour later, the men returned to the compound. There were no clues—no tracks of any kind to help solve the mystery. Bloundt's head spun as he walked back to his quarters to lie down. After twenty minutes, he gave it up and admitted that stress was beginning to take its toll on him. Setbacks were to be expected, but he was beginning to think that chance had reshuffled the deck and stacked it against him.

It figures, he thought, just when they were down to their last thirty days. Everything seemed to be going like clockwork up until today. His mind started to clear, and he began to consider his options. He would tolerate no laxness. Now was the time to tighten the nut on discipline, he decided. Crack the whip.

The lone man watched from his vantage point high on the mesa. He had seen the truck, and he saw the blanket and what lay in it. He had watched the truck leave again with more men and return an hour later.

Curious, he thought, and he settled back to watch the rest of the day's events.

CHAPTER 16

'Another date,' Kip remembered Lisa's words from yesterday, and how she looked when she walked away from the hanger. She might just as well have said, 'I'm sorry, but I can't be expected to wilt away, and be ignored by a broken-down pilot.'

"Damn!" He smashed his fist down on the small workbench. Some of the tools jumped, and a few clattered to the cement floor with the sound of hammer-struck bells. "Crap," he said, and sighed as he bent to pick them up.

Doo avoided Kips outburst by answering the ringing phone in the office.

Just as Kip finished picking up the tools, Doo stuck his head out and hollered, "Hurry up, it's your Aunt Vicki on the phone."

As Kip picked up the receiver, Doo stood in the background waiting to hear what the call was about.

"Hi Aunt Vicki, how are you?"

"Oh I'm just fine Kip. Bob's the one that isn't doing so well."

"Uncle Bob? What's wrong?"

"He sprained his ankle two days ago working in the barn, and I had to take him into town to have the doctor look at him. He's back home now, lying in bed all bandaged up in a cast."

"He's going to be alright, isn't he?"

"Oh sure, but it's going to take a while to mend, and…well…we're in kind of a bind. Our neighbor would come over and help with the chores, but he's out of town for a couple of weeks. You know honey, I hate to ask you this, but I'm having a heck of a time trying to do everything around here and take care of Bob too."

"Aunt Vicki, do you want me to come out and help for a while?"

"Oh could you Kip? It would only be for a few weeks. I could even pay you a little."

"Aw, Aunt Vicki, you don't need to pay me. I'm more than happy to help. Are you sure he'll be up and around in a couple of weeks?"

"Yes, that's what the doctor said. Besides, our neighbor should be back by then too. Oh, Kip, I just don't know what else to do."

"Don't worry about it. I can fly out there tomorrow and stay as long as you need me. Besides, business is slow here anyway, and Doo can handle any repair work that comes up."

"Oh, Kip dear, that's so kind of you. I'll even bake an apple pie and have it waiting for you."

"Okay, just don't let Uncle Bob get anywhere near it until I get there."

He heard the relief in his aunt's voice, as she swore she would lock the 'old coot' in his room, if necessary, to keep the pie safe until Kip arrived. They both laughed and said their goodbyes.

Kip looked at Doo as he hung up the phone.

"I guess you heard. Uncle Bob sprained his ankle, and he's laid up for a couple of weeks. Aunt Vicki doesn't have anyone else to help with the farm. Do you think you can handle things around here by yourself for a while?"

CHAPTER 17

With the first blush of dawn, fatigue weighed heavily on Dan Yazzie. This was to be his journey: to walk the Earth during the day, and travel the spirit world at night. It made sense. He was on a quest for revenge against the spirit monster Ye'iitsoh: a God who came to Earth from the spirit world to feed upon lesser beings.

Dan's courage grew as he started to sing a warrior's chant learned from his grandfather. "Ye-aa-hey..." He sang louder, and as he shouted it to the sky, it echoed back from the canyon walls.

When the corona of the sun appeared above the horizon, Dan held his grandfather's medicine pouch before him and greeted Father Sky. He built up his fire and cooked bacon for breakfast. Afterward, he used the grease and ash from the fire to paint broad lines across his cheeks, forehead, and chin. Today, he would go out as a warrior, and he would show Ye'iitsoh that he was hunting him.

Dan still had not found any clear tracks to follow, so he decided to try another method. Every creature required food and water. The monster had eaten, and it would need to drink. Dan opened the map Sam had given him. He saw where the nearest watercourses were, and places where floods had cut deep canyons into the soft sandstone. Many of the washes would be dry, but some would hold small pools of water. Some might even shelter a few small fish.

There had been no rain since the creature had attacked his family. The chance was good, that if the demon had passed this way looking for water, there would be some sign.

He coaxed his horses over a rough hump of rock and into a shallow canyon. He remembered his grandfather's words, teaching him how to hunt and track.

"Often, the rabbit and the deer do not leave their footprints. They are both swift and cunning. They can walk across places that do not hold a print, but you can still find signs of their passing. Look for the blade of grass that is bent the wrong way; keeping in mind that the deer bends the grass backward in the direction it has come from. Find the twig recently broken or scuffed. Find the pebble that has moved from where it has slept for an age. Look for the things that shouldn't be."

Dan made his way through the sandy gully. Often, he had to lead both animals around some deeper cuts and narrow canyons. By early afternoon, he climbed into higher country. He picked his way through stunted juniper and greasewood, and then back down through a twisting path of crumbled shale.

By late afternoon, he had seen other vacant hogans; none showing damage. The homes all had one unusual thing in common, however; they all showed signs of haste in their abandonment. Food and personal belongings had been left behind, a child's toy, a good knife, a woman's velvet dress; none likely to have been forgotten or discarded.

Why abandoned? Did the monster scare the people away? At the end of the day, Dan had many more questions and still no answers.

He coaxed his horses into a sheltered draw with a small stand of pinon, and staked them out near some grass. Sighting a family of quail, he took up his bow and soon dispatched two fat ones with as many arrows. Dan returned to the horses to prepare supper.

An hour later, with darkness falling, the aroma of roasted quail rose from the small cooking fire. Dan reached to one of the birds on the spit and cut away a slice of sizzling meat. He savored the hot, wonderful taste. He reached forward to cut another slice and heard a faint sound behind him.

He spun around, rifle instantly in his hands pointed in the direction of the noise. He held his breath and listened, as a small, furry head appeared from behind a rock. The animal took a few tentative steps into the open and lay down, as if waiting politely for an invitation into the camp. The dog panted as it watched Dan, and then it rested its chin on its forelegs and whined.

With his rifle still pointing at the mutt, Dan stole quick glances around him. He didn't see any other movement, and he soon brought his attention back to the animal. He could see it was thin; its fur matted. Nearly starving, he thought.

"So you're hungry eh?" Dan glanced again at the brush and the shadows around him.

The dog whined, answering his question, and Dan crouched and motioned for the animal to come closer.

"C'mon boy."

The dog began to take tentative steps toward the man. It was tame, probably left behind by one of the families from the empty houses.

"That's it boy."

The dog's tail wagged and Dan reached out to pet the shivering animal. He gave it a sliver of meat. It hungrily gulped it down as Dan went back to eating. He removed the second quail from the spit, and then froze as a raspy voice spoke from the low embankment behind him.

"This old man is hungry, and he would ask if you have enough food to share."

Dan turned, hand resting on his rifle.

"Sure old man, I heard you crawling up behind me for the last ten minutes. I wondered if I would have to call out and invite you, or if you'd finally speak up."

A thin, ragged-looking Indian stood in the bunch grass at the top of the bank, and then he slid down to the camp below. The sweat on his wrinkled face showed brightly in the light of the fire. An old rag held his long hair back, and he clutched a small sack, probably containing all that he possessed.

Dan tore the second bird apart, and gave half to the old man, who began to devour it instantly. The dog whined and received another morsel.

"I circled your camp twice, and when you didn't invite me in, I decided I had to let you know I was here."

Dan understood. "Funny, the mutt didn't act like it heard you moving around. Your dog?"

"Yes." The old Indian smiled and wiped grease from his mouth. "I thought it best if he went in first, being the smaller target, to see how trigger happy you were."

The dog yipped as if in agreement.

"Ho grandfather, you are a great hunter and a wise man." Dan chuckled heartily. "It gives me pleasure to offer food to such a warrior as you—and to your brave little friend."

The dog gave another yip.

Night was falling and stars began to fill the sky. Dan poured coffee into a tin cup, and handed it to the old man. He had many questions he wanted to ask of his visitor, but he also remembered the polite way of beginning conversation. He began with his name, his parent's names, and then their family connections, beginning with his mother's clan. When done, the old man replied in a similar fashion. Dan waited a few moments before speaking.

"There are many strange things happening in this desert." He watched the old Indian, who nodded sagely and held his coffee cup to his lips. "I am on a spirit journey," Dan said. "I seek revenge upon a creature that has killed my daughter and my grandfather." He paused to see how the old man reacted to his next statement. "I seek to kill a monster."

The old man's eyes glanced knowingly at Dan, and he nodded slowly. "Revenge is a worthy thing for a warrior." The elder paused. Dan remained silent, waiting for him to continue.

"I know of this monster." The old Indian said. "I also know of other strange and evil things that have come to this land. If you seek the monster, you may find him. You may also find the other evil things. Over these past moons, I know of many people who have been taken away by strange Balagaana (white men) who drop from the sky. The people are never seen again."

Dan immediately thought of the strange apparition he saw last night. He waited tensely for the old man to continue.

"I have seen this creature you seek. I have seen its bent shape along the edge of the mesas at night. You will need many arrows for your bow and many cartridges for your rifle if you wish to kill it. Still, they may not be enough."

The old man lapsed into silence. When Dan was certain that he had finished speaking, he asked his single, dreaded question.

"Old Grandfather; the monster…is it Ye'iitsoh?"

"Yes."

If Dan had ever needed more proof that his journey would take him beyond this Earth and into the land of the Spirits, the old man's words of warning were all it took.

The small fire barely kept away the chill of the night. Dan gave the old man one of his blankets, and then sat back against his saddle clutching his rifle to his chest. He soon heard the old man snoring, becoming part of the other noises of the night. Dan's eyes grew heavy, and sleep finally overtook him.

CHAPTER 18

When Dan awoke the next morning, the sun was high enough for its rays to touch his face. He realized he had slept without dreaming.

He suddenly remembered the old man and looked where he had bedded down, but he saw nothing there. Dan sat up and glanced around nervously, as he pulled on his boots and grabbed his rifle. Everything seemed to be in place around the camp, including the two horses; but there was no old man, no dog, and no spare blanket. He consulted his memory to make sure he didn't imagine it all, and then he slowly walked around the area looking for tracks. He found none.

"Nothing." he said as he pushed his hat back. "No sign, except a missing blanket."

Dan looked at the clear sky, and he greeted the new day in his customary manner. He rebuilt the small fire and prepared coffee and a quick breakfast of beans. While he dabbed up the last of it with a dry biscuit, he ran through the morning's mystery in his mind.

"Well, I can't figure it," he said to his horses.

Birds made their scolding noises as Dan mounted up and headed south. The day pressed on. The creak of saddle leather, and the sharp smell of horse and sage, helped him keep his focus.

Eventually, he came to understand what had happened last night. The old man had tested him. The spirits, knowing of his quest for revenge against a God, had sent two lesser spirits to see if he was worthy. It was natural that these spirits would take a human or animal form.

Well, so be it. He gazed at the uneven line of the Continental Divide. There would be water in the canyons ahead, and perhaps, a monster.

Around mid-morning, he came upon a small, brush-choked wash, and walked above it, leading the horses. He came across a few tracks of small rodents and the larger prints of a coyote. When he saw the tracks of a young deer, he followed them in the soft sand and soon came upon some larger, blurred prints.

Dan turned around in a full circle, and looked again at the scuffed sand in front of him. The other creature probably startled the deer. The new prints were of something heavy, and it walked on all fours. The soft sand did not hold a clear print, but both signs showed the quick movement of flight and chase. Dan left the horses and walked ahead, levering a shell into the firing chamber of his rifle.

The prints ran out of the wash, and then over an embankment into some creosote and sage. He stopped when his ears picked up a buzzing sound. Dan crept ahead for another twenty feet, and he saw a pulsating, black cloud of flies. He smelled the stench of rotting meat. His face was grim as he moved in for a closer look. It was the small deer, or rather, part of a leg and a crushed skull. He studied the bitten end the limb, and he saw that the skull was mostly intact, but crushed at the back. When Dan walked back to the horses, he watched for any other movement.

He had learned several things about the creature that had killed the deer. It was cunning, and fast and nimble for its size. He figured the small deer would have done nothing but sharpen the animal's appetite for larger game. He had tried to envision the creature in terms of the spirit monster, but the grisly clues only gave him an indistinct picture.

Late in the day, Dan came upon a group of houses in a draw along a lava wall. There was no movement anywhere, but as he rode closer, he noticed a portion of the top of the cliff detach itself, change shape, and disappear. The hair stood up on the back of his neck. It was something large, and it moved in a way unlike any animal he had ever seen.

Dan halted the horses, and watched the cliff for an hour, hoping to catch another glimpse. When nothing appeared, he rode warily toward the houses. There were three small dwellings, and a log hogan. He rode past a junked pickup truck at the edge of the compound, and he tied the horses to the rail of a broken-down corral. Dan carried his rifle as he walked warily to the first house. The door hung open, and he found the interior to be a jumbled mess of overturned chairs and strewn clothes. The second house looked the same. The third had its door completely torn off the hinges with a similar mess inside.

As Dan stepped away from the third house, his foot accidentally kicked a small rubber ball. It skittered away and bounced off a corral post, spooking one of the horses. He looked around and then continued to the hogan.

An old rocking chair lay on its side by the door. He noticed a dark stain on the cracked white paint of one of the arms. It was blood. He peered inside the small dwelling, but he found nothing remarkable.

As Dan turned to walk away, a small, lisping dust devil whirled through the yard, conjuring up a ghostly image in his mind. One of the horses reared and screamed, and Dan spun around, rifle at his hip, ready to fire. There was nothing but the wind.

He pushed his hat back from his forehead, and he approached the nervous horses, speaking to calm them.

"That's okay mustang, just the Blue Flint Boys playing one of their games; just the wind talking."

He patted each horse on the neck before mounting up, and he followed a vague path from the structures to the lava wall. It rose sharply, twenty feet above him. The black, pitted lava rocks showed reddish-brown where slabs had cracked and fallen away. The wall gradually became lower, and soon the path led up the rock and across the upper surface.

He found some partial tracks in the sand above, and followed them until they disappeared at the edge of a drop off. He looked around but found no other tracks.

At the end of the day, with a fire started, Dan put together the makings of jerky stew; some wild onion and other tubers, and some beef jerky and water. He sat in the sand against his saddle and pondered what he had seen today, and what it meant.

The last tracks he had found were large and oddly shaped, but they were not distinct. He could not confirm that they were the same as the clear prints Sam Begay had shown him at his grandfather's house. The shape he had seen on the lava cliff had been too far away, and the sighting, too brief for him to make out. The vacant and vandalized houses continued to disturb him though; he had found two more later that day in the same condition.

It was not uncommon for a Navajo family to take their sheep to higher pastures in the mountains, and then stay with them for the summer, but

Dan hadn't seen evidence of sheep around any of the houses. It did not make sense for families to abandon their homes for no reason.

Not one, but two mysteries; were they related? Dan's grandfather taught him that everything was connected; everything happened for a reason. If he could not discern the reason, then he would have to think about it some more.

CHAPTER 19

The lone man continued to watch the mine from his vantage point on top of the cliff. He napped occasionally during the day, and when night fell, and the lights in the compound created dark shadows, he dropped his rope down the inner wall. He slipped nimbly through the darkness at the bottom, timing his dashes across the open areas with care.

His first destination was where the mangled body was taken earlier in the day. He crept behind the backs of the buildings until he came upon the one he wanted. The doorway was deep in shadow. Once inside the building, he took out a small light to locate what he was looking for. He lifted the edge of the canvas and grimaced as a strong smell of rotting meat engulfed him. He held his breath as he quickly examined the lacerations and bite marks, and then he left to continue his investigation.

He entered a larger building that appeared to hold some kind of machinery. He wound his way past conveyer belts and crushing equipment, and at the far wall, he found rows of stacked steel drums. The sound of a closing door echoed through the building, and he quickly turned off his light.

He hid in the shadows as a worker walked past him, his own light playing across the machinery. The worker eventually exited through a side door, and the lone man turned on his flash again and pulled a small device from his pack. He held it near one of the drums, thumbed a switch, and watched a dial move. The man did this to several drums before putting the instrument away. He slipped out through the same door he came in.

He was almost to the next building when a siren began to howl. The entire area was lit up, and he quickly hid behind some boxes as he heard men running. There was a commotion near the mine entrance. He heard shouts, and then the sounds of a scuffle. When he heard the sharp crack of a whip, he crept forward to see what was happening.

A handful of men shoved two Indian males around. They beat them repeatedly, and struck with a whip until the two lay moaning in the dirt. He continued to watch as they roughly dragged them into the mineshaft.

In a few minutes, the other men were gone, and most of the lights extinguished. The hidden man felt his best move was to withdraw. He carefully made his way back to the rope and pulled himself to the top of the cliff.

As he retrieved his rope, he noticed a bright sliver of light appear on the dark rocks across the compound. The light expanded into a rectangle, revealing the silhouette of a man. The light abruptly disappeared, and in a moment, the figure stepped from the shadows and walked away.

CHAPTER 20

Kip and Doo showed up at the hanger early and talked about the work that needed doing around the shop. Doo insisted he was more than able to carry on while Kip was out of town.

"Besides," Doo said, "It'll be good for you to get away from Lisa for a while."

"What's that supposed to mean?"

"Oh nothing, just that she seems to get under your skin every time she's around you. Honestly, I don't know what goes on between you two. A year ago you were both lovebirds, and then something happened, and now you can't be together for two minutes without snarling and spitting at each other like a couple of alley cats."

Kip's back was up. "Aw just shut it off will you. It's none of your business anyway." He couldn't help his anger, even though he knew the truth in Doo's words.

"Oh that's right; it's none of my business. I just do my work while you go off on your moody snits. Well I'm tired of it! Go on, get out of here; it'll be a relief not having to listen to the two of you fighting for a couple of weeks. The time away will probably do us all good."

Kip felt taken aback; Doo had never spoken so bluntly before. Maybe he pushed him too hard. Maybe he was growing up. Kip still thought of him as the young kid that pulled him from his plane crash a few years ago. He swallowed hard as he also remembered the reason Doo walked with a limp.

"Doo, I know it's not easy getting around...with your ankle. I...I'm sorry that it happened. I don't mean to make things more difficult for you."

"More difficult? Do you think that this…this limp is a difficulty for me? Did you ever think that I might consider it proof that I did something that mattered once; helping a friend when he needed it? The same friend who thinks I'm not worthy of being honest enough to tell him how his life is going? Well phooey!"

Doo stormed to the back of the hanger and started tossing around pieces of scrap metal and wood.

Kip's shoulders sagged with the weight of the truth. He walked up to Doo, who turned away to hide the tears filling his eyes.

"Doo I'm sorry. You're right, I have been moping around here for the last few months—well, maybe for the last year. I owe you better than that. I've never had a good friend like you before, and I guess it's time I told you so."

"Aw that's alright." Doo said, with his back still turned. "I could use a little less excitement around here anyway; what with you getting the plane all shot up, and racing around with your motorcycle, punching out Lisa's boyfriends."

He turned and grinned. "You're probably looking forward to sitting on your aunt's porch with your feet up, sipping lemonade while I do all the work around here."

Kip rolled his eyes and smiled. "So you're on to me then."

The damage to the wings and fuselage repaired, Doo helped Kip stow his duffel into the front cockpit of the Jenny.

"I'll give you a call whenever I get a chance. There is no electricity or phone service that far out of town, so I'll have to go to Gallup to do it. I hope you'll have enough work to keep yourself busy while I'm gone."

"Not a problem; Captain Jack has a customer that needs some engine repair done. I'll be up to my elbows in pistons and grease while you're out napping in a stack of hay."

Kip climbed into the rear cockpit and worked the flaps and rudder. He looked down at Doo.

"Thanks buddy."

"Yeah, yeah, get out of here," Doo said, and walked to the front of the plane.

Kip nodded, and Doo grabbed the prop and gave it a pull. The engine started with a ragged, flatulent roar. Doo backed away and waived as Kip taxied, and then climbed into the cool morning air.

"And bring the damn plane back in one piece!"

CHAPTER 21

At the other end of the airstrip, Lisa watched the Jenny until it disappeared over the west mesa. She was lost in her thoughts for a few moments, and then she took a deep breath and stepped back inside her uncle's office.

Kip gained altitude as he aimed for the distant peak of Mount Taylor. The cold morning air chilled him, and he felt the contrasting warmth of the sun on his shoulders.

He had to admit he was looking forward to seeing his aunt and uncle. He hoped Bob's injury would heal quickly, though he didn't mind farm work at all. He enjoyed the rural McGaffey area with its tall pines and grassy meadows. The living was simple without electricity, just like it was when the area was first settled a hundred years earlier.

Out of the Rio Grande Valley, the desert was dotted with low trees and shrubs. Kip was soon daydreaming, and his thoughts came to Diana Witherspoon: tall and trim, and annoyingly sure of herself. He felt his heartbeat quicken, and he thought briefly of changing course and dropping in on her. He could easily be at Chaco Canyon within an hour.

Would she be glad to see him? What would he say to her? What would she say? What reason would he have to see her? If only she had left something behind to give him an excuse to bring it to her.

He moved the stick and rudder and flew northwesterly for ten minutes, then he sighed, and he reluctantly returned to his original course. He had forgotten about Carl, her tanned, smiling boyfriend. She called him her 'assistant.'

"Sure, I'll bet," he said aloud.

The spectacular scenery helped dissolve Kip's gloomy mood. At the halfway point near Grants, passing south of Mount Taylor, he picked up the east-west highway and followed it as it bent slightly northwest on its way to Gallup. To the left, he saw miles of black, hardened lava flows, called the El Malpais (badlands). The landscape gave evidence to Mount Taylor's spectacular, volcanic past.

The highway wound its way through the high desert, and it soon crossed the Continental Divide. To the right, canyons carved deeply into the tall, red cliffs, and the jutting rocks looked like the prows of naval ships parked at their pier.

Miles of rugged scenery passed, and Kip's mind wandered. He thought of his Aunt Vicki: his father's only sister, and how he'd come to New Mexico to live with her after leaving the Navy Air Corp. She was sure something back then: a darling of the barnstorming circuits, and a heck of a good pilot. She taught him all he knew about stunt flying, but things had been changing for the aerobatic thrill shows, and his aunt was getting older. Vicki figured it was time she had settled down and gotten married. She gave Kip her old Jenny, married Bob Johnson, and went to live with him on his family farm.

When the layout of Fort Wingate appeared along the railroad tracks on his left, it was time to head south. He gained altitude and flew over the wooded hills into the area known as McGaffey. Up ahead, a patchwork of small farms soon came into view. He buzzed the familiar buildings and rejoiced in seeing his aunt come out from the porch and wave. The narrow dirt road in front of the house was the only place to land, and after another low pass, he turned, throttled back, and touched down, taxiing into the yard.

Aunt Vicki ran up to the plane as Kip cut the engine and jumped to the ground. They clung together like old friends, his aunt clucking her joy as he kissed her cheek. She cooed with delight as she held him at arm's length to get a good look at him.

"Come into the house," she said taking his arm, "before Bob has a fit, waiting to shake your hand and tell you all about his accident."

"How's he doing?"

"Oh, he's just fine, but the darn old coot won't sit still and let his leg heal."

"He hasn't gotten into my apple pie has he?" Kip's face showed mock concern.

Aunt Vicki took the cue and feigned a worried look. "You know, we better hurry and make sure he doesn't."

They both ran, laughing, up to the porch and into the house.

Bob stood on crutches in the living room; his foot and lower leg were in a cast.

"Hey, KJ."

Bob always used Kip's first two initials rather than his name. He balanced on a crutch and stuck out his hand, as Kip walked up and shook it.

"Now you just sit right back down before you fall down and break something else, you…" Vicki scolded.

She positioned a small hassock underneath his leg, and said to Kip, "Why don't you take your stuff upstairs and freshen up, I'll get us some lemonade, and then we can talk and catch up on things."

Later, after supper, they sat on the porch and listened to the crickets while the stars popped out.

"KJ, it's like a breath of fresh air to have you here. I don't know how to thank you enough for coming out to help. This darn leg of mine…"

"Aah," Kip replied with a shake of his head. "I'm glad to be here. Goodness knows I owe you both a lot."

His thoughts turned briefly to the airstrip and Doo, and then to Lisa Ann. "I think this time is going to be good for me too. I feel like a weight has been lifted from my shoulders."

"What do you mean Kip?" Vicki had a strong, female's inquisitiveness.

"Oh, with the way business has been lately, and Doo being such a great kid, I just wish things could be better for him."

"I don't think you need to worry about Doo," she said. "Ever since he found you in that plane wreck, he's stuck to you like glue. I'd say you were just the friend he was looking for."

"Yeah, I guess you're right, but things have been weird lately. Like Lisa Ann: It seems she's been hell-bent on getting herself tangled up with every guy that waves his money around. I don't know what I ever saw in her."

"Now KJ," Bob said, "a girl like Lisa can't help but attract men. She's a real fine thing to look at, and there isn't anything wrong with that, but she just doesn't seem to be the kind of gal to want to settle down and get hitched."

Kip chuckled, thinking of Aunt Vicki in her younger days.

"I guess I've just got to give her time to mellow, eh?" He glanced knowingly at his aunt and uncle, until they caught the joke and grinned at each other.

"You can sure say that again," Bob said, rolling his eyes. Vicki gave him a teasing swat on the arm.

"Oh, here's a weird thing, I got shot at by a Sparrowhawk fighter north of Grants yesterday."

"That is weird." Bob looked to Vicki, and then back at Kip. "You were minding your own business flying in open country, and the plane came up and took a pot shot at you?"

"Exactly! And it was a Sparrowhawk; a Curtis F9C-2! Nobody is supposed to have those planes except for the Navy, and I thought they were all lost when the two dirigibles sank in the ocean. This plane even had a mooring rig attached to the upper wing. I saw it!"

"Mooring rig?" Bob's brow wrinkled in confusion.

"Yes, the planes were kept inside the dirigibles, and to deploy them, they were hooked to a trapeze tower and lowered outside the ship. The pilot then starts the engine and releases the hooking mechanism when he's ready to take off. They return the same way. I used to fly them in the Navy. They're small, with a lot of power, and they're very fast."

"So how did one of them find its way into the desert?" Bob asked.

"Good question!"

The night sounds soon replaced their conversation. The darkness seemed to deepen the mystery.

"We've had our own weird happenings around here these past few years, haven't we Vicki?"

The silence lasted for several minutes until Vicki spoke.

"A couple times in the early morning before dawn, we've heard some things. Things like…faraway moaning sounds; almost like humming. The sound fades in and out, and you can't tell where it comes from, exactly. Sometimes when you hear it, if you look up at the stars, you can see a big patch of sky go black, just like the stars went out. Maybe it's the clouds."

"Then one time," Bob said, "the stars went out on a clear night, and we heard the humming…and I swear we heard voices too. Maybe from another dimension, eh, like in the dime, science fiction books."

Bob laughed, but the hair stood up on Kip's neck.

That night, after they had all gone to bed, Kip lay awake trying to put together the oddly shaped pieces of this puzzle.

CHAPTER 22

Commandant Thomas Bloundt stepped from his quarters with his back straight and his head up. He felt more refreshed than he had for days, and he eagerly began his morning inspection of the facility. On his way across the grounds, he noted the sloppy look of the men. This would end now. The need for discipline was far greater at this point, than it had ever been.

When he crossed the path of two mechanics who were sauntering lazily along their way, he halted them with scathing words and impressed upon them the need for focus and speed in their assigned duties. The two dashed off, and Bloundt smartly swatted his gloves against his leg.

"Richard I want your report!"

The head of the section stood up quickly from his desk and addressed his superior.

"Sir, we are working on schedule, sir. We have repaired the equipment and are nearly back to capacity. We will be ready when the end of the month arrives."

"That isn't good enough Richard! We could have another breakdown. What if we suffer another loss of manpower or the quality of the ore diminishes?"

Richard was wary of Bloundt's moods. "Well sir, our section can't be held responsible for the work crews. It's our job to refine the ore once it's extracted."

"From now on mister," Bloundt said with a snarl on his lips, "it's every man's job to make sure nothing happens to slow down our work. In fact, I want to be ready to leave a week ahead of time. You will inform your crew to do whatever is necessary to meet the new deadline. This means the ore must be refined, stored in the drums, and loaded onto the rail cars. I want a full report tomorrow, and I expect everything to be on schedule exactly as I have just described it."

The station chief knew better than to voice any disagreement. He saluted with a brisk, "Yes heir Commandant."

Bloundt abruptly turned and strutted out of the building.

"Pompous swine," the station chief said under his breath.

Bloundt felt invigorated by his newfound purpose. He walked into the yawning maw of the mine, and continued down the tunnel, eventually turning into a shaft that led to a wide area lined with iron cages. The light was poor here, and the stench of sweat and sick humanity filled his nostrils. Low moans and weak crying came from the cells.

Bloundt announced himself with a loud "Frederich!"

His voice echoed through the chamber, and the small, sad voices became still. A man answered from the other end of the corridor and rushed to join the officer.

"Yes Commandant Bloundt, what can I do for you sir."

"Frederich, how many workers do you have here now?"

"Counting the new batch, we have fifty workers, but some are in poor condition."

Bloundt walked slowly past the cages, noting the blank expressions of the dispirited captives. Children held on to their mothers and whimpered softly. Bloundt saw only a mass of smelly animals. This was his gift; he found it easy to dehumanize others. He would complete the mission on time in spite of the wretched things he had to do to make it happen. To him, there were only three kinds of people: himself, his men, and those who were expendable.

"Frederich, I've announced a step-up in our schedule. This means I want your work done here within the next two weeks."

"Two weeks, sir?" The man appeared puzzled. "But we'll have to work the captives much harder, and no doubt, we'll lose more of them than usual."

"Enough man; you don't really care do you?"

Frederich's face slowly formed an evil smile. "Why no sir, we'll be ready on time." He clicked his heels and saluted.

When Bloundt left the mine, his purposeful smile vanished when he saw two men carrying the blanket that held Schultz's remains for burial. His stomach knotted as he thought of the bizarre incident. How could this kind of thing happen? It was a large animal no doubt: a cougar or a bear.

CHAPTER 23

The hot days passed slowly at Chaco Canyon. The students methodically dug through the dirt mounds and found the usual abundance of pottery shards, small animal bones, and beads. Diana spent most of her time photographing the strange wall paintings in the cave at Fajada Butte. When done, she attempted to locate similar designs in her reference material.

Carl was beginning to get edgy. He hated waiting, and he hated the pompous, Commandant Bloundt. He knew the man was plotting to steal the glory of this mission away from him. As far as Carl was concerned, a valuable spy, like himself, was worth two administrative asses like Bloundt. The fact that Bloundt had amassed a large cache of Indian jewelry he had stolen from the captives, also annoyed Carl. He would have it for himself before this mission was over.

Another man he hated was Nicholas Ells. He broke out in an evil smile as he thought of the Commandant's squat toady working away at latrine and janitorial duties. He was pleased to hear that old "Nick the biter" got bit in the ass by his own stupidity.

The recent killing and mutilation of the guard had put him on edge. The remains had been excessively gory, even for Carl's relaxed standards. He also felt there were other strange things going on in the desert lately. He sensed someone watching him at times, but he never found evidence to support his suspicions.

He had made another secretive trip to the small mesa in search of the professor's journal. He could see it plainly in his mind, and he knew the professor had never let it out of his possession, but where was it now? The old fool had died before Carl could make him tell where he had hidden it. It had to be at the mesa somewhere. He was certain the pages contained the location of a special find that the old archeologist had hinted about.

That afternoon at Fajada Butte, a lone man stepped among the rocks and disappeared into the crevice leading to the recently discovered cave. In addition to following Carl, he also kept his eyes on the comings and goings of the students, and of the young woman who led them.

Edging through the narrow passage and into the open area, he removed his pack and looked around. The dimly lit space was cool and comfortable. He walked back to the sunken area and held his light on the wall markings again. He slowly illuminated each painted design, and even though he had already committed every line and color to memory, he became lost in the amazing story it told. It was because of his concentration, that he didn't hear the quiet tread behind him.

"Who are you?" An angry female voice demanded.

He nearly dropped his light, and then he turned it on the woman. He recognized her as the archeologist from Chaco.

"I said; who are you and what are you doing here?"

The man took a step toward her, and Diana instinctively stepped back, wondering if she should run for assistance, rather than confront this stranger on her own.

The man noticed her fear, and he spoke in a soft voice, "Please; you are in no danger. I was only curious."

"This is a protected archeological site, and you are trespassing. Did you know that?"

"Yes, I suppose I did. But can't we just go out in the other room and talk where the light is better?"

Diana thought for a moment, then quickly turned and walked back to the larger chamber. She stood at the far end of the room and watched the man. He was slim and athletic looking. His straight, blond hair was a little longer than normal, and he appeared confident, but unassuming.

"Won't you have a seat?" The man motioned to a flat rock next to her. "I suppose I should explain myself, but first, my name is Val. And you are...?"

"Diana."

He smiled. "Diana, have you had a chance to study the drawings in the other room?"

"Yes. Why?"

Val smiled again, "A two word answer this time. I can see that you can be quite a chatterbox when you get going. We'll get along famously."

Diana frowned, but found herself drawn to his smile and pale blue eyes.

"Diana, may I ask what conclusions you've made about the origin and meaning of the drawings?"

Diana was interested now. "Conclusions? Why, none at all. There are some vague resemblances to a few ancient cultures around the globe, but nothing concrete. Why do you ask?"

"Because I know who made them, and why."

CHAPTER 24

Elsewhere, Carl Walker's long awaited turn of good luck had finally come. He had found the Professor's journal by accident while checking out a small ruin he'd found on the top of the mesa. A flat rock seemed out of place, and he had found the worn book hidden in a hole underneath it. The old man had been secretive about his explorations here, and Carl suspected the journal would surely contain the information he sought. With the notebook in his pack, he went back to Chaco Canyon, preparing an excuse to be away for a few more days.

"What do you mean, 'you know who made them?'" Diana said. "There is no one in today's archeological community that can say exactly where the Chaco culture came from, much less what these designs might mean. Are you some kind of scam artist or just an antiquities thief?"

"Now, now…" Val motioned calmly with his hands. "Would it help to say that you're right about one thing?"

"Just one?" She said, with her hands on her hips.

"There is no one in 'today's archeological community' that knows what those designs mean…but I do."

"But…"

"Diana," Val cut her off, "the people who made these designs are my ancestors."

Diana had heard enough, and she stuck out her chin. "That's a load of crap, buddy. If you have an ounce of Indian blood in you, then I'm a duck."

Her temper boiled, and she glanced around, ready to bolt.

"Diana, please, you're not a duck, and I'm not trying to con you. Let me show you something. Follow me."

He strode back to the room with the painted designs. Diana hesitated: not sure what to do. She finally made up her mind and followed him.

Val crouched near the wall with his light. "This room was a nursery; it was meant to be a safe place for a child."

His unexpected statement spurred her curiosity. "Why do you think that?"

"Because these pictures tell a story meant for children. It's the story of a pretty blue planet, and of a family that traveled a great distance to make it their home."

Diana eyes narrowed. "Who are you? Why are you telling me such outrageous things?" She felt a strong urge to run again.

"I know, I know," he said. "It is a pretty outrageous story, isn't it?"

Val's eyes searched hers. He desperately wanted her to believe him. He needed someone he could trust and take into his confidence.

"You don't have to believe me Diana, but it is true. Open your mind and let me tell you the whole story. If you still don't believe me when I'm done, I'll go away. You will never see me again. In the meantime, please allow me to stay here for the night, so I can catch up on some sleep. Come back tomorrow, alone, and I'll tell you everything you want to know."

Diana's face felt flushed, and she knew he had hooked her. She wanted to know more about the drawings, and more about this mysterious and interesting man.

"I'll be here tomorrow morning," she said.

As she walked back to camp, she felt confused about her feelings. The man's story was absurd. On one hand, she suspected he was a scoundrel, but on the other, he was good looking, and his blue eyes seemed to capture her.

Great, just great, she thought. I've gone too long without a man, and what do I do? I get all tingly over some crazy stranger with a story he took out of a science fiction book.

CHAPTER 25

Val woke up early, and his first thought was how lovely and headstrong Diana was. He feared he had told her more than he should have, but she was the Professor's daughter, and he felt he owed the gentle, old man to look out for her. In addition, the circumstances surrounding the man's accident and death had aroused his suspicions.

Lifting his pack, he stepped through the entrance of the cave and blinked in the bright sunlight. He set out southward, and within a few miles, he spied another man hiking ahead of him. The other man stopped frequently to look around, as if to see if someone was following. Val kept behind cover, and soon realized that they both had the same destination.

Carl could barely contain his excitement. The professor's journal contained some crude maps with landmarks and measurements. To his dismay, however, most of the writing was in indecipherable shorthand. He mentally cursed the secretive fool, and he regretted killing him before he could force him to divulge the secrets contained in his notes.

With book in hand, Carl sought to match the sketches with the weathered rocks and cliffs around him. When he passed a formation with an oddly shaped cap rock balanced on an eroded pillar, he flipped through the pages until he found a rough drawing that looked similar to it. This was it! There were some numbers and a compass heading on the page. Soon, he was at the northern face of the small mesa. He looked high up the slope and saw the rock fall. Of course, the cliff looked different now. Carl soon found another formation that matched a drawing in the journal: an overhanging slab that sheltered a small pile of brush and tumbleweed.

There were more pages of shorthand, and then a drawing of a square stone with three even grooves. Carl recognized this specimen, and he remembered when the professor had brought it back to the camp. Carl saw it last in Diana's tent, and he planned to take a closer look at it when he returned.

He found a few more locations similar to the sketches, but nothing that was more helpful. Why did the old man make these cryptic marks and drawings? He closed the book in frustration and placed it in his pack. He started to retrace his steps, wondering how much Diana knew about her father's code.

Carl was nearly back to camp when he noticed a furtive movement in the hills behind him. He quickly hid, and watched as a tall, blond man hiked closer, before angling off and passing him to the east. Carl followed the stealthy figure and saw him disappear in the rocks at Fajada Butte.

Turning to return to camp, he had to duck again when he saw Diana walk up to the rocks where the other man had vanished. Carl didn't know what to make of this, but it was a good opportunity to examine the professor's stone in Diana's tent.

"I was here earlier," she said, "but you were gone."

Val was putting away his pack when her voice startled him.

"Yes, I got up early and went out to do some exploring. I was out longer than I intended. I'm sorry you had to wait."

Val motioned for her to sit down. "Okay, you kept your bargain, now I'll keep mine. What do you want to know first?"

"That's easy," she said. "Tell me who you are and where you came from."

"I'm Val Tannin. That's short for Tanninchevsky. My parents came from Eastern Europe when I was a baby, and we lived in a small town in New England…"

"What town?" She quickly interjected.

"Well, it's a small place. You wouldn't know it. Do you want to know why I'm here?"

"Very well," she said. "Why are you here…in New Mexico…at Chaco Canyon…in this cave?"

Val drew a deep breath as he studied her face. "My parents were ancient history teachers, and I guess I just naturally grew up interested in the subject. I studied the migrations of early cultures from Africa to the

Far East, and finally to Alaska and across Canada to the North American Southwest. I have a theory that the people who first lived in this part of the country came here 50,000 years ago."

Diana's eyebrows rose, but she let him continue talking. She watched his eyes as he spoke, and realized she was becoming more and more interested in this annoyingly attractive man.

"My studies brought me to New Mexico, or to be more exact, Chaco Canyon."

"Why Chaco Canyon, the ancient Anasazi culture isn't anywhere near that old."

"Yes, I know, but I believe there were people here much earlier. And imagine my surprise," Val smiled, "when I got here and found you."

She narrowed her eyes, "Stick to the subject Mr. Val Tannin." She hoped she wouldn't blush.

Val hesitated to tell her the rest, and then relented.

"I met your father a month ago…" He saw her posture stiffen. "I liked him, he was a good man, and I told him about my search. He agreed that there was something else hidden in the desert here. I was saddened to learn that he died."

Diana stood up. "He was killed, Mr. Tannin, he didn't just die. Someone pushed him off a cliff."

"I suspected it."

"You did?" She stepped closer to Val, desperate to know more. "What made you think that?"

Val's expression changed. "I can't say for sure yet, but I have an idea or two. By the way, have you seen your father's journal recently?"

"No, it wasn't with his things. Why?"

"No real reason, but if I find it, I'll let you know."

Diana felt off balance talking about her father. She decided she needed to leave.

"Well then, I should be getting back to my students. Perhaps we can talk more at some other time."

"How about tomorrow?"

She almost blurted an eager 'yes' but she caught herself.

"I don't know; I'll have to see. I have a lot of work to do…but I might be able to come by sometime in the morning."

Carl was waiting for her when Diana returned to the camp. He noticed that her face was flushed, and he was certain it wasn't all from her long walk. He had to find out what she knew about the man who had followed him.

"Oh Carl, you're back."

"Diana have you seen a stranger around?" He caught her off guard by being direct, and he saw the guilt on her face.

"A stranger?" she hesitated and shifted her eyes.

"Yes, a rather tall, blonde man, perhaps in his thirties?"

"Hmm," she frowned. "Well there was a fellow I ran across a week ago who said he was hiking to the Bisti formations. He could match your description, but I haven't seen him since. Why?"

"Just curious, it seemed rather odd to me to see a lone man walking in the desert."

Diana brushed back a strand of hair and changed the subject. "Are you finished with your work away from camp yet?"

"Yes for today, but I'll be going out tomorrow to do some additional mapping. By the way, have you had any luck in finding your father's journal?"

"No, I haven't." She wondered why the two men had such an interest in the book.

"Well, no matter. He said that he wrote in some kind of code. I guess if somebody found it they couldn't decipher it anyway."

"Yes, only he and I could read it."

Carl reached into his pocket and handed her a piece of paper that appeared to be torn from a book. It had one short line of cryptic writing across the top.

"Is this his writing, by chance?"

"Yes, yes it is; where did you find it?"

Carl had copied the line on another page in the journal, and then tore out this page to show Diana; hoping to coerce her into helping him read it.

"I was out this morning towards the Bisti, and I found this slip of paper near some rocks."

Diana glanced at the page. "This is odd."

"How so?" he said, feigning only mild interest.

"It's his writing alright. It says '*The God's Tomb*,' and then he initialed the page like it was the end of a chapter or something."

"That does sound odd," he said. "Does it mean anything to you?"

"No, it doesn't. You didn't find the journal or any other pages?"

"No, I found just this one page. You don't think the guy you saw hiking, found the journal, do you?"

Diana did not reply.

"Well, it just goes to show that we should be careful of strangers; being so far away from civilization. You never know who they might be. Would you like to keep the page?"

"Yes I would."

Carl grinned wolfishly as he watched her take long strides toward her tent. Now, he knew that the professor's daughter could decipher the journal.

The next morning Carl went looking for Diana. One of the students said she was probably over at Fajada Butte, at a new site she was studying.

Carl grabbed his pack and muttered under his breath, "New site, my ass."

She lay atop Val, his strong arms wrapped around her; both lost in the afterglow of their lovemaking. Diana's black hair lay matted across her forehead, covered with sweat from their exertions. She had been coy at first, and then when she had seen him look at her with such sad longing, she had become the aggressor, giving in to passions too long denied. Val was a willing partner for his own reasons. She hardly knew him, but somehow she trusted him.

"I found something yesterday," he said, as he lazily stroked the narrowness of her waist and the soft swell of her hips.

"Mmm?" she murmured. "What is it?"

He groaned as he slowly got up. She rolled over and watched him dress. When he left the room, she put on her own clothes.

"Here," he said, returning with a wrapped object. Removing the cloth, he placed a round crystalline ball, about two inches in diameter, into her open hands.

"Oh, it's beautiful. What is it?"

She gazed intently at the designs etched into the surface of the sphere, and then reacted with surprise.

"It's the Earth!" Where did you find it?"

Carl could hear voices coming from the chamber as he walked up, and he decided to announce himself.

"Hello? Diana? Are you in there?"

She quickly gave the sphere back to Val.

"Hide it," she hissed, and stepped toward the entrance calling out to Carl.

"We're in here Carl, be careful where you step."

Carl ducked as he entered the room and feigned surprise at seeing Val. "Oh, you have a visitor."

"Carl, meet Val. Val is a…early civilizations specialist. He, uh, comes from back East. Val, this is Carl, our site manager."

The two men nodded in acknowledgement. Val was inscrutable, while Carl took an obvious interest in the stranger.

"From back East, eh, you must have gotten here just recently?"

"Yesterday," said Val.

An uncomfortable silence ensued until Diana spoke. "Well Carl, are you going out again?"

"Yes. I'm leaving right now as a matter of fact. I just wanted to tell you that I'll be gone for a day or two." He glanced at the rumpled bedding, and then meaningfully at Val.

"You'll be alright, won't you?"

"Yes, I'll be fine," she said quickly. "The students are doing quite well at the new site. When you get back, we can start packing up some of the artifacts they've found."

"Alright," he said and turned abruptly and left the cave, knowing he would have to kill this man when the first opportunity arose.

"Whew." The girl exhaled the breath she had been holding, and then she giggled. She glanced devilishly at her stony-faced companion.

"What's wrong?"

"Nothing," Val said, staring at the entrance to the cave. His expression told her something altogether different.

"I'll be leaving for a few days myself. When I get back, I think we need to have a long talk."

CHAPTER 26

Carl knew there was trouble brewing. The stranger did not look like the studious type, or any expert on early civilizations for that matter. He looked muscular and confident, just like himself. He also didn't like the way Diana seemed to be attracted to him. He's probably a government agent, he thought. Bloundt is not going to like this.

Carl left the camp by a different route this time. He took care to hide his tracks and make sure he wasn't being followed. Unknown to him, Val was following, but he saw the extra precautions Carl was taking. Val figured the small mesa would still be the man's destination, so he headed directly there and found a place to hide before Carl arrived. Confident that no one pursued him, Carl continued past the small mesa, straight for the larger one, to the gates of the mine.

Bloundt was having a bad day; another two workers had died overnight, and they were still behind his new schedule. Sleepless nights were taking their toll on the man, and he was tired and short tempered when Carl's knock came at his door.

"How's it going Bloundt?" Carl noticed the Commandant's bloodshot eyes. "I came by to tell you that we've got another problem."

"Another problem," Bloundt sneered. "Like what?"

"Like, a hard looking stranger at the Chaco camp, that's what. He's nosing around, and he followed me yesterday while I was scouting some new sites."

"Followed you? Did he follow you here too?" Bloundt's voice rose as he spoke, and he jumped to his feet.

"Relax; I made sure I wasn't followed. Besides, I think he has another distraction at the camp."

"What kind of distraction?"

"I think he's banging the boss lady. I saw them…"

"That's enough!" shouted Blount: spittle flying from his lip. "If he's at the camp, then he's *your* problem; that is, if a *master spy* like you can handle it."

Blount knew he needed a successful field command on his record in order to advance in rank. To his dismay, he found nearly everything about this mission to be a problem: especially this smirking ass standing in front of him.

Carl felt amused by the bundle of nerves his counterpart had become. He never did like the man, and had objected strongly to his superiors. Thomas Blount had come from a long line of desk-bound officers; Carl on the other hand, was a man of action.

"Okay Blount, I'll take care of him, seeing as how you asked me so nicely. I doubt you could do much about him anyway. Just make sure you carry out your side of this mission." Carl saw the chance to lay out his trump card. "And if you screw up like your father did, I'll make sure you never get the opportunity to command again."

The effect on Blount was like gasoline thrown on a fire.

"Get out, you stinking dog, or I'll have you shot!" Blount shook like a leaf in the wind, and when he dragged his arm across his mouth, it left a wet mark on his sleeve.

Carl smirked. "I'll leave in the morning when I'm good and ready."

"Get out," Blount hissed. The memory of what he'd heard said about his father ate at him like acid: 'A reasonably good statistician, but a coward in the field.'

From his vantage point overlooking the compound, Val watched Carl walk to the bunkhouse. He settled back to wait for nightfall, hoping he would see the strange sliver of light again. With time to think, he went through the list of things he knew about this place.

First: Carl was obviously part of the group. Val suspected that the man's duties at Chaco Canyon were part of the subterfuge. Second: there was the odd, gruesome killing of the guard by something…unknown. Val had to admit he kept a more watchful eye on his surroundings since then. Third: the two Indian males beaten, and dragged into the mine must have been trying to escape; which meant they were prisoners instead of workers. Fourth: a huge dirigible somehow connected to this facility, and it had some uncanny way of vanishing.

Throughout the day, he saw men loading metal drums on railroad cars. Supply trucks came and went, and mechanics worked on the planes in the hangers. Val took short naps during the day, and when darkness fell, he dropped his rope into the compound again.

He wanted to accomplish two things tonight. He hoped for a chance to investigate the sliver of light, and he was curious about one of the hangers that the headman seemed to visit more than the rest.

Keeping to the shadows as much as possible, he made his way to the hanger and stole inside. He found a few lights on, and moved carefully and crouched under the stubby wings of a biplane as he listened for any other movement. Hearing nothing, he moved past its tail to a wall separating the front and back of the building. He stole through a doorway, and found something big in the center of the room covered by a large tarp.

Something about the shape set off a signal of recognition in his mind. It was an eerie feeling, and he felt drawn to the object before he even knew why. He lifted a corner of the tarp, and he took in a quick breath when he saw the lines of the thing.

"It's a scout flyer," he whispered as his hand reached out to touch the familiar shape. He was shocked to find that the surface was rough and pitted. It felt scoured by acid, and he suddenly knew that the rough treatment of 50,000 years had done this to the once sleek machine.

Val sat down as realization washed over him like the surf on a beach. I am here, he thought. This is the place. He ducked underneath a pitted wing edge and found the lower hatch open. With his light in front of him, he climbed into the ship and was saddened to find the interior in poor condition. When he exited, he noted that one of the large stabilizing fins was missing, presumably torn off eons ago.

In a few moments, Val crouched in the darkness outside the hanger. He had seen the sliver of light somewhere along the rock wall further down the plaza. With nothing else to do, he found a place behind some discarded pallets and waited for something to happen.

He didn't have long to wait. Within ten minutes, two men walked across the yard toward the section that interested him. When they reached the rocks, the bright sliver of light appeared and opened into a doorway. Both walked through, and it closed behind them.

Val was stunned. He didn't see a door there, yet the men were gone. He moved along the cliff wall to the spot, but it was too dark to make out any marks or details. He was about to back up and retrace his steps, when the door opened, and a sleepy worker stepped out and ran into him. Val dispatched him with a quick blow to the head and dragged the body to the side.

He soon found the recessed handle and entered the room. Val found himself in a small foyer with a double door at the end of a short hallway. He went to the doors and stepped through them, and couldn't believe his eyes. The area beyond was a vast chamber with its farthest boundaries hidden in darkness. In the space, nearly filling it with its bloated shape as if it were a fat insect in its cocoon lay the largest dirigible he had ever seen. It towered above him into the darkness of the ceiling, and it stretched back beyond sight for hundreds and hundreds of yards.

Val backed away in awe and noticed something that puzzled him. There were forces at work here that he didn't fully understand. He remembered the two Indians again and knew some action was called for soon. He retraced his steps, and ducking quickly out the front door, he ran into a stocky man who bellowed his complaint.

"Watch where you're going you…"

Val cut off the words with a sharp blow to the side of the man's thick neck. The man grunted and fell to one knee, and Val hit him again. This time the man slumped to the ground and did not move.

A half-hour later, the yard was lit up, and groups of men searched the entire compound. Carl and Bloundt questioned the stocky man in the Commandant's office. Val was long gone, and the bully, Nicholas Ells, was seething with anger, knowing that someone had knocked him unconscious.

"So Nick old buddy," said Carl, chuckling, "this guy was tall and blonde, eh? Are you sure it wasn't a woman?"

Nick glared at him. He had to take this kind of abuse from Bloundt, but not from this swine. He glanced at the Commandant behind the desk, and physically cowered from his piercing gaze. Bloundt put his palms together touching his lips with the tips of his fingers as he spoke. "Nicholas, I believe Carl may be right. You must be slipping. There was a time when I could depend on you to react quickly and decisively to any kind of provocation."

Nick the biter looked at Carl and ground his teeth.

"Enough Nicholas, I'm sure Carl would love to teach you some of his moves, but I believe we have a better use for you and your anger. I am going to give you a chance to redeem yourself. You do believe in second chances don't you Nicholas?"

He blinked his pig-eyes as Bloundt continued. "I want you to select five other men and report with them to my office at 8:30 tomorrow morning. I suggest you select them for their abilities with their fists and not for their brains. I'm going to put you in charge of your own squad. In fact, we are going to call it the Goon Squad. I have some special work for you and your team."

Bloundt dismissed Nicholas and looked at Carl. "Are you sure it was the man you met at Chaco Canyon?"

"Who else could it be?"

CHAPTER 27

Within a week, Kip had most of the work caught up at the farm. Bob's leg was healing, and Vicki began to appear more relaxed. They finished their breakfast with a warm-up of their coffee.

"Kip honey, you've been working harder than a team of horses since you first got here. Why don't you take the day off and go into town; let off some steam or something."

"Yes," Bob said, "you've got to take a break once in a while or you'll make us feel like slave drivers; besides, I think your aunt wants some time alone with me."

He gave Kip an exaggerated wink.

Aunt Vicki gave Bob a sharp rap on the shoulder with her wooden spoon. "Yes I do want to be alone with your uncle so there'll be no witnesses when I kill him."

Kip smiled, "I haven't been working that hard. After all, I owe you."

Bob rubbed his shoulder and gave his injured and innocent look.

"You know what?" Kip said, "I think I'd like to take the Jenny up for a quick trip to Chaco Canyon. Maybe come back late in the day, or even stay overnight."

Vicki shared a knowing glance with her husband.

Bob said, "It's a beautiful place. I was there once, and even read some magazine articles about it. Say, you could see if that girl archeologist is still around. She sounds like a looker, and she would probably appreciate the company of a dashing young pilot like you."

Kip set his coffee down. "Okay, okay." He didn't even try to hide his guilty smile. "I'll prep the plane today and set out tomorrow morning to see how she's been doing."

Shared laughter rolled out of the kitchen, and their old dog, Charlie, lifted his head from his morning nap on the porch.

CHAPTER 28

Sam Begay closed his notepad and stood up from the sagging couch. He thanked the old woman and her daughter for speaking with him, and then walked outside and put on his sunglasses.

He had driven east from the trading post in Blanco, just north of Nageezi, to the old hogan, hoping the family could shed some light on the disappearance of their neighbors six months ago. It was the same story he had heard all week; no one knew where the missing people went.

He had spoken to twenty-nine individuals who personally knew of a friend or family that went missing. In addition, he'd listened to anecdotal rumors of thirty-two other disappearances. A few said they'd heard unusual moaning or growling noises at night, but only one responded to his questions about killings and mutilations, or the sighting of a monster. In that one, the monster turned out to be a cougar, and someone had shot and killed it two months ago.

He stepped into his dusty truck and pulled the door shut. The cab was hot even with the windows open. In the glare of the bright afternoon, the spark of an idea bounced around in his mind. He drove away on the trail toward Cuba, and then south to Albuquerque. He wanted to get some maps from the BIA and lay out his findings from the last seven days. He also wanted to see Jim Avery, the head of the FBI office.

This past week he'd driven from Gallup to Zuni, over to Grants, back up to Crownpoint, over to Coyote Canyon, and then up to Newcomb and Farmington. A few days ago, he had called law enforcement offices in southern and eastern New Mexico and western Arizona, but he found no reports similar to the ones he was investigating.

Sam was tired and frustrated; he had no viable clues to help solve the mystery yet. He did have an idea however; a lawman's hunch. It seemed that all the disappearances happened in the northwestern corner of the state, on or near the Navajo Reservation. He pondered this as he drove into the glaring sun on his way to Albuquerque.

He would check in with old Jake at the trading post on his way back to Gallup tomorrow and see if Dan Yazzie had shown up. Sam wondered how his hunt for the monster was going. He had faith in Dan in spite of his trouble with the law. He knew the man was resourceful and a good tracker. He didn't doubt Dan's bravery, but his quest was one steeped in the supernatural and the spirit world, and also had proven to be deadly.

The Sandia Mountains glowed pink in the late afternoon sun, and Albuquerque lay dust-covered in the valley below. Sam approached the city along the high bluffs west of the river. The hot summer had turned the wide flow of the Rio Grande into a ribbon of shallow water. It meandered south through mud flats past the city toward El Paso. Not so grand, he thought.

He picked up the maps from the BIA office, and after stopping for food, he rented a room at a small motel near Old Town. He took off his shirt and boots, and spread his papers across the sagging bed. Sam ate a burrito as his eyes wandered over the large map.

When he finished eating, he picked up his notebook and began to make circles on the map at the locations of confirmed abductions. He used a different colored marker to note the anecdotal incidents. When he was done, he stood back and looked at his handiwork. The colored marks formed a pattern, like an irregular circle, in the northwestern corner of the state. No, not like a circle—more like a donut.

Sam raised his left eyebrow as he looked closely at the area in the center of the hole. He made a small snort of surprise.

The next morning he went to see Jim Avery at the FBI office downtown. He gave his name to the receptionist and he was ushered through a door with the man's name stenciled on the glass.

Jim got up smiling, and walked around his desk to greet the Indian Officer. He was a smallish, middle-aged man, with short, red hair, and enough energy for two people. He pumped Sam's outstretched hand and offered him a chair.

"Sam you old Indian," he grinned, "what takes you off the Reservation and brings you to big town? You're not hunting another monster are you?"

Sam cringed at Avery's words. "I see you've been talking to the two agents that came out to the Res. a few weeks ago."

"*Pffttt*, those two knot-heads? I wouldn't give a poached fart for either of 'em. College educated know-it-alls, is what they are! Suppose you tell me what's on your mind?"

Sam smiled at the Director's remarks. "I've got a mystery on my hands, and I figured I might need the brilliant minds of the FBI to help solve it."

"Bullshit!" Avery said with glee, "brilliant minds of the FBI? Where did you ever hear such a thing? No Sam," Avery narrowed his eyes and stared at the Indian, "you've got a problem, and you wrapped it all up with a ribbon to give it to me, like it was a present. You just want me to have my men stumble around and make a bunch of noise, and spend a lot of government money on it, while you sit back and solve it yourself, and rake in all the glory."

It was Sam's turn to say "bullshit!"

The two men laughed like kids, and then Sam told Avery about his mystery.

"Coffee?" Jim asked, without commenting on Sam's story.

Sam nodded and accepted a lukewarm cup from a carafe'. They both sipped and made faces at the horrible tasting brew.

"Abductions you say? Navajo families? Why would anyone abduct Navajos, Sam?"

"That's what I can't figure out. The people are unrelated. They have nothing in common but the general area they live. And here's another thing." He reached into the folder he brought with him, and then spread out his map on Jim's desk.

"Say, it does look like a donut. What's in the center?"

Sam said, "Chaco Canyon, the Atcitty hogan, and the Blacksparrow Mine."

After ten more minutes of talk, Jim Avery agreed to gather all the information his office could find out about the Mine, and then call him back.

The sun was climbing overhead when he left Avery's office. The soles of his boots stuck to the hot asphalt as he walked to his truck. Sam drove west out of town. He made it to the top of Nine-Mile Hill before he turned around and headed back down the long slope to the city. He then turned northeast toward Santa Fe, the State Capital, where most of the government offices were, including the Bureau of Mines.

CHAPTER 29

Kip was in a buoyant mood. He waved to his aunt and uncle as he taxied down the narrow road in front of the house. The Jenny took to the air like a kite caught in a stiff breeze and he headed toward Gallup to fuel up. The old biplane was running well, and Kip was grateful to be up in the air again.

Within fifteen minutes, he landed at the airfield and took on fuel. With the dual tanks topped off, he took to the air again, and left the dusty railroad town behind. He passed over the hogback with Churchrock on his right. The rugged desert made the shadow of his plane dance over the hills and canyons below. This was where he loved to be; he should have been a bird.

Kip marveled at the ageless desert stretching from horizon to horizon. Sparse, twisted vegetation dotted the ancient hills, and he occasionally saw a small house connected to civilization by a thin winding two-track. Many Navajo lived a primitive and secluded life: undoubtedly lonely at times, but certainly free.

He traveled about forty-five miles, and with Chaco Canyon just over the horizon, he noticed the small speck of another aircraft coming toward him from the east.

"Oh no, not again," he said aloud, getting ready for danger. "Please don't let it be another…Oh shit!"

Kip kicked the foot controls savagely and yanked the stick over. It was a Sparrowhawk, and it screamed past like a rocket as he frantically maneuvered the Jenny. The other plane circled as Kip glanced below. He was dismayed to see no cliffs or canyons to offer cover. The fast biplane tore past him again, and Kip dove for the ground, leaving his stomach a hundred feet above him. He knew he couldn't evade the faster plane for long.

"Bastard," he yelled, and climbed again for maneuvering room. He watched the Sparrowhawk loop above and come back at him head on at full throttle. He hoped the other pilot wouldn't fire his guns.

Kip barely had time to push the stick over, when he heard the snap of bullets hitting the fuselage. His controls immediately went sloppy. Kip twisted around and saw the tail torn to shreds.

"Son of a bitch!"

The Jenny was barely responding to the stick, and Kip struggled to keep the craft from falling into a tailspin. Kip used every trick he knew to regain some control, but the biplane continued to fall drunkenly toward the ground. His sweating hands jockeyed the throttle and stick, and he howled like an animal when he barely cleared the top of a small butte.

The doomed plane stalled and nosed over. It dropped down the steep talus slope like a rock, tearing off the prop and undercarriage, and kicking up a cloud of dust. It stopped abruptly at the bottom with Kip jammed into the padded rim of the cockpit; his flight harness tearing at his chest, his arms and legs tangled in the broken controls. Dust sifted down and covered the wreck.

Kip teetered on the edge of consciousness, noticing his arm bleeding down over his right hand. He unfastened the restraints and crawled out of the cockpit, dropping painfully to the ground and dragging himself away from the plane. There was always the danger of a fire. Kip managed to crawl over some rocks and fall headfirst into a shallow ditch, just before the hammering guns of the Sparrowhawk shredded his plane. It passed two more times, strafing the Jenny to ribbons before it finally disappeared.

Kip's body twitched as he regained consciousness. He groaned and rolled slowly onto his back, trying to sit up. His right arm hurt, and something was stuck to his forehead. Kip looked at his bloody right hand, and used his left arm to wipe at his brow. He pulled it back quickly when he felt a sharp pain. Sand and blood oozed over his eyes, and he clumsily reached for his bandana to try to staunch the flow.

He peered at the shredded canvas and broken wood of the old plane, and his heart sank. The Jenny was done for. Kip grimaced and took a deep breath, quickly doubling up in pain.

Okay, some cracked or broken ribs, something bleeding all over my hand, and a scalp wound that hurts like hell. He struggled to his knees and staggered for a moment when he got to his feet. Kip walked gingerly to the wreck and retrieved his frayed pack from the cockpit. He painfully hoisted it over one shoulder and then stumbled off in the direction of Chaco Canyon.

CHAPTER 30

Sam Begay mentally shuffled through his deck of clue cards as he drove toward Santa Fe. He only had three; a deadly creature, reports of missing persons, and something suspicious going on at the Blacksparrow Mine. Everything occurred in the same general area; was it related? He wanted to say yes, but he shrugged instead and decided he needed more cards.

The peak of Santa Fe Baldy stood high in the Sangre de Cristo mountain range, guiding him to its namesake town. He drove past a sprawl of adobe shacks and motels on the outskirts and eventually found his way to the narrow streets of old town. Sam knew of many cities that boasted about the age of their old town districts, but Santa Fe had them all beat; being established in 1610.

He parked in the central plaza and walked past the street venders displaying their brightly colored blankets and silver jewelry. He found the government offices and walked up the steps of a large adobe and stucco building. Sam hoped to find some useful clues in the records of the Bureau of Mines.

The air was musty inside and it smelled of old varnish. At least it was cooler than out on the street. Sam received directions to the second floor, and he found the door he wanted at the end of a long corridor. When he walked in, a pretty, Hispanic girl rose from her desk behind a worn counter. She asked if she could help, and Sam described the kind of information he was looking for.

She took him to a storage room with rows of file cabinets and tall shelving. After helping him locate the section with the type of records he was looking for, she left him to his search.

An hour later, Sam was ready to give up. He hadn't found anything that covered the area around Chaco Canyon. He went back to the counter to ask the young woman for help again.

As he explained his dilemma, a balding man with a bolo tie strode from the office behind her and interrupted them.

"Did I hear you say that there are some records missing?" he said in an officious tone.

Sam sized him up with a police officer's stare. "No, I didn't say they were missing, I just said I couldn't find them."

"Oh, well let me see if I can help you. Miss Ortega, please finish the typing I gave you this morning. I'm sure you could get more done if you didn't spend all your time visiting with the customers."

The man led Sam back to the storage room. Sam glanced over his shoulder and saw Miss Ortega stick her tongue out at her boss's back.

"Now what is it you're looking for?"

"I'm looking for information on a mining operation north of Crownpoint." He watched for any reaction on the other man's face. "It's called Blacksparrow."

Bolo tie was good, but Sam saw what he'd hoped to.

"Blacksparrow...Blacksparrow? I'm not sure I know of any mining operation by that name. You say it's near Crownpoint? By the way, my name is Esteven Gallegos, I'm the records manager. And whom, may I ask, are you?"

"Officer Begay, Federal Indian Officer."

Gallegos looked perplexed. "Well let's see what we can find."

They searched the room, but after twenty minutes, the manager admitted that the records appeared to be missing. They went back to the counter.

"Rosa, did someone borrow any of our record books recently?"

"Why no, Mr. Gallegos, we're not allowed to let any kind of records leave this office without your permission."

He cleared his throat. "That's correct, but some of the records seem to be missing just the same. How do you explain that?"

She turned white with shock.

"Why, Mr. Gallegos, I just started working here two months ago. They must have been missing before I came here. I assure you I would never do anything against the rules."

"Alright Miss Ortega, I believe you. The girl you replaced was sloppy with her work. I'm sure she just misplaced them somewhere. Next week we'll start looking for the missing books."

Bolo tie said to Sam, "I'm sure they're misfiled somewhere. If you'll give me your phone number, I'll be happy to have Miss Ortega call you when we find them."

Sam gave the man his office number, tipped his Stetson to the young woman, and left the building. A slight itch tingled across the back of his neck as he walked to his truck. In a second story window, bolo tie watched Sam as he drove away. He picked up the phone, and a moment later a voice said, "Jim Avery."

When Sam Begay pulled up to the Thoreau Trading Post, a few small clouds were building in the west. He doubted they would bring any rain. There were three vehicles in the lot, and he waited in his truck for the customers to leave. He greeted the old storekeeper with his usual teasing before getting to the question he wanted to ask.

"Jake, what do you know about the Blacksparrow Mine north of here?"

Old Jake considered his words while he wiped some dust off a shelf behind him. He put the rag down and looked directly into the Navajo's eyes. Sam ignored the cultural rudeness and waited for his response.

"I think they're a bad lot. They don't come in here much, except for the occasional can of tobacco or some candy. Tough looking men and they talk a little odd."

Old Jake leaned against the counter and stuck his face closer to Sam. "So what's your interest in the mine? Something to do with the missing people we were talking about?"

Sam smiled and stood his ground. Jake was old but he wasn't stupid. He had his suspicions about the people at the mine all along, but it took Sam to ask before he said anything about it.

"Sam I don't know much about the place, except that one of the men came in a few weeks ago and showed me a squash blossom necklace. He asked me what I thought it was worth. He said he traded for it and wanted to know if he got a good deal. To make a long story short, I recognized the jewelry; it belonged to Sarah Bitsilly out by Haystack. I haven't seen her around for a while, but I know she wouldn't part with that necklace. She wouldn't pawn it either; it had some special meaning for her. Then this rough looking white guy comes in and says he traded for it? I don't think so."

CHAPTER 31

Kip Combs took a sip of warm water from his canteen. He decided to save it for drinking rather than cleaning off the blood on his face and arm. He didn't want to run out before he could find help. The camp at Chaco Canyon was his closest chance, and besides, it was where Diana Witherspoon was. The sun beat down unmercifully as he stumbled over the rough landscape. He imagined Diana coming to his aid with cool, tender hands. He imagined her soft lips brushing his injured brow…he could see the concern in her sparkling, green eyes…

"Sheesh," he croaked, after stumbling to his knees. "Wake up boy; you're getting a little sappy out here in the sun."

He put away his thoughts of the girl and took his bearings. Another mile as the crow flies, he guessed. He staggered into a dry wash and shuffled along until he saw the sandstone cliffs that were the backdrop of the Chaco Valley.

When he finally staggered into camp, he collapsed in front of a large tent and a handful of students rushed to his aid. He woke up thinking he was hallucinating. Diana sat next to his cot pressing a wet cloth to his forehead. He closed his eyes and realized he was actually hearing her voice.

"Mr. Combs…Kip wake up. Can you hear me Kip?"

He blinked and tried to sit up, but she pushed him back down.

"Just stay still; you've had a nasty fall. You've gouged your arm, and you have a bad cut on your forehead."

A thought suddenly crossed her face. "Your plane—where's your plane?"

"M-my ribs...hurt."

"You probably bruised them when you fell." She waited for his response, and then asked knowingly, "You didn't fall did you?"

Kip closed his eyes and slept for another hour before waking again. He managed to sit up this time, and he was putting his feet into his boots when Diana opened the tent flap. Sunlight and a warm, sage-scented breeze came in with her.

"I wish you'd lie back and rest," she said.

"No its okay, I'm pretty clear headed now. All I've got are some cuts and bruises anyway."

"Cuts and bruises? You crashed your airplane didn't you? How did it happen?"

"I was shot down by another plane." He held his head in his hands, "Probably the same one that shot at me when I flew you out here a few weeks ago."

"Someone shot at you? But why would they do that?" Her brow wrinkled with concern.

Kip scratched his head and winced. "Sister I don't know, but I'm sure going to find out." His gave her a lopsided grin. "You don't happen to have a jealous boyfriend with an airplane do you?"

Nicholas and his squad arrived at the crash site on horseback. They searched for the body of the pilot, but only found a few tracks and some blood. Nick had an evil look on his face when he recognized the numbers on the plane's tail. It was the same one he had shot at and got in trouble over. He ground his teeth and hoped the fool pilot wasn't dead yet. He had his own revenge to satisfy first.

Working quickly, the men dumped the pieces of the broken Jenny into a nearby ravine. They covered it with a canvas tarp and then with dirt and rocks until it looked just like any other part of the desert a hundred miles in any direction. When they rode back to the mine, they noticed a plume of dust and a pickup truck heading toward the gates.

Two armed guards watched the truck coming. The brakes of the Plymouth squealed loudly as it stopped in front of them. Sam waited in the cab for the dust to blow away, and then he stepped out. The guards appeared nervous, and the smaller of the two acted as if he had something to prove.

"You might as well turn around and go back to your hogan Chief; didn't you see the sign back on the guard shack? No visitors allowed unless they have an invitation," he moved the barrel of his rifle toward Sam, "and you're not invited, so scram!"

Sam pushed his hat up from his forehead. "Look boys, I'm a Federal Indian Police Officer, and I want to speak to your boss."

Just then, a gaunt looking man stepped between the two guards. "What's going on Ernst?"

"This Indian Cop wants to talk to you."

Sam was used to dealing with superior-acting white men. "Yes I do. I haven't had the chance to properly introduce myself to the owner of such an important industry in my jurisdiction. My name is Officer Begay, would you be the owner?"

Bloundt stood stony quiet for a moment before addressing the policeman in his most condescending voice.

"Officer…Begay you have arrived at a time when I cannot give you even a moment of my time. I have a tight schedule to keep, and I will not tolerate trivial distractions."

Bloundt turned to leave, and Sam gritted his teeth and said, "It pains me, but I may have to be more than a trivial distraction."

Bloundt regarded the Indian with an icy glare.

"Officer, I suggest you go find yourself some sheep to talk to; or whatever it is that you Indians do with them."

The guards smirked at the crude remark.

"This is checkerboard territory, and you're on white man's property. You have no jurisdiction here. Now get off before I have my men throw you off."

Sam ground the truck's gears and threw dirt and dust at the gate as he spun his vehicle around. His face was a fierce mask of rage. He gripped the steering wheel and wished he were choking the neck of the wise-ass white man who called his bluff.

Stupid law. He was a trained Government Police Officer; a native assigned to handle Indian Reservation matters, but forbidden to meddle in non-Indian jurisdictions. This part of the reservation was problematic because it was divided into a checkerboard of Indian and non-Indian parcels.

"Stupid law," he said with feeling.

Sam quickly reached the guard shack at the Chaco Canyon intersection. He jerked the wheel and made the truck slew around as he downshifted and stomped on the gas. He accelerated north toward the ruins, and when he hit a large pothole, his head hit the roof and crushed his hat. He finally slowed down and began to cool off.

Bloundt walked back to his office and called a certain number in Albuquerque.

"James," he said when the man came on the line, "I have just met the Indian Officer you called about earlier. He came here and I told him to leave. Listen, I can't afford to have him around here again."

"Just what would you like me to do about it?" Avery said with a petulant note in his voice. He disliked the demeanor of this man even though he was obliged to follow his orders.

"I want you to call him and set up a meeting between the two of you. Make it somewhere in the desert around here, but not too close. Here's what we'll do..."

James Avery listened, and then he stammered his strong objections.

"Just do it," Bloundt shouted. "Just shut up and do it!"

The line went dead, and Avery slowly hung up the phone. His face turned white as he contemplated what he'd been told to do.

CHAPTER 32

Kip felt well enough to walk around the camp by mid-afternoon. His ribs still ached, as did his head and arm, but he found the company of Diana Witherspoon to be an elixir of strong, recuperative powers. Broken shards of pottery crunched underfoot as she led him on a tour of the excavations. The soft wind brought Diana's earthy scent to him as she talked of the ancient inhabitants of the valley. Kip saw her face light up as she pointed out the various ruins, and he wondered if he could ever excite her the same way her work obviously did. She stopped and pointed to a small hill

"Do you feel well enough to walk up there? There's a section of wall from an old village and a perfect view of the entire area."

When they reached the top, Diana sat down and pulled two apples from her pack. They ate while they feasted their eyes on the majestic panorama before them.

"It must have been something," Kip said with feeling.

"See the Pueblo Bonita walls over there near the cliff. Across the riverbed is Casa Renconda. Behind us, there's a stairway cut into the rock leading to the top of the plateau. Ancient roads are still visible up there. The valley inhabitants traveled and traded with other cultures as far north as Mesa Verde."

As she spoke, Kip noticed a subtle change come over her face. He asked, "What could bring on a sad look like that?"

Diana looked away as a small tear ran down her cheek. She wiped it away in frustration.

"My father used to take me all over this part of the state when I was a young girl. He worked for the university, and I spent most of my summers with him at one Anasazi site or another. It was lonely at times, but I didn't mind because we were together. He was always so excited when he found something new."

Another tear dropped down her cheek and Kip gently touched her shoulder.

"I'm fine," she sniffled. She took a deep breath and wiped her eyes. She set her jaw and looked out across the valley. "No, I'm not fine. My father was a kind and gentle man. He wouldn't harm anyone. He lived his life to discover, and to understand how the ancient Indians lived," she hesitated for a moment, "and he was killed out there almost a month ago."

"Killed?" Concern and alarm showed on Kip's face.

"Yes, his body was found at the bottom of a cliff near the Blacksparrow Mine. He was always afraid of heights and would never go anywhere near a steep drop—so how could he fall from one? I was away at a seminar when it happened and just came from his funeral when you flew me back here. Carl found him, and he told me he saw evidence that my father was beaten and pushed to his death."

"I'm sorry," Kip said softly, "and here I was so rude to you when we met at the airfield."

"Oh don't apologize," she sniffed. "I was the one with the chip on my shoulder."

Kip gently reached for her hand. "Diana, I've thought of you almost every day since then. I...I just wanted to come back and see you today."

She turned and their eyes held. He gently kissed her lips. She responded briefly, and then pulled away. She noticed something in the distance over Kip's shoulder.

"What in the world...?" Her voice trailed off, and Kip turned to look. A grey truck drove into the camp and stopped, while the inevitable dust cloud drifted away to the east.

"I'd better see what this is all about," she said.

As they walked down the hill, a man in a uniform got out of the truck and approached a couple of students. They pointed at Diana and Kip, and the man walked over to meet them.

"Are you in charge here ma'am? My name is Sam Begay." He tipped his hat to her.

"How do you do Mr. Begay, I'm Diana Witherspoon; the head of this expedition. This is Kip Combs."

"Do you work here too?"

"No, I'm just a pilot." Then showing his bandages, "A pilot without a plane now, unfortunately."

Begay looked thoughtfully at Kip, and then turned back to the young woman. "Miss Witherspoon, I came to ask if anyone in your group has noticed anything unusual around here lately."

"Unusual? Like what?"

"Oh nothing specific: just strange noises, odd occurrences, that sort of thing."

"Well," she nodded at Kip, "this man just had his airplane shot down this morning."

Sam looked questioningly at Kip who recounted his experience. When he was done, Diana described the mysterious death of her father.

"Have either of you had any contact with anyone from the Blacksparrow Mine?"

They both shook their heads and said, "No."

Diana was called away just then by one of her students. She excused herself, and left Kip and the officer to talk. When she rejoined them a few minutes later, Sam said he was finished. He thanked her for her help and walked back to his truck. Kip stayed behind with Diana for a moment.

"He's going to give me a ride back to my aunt and uncle's place in McGaffey. I've been staying out there helping them with their farm for a few weeks." He looked into her eyes. "I'm glad I got to see you today. I don't know when I'll be able to get back again, but I hope it'll be soon. Is that alright with you?"

She leaned over, kissed his cheek, and smiled. "Yes, that would be alright with me. You might want to try driving next time though."

Diana waved at Kip as the vehicle left the camp.

She watched for a moment, and then looked east toward the familiar outline of Fajada Butte.

"No man in my life for more than a year, and now I've got two of them." She smiled and shook her head.

CHAPTER 33

When Nicholas and his goons returned to the mine, he immediately sought out Commandant Bloundt and told him about the identifying numbers on the plane they had buried.

"Are you sure it was the same aircraft?"

"Yes sir." Nick barely kept control of his rage over the humiliation he had endured from his previous encounter with the aircraft.

"And you say there was no sign of the pilot?"

Nick squirmed, and his eyes dropped to his boots. "We saw a few tracks and some blood, but we couldn't find a trail."

"Of course not," Bloundt said after a pause, the familiar sharpness was back in his voice.

"And do you know why you couldn't find it?"

Nick flinched as if the words were a snake ready to strike. He had trouble finding his voice.

"I'll tell you why you couldn't follow the tracks Nicholas." Bloundt's voice was surprisingly gentle now: even reasonable. "It is because you are a blunt tool. A blunt tool cannot be expected to cut." He continued calmly. "Let's face it, Nicholas; you are only good for one thing. You are a club. You will never be a sword."

Bloundt dismissed the man. A confused and relieved Nickolas Ells darted away.

The Commandant went back to his desk and picked up the phone.

A hundred miles away, James Avery jotted down the number of the downed aircraft.

"Yes, I'll check the registry and find out who owns it. I'll call you back when I have the information."

CHAPTER 34

Sam Begay and Kip Combs jostled in the cab of the pickup as Sam tried to steer around the biggest rocks in the road from Chaco Canyon. Like a good lawman, Sam quizzed the pilot over and over again, pulling out every detail of both encounters with the mysterious airplane with guns. Kip pointed to a group of low buttes and mesas to the west where he thought his plane may have crashed. There wasn't an easy way to get to the spot except on horseback. Sam made note of the location in case he wanted to investigate it later.

At the Chaco ruins, Carl walked out of concealment. He had seen Diana and the pilot talking to the Indian cop. He approached her now to find out the subject of their conversation.

"Was that the same guy that flew you here after your father's funeral?"

"Oh, there you are Carl. Yes, he's the same one. He told me he was shot down on his way here earlier today. He walked into our camp with his injuries this morning. Carl have you seen anything strange around the area recently?"

Carl stared at her wolfishly. "Do you mean other than the guy at Fajada Butte?"

"Yes, well...," She stopped and considered his meaning. "The Indian policeman that was here asked me the same question. I told him about dad of course, and the pilot told him about his plane being shot down. Funny thing, he said he'd been shot at on his way back to Albuquerque after he dropped me off that day, too. The policeman asked me what I knew about the Blacksparrow Mine."

"Hmm, that's odd," Carl said. "That mine is quite a bit south of here. I wonder why he would he be asking about that?"

"I don't know, he didn't say."

With that, Diana turned her attention to other matters.

"We need to move some of our equipment to the Bonita site before tomorrow. Can you ask a couple of the boys to help you? They'll show you what they need."

"Will do," Carl said. "I'll get at it right away."

Later, Carl left the camp and headed for the mine again. He was concerned about the Indian nosing around and very disturbed about the pilot living after the men shot him out of the sky. Something needed doing so the mission wouldn't be compromised by these recent events.

A few hours later, he approached the small mesa and saw someone nosing around where he had been searching earlier. Carl sought cover and used his binoculars to identify the other hiker. In his gut, he already knew who it was, and his eyes confirmed his suspicion.

Val Tannin stepped carefully on the slope, poking around where he saw Carl before. He was watching earlier and saw the man ducking to avoid the riders returning to the mine. Why would he hide from them when he was a regular visitor to the mine? Perhaps he had his own reasons for exploring this place and didn't want anyone else to know about it. Would it have anything to do with the death of the Professor? Val strongly suspected Carl had a hand in it, but how could he prove it beyond any doubt?

Carl watched Val from cover and cursed under his breath when the man climbed up a narrow path and looked around some rocks. He nearly swore aloud when he saw Val reappear with something in his hand. He put the binoculars down and picked up his rifle. While Val investigated his find, Carl rested the barrel of the Winchester on a rock and framed the man's back in his sights. The rifle kicked and the body fell beyond the top of the ridge. Carl picked up his pack and sprinted to where his target had fallen.

Val tumbled down the slope as he struggled to breathe. He felt numb all along his back and right shoulder. Knowing that whoever shot him would be along to finish him off, Val scrabbled across the rocks looking for a place of concealment. The numbness was beginning to turn into a sharp pain, and he had to gasp for each breath.

He found a slight overhang with a gathering of tumbleweed choking the shallow opening. It didn't look like much cover, but he could see no other options. He stepped behind the brush and the ground dropped from underneath him.

Carl reached the top of the ridge a few moments later and looked expectantly for the body. He was sure of the hit, but though he saw signs of the initial fall, he couldn't find the man. Carl paced back and forth in desperation. He was so upset, that he began to curse. After a thorough search, he found no trace of Val and no blood. Realizing he had to tell Bloundt about the Indian policeman and the pilot, he reluctantly moved on toward the mine.

Carl, usually in total control of his environment and confident of his abilities, began to feel the soft touch of doubt enter his mind like the slow crawl of a hairy spider.

CHAPTER 35

It was late evening when Sam finally reached Gallup. Kip introduced him to Bob and Vicki Johnson when he took Kip home to McGaffee, and he ended up staying for supper. He listened with interest to the couple's accounts of hearing strange moaning noises in the night and mentally added their location to his map of suspicious events.

Kip came down to breakfast the next morning feeling rested, but quite sore. Aunt Vicki clucked over him like a mother hen, but his thoughts were of his broken plane, and of Diana. He didn't want to read too much into their parting kiss, but his heart was buoyed up, and he couldn't get her out of his mind.

For some reason, Bob was beaming at him from the other side of the kitchen table like the cat that ate the cream. Finally, Kip could stand no more of it.

"Uncle Bob, what is going on this morning? You are certainly in a rare mood. Am I missing something?"

"No," Bob said innocently, still smiling. "I'm sorry about your plane, but I did make up my mind about something last night that I think will lift your spirits."

"Yeah?" Kip was interested but doubtful. "It's going to take something pretty big to make me forget about the Jenny. Don't get me wrong, I'm grateful to be alive, and thankful to have you both here to care for me, but I just don't know what I'm going to do without some wings."

Bob set his cup down and pushed away from the table.

"Finish your coffee and follow me over to the old barn. I've got something to show you."

Kip lifted his cup, studying his uncle's face over the rim. He glanced sideways at his aunt and was surprised to see the same expression on her face. Something was up.

"Okay, what's going on?"

Bob stood up. "Finished?" he inquired. "Let's go."

Vicki didn't say a word. She wiped her hands on a towel, took Kip's arm, and walked with him and her limping husband across the yard to the barn.

Kip helped Bob open the sliding door, and they stepped into the musky shadows inside. Bob lit a lantern and led them around some rusty machinery toward the back. There were stacks of crates and discarded items, and a dusty tarp covering something large and angular.

Bob set the lantern down and motioned to Kip. "Help me move some of this junk out of the way."

They spent a few moments removing the crates and some boards and tires. Then they both grabbed a corner of the tarp and pulled it back to uncover the unmistakable shape of an aircraft fuselage.

"Wha...what is it?" Kip stammered in surprise.

Bob turned his beaming face to Kip. "It's a de Havilland DH-4 mail plane. Now let's get it uncovered. We've got an engine to tear down and a lot of assembly to do, but I think we can make it airworthy in a few weeks."

Aunt Vicki hugged Kips arm, as he stood speechless.

"Bob decided to give it to you Kip. We talked about it last night, and we think you should have it."

Bob crawled around the disassembled biplane and said, "We'll need to go to Gallup tomorrow and get some parts and things...here, help me move this wheel assembly."

Vicky watched as the men lost themselves in their new project. She couldn't help but share the excitement they both showed on their faces.

Back in Albuquerque, Doo heard the phone ringing in the office. He set his wrench down and walked through the shop to the front of the building.

"Hello?"

"Hey Doo it's Kip, how are you doing old buddy?"

Doo's eyes lit up. "It's about time you called. I'm bored to the gills, how about you?"

"Well the truth is…I crashed the Jenny."

"*What?*"

Kip told Doo the whole story including the gift of the de Havilland. "Uncle Bob and I started putting the airframe back together yesterday. I'm calling from Gallup right now; we had to come to town to get some parts."

"But are you okay?"

"Yeah, yeah: just a couple of scratches and a bruise or two. Are you working on anything?"

"Well, I've been straightening out some sheet metal and replacing a piston or two, but it's barely enough to keep me busy."

"How about Lisa Ann, has she been bugging you with all her chattering?"

Doo looked up, just then, to see Lisa Ann walking into the office wearing one of her (and his) favorite blouses.

"Aw Kip," he grinned devilishly and raised his voice, "you know Lisa Ann. Why, just this morning, she said that she misses you to distraction. She's been moping around ever since you left, and she's starting to act a bit peckish…"

"*Shriek!*" Lisa screamed from across the room, and she ran up and snatched the phone from Doo, pushing him away with her hip.

"I did not!" she said loudly. "Why, I haven't even noticed you've been gone. I mean, I've been so busy with shopping and work and such."

"That's a lie!" Doo hollered from across the room and quickly dodged the pencil Lisa Ann threw at him.

She put a hand on her hip and started scolding. "Kip you didn't even say goodbye when you left, and I bought a new two-piece bathing suit, but you weren't even here for me to show it to you." She stuck out her tongue at Doo.

"Are you saying you miss me?" asked Kip.

"Miss you? Well, I wouldn't say that, but I guess I am used to you being around in case I…need something…" She purposely drew out the words so Kip could use his imagination about what that might be. "Of course, maybe I could ask Doo to help."

"Well, you know Doo is busy most of the time," Kip said, thinking quickly, "and I guess I'll be back there pretty soon; maybe a week or so.

I could probably help you when I get back. So…tell me about your new bathing suit."

She gave the receiver back to Doo without saying another word—a big smile crossed her face as she rushed out of the room.

"Okay, she's gone." Doo said.

Kip was still thinking about the bathing suit. "Look, there's something weird going on around Chaco Canyon. There's even an Indian cop looking into it. Anyway, Bob and I figure to have the new plane ready to fly in about a week, so it shouldn't be too long before I get back."

"Oh good," quipped Doo, "I'll try to help out Lisa Ann as best I can until then."

"You shit!" said Kip.

Doo laughed. "Yeah, yeah, just get back here as soon as you can. Even the chickens aren't laying two eggs together for fear that Lisa Ann will go digging around to see what they're attached to."

Doo snorted over the phone, and Kip laughed so hard he had to gasp for air. As soon as he could talk again, he said, "I'll be back real soon."

CHAPTER 36

Sam Begay heated the last of the mutton stew left over from two days ago. It was a sturdy, bachelor's breakfast, and while he ate, he thought over yesterday's events.

It seemed odd that the office manager in Santa Fe didn't recognize the name of the Blacksparrow Mine. It was unlikely that he was not aware of it, and it was more than likely that he had a reason to divert attention from it. Then there was that pompous ass at the mine, and then the guy who had his plane shot down, and the woman whose father died under suspicious circumstances. Sam was sure he was on to something, but what was it?

He added these new cards to his deck of clues and shuffled them. They had nothing in common except for the general location.

When he finished eating, he got dressed for a trial he had to attend in Gallup. He was the arresting officer, and he had to give testimony about a string of thefts in the Tohatchi area. It involved two teens and their old grandmother. Though Sam felt a need to uphold the law, he also felt sorry for the family. They were poor and starving, and the two grandsons had taken to theft to put food on the table.

With a deep sigh, he put on his hat and reached for the door when the phone rang.

"Sam this is Jim Avery. I've got the information you wanted on the Blacksparrow Mine."

"That was quick work. Hold on, let me get a piece of paper and a pencil."

Sam looked around to find something to write on.

"No Sam, I've got papers and maps, and a whole bunch of other stuff. I'd rather give it to you in person. Can you meet me this afternoon?"

"Sure Jim, but I won't be able to get to Albuquerque until late."

"I'll meet you half-way then. Do you know the road by Prewitt that goes out to Ambrosia Lake? I have to be in Grants for a lunch meeting and I can meet you afterward. Go north on the Prewitt road about ten miles where the canyon area begins."

"Yes, I know where that is. But why so far in the boonies?"

Jim's voice became quiet and secretive. "Sam I can't tell you now, but there are some things going on with that outfit, and it seems they've got connections. It'll be safer if we meet away from the beaten path. Can you be there about three o'clock?"

"Yeah, sure Jim, three o'clock it is."

"Okay, see you later; and Sam, don't talk to anyone about this."

Avery set the phone down and stared at the photo of President Roosevelt on the wall. After a moment, he abruptly picked up the phone again and dialed another number.

"Bloundt, this is Avery. It's done. He'll be out there at 3:00 this afternoon."

The trial was short, as it usually is for an Indian. Sam showed up just before the proceedings at 9:30 a.m. By 11:30, with all of the witnesses sworn in, and testimony given, the judge rendered a verdict. Of course, the teens were guilty, but at least the sentencing wouldn't be done until Sam had a chance to talk to the judge about the family. He walked into Judge Reilly's chambers after the trial and invited him to lunch.

As they ate, the two old friends caught up on personal matters as well as the trial.

"Judge, I know those kids are guilty, but I also know how the family has struggled since their mother died. She was supporting all three of them; her mom and the two boys."

"Yeah Sam, I know about that. Fact is, one of the uncles came up to me before the trial and offered to pay back what the kids took. He said he would be looking after them from now on. I'm thinking I'll take him up on that and let the boys off."

"Oh," Sam was relieved. "I didn't know they had any other family. That's great."

"I'll have to talk to the prosecutor first, but it should be okay with him." Reilly glanced out the window from their booth. "Say, what's with the new truck you're driving? You're really coming up in the world."

Sam hung his head in mock resignation and shook it slowly.

"It's this white man's world Judge. I told them all I wanted was a good horse, and they made me take the truck."

Reilly chuckled. "Don't lie to the Judge Sam. You know damn well you'd never keep your boots shiny enough riding a horse."

Sam just rolled his eyes, feigning the long-suffering and misunderstood Indian.

When they left the restaurant, Sam glanced at his pocket watch and saw there was enough time to gas up the truck and make a quick stop home for a change of clothes, before he headed east to meet Avery.

An hour later, he turned north on the Prewitt road. A few miles in, he passed two men in a wrecker headed toward the highway. He watched his odometer click off ten miles and stopped at the edge of a wide curve looking out over the canyon land. Sam turned off the motor and waited.

Three fifteen, he noted, and put his watch away for the third time. Jim must be running late. He opened his door and stepped out. He heard the sound of a loud motor echoing somewhere down the canyons. It seemed to get louder, and Sam thought he could now discern the sound of two engines. Suddenly they were on him. Two fast moving planes appeared and fired their machine guns as they flew past. Sam dove into the truck headfirst as .30 cal. loads stitched across the hood and roof. He felt his leg go numb, and he reached for the passenger door latch and pushed it open. He crawled out and kicked the door shut, and then dove over the edge of the embankment.

Sam dropped five feet to a narrow ledge and crawled until he found some cover behind a bush. The two planes roared past again spraying the truck with more hot lead. This time the guns must have hit the fuel tank, because Sam saw black smoke rising over the ledge. He lay there waiting for an explosion, but none came.

The planes buzzed over two more times, and he heard an engine laboring from a different direction. It sounded like the wrecker. For some reason Sam decided to stay under cover. He heard it stop and then start up again in low gear. Suddenly, the sound of crumpling metal and shattering glass came to him, and in a moment, the dented and smoking pickup teetered over the edge of the ravine and rolled downhill.

The air was full of noise, dust, and smoke. When the truck hit the bottom, a loud *whump* announced that the gasoline tank had finally exploded. The wrecker revved its engine as it maneuvered above him, and then it drove away.

Sam waited until he heard only the roar and pop of the fire over the sound of his pounding heart. His leg was still numb, and he saw that his boot and pants were soaked with blood. To his dismay, he also realized that the sandy ledge was slowly crumbling beneath him. He clawed at the bush for a better grip, but his eyes lost focus, and he realized he was falling.

When he started regaining consciousness, he heard the wind whistling, and felt sand blowing on his face. He heard the sound of running, and then someone spoke to him.

"Easy Sam, don't try to talk." He felt his head being raised, and then tasted warm water trickling over his lips and his chin.

He figured it was Jim Avery and tried to say his name. As his eyes began to focus, he saw a big, Indian nose and dark, arching eyebrows. He soon recognized the face of his friend, Dan Yazzie.

"Dan?" he whispered. "How did you get here?"

CHAPTER 37

The two Sparrowhawks touched down on the landing strip at the mine. The pilots left their planes and walked quickly across the compound to the Commandant's office. He would be waiting for their report.

"Come in," Bloundt growled impatiently. "Well?"

The pilots wore great smiles. "We got him sir. We caught him in his truck and threw lead all over him. We made a few more passes until we saw the vehicle catch fire. When the wrecker pulled up, we took off."

Both men were waiting for words of praise, but Bloundt didn't look quite as pleased as they thought he would be.

"You didn't actually see the body did you?" The Commandant spoke in a reasonable voice, but his eyes bored holes through their skulls.

Both pilots began to sweat. "We saw our boys come up and push the burning truck over the edge. We could see the smoke from the explosion."

Bloundt considered this for a moment. "Yes, I believe you have been successful."

The pilots appeared noticeably relieved by his words.

"Well done men. Dismissed."

Dan Yazzie rode double with his wounded friend. He picked his way carefully down the narrow trail as they made their way to his camp. It was near a place where Dan had noticed signs of the creature.

They rode up a dry wash that wound its way through the rocks. There were cottonwoods and olive trees along the banks and a few small pools of water hidden in the shady spots.

Dan could tell that Sam was becoming weaker, and he was relieved when he saw the camp ahead. It was set in a shallow opening resembling an amphitheater. They climbed the slope of weathered sandstone, and Dan helped Sam from the horse. He took him to the lean-to in the back of the shelter and brought him some blankets.

Dan attended to Sam's leg first, and then made him comfortable while he unpacked the horses. He left the animals staked out where they could forage and drink from a small pool, and then he gathered some dry wood and started a fire.

"How did you find me?" Sam said as he propped himself up on a pack.

Dan prepared some canned stew and he answered while stirring the pot.

"I saw the airplanes and heard the machine gun fire. When I saw a black cloud of smoke, I knew something bad happened."

"Bad is right," Sam said. "You didn't see anyone else around did you; no other car, a white man in a suit?"

"No one." Dan looked at his injured friend with concern. A single bullet hit Sam, and though it didn't go through his leg, it left a long, deep gash through the skin and muscle. He would have to wait to see if it would heal or get worse.

Dan decided to tell him his other news.

"Sam, I finally found it. This whole area is full of tracks from the monster. I even saw its shape on a ridge a few miles away. It's here somewhere."

Sam stiffened, and glanced around nervously.

Dan chuckled. "Oh no, not right here. I meant in the general area. We're really on the outskirts of where I think it makes its home. It leaves from time to time to look for food, but it always comes back. Here, I've got something to show you."

Dan reached into a pack and pulled out a rolled piece of cloth. He brought it over to Sam and opened it to show a ten-inch, brown and black feather. It wasn't like a bird's feather; it was longer and more narrow, and it had thin hairs, almost like a quill.

"I figured this was a good place to stay while I looked around to find it and kill it. I went for more supplies, and was on my way back when the airplanes buzzed overhead. I heard the guns, and I saw the planes circling around again. I stayed behind cover, and waited until they were gone before I rode up to see what was going on. I found you lying about twenty feet away from your burning truck. It looked like you got out just in time; there isn't a burn mark on you."

"There was no other vehicle around?"

"Nope," Dan said, "Why?"

Sam thought of his planned meeting with Jim Avery. He expected him to arrive a few minutes early, if anything and he would have waited until at least 3:30 before leaving, thinking Sam was late. He wouldn't arrive so late that he and Dan would've already left.

"Dan, I came out here to meet someone I know from the F.B.I. office in Albuquerque. He didn't show up."

"Do you think something happened to him; a breakdown maybe?"

"Could be, but it isn't likely. I guess he could have been attacked, too. The thing is, as far as I know; only he and I knew we were meeting there."

Sam's concerned expression changed to a frown as he considered a darker thought.

"There's another possibility," he said slowly. "Let me ask you this: if only two people know of a time and a meeting place, and one doesn't show up, ruling out bad luck, why wouldn't he?"

"Because he didn't want to?" said Dan.

"And why wouldn't he want to?"

"Because he knew it was a set-up?"

Jim Avery's phone rang at his desk. He had been nervously awaiting the call, and he quickly lifted the receiver. "Avery."

Bloundt's gruff voice spoke three words before he hung up. "We got him."

Avery softly replaced the handset and sat staring at the phone for a moment. Beads of sweat began to form on his face, and he ran to the bathroom and threw up.

CHAPTER 38

Commandant Bloundt called Nicholas to his office a few days after the Sparrowhawk attack on the Indian policeman. He had just received a call from Jim Avery with the information he wanted about the owner of the biplane.

"You wanted to see me sir? Nicholas was still leery of the man even though he seemed to be back in Bloundt's good graces.

Nicholas, I may have some good news for you. I have just been given the address of the person who owned the biplane you and your squad buried the other day. It's a flying service at a small airfield north of Albuquerque. What I want you to do is, pick another man and both of you drive over there and find out if the pilot made it home after the crash.

Nicholas and Gunter arrived at Mathews Airfield in the middle of the afternoon. Doo was working in the back of the hanger when he noticed the two men in the office snooping around. He quickly wiped his hands on his pants and walked to the front. He didn't like what he saw. The men stared at him with unconcealed predatory looks.

"Can I help you?" He said, keeping some distance away from them.

"Well I sure hope so," said Nicholas in a loud voice. He looked the most threating because of his size, and his dark beard.

"Gunter, go have a look in the back."

His thin accomplice left the room.

"Hey you, get back here. Customers aren't allowed in the shop."

"Sonny," Nicholas said with a sneer, "we ain't customers. In fact we might be your worst nightmare if you mouth off again."

"It's clear Nicholas," Gunter said.

Doo looked over his shoulder as the man took a position behind him.

"Now sonny, said Nicholas, "we're looking for a pilot who flies an old biplane. We understand he works out of this hanger. Where is he?"

"What do you want him for?" Doo licked his lips and glanced nervously at the man behind him again.

Nicholas shook his head in mock sadness. "Now you see sonny, that's just what I was talking about. You mouth off, you get nightmare."

Gunter quickly grabbed Doo's arms as Nick approached still shaking his head.

"Maybe you didn't under—*stand!*"

On the last syllable, Nicholas drove his fist into Doo's unprotected stomach, and then watched him collapse, coughing, and retching on the floor. He grabbed the boy by his hair and jerked his head up. Doo's chin was moist with spit.

"I'm going to ask you again; maybe you should think first before you answer."

"H-he isn't here," Doo struggled to breathe.

"See how easy that was? Now here's the hard part; where is he?"

"I-I don't know."

Nicholas gritted his teeth and pulled back his clenched fist.

"I don't know, I don't know!" Doo stammered. "He isn't here. He's somewhere out by Gallup. I don't know where, I swear it."

Nick bent down looking at the kid, and then nodded to Gunter to pull him back to his feet. Gunter started to lift him, and Doo grabbed his arm and threw him over his shoulder. Nicholas danced out of the way and stepped in to throw a punch that put Doo on the floor again.

Nicholas turned to his partner who was just getting to his feet. "Let's have a good look around before we go."

Gunter made sure his foot rapped Doo on the head as he stepped over him.

Ten minutes later, Lisa Ann watched from a window in her uncle's office as the two men got into their car and drove away. Her curiosity aroused, she left the building and walked over to the hanger.

"Doo!" she shouted as she saw the boy on the floor. She ran to his side. "Doo, Doo wake up!"

Doo was stirring a little. She ran to the water cooler and brought a cup back to the boy, gingerly cradling his head while she lifted the water to his lips. He coughed painfully and took a small sip. When he could finally get up, Lisa Ann helped him to a chair.

"What happened, Doo? Why did those men do this to you?"

"I don't know," he ran a hand slowly through his mussed hair, and winced as he touched a knot that was beginning to swell.

"These two goons showed up and started asking about the guy who owns the biplane, and then they punched me out."

"What did they want Kip for?"

Doo looked at Lisa and shook his head carefully.

"They didn't say."

CHAPTER 39

Sam Begay slept fitfully near the fire that night, and when Dan changed the bandage on his leg the next morning, he told Sam he didn't like the look of it. He applied some iodine and rewrapped the wound as Sam stoically endured the pain and tried not to move.

Dan talked about his journey while they ate a breakfast of biscuits, beans, and hot coffee. He told Sam about the vacant houses and the tracks of the elusive creature. He told him, that though he had only seen its shadowy silhouette, he did find the odd-looking feather, and it gave him its look, and its scent.

They spent the rest of the day talking about the creature, as well as Sam's mystery, and the clues he was shuffling in his mind. Dan offered no comments. That evening, they shared another can of stew as they sat next to the warming fire.

Dan cleared his throat, "I forgot to tell you about something. I think this monster keeps a regular feeding schedule." Dan paused as he gathered his words. "I think this creature Ye'iitsoh only feeds once every ten days."

Sam appeared confused as Dan explained. "I've been thinking back to when my family was killed, and then later when I found an animal carcass in the desert. One day I found the creature's tracks leaving this area and then coming back the next day, and I've been adding it all up."

"So according to this schedule you've worked out, do you know when the creature will feed again?"

"Yes, today or tonight."

"Shit!"

Shadows gradually turned to darkness. The two men sat near their fire with weapons at hand; their faces bright in the glow of the flames. They staked the horses nearby for the night.

A short while before midnight, a shadow from the depths of the canyon moved soundlessly up the slope toward the camp. It stopped frequently to listen to the night, its grotesque shape hidden in the darkness. It arrived downwind to give no scent to betray its presence. It lifted its snout and took in the smell of the men. The creature would feed tonight. There were two; it would take only one. Still downwind, the shape moved without a sound as the night seemed to hold its breath. The beast crouched in darkness fifteen feet from its prey.

Sam moved a hand, gesturing to Dan, who warily lifted his rifle.

"Listen. Do you hear it?" he whispered.

"What?"

"Nothing."

Both men sat unmoving as they peered into the gloom, realizing that the light of the fire hindered their night vision. They could feel the sweat forming on their hands as they clutched their rifles. Ten minutes passed, and then an owl sounded from somewhere down the canyon.

The creature chose its victim and crouched ready for the kill.

Sam slowly turned to Dan to suggest that they separate and move from the fire, and both men jumped as a shrill scream tore through the night.

Dan yelled, "It's after the horses!"

The night was full of the terrified screams of the two animals and the horrible, piercing cry of something else. The rocks above the camp echoed with noise as blood froze in the men's veins. Standing in the shadows near the campfire, they tried to see through the thick veil of dust kicked up by the struggling horses. They were reluctant to fire their guns for fear of hitting one of the animals.

Dan fired high and Sam joined in. They heard a horse running away as a weird bubbly breathing came from beyond where the animals were tethered. The sound of crunching bones came to them, and then a wet noise like something meaty dragged away. They both began firing again, stopping only when their rifles were empty.

The men reloaded with shaking hands, and they built up the fire and stayed vigilant for the next hour. Everything appeared quiet now, so they fashioned two torches and went into the darkness where they'd left the horses. They found the carcass of one of the animals torn apart; its hairy skin shredded and splashed with blood. The hindquarters were missing; presumably dragged off by the creature. The other horse, they hoped, had run to escape. They would need to find it. The men took turns keeping watch for the rest of the night while the other tried to sleep.

When dawn came, they went to view the evidence of what had happened. Flies covered the ruined carcass of the horse, buzzing a weird homage to its demise. The men saw a thick smear of blood and drag marks leading away from the animal. They followed the marks to a sheltered canyon a half a mile away and found where the creature had eaten its prey. A few splintered bones and some strings of gore were all that remained. Tracks of the creature were plain to see here, but when the men began to follow them, they soon vanished in the rocks.

The morning wore on, and they eventually found the other horse eating grass near a small seep. It was still nervous but it let the men approach. The animal was in sad shape, having run blindly into the night. Its flanks were bloody from scraping against sharp thorns and branches in its fearful, headlong flight.

As the men led the animal back to camp, Sam said, "Ten day feeding cycle eh? Remind me to be home in Gallup before then."

Dan looked at Sam. "But just think, we have nine whole days to track it down and kill it before it gets hungry again."

CHAPTER 40

Miles away to the west, Val Tannin awoke to pitch-blackness. His shoulder and back burned as if a firebrand had touched it, and his head throbbed with a dull pain. He gingerly lifted his arm and touched a painful lump on his forehead. He croaked a few words and heard his voice echo faintly. Swallowing with difficulty, he lay back again and tried to piece together how he came to be here. The ground beneath him was hard and flat, and covered with a thin layer of sand littered with small twigs.

Val knew that a bullet had hit him. He'd felt the impact and heard the sound of the gunshot as he rolled downhill. He remembered getting to his feet and running…but where was he now?

Then, he remembered climbing into a pile of tumbleweed and the ground opening up beneath him. He must be in a cave of some kind. How far did he fall, and how long ago? He tried to move again and managed to sit up against a flat wall. His pack was still on his shoulders, and he began removing it with some difficulty as sharp pain flared across his back. He had to rest several times and slowly suck air through his clenched teeth, but he finally pulled the pack in front of him.

Val could feel a slight breeze as he fumbled for his flashlight. When he found it, he thumbed the switch, but it didn't work. He searched for some matches and struck one. In the small flickering light, he could see what looked like squared off walls. Thick, dusty spider webs covered everything, and he noticed small bits of brush scattered all around him on the floor. He lit another match and noticed something nearly out of reach of the light. He couldn't be sure, but they looked like dust covered bones.

Clenching his teeth in pain, Val gathered some twigs and made a small fire. When the flames grew, he could see that the walls definitely appeared to be manmade. The place looked almost like a hallway; the sides were fashioned too regularly to be a mine tunnel or a natural cave. He noticed it ended abruptly in a rockslide near where he sat, and it continued into darkness in the other direction.

His heart beat faster as he dared grasp the origin of this strange place. He had only hoped for a stroke of luck like this. He remembered the dusty bones lying nearby, and in the dancing shadows of the small fire, they almost appeared to come to life. He crawled over to examine one, and it crumbled to his touch.

Val took a closer look at his flashlight and saw a deep crease along one side where it had come apart. He managed to snap it closed, and he tried the switch a few times until a weak beam cut into the darkness. Val pulled himself painfully to his feet and began shuffling slowly down the tunnel. He found more bones a short distance away. A pale, grinning skull in one crumbling mass told him that they were human. As he moved further along, he found another skull that was not. The sight of it shocked him, and he couldn't identify the kind of animal it once was.

His light became alarmingly dimmer, and he shook it with no better result. Val reluctantly shut it off and returned to the small fire.

CHAPTER 41

Sam Begay's leg bothered him throughout the next night, and when morning came, it hurt even more. With too little sleep, he felt listless and groggy. A soft, female rain created a din as it fell from the lip of the rocks above their campsite and made their voices sound disembodied. The moisture in the cool air chilled their bones and drained the blood from their faces.

Dan dug at the ashes of last night's fire and placed a few dry sticks on the coals. When the fire came to life, he made coffee. Sam sat with a blanket across his shoulders, staring bleakly at the sheet of water falling like a curtain in front of them.

Sam thought of the monster again and how close they had been to it. Yet they still lived. What if Ye'iitsoh wasn't so invincible? What if it wasn't a demon, but instead just a large creature that had to abide by nature's laws, just as any other animal must? He shared his thoughts with Dan who shrugged noncommittally.

In Dan's mind, he believed the beast to be the ancient Monster: a God with near-immortal powers. It was also his personal demon, since it had come to him as he slept a week ago.

He thought he might have been dreaming at the time, but he knew now that Ye'iitsoh had come to him that night. It had stalked him silently in the darkness, and it brought its evil face close to his as he slept. It had stared at his closed eyes. Dan remembered waking later and smelling its foul scent. He'd looked around, and glanced down at the front of his shirt where a wet smear of drool hung across his chest.

The creature had really been there. It had somehow entered his mind and told him of the horrible things he would soon experience. Dan had thought of his daughter and grandfather afterward, and a fire grew inside him warming his resolve. He realized two important things that night: the monster had not been hungry, and the monster feared him!

Dan changed Sam's bandage after the two men finished their breakfast. "Your leg looks infected this morning. You need to see a doctor before it becomes a bigger problem. The rain has stopped, and I think I should get you to the hospital in Gallup."

Sam frowned and nodded. "I know. I just wish I could be more help right now."

"That's alright; I'll take you to town and then come back here to do some more looking around."

"What if you find Ye'iitsoh?"

"Well, if he's not hungry, I'll poke him with a stick and tell him I have come to kill him."

"And if he is hungry?"

Dan just looked at him grimly.

Sam said, "I saw a movie in Albuquerque last month before you got out of prison. It was about a detective named Charlie Chan who was a very wise Chinaman."

Sam got up and brushed himself off. "He caught a murderer by tricking him into admitting his crime. I just remembered something he said. 'A wise man does not poke a sleeping tiger with a stick.'"

The two men were saddling the horse when Sam got a strange look on his face.

"Dan, there was something in the newsreel, before the movie, that just came to me. Didn't you tell me that you saw something eating the stars one night as it moved across the sky? Would you say it was round, or more like a long football?"

Dan thought for a minute, "More like a football I guess. Why?"

"And it was pretty big, huh?"

"Yes, it had to be."

"Well, the newsreel was about Germany and a man called Hitler. They had huge, gas-filled balloons that were hundreds of feet long and carried passengers across the ocean. They called them dirigibles. Just think; what if one flew across the sky at night and was close enough to blot out the stars behind it as it passed. Would that look something like what you saw?"

Realization spread slowly across Dan's face. "That could be it. There was a weird moaning sound in the air too, like something far off. What did you call this thing?"

"A dirigible and you might have heard the sound of its engines and propellers."

"Just think," Dan said, "a big cloud with motors."

Sam stopped dead in his tracks. "A growling cloud…a growling cloud! That's what some of the witnesses said. A growling cloud with white men climbing down ropes, taking people away."

"Do you think the monster has something to do with it?"

"I don't know, but I'm starting to think the Blacksparrow Mine does."

The men rode down the canyon and across the hills of the Continental Divide. The sun quickly took back the moisture in the soil, and the vivid colored rocks lost some of their brightness.

Dan said he had a cousin living at Crownpoint about fifteen miles away. They arrived at his place in the early afternoon. There was a sorry looking truck sitting in the front yard, and Dan's cousin assured both men that he could get Sam to the hospital in Gallup.

With the engine clattering like a can of rocks, and the exhaust rising in blue clouds from the floorboards, Sam bid Dan good luck.

"I know you are doing what you must do. Soon I will also have to do something I must. After I get my leg taken care of, I'm going to find some good men and pay another visit to the mine. But before that, I'm going to call someone in Albuquerque, and ask him why he didn't meet me on the Prewitt road."

CHAPTER 42

Sam Begay's leg throbbed painfully all the way to Gallup. Exhaust fumes and dust seeped through the cab of the ancient, clattering truck, but thankfully, the open windows let in enough air to keep the two men from losing consciousness.

Sam's head lolled side to side as the truck labored past Rehoboth, and then through the hogback ridge at the eastern edge of Gallup. Dan's Cousin Billy drove up to the Indian Hospital and helped Sam out of the vehicle and into the building.

Billy wanted to stay, but Sam thanked him and sent him back home. He took a chair in the crowded waiting room and dozed off until someone called his name.

The leg was worse now. They scrubbed and disinfected his wound, and gave him a shot and then assigned him to a room. The doctor told him if the wound looked better in a week, he could go home. Sam didn't like waiting, but he knew he needed rest. If anything, he felt worse now than when he first limped into the hospital.

In his room, he glanced at the man lying in the bed next to his. There were bandages around his head and arms, and he appeared to be asleep. Just as well, he didn't feel like making conversation.

Sam slept and dreamed of the events of the past week. It all became a distorted nightmare where he ran from a speeding truck and dodged bullets that hissed at him as they sped past. Each time he thought he found a place to hide, a demon blocked his way, and its drool-flecked teeth morphed into Jim Avery. Sam had a temper, and he displayed it in his sleep with his clenched teeth, and his sweating face hot with rage.

He awoke with only one thought in his mind. He wanted to hear the crooked bastard's voice on the phone when he called him and said, "Hi Jim, this is Sam Begay." He knew, to Avery, it would sound like a voice from the dead.

Sam savored the thought and reveled in what the effect on the man would be. He stiffened suddenly, his eyes open in the dark. He thought of one response Avery was sure to make. It wasn't so much what Jim would say that was important, it was what he would do. His reaction would be to rush agents to Sam's house to find him. They would probably kill him while resisting arrest or attempting to escape. Sam wasn't in a position to be ready for anything like that yet. No, he wouldn't call Avery until his leg had time to heal.

Sam knew he was set-up, and the man in him wanted revenge, but he also knew he had to carefully choose the right time and place. Yes, it would be better if he were to appear to be dead for now. There were things to find out, and things he must do before he made his call to Jim Avery.

CHAPTER 43

Diana Witherspoon walked toward the Fajada Butte cave hoping to find Val there. He had been gone for three days now, and she climbed the uneven slope late in the afternoon with fading hope of his return.

She squeezed through the narrow passage into the inner room and saw the familiar possessions he had left behind: a bedroll, some extra clothes, and some cooking utensils. Would he leave his things if he didn't plan to return? Her eyes misted over with tears, and she put a hand to her mouth and cried.

A weak voice spoke softly behind her. "Is that for me?"

Her heart jumped, and she spun around and ran to his arms. When he recoiled with a sharp yelp of pain, she quickly jumped back.

"What's wrong?" she cried, reaching out to touch him gingerly. "Are you hurt?"

"Help me take off my pack and shirt," he whispered.

When Diana removed the pack, she sobbed as she saw the dried blood covering the back of his shirt. "What happened?"

"I was shot a few days ago," he said, fighting the pain and fatigue. "Help me over to my bed and please heat some water."

She lit a small fire and put on a pan of water, and then she carefully removed his shirt. When she saw the festering wound, she nearly fainted.

Diana worked quietly, cleaning the caked blood from his shoulder and back. Her cheeks were wet with tears and an occasional soft murmur of sympathy escaped her lips. After she helped Val view the damage with a small mirror, he asked her to get his first aid kit. He gave her instructions on how to scrub the wound and to apply an ointment. He swallowed some pills, and afterward, Diana wrapped his wounds. Val sat back gingerly when she was finished. He took her hands to his lips and tenderly kissed them.

"The bullet knocked me off my feet. Fortunately, some things in my pack slowed it down or deflected it and kept it from passing right through me. It looks like it struck bone and glanced off. Made a mess of my back and shirt though" he smiled weakly. "I'm tired and very sore, but I should heal alright thanks to you."

He pulled her closer and kissed her lips. She didn't know where to hold him without causing more pain and just touched his face lightly with her fingertips. First, someone killed her father, and now someone shot Val. Suddenly, she realized someone had shot at Kip at too. In a moment, she was over her tears, and she began to burn with anger.

"What kind of gun-happy maniacs are running loose around here? We've got to report this," she said. "A few days ago an Indian policeman was here asking questions about the Blacksparrow Mine. There was a pilot here too; his plane was shot down nearby." She thought for a moment, "Were you anywhere near the mine when you were shot?"

"Not too far from it; somewhere near the smaller mesa north of there. Why?"

"Val, my father was killed at that same mesa. Carl and I went there recently, and he showed me where he thought Dad had been pushed from the cliff. Now you almost died there. I've got to find Carl and tell him…"

"No!" Val startled her with his abrupt response. "Don't tell Carl anything about this. Don't even tell him I'm here."

"Why?"

"Diana, Carl is the man who shot me."

Diana stepped back in shock. "But…my dad knew him well. He's worked with us at Chaco for a long time. I…"

"I've seen Carl at the mine Diana. I followed him and saw him go inside the compound, not once, but several times."

"Carl? Are you saying he might know who killed my father?" She stood up, anger welling inside her again. "That son of a bitch, wait 'till I get ahold of him."

"Diana," Val said softly. "I saw him with your father's journal. It's likely that Carl is the one who killed him. There is something bigger going on here than we are aware of, and you are in no position to stop it by yourself.

Let's not tip our hand and let him know we suspect anything just yet. We can both be of more help by watching his comings and goings. We can report our suspicions to the authorities when the time comes."

Diana searched Val's eyes and saw the wisdom of his words. "But we can't just sit here and do nothing."

Val swallowed and said, "That's exactly what we're going to do. You are going to pretend that nothing has happened. You found me here injured from a fall, and you patched me up. I gouged my back on a rock. Diana, I need you to be aware of his movements for the next few days, but not so that he would ever suspect you of watching him. I'll be better by then and can take over the surveillance. Can you do that?"

CHAPTER 44

Thomas Bloundt noted that two of the rail cars were fully loaded now. He felt relieved to see some positive results from his new scheduling. The men grumbled, but the captives did most of the work. He cared little for any of them, but he didn't hate. It wasn't their fault; it was just that he was raised to look down on people who were different than he was.

If Bloundt despised anyone, it was his own men. In the first year of the mission, he came to believe that his superiors had recruited the human dregs of Munich to serve on this team. The men were lazy, most were ignorant, and many were criminal, but Nicholas Ells was a true sub-human product of the mating of an ox and a charwoman.

The men lacked initiative, unless you called bedding the captive women, initiative. He would never drop low enough to copulate with the natives, as the others did. He still had his needs, but he preferred to wait for when the soft, perfumed bodies of German maidens would be his for the taking. They would be proud to hang on the arm of a military officer who had completed a successful mission in America.

He completed his inspection of the drums. Who would think that a pale yellow rock could be so important? Who would have thought that handling it could be so deadly?

He'd lost men in the early days due to prolonged contact with the ore, and had to replace them with the only other resource available. Actually, the reservation natives were a perfect find. Due to them living in the remote northwest corner of the state, Bloundt doubted that anyone would miss more than a few of the families.

They forced the captives to work, and they ultimately became ill. None lasted very long. The work crew was at a minimum right now, and he preferred to work the current group harder, rather than make more flights of acquisition.

He had few real concerns until the Indian officer showed up at the gate. The missing pilot was more of an irritant, but like a painful sliver, he had to remove him.

Bloundt entered the hanger and strode to the back to view the thing that thrilled him most about the mission. His eyes took in the familiar shape of wing and fuselage, and he wished again that it were a working machine, and not just a restored artifact. No matter, it would still astonish the greedy eyes of the Fuehrer.

Stepping from the building, he strode purposefully toward his quarters. The earth suddenly shook from a loud explosion and threw him to the ground. A thick belch of dust and smoke came from the mineshaft, and he choked in the dust as men ran to the scene of the blast. He numbly wiped the dirt from his eyes and felt his skin turn cold with dread.

Hours later, Bloundt received the final assessment report from the explosion. He went to his room and collapsed on his bed. The damage could have been worse. The main tunnel caved in, but a secondary shaft still led to an adequate amount of ore to complete their work. Two more of his men were lying under the rocks along with two dozen of the natives. He had to replace them quickly in order to complete the mission on schedule.

The twin demons of fear and inadequacy flew through his mind like screeching bats. He got up, and sat at his desk and pulled a bottle of Ouzo from the bottom drawer. He sloshed the clear liquid around in the bottle before pouring a glass and tossing it down. The harsh spirit made him gasp and exhale through his mouth; his face flushed as the warmth spread through his body.

Bloundt felt himself starting to relax, and he began to consider his circumstances, and his next move. Fortunately, the dirigible was safe in its hidden hanger and the winged artifact and the other planes were undamaged. He washed his face and changed clothes, and then he sent for Nicholas Ells.

"At ease Nicholas," he flashed a disapproving glance at the dull-witted toady. "We find ourselves in a tight spot; one that calls for your special skills."

Nick perked up as he heard the man's words.

"We have lost too many of our laborers in the explosion today, and we don't have time to scour the countryside searching for others to take their place. However, we have a sufficiently large and healthy group of young men and women nearby who can satisfy our urgent needs. Ready your men to ride to Chaco Canyon late this afternoon. I am expecting Carl to show up soon, and I'll have him go back to the camp ahead of you to ensure that every individual will be there when you and your men arrive. I will send the airship to the site before midnight to bring the prisoners back. Is that clear?"

Nicholas grinned broadly and said, "Oh yes sir, it sure is."

When Carl arrived at the mine later that morning, he roared his disbelief and displeasure at Bloundt.

"Take the Chaco students captive? Are you out of your mind? These are privileged young men and women. They have parents: important people with connections. Do you think they won't be missed?"

Bloundt glared at the man, and his voice dripped with venom when he finally spoke. "I think I've had enough of your insolence Carl. I'm of the opinion that your value as an asset to this mission has become questionable as of late."

Carl began to tell Bloundt exactly what he thought of his opinion, but the man shouted him down.

"You will follow my orders to the letter, or you will be placed in chains to work alongside the captives! The students won't be missed—at least not until after we are gone. You said before that there are rarely any visitors to the Chaco site. I'm sure you can sidetrack any inquiries from meddlesome tourists for a few weeks."

"You..." Carl began.

"You will shut your mouth!" Bloundt shouted. "After the airship brings the captives here, you will stay at the camp and tell any snooping tourists that the students have gone to a remote site and won't be back for two weeks. I'll leave Nicholas with you to keep you company just in case you run into something you can't handle. Understood? Dismissed!"

Carl strode angrily out the door. He was certain that the mission was doomed. "Pompous ass!" he said loudly.

He left the mine still seething and hiked back to Chaco Canyon. He passed the area noted in the professor's journal and wondered again what happened to Val after he had him in his sights earlier in the week. It was a clean shot. The bullet hit the man solidly and knocked him off his feet, but where did he go? He searched for two days and couldn't find him. He even checked the cave at Fajada Butte.

When Carl reached camp, he meandered through the area and accounted for all of the students except for Diana. She eventually showed up at the mess tent before supper. She seemed to act a bit coldly toward him, but he ignored her.

Men on horseback arrived midway through the evening meal and took everyone at gunpoint. Ignoring the angry questions, they gathered the students outside the tent. Diana was furious and worried. She saw more than just the crude leering looks of the gunmen; she saw cold discipline in the way they worked together. She feared that the reason for this holdup was not for mere robbery.

They tied the captives' hands behind their backs, and placed them in a row on the ground. None wore a gag, but the guards told them to keep quiet. Those who spoke were gun-whipped to silence. Diana tried to make some sense of this brutal intrusion. She noticed that Carl was not with the group. Good, she thought, he escaped, and maybe he could find help. Her hopes vanished, however, when Carl showed up with a gun strapped to his hip.

"Carl, you…you're not with these men are you?"

He cuffed her on the head and growled, "Shut up."

Darkness fell, and the students were tired and frightened to death. Some of the girls cried softly. There was a smug look of pure enjoyment on Nicholas' face as he grinned, watching them writhe in discomfort.

When it was well after dark, the men lit spotting fires around their position. Soon a strange moaning sound came with the wind. The moaning became louder and they could sense the presence of a giant shape overhead. A bright light stabbed down from the darkness and ropes with harnesses dropped as if from the sky itself. The students were roughly strapped into a sling and hoisted into the dark dirigible above. When the airship rose and left the area, Carl and Nicholas stayed behind while the other riders headed back to the mine.

Carl told Nicholas to take a tent across the main grounds from his. He had no doubts as to why Nicholas stayed behind. The Commandant was playing it cagy, and Carl knew that the big brute had been given orders to do away with "disrespectful Carl" as soon as he wasn't needed any longer.

Carl rose from his cot and slipped from his tent through an opening cut in the back. He crept away a short distance from camp where he could be out of sight and still keep an eye on the tents. He didn't trust anyone but himself at this point.

Thirty feet away, the hulking Nicholas also kept a vigilant eye on the tents. He thought of how much he would enjoy killing Carl who had taunted him for so long. Nick was, after all, easy to please; he liked his revenge hot or cold. He would relish the fear he would see in Carl's eyes as he slowly took the life from him.

CHAPTER 45

Huddled in a guarded corner of the aircraft deck, the captive students endured an uncomfortable and fearful flight from Chaco Canyon to the mine. Ordered to be silent, only muted sobbing came from the students over the low rumble of the airship's diesels. Diana tried to calm her group and someone cuffed her across the face for her trouble. When one of the boys stood up to protest, a guard clubbed him down.

The floor beneath them rolled and twisted slowly like the deck of an ocean liner at sea. The powerful engines buzzed like giant bees inside the huge hive of girders and lacquered cotton skin. The captives soon felt the ship turning and then lose altitude. The pitch of the engines changed as the *Nighthawk* jockeyed down for a landing.

With the craft secured inside the Blacksparrow compound, the guards took the human cargo off. The prisoners could see very little of their surroundings in the darkness and the glare of the floodlights. They were marched into the mine to the underground prison, and sickened by what they saw and smelled. If the other prisoners were curious about the new arrivals, they didn't show it.

Diana was horrified to see the suffering men, women, and children. How could anyone treat people like this? It was inhuman. She stumbled ahead from a shove by the guard. They separated the men and the women, and pushed the group into some empty cages. Filthy blankets and soiled piles of straw lay at their feet. In one corner, a large bucket lay on its side, spilling an evil smelling pool of excrement. One girl vomited and two others followed her lead. Diana moved to a far corner and sat on the floor holding her knees. She shivered with fear. With most of the lights turned off, they sat in semi-darkness to sort out their own demons.

The next morning, Bloundt spoke with the captain of the airship. He instructed him to have his crew prepare for an evening departure to the secret location in Mexico for final provisions and fuel. Afterward, he went to the officer in charge of the mining operations and asked about the new captives. The officer acted ill at ease.

"Speak up man, I asked you if the captives were ready to perform their work?"

"Sir," the officer stood at attention. "Some of the men, sir, were thinking that the new women were…quite attractive. They thought that since they hadn't seen white women for a few years, they would take them aside and… comfort them, sir."

Bloundt stared at the officer. When he finally spoke, it was in a low growl.

"Frederich, I am going to walk to my quarters and strap on my pistol. Then I am going to walk back to this building. When I return, I expect to see every man who took part in this 'comfort detail' to be standing in a line against this wall. I want the women here also, to the side over there."

The Commandant was shaking with anger when he turned and strode away. The fearful officer ran in the opposite direction.

Bloundt found eight miserable men standing at attention when he returned. None of their eyes met his as he mentally bored holes through each of their skulls. He glanced at six disheveled young women gathered together in the corner. Bringing his attention back to the men, he spoke softly at first but then allowed his voice to rise to a shout.

"We have two weeks left before we leave this flea-infested shit hole," he shouted. "We've all worked hard. We have all sacrificed. Now that we are down to our final days we find ourselves having to pick up the pace and bring in additional workers to help us meet our schedule."

He paused for his words to settle in before he screamed, *"You all know this!"*

He drew his gun in a quick, practiced motion and held it down at his side as he walked past the men again. "Now, a truthful man, who feels that what resides in his loins, is more important than the work that needs to be done, can step forward and receive his punishment."

Bloundt spun around and waited but no one stepped forward. He walked back to the middle of the line and spoke damningly.

"Then each one of you is a liar."

He quickly lifted his gun and shot the man in front of him in the face; he crumpled dead to the floor with a hole in his forehead. The rest of the men recoiled in horror. The women screamed and cried pitifully in their corner. Bloundt, annoyed, glanced at the females, and then spoke to his men again.

"I said, a truthful man can step forward and receive his punishment!"

Seven trembling men stepped forward, shaking as they stood with their eyes wide with terror. Bloundt spoke to the officer in charge.

"Captain, see that these men are put to work immediately. I want them digging in the mine on twelve hour shifts until we leave this desert toilet."

"And the women sir?" the officer asked.

Bloundt gazed at the six females, taking time to appraise each one. "Put them to work."

Back in his quarters, the Commandant removed his sidearm and stood at his window overlooking the busy compound. Men hurried about and appeared to move with renewed purpose. Word of his new method of discipline had gotten out quickly.

He put a hand to his eyes and rubbed them to ease the strain. He figured the next two weeks would be enough time for his crew and the new workers to process enough uranium ore to put their end game into motion. He would have a few loose strings to tie up by that time. Carl was one of them, James Avery was another, and of course, the captives.

Carl Walker, he considered, dared to insult him more than once. His contribution to the mission was finished as far as he was concerned. Nicholas and Carl were at the Chaco site for the time being, but soon Nicholas would execute the orders Bloundt had given him and the problem of Carl would be over.

Bloundt frowned, he had been here a long time without having a woman, but since he'd given the men such an extreme example of his discipline, he couldn't very well show them that he was above his own orders. He longed for female companionship, but the new captives were off limits to him also.

He could wait two weeks. One dark-haired woman caught his attention, perhaps more for her dignified appearance than her obvious charms. Two weeks, he thought, two long weeks to keep all the threads from unraveling.

CHAPTER 46

The *Nighthawk* lifted off in the calm, starry hours before midnight. Bloundt watched from his porch as it rose from the compound and headed south.

The dirigible leveled off at four thousand feet. She was invisible in the darkness with her black skin. The captain tacked westerly to compensate for a twelve-knot wind while the powerful Maybachs hummed, each engine taking its share of the load. Nearly a mile below, no noise could be heard as the airship plowed through the clouds. In the high wooded hills and valleys near the Johnson Ranch, the night breeze picked up to a brisk twenty knots. The Captain brought the engines to bear against the heavy crosswind, and the soft purring grew to a moan that sounded like the wailing of a host of lost souls.

Kip was asleep when the airship passed high overhead. He dreamed that he was in a room, not unlike the bedroom he was in now, and he thought he heard someone moaning behind the walls. In his mind, he drifted to the door and then to the window trying to find where the noise was coming from.

He woke up and jumped from the bed, putting his face to the screen of the open window. He listened as he took in the fresh smells of the night. What was the noise, he wondered? An answer popped into his mind: a dirigible. But there were no dirigibles in the United States anymore; and except for a few German airships like the Graf Zeppelin, there were no other dirigibles in the entire world. He listened, holding his breath as the moaning became fainter and then was gone.

That morning, Kip came down the stairs and found Bob and Vicki at the kitchen table. He sat down and Vicki poured him a cup of coffee.

"Did either of you hear a moaning sound late last night? It happened around midnight."

Bob said "no," but Vicki said, "I certainly did. It was the same thing I've heard before."

"I think I know what it is," Kip said. Both Bob and Vicki looked at him. "It's a dirigible; a big one."

The couple looked stunned. "Are you sure?" Vicki asked.

Kip nodded, "Didn't you say that it usually came back again in a few days?"

"That's right KJ. What was it Vicki, about two or three days later?"

Vicki nodded and turned her attention to her oven. She put on her mitts, pulled out a steaming pot, and set it on a cutting board.

"Uncle Bob, do you think we'll have the de Havilland finished by tomorrow so I can take it up for a practice flight?"

"Probably," Bob said warily. "The chances are we'll get it done by then, but we'll have to go into town again to get some cable and a few other things. KJ, you don't intend to fly after that thing in the dead of night do you?"

"I don't know, maybe. There'll be a three-quarter moon, and I've flown in darker skies than that before."

Bob & Vicki exchanged worried glances as Kip finished his coffee. He set the cup down and noticed their looks.

"Geez, you'd think I was going to fly to the North Pole or something. Look, the airplane is sturdy, and built to fly at high altitudes. Isn't that right Bob?"

"Yes that's true. The DH-4's were designed for high altitude observation and bombing. They weren't worth spit as a fighter, but they were built well and could outfly most of them.

"How so?" Kip asked. He was always interested in hearing about anything having to do with airplanes.

"Well first, the plane has always been sturdy because of the tubular steel frame, and the one in the barn was renovated for the airmail service. It's a lot better plane than the early models in the war. The early ones placed the pilot in front just behind the engine. It was dangerous in a crash. They used to call them flying coffins."

Aunt Vicki gasped and her husband added quickly, "But they were re-designed, and they moved the pilot to the rear cockpit. They did a whole lot of other stuff too."

"Like what?" Vicki's concern was obvious and not so easily mollified.

"They replaced the fabric on the fuselage with plywood and extended the exhaust stack behind the cockpits. They moved the landing gear too, and gave it bigger tires and better instruments. With all the changes, they called them DH-4B's. Heck Vicki, they built them so well, back then, they could crash the things and walk away from 'em."

Vicki took this information with a grain of salt. "Well, it's a good thing they're built sturdy, the way this boy crashes airplanes."

She skewered her nephew with a stern look, and turned back to the stove.

"Aw Aunt Vicki, I'm always careful; it's just that I'm not used to being shot at."

Vicki regarded her deceased brother's son with frank concern.

Later out in the barn, Kip and Bob hooked up the exhaust and external parts to the rebuilt engine. Bob stepped back from the aircraft and said to Kip.

"Let's take a break and go into town. We'll get the things we need to finish it up. When we get back, we can go over the wiring and test the engine. When that's done, we can push it out of the barn, attach the wings, and with luck, you'll be flying tomorrow."

After being handed a small list of wants from Vicki, they jumped into Bob's old Ford and headed south on the two-track. They both had their arms out the windows, grateful for a breeze to help cool them off.

Bob picked up the items they needed, and Kip found a phone and called Doo. He brought his friend up to date on the rebuilding of the de Havilland.

Doo changed the subject as soon as Kip stopped talking, and asked with a little hesitation, "Kip what kind of trouble are you in out there?"

Kip was confused. "What do you mean?"

"Well, last Friday at the hanger, I got a visit from two toughs, and they asked all kinds of questions about where they could find you."

"Find me? Why? Who were they? Were they cops?"

"I don't think so. Cops are tough, but these guys were just plain mean. They beat me up when they couldn't get anything out of me, except that you were out west somewhere near Gallup."

"Beat you up? Are you alright?"

"Yeah, yeah, I got a couple of bruises and a fat lip, but otherwise I'm okay. What are you mixed up in anyway?"

Kip thought for a moment. "I didn't think I was mixed up in anything, except that some idiot in a Sparrowhawk wants to shoot my butt off every time I fly out towards Chaco Canyon. Did they say anything else?"

"Nope, it was just these two guys and their bad attitudes. I remember one guy's name was Gunter, and he called the other one Nicholas. They took off pretty quick after they pounded me, and I don't think they'll be back."

After a few more minutes of catching up, Kip went back to the truck to wait for Bob. On their way back to the farm, Kip told him about his conversation with Doo.

"So what do you make of it KJ?" Bob was becoming more and more concerned about what Kip was getting himself into.

Kip stared out the windshield, eyes unfocused as he thought of the two names Doo had mentioned. He recognized the names Gunter and Nicholas, but no, it was too much of a coincidence.

Finally, he said to Bob, "I don't know…I just don't know."

CHAPTER 47

Val was still in pain when he woke up, but he was glad his head was much clearer. A narrow shaft of light beamed into the cave and warmed the ground where he lay. He dressed gingerly, favoring his wounded shoulder, and he wondered where Diana was. He hadn't seen her at all yesterday.

The sun was high overhead when he stepped out on the talus slope. He squinted in the sunlight. Below, the dry wash wound out of sight behind high, red cliffs. A quiet, scented wind whispered secrets that made his heart sigh with the weight of the ages.

He made his way down the valley. None of the students was aware of his presence here, so he still took care not to let anyone see him. He saw none of them along the way and thought they might be working further down the canyon.

He approached the camp behind a shoulder-high embankment and searched for Diana's familiar shape. No one was about. The camp appeared to be deserted. He followed the riverbed a little further and finally saw two men in the shadows of the mess tent.

Val worked his way closer and tried to hear what they were saying. He could catch only a few words, but he noted one of them becoming more and more belligerent. A stocky man sat calmly listening to the other one who stood waving his arms. The stocky man abruptly jumped to his feet and grabbed the neck of the other. He swung a fist into his face, knocking him across a table.

Val recognized the man who'd been hit. Chairs scattered as Carl fell backward over the table into the dirt. Nicholas came quickly around the table tossing aside the chairs in his way. Carl kicked savagely at the man's knee and landed a solid blow that spun Nicholas to the ground. Carl jumped to his feet and pulled his gun.

"I should kill you now," he shouted. "A stinking pig like you deserves to die."

Nick stood, gingerly rubbing his knee as he limped to a chair. "You could kill me, but then you'd have to answer to Bloundt."

"He doesn't scare me," Carl said, knowing in his heart that he did fear what the evil bastard could do.

He knew the Commandant was planning to have this man kill him soon, but Carl had his own plans for escape before then. He decided that this disgusting slug Nicholas had fouled the Earth for far too long. He would kill the man, but not yet.

As Val listened to the men argue, he began to feel a growing concern for the whereabouts of Diana and her students. The stocky man was not part of the dig, and since Carl worked with the people at the mine, Val suspected the other man did too. He knew their presence here did not bode well, and he quickly crept away and returned to the cave to retrieve his gear and set out for the mine.

As Carl walked off his anger, he thought again of the man he'd shot earlier in the week. He decided to check the Fajada cave one last time. It also gave him a chance to get away from Nicholas, and cool down and think.

When Carl reached the cave, he noticed some of Val's things were gone. He cursed his bad luck and knew the man had been here recently. How could he have missed his shot? He searched the dim space more carefully and found some soft dirt that had been recently disturbed. He dug at it with a stick and came up with a wad of bloody clothing. His smile was wolfish as he realized he had hit his missing quarry after all.

CHAPTER 48

Kip and Bob finished turning the last bolt on the engine assembly and began to clean up the mess around the plane. They wheeled the airframe out of the barn, added fuel, and checked the oil level. The reliable, old Rolls Royce engine fired and ran roughly at first, but with some tuning, they got the motor to smooth out. Kip shut it off, and the men went back in the barn to bring out the wings.

The sun was touching the western tree line when they secured the last section of wing to the fuselage.

Kip stood back to admire their work. "It looks like we've got it."

"Yep," Bob said as he wiped his forehead with his shirt. "Come morning we'll give her a full flight check and see if she's ready to fly."

Kip loved the businesslike look of the aircraft. In a way, it resembled the old Jenny, but having worked on both, he knew there was no comparison. The Jenny was a toy compared to the sturdy de Havilland. Kip couldn't wait to see how it responded to the stick and rudder.

Vicky watched her men as they stood around the old mail plane. She felt the excitement herself, and remembered the days when she traveled with the flying circus and performed loops and barrel rolls for the crowds. She remembered the locals paying money for a ride high over the tents and arcades. Her nose wrinkled as she also remembered how some of them would get sick and spray their cotton candy and corn dogs all over the cockpit. A hazard of the job, she shrugged, and then she went back into the kitchen to finish getting supper ready.

Vicki had given her old Jenny to Kip when she and Bob got married. She remembered how they decided it was time to give up flying and spend their days together with both feet on the ground. She would occasionally see her husband go into the small barn to look at the pieces of his old plane. It had been a part of him just as the Jenny had been part of her. She understood, because she too felt the occasional longing for the thrill of climbing into the clouds

Vicki rang the dinner bell, and the men came in to clean up for supper. After eating, they all sat on the porch sipping lemonade while they waited for the stars to come out. It was a hot August evening. Long shadows from the trees and buildings crept across the yard to where the de Havilland cast its own angular shadow. The men slept hard that night while Vicki tossed and turned, worrying about her nephew.

The next morning after breakfast, the men spent an hour inspecting every inch of the plane before starting it up. Kip was eager to see what the big Rolls engine could do.

Bob had coached Kip about the strengths and weaknesses of the plane for weeks as they reassembled it. It had power, yes, and the rigid frame could take the strain of hard flying, but it needed more room to complete maneuvers than the Jenny did. Kip hoped the plane would make up for that by sheer horsepower and speed.

When Bob was satisfied that Kip knew what he needed to fly the plane and land it safely, it was time to start the engine and let him learn the rest by himself.

Kip strapped in and Bob gave the prop a hard pull. The engine roared to life. Kip let it warm up while he worked the rudders and flaps. Before he advanced the throttle, he gave a quick wave to Bob and Vicki. The plane bounced across the yard to the primitive road in front of the house. He opened the throttle, and the engine roared as the plane picked up speed. Finally, the wings lifted him skyward.

"Oh Bob," Vicki said, "Are we doing the right thing?"

Bob looked at his wife, a firm, warm shape standing next to him. He put his arm around her waist. "What do you mean darlin'?"

"Is this what my brother and sister-in-law would have wanted me to do? Would they want me to let their boy go up in a rickety old plane that was nearly as old as he was?"

"Now Vicki, I'm not going to argue with you. Will Rogers once said that there are two theories about arguing with women, and neither one works." He hugged her waist.

She frowned at him and said, "I recall that he also said to never miss a good chance to shut up."

The old de Havilland climbed smoothly as Kip made a wide circle of the area. He noted the small fishing pond a half-mile north of the farm, and he could see the mesas and cliffs to the west and the dark green pine forests stretching to the east.

He came in low over the farmhouse and waggled his wings as he passed. Kip pulled back the stick and climbed effortlessly for the clouds. For the next thirty minutes, he took the biplane through turns and maneuvers to get a feel for its capabilities. When he came in for a landing, he brought it down as if it were as light as a feather. He taxied into the yard and cut the engine.

Bob hobbled up with a big smile on his face.

"Ye-ha boy, you sure know how to coax this baby down. What do you think KJ? Do you like how she handles?"

Kip tried to hide his exuberance behind his best poker face, but Bob's infectious grin forced him to give up with a loud laugh.

"What a *plane!*" he shouted.

Throughout the day, the three of them told their old flying stories, and when they went to bed that night, it was with tired smiles and heads full of happy memories.

CHAPTER 49

A mile above McGaffey slowed by headwinds, the captain of the *Nighthawk* increased airspeed to insure that they would reach the safety of their hanger before dawn. Arriving after daybreak would make the dirigible visible to any inhabitants in its path. The timing would be close. He opted to use the additional fuel even though they might need it when they took to the skies for their flight back to Germany. It would come about in two short weeks, and as far as he was concerned, it couldn't be soon enough. In his estimation, Bloundt was slowly going mad. The sooner they finished this jinxed mission, the better.

The sound came in the silent hours before dawn. It came like a whisper of wind through a tree, and then changed to a moaning, like that of a lost soul. Kip heard it as he dreamed, puzzled by the faint sound that slowly grew in volume. His eyes opened abruptly, and he sat up. It's the dirigible.

"It's the dirigible," he shouted as he ran through the house waking Bob and Vicki. When Bob caught up with him, Kip was already putting on his flight gear. Kip rattled on as he finished dressing.

"That explains the Sparrowhawks too. They used to fly reconnaissance from the *Akron* and the *Macon*. Do you know what this means? There must be another dirigible; one that the government somehow hid from the public after the other two crashed into the sea."

"That would explain why they didn't want anyone near where it was anchored." Kip paused for a second. "But that doesn't explain why I was shot at. For crying out loud, I'm an American citizen!"

Bob finally found his voice. "KJ, you can't take off in the dark, it's too dangerous. You'll become disoriented."

"Aw Bob," Kip said, as Vicki came into the room wrapped in her robe. "I've taken off dozens of times before dawn. It's not far off now, and I'll be able to see over the horizon as soon as I gain altitude. It'll be lighter up there, and besides, I've got to find out what's behind this mystery. Something is not right, and I'm just mad enough to want to find out what's been going on. I have to hurry or I might lose my chance to catch the thing."

"That's what we're worried about," Vicki said softly.

Kip looked into the concerned eyes of two of the most important people in his life.

"Aunt Vicki, Uncle Bob, I've just got to do this. Trust me, I'll be safe."

Bob dressed and hurried out of the house with Kip. They went through a quick pre-flight check in the glow of their lanterns.

Vicki joined them shortly and gave Kip a sack of sandwiches and an apple. "You'll need this," she said.

He took the bag and kissed her on the cheek.

Kip turned to Bob. "Are you ready to fire this thing up?"

Ten minutes later, the wheels of the old de Havilland left the bumpy road. Kip squinted at the compass, and guessed that the dirigible was heading northeast. That would take it toward Chaco Canyon. The engine roared in the darkness as he gained altitude, and the cold air whipped at his jacket and face. Kip's leather helmet and goggles helped him endure most of the discomfort.

He flew over the dark McGaffey forests and then over miles of twisting canyons that slowly materialized in the coming dawn. The sculptured desert lapped against the rocky monoliths like frozen waves against a dead shoreline.

Kip thought he saw a glimpse of a large shape dipping below the horizon, but as he neared the edge of the plateau, he found no trace of it. He continued on to Chaco Canyon, and when he still hadn't found the dirigible, he circled the valley and retraced his route.

Where is it, he thought as he flew over the maze of canyons and buttes. He recognized a section of the plateau where he'd been attacked many weeks ago, and he saw some buildings tucked into an open area encircled by the walls of a mesa. It looked like the mine. The sun rose above the horizon as he circled to get closer, and then he saw flashes of light gleaming from the wings of three aircraft climbing to meet him.

"Planes—shit!" He kicked the rudder and pulled the stick back to gain altitude. "Shit, shit, shit." He said the words aloud, like a mantra. He was climbing, but the Sparrowhawks were gaining on him.

"Come on you old mail plane, you were a bomber once, let's show them how you can climb."

The Rolls Royce engine screamed as the rpm's increased, pulling the plane upward at a steep angle. Kip noticed he was sweating in spite of the cool air, and he was startled to see a line of bullet holes stitching across his left wing. He tipped right and dove toward two of the planes approaching from below. He aimed between them and pulled out the handgun Bob had secretly given him. He fired two shots at the closest plane as he passed.

Kip pulled for the sky again and was overjoyed to see one of the Sparrowhawks winging away from the fight trailing a dark cloud of smoke. Just then, the first plane cut across Kip's wing from his 11 o'clock, stitching another line through the midsection of the aircraft. He fired two more rounds at the passing plane but was sure he missed.

Kip felt his leg tingling after more lead tore through the fuselage. When he had a chance to look down, he saw blood seeping through his pant leg above his boot. Kip also noted that the Rolls engine had developed an odd stutter.

He shook off his distractions as the two remaining planes approached from below and to the right. Kip's airspeed had dropped alarmingly, and he could smell oil. The Sparrowhawks were coming up quickly, and Kip tucked the revolver under his leg and fiercely kicked the rudder, pushing the stick over, nearly stalling the old bomber. He dove directly at the two fighters and gave the throttle all it had.

The Sparrowhawks flew in close formation, and at the last minute, they fired their guns and peeled away to let the de Havilland pass between them. Kip jigged the controls, attempting to stay away from the lead, but to no avail. As the two planes parted, Kip took his last two shots at the fighter on his right. The gun fell from his hand, and his arm and right side went numb. All Kip could do now, was to stay conscious and try to land.

He looked for the plane he had taken his last shots at, but thick oily smoke sprayed from his engine, covering his goggles and burning his face.

He thought of Doo and Lisa Ann, and time seemed to slow down. He suspected he was going to die, and he never knew that his last two shots hit the other pilot through the side of his chest, puncturing his lungs and nicking his heart. The Sparrowhawk spun out of control and hit the side of a small butte in a flash of fire. Pieces of the aircraft rained over the rocks like confetti.

The last fighter caught up with the damaged de Havilland and spat round after round of hot lead into the airframe. Kip was barely conscious, trying to maneuver, when a slug grazed the side of his head. He blacked out still holding the stick.

The old bomber weaved drunkenly away. Oddly, the plane succeeded in avoiding the next few passes of the fighter, due to its erratic flight and thick black smoke. Finally, it pancaked down on the wide expanse of a dry wash. The plane immediately hit some debris and flipped, losing the undercarriage and most of the right wings. The stout fuselage stayed together and rolled, strafed repeatedly by the relentless Sparrowhawk. The gas tank in the old plane finally ruptured. The fighter made three more passes spitting hot .30 cal. loads. When the fuel ignited, the downed craft began to burn, and the Sparrowhawk left the area.

The sound of the fighter diminished in the distance, and in a while, the flames slowly dwindled into smoking ribbons.

Kip was unconscious, tangled in the roots of a dead cottonwood that had been in the path of the falling de Havilland. Fortunately, he'd been thrown out and covered by dirt and branches as the plane spun and rolled on for another sixty yards before coming to a halt. Now all that was left of it was a smoking pile of twisted metal.

A bird tentatively chirped from the trees along the banks of the wash. The sun climbed overhead, and the afternoon passed with clouds gathering to the north. Soon, their dark billows lit up with flashes of lightning and the low rumble of thunder echoed for miles across the desert.

Evening came and the gathering dusk took away the colors of the desert. Kip moaned weakly and tried to move. He painfully gasped for air and passed out again. With dusk, came a low rumbling—not thunder, but growing nearer. Kip was vaguely aware of this phenomenon. He imagined he felt the ground shaking, and he tried to open his eyes as a wall of debris-laden water hit the old cottonwood. He cartwheeled away, conceding to the wet, bony hands of death.

The bony hands clutched at him; jabbed him, pulled at him, and he couldn't breathe. He tried to move and immediately felt silly; dead people don't move. The hands pulled at him more insistently, and one slapped him across his cheek. He became conscious in a fit of painful coughing and nearly passed out again. He heard a voice and felt hands clutching at him, dragging him.

When he opened his eyes, it was near dark, and his vision was blurred. A shape moved around him, and he wondered if this was what dying was all about.

"Wake up," an insistent voice said. "You must wake up and tell me if you can feel anything."

Kip blinked several times, his eyes still grainy with sand. He made out the blurry shape and face of a man ministering to his wounds. He moaned weakly and choked as he tried to speak. He felt wetness on his face, and then the warm water from a canteen trickled over his lips.

Soon Kip understood he was conscious and alive. His cold body screamed with pain when he tried to move. He attempted to speak again.

"Who…are…you?"

"We'll talk after I've tended to your wounds."

Kip passed out, and the cold, silent stars took over the night.

CHAPTER 50

Sam dozed on and off in his hospital bed. When a nurse came by with some bland food, he was surprised that he felt like eating for the first time in days. He noted that the bed next to him was empty, and he didn't want to dwell on what that might mean. After he ate, he slept again; his mind drifting through his fevered dreams like a ghost through a series of doors.

When he woke the next morning, his mind was clear, and he knew exactly what he had to do. He felt much better, and when his bandage was changed, he saw that his wound had already begun to heal.

He was just finishing breakfast when a familiar raspy voice called his name from the hallway.

"Sam, is that you?"

Judge Reilly's eyes were wide open as he came into the room.

"Sam what's going on? Are you all right? What happened to you?"

"Hi Judge, it's just my right leg. I got an infection from a gunshot wound a few days ago on the Res., but I'm okay now. They said I could go home as soon as I see the doctor, and they finish up some paperwork."

Sam and the Judge exchanged local news for the next fifteen minutes, and Sam asked his friend if he could find him a car to use for a few days.

"What about your new truck?" Reilly said, puzzled.

"It burnt up. I need to do some checking around, and I don't want to be recognized. Say, have you seen my office partner Charlie?"

Sam was referring to the young FBI rookie that shared space with him in Gallup. "He went out to Lukachuki late last week, and he said he'd be back sometime this week."

"Burnt up?" Judge Reilly asked. "No I haven't seen him lately."

The Judge helped Sam sit up on the side of the bed.

"How about I just hang around until you're cleared to go, and then I'll take you home so you can change your clothes. We can go check up on Charlie after that if you want, and then go pick up a car for you. The Judge asked again, "Burnt up? Are you talking about your new government truck?"

Sam regarded the judge with a patient look. "It's a long story Judge, I'll tell you later. What brings you to the hospital?"

"It's my day off, and I came here to visit a young man down the hall who was beaten by his uncle. It's a sad thing Sam,"

Judge Reilly dragged his fingers through his thick, grey-white hair, "Another victim of a door jumping out and hitting someone in the face."

Sam nodded knowingly.

It was after one o'clock when they drove to Sam's small house east of the hogback. The Judge followed Sam inside, and they walked into a scene of scattered furniture, strewn papers, and broken items.

Sam's face was grim as he looked around.

"I'll pick up a quick change of clothes and get my guns if they're still here. We should leave right away."

"What's going on Sam?"

"I'll tell you when we're out of here."

Sam decided to forget about Charlie for the time being, and they drove to Judge Reilly's house in a small canyon east of the Zuni road, just south of Gallup. They walked in through the kitchen door, and the judge's wife Betty greeted them with a smile and many questions. She fixed a quick snack and served it on the back patio.

Sam told them all about his activities over the past month, beginning with Dan Yazzie coming home from prison to find his daughter and grandfather killed by a large animal. Sam appreciated the opportunity to lay out his clues to both of them and to hear their thoughts.

He knew Mrs. Reilly was the intellectual equal of her husband, having been a sought-after corporate lawyer in Albuquerque before she consented to wed the Judge who was an attorney in Santa Fe at the time.

After Sam finished describing his suspicions about Jim Avery, Mrs. Reilly tossed her red hair and leaned forward to speak.

"Well, for one thing, you sure can't go to the FBI for help." She snorted and exchanged a concerned look with her husband.

"Yes," the Judge said. "You might find some Navajos who would help you go after these people, but I don't think it would be a good idea for a group of armed Indians to go riding around *on or off* the reservation."

"I've got to get help from somewhere."

"What about Charlie Redman," asked the Judge?

"But Charlie's the local FBI man isn't he?" Mrs. Reilly was surprised her husband would suggest such a thing.

Sam looked at the Judge and began to nod his head slowly.

"Yes, Charlie Redman. He's part Dakota Indian, and we've shared an office for almost a year now."

The Judge added, "Yes, there was that murder out by Naschitti and the Window Rock investigation. He seems to be a pretty level-headed man, being as young as he is."

Betty regarded them as if they had both lost their wits. "I thought you said you couldn't trust the FBI for help? Didn't you just say Jim Avery tried to kill you?"

"That's just the thing Mrs. Reilly, he tried to kill me, but Charlie has been out of town for over a week. He doesn't get along very well with Avery or the rest of the Albuquerque crowd to start with; heck that's why he was sent to Gallup in the first place. They found out he was part Indian, and they sent him here to work with me. He's a good man, and I'll bet he hasn't heard a word about any of this."

Yes, Sam thought. If he could count on anyone to help him right now, it would be Charlie Redman.

CHAPTER 51

Sam followed the Judge to an old barn behind the house, and when they went inside, the Judge walked up to a dust covered sedan.

"It's a '29 Ford," he said. "Kind of beat up, but she still runs. The tires are low, so we'll have to put some air in them."

Reilly flashed a sly smile. "I keep it for sentimental reasons, on account of it's where the misses and I got to know each other better."

"Ah youth," Sam smiled and nodded, remembering his first pickup truck.

It was late afternoon when the men finished and Mrs. Reilly called them in for supper. They talked some more at dinner, and Sam agreed to stay the night. He had a belly full of fried chicken and apple pie and was asleep within a minute of his head hitting the pillow.

When he got dressed the next morning, Sam found the couple already in the kitchen drinking coffee. Eggs and tortillas were on the stove, and he ate quickly, and thanked them both for their hospitality and the loan of the Ford.

Sam drove into Gallup and parked in front of his office. When he unlocked the door, he found his desk covered with papers and other items scattered on the top, but his partner's desk showed no sign of tampering. He went to the back to put on a pot of coffee, and a short while later, he heard the front door open and close noisily.

"Anybody home? Sam is that you?"

Sam peered out and saw Charlie Redman drop a briefcase and a traveling bag on his desk.

"Ya-ha-tey Charlie."

The young Agent raised his arms and stretched. "Ya-tey yourself, you old Indian. I hope you've got some coffee going 'cause I've been driving all night, and I'm likely to fall asleep right here without it."

He noticed Sam's littered desk top. "Jeez, what a mess."

Charlie walked to the bathroom, and when he came out, Sam poured him a cup of black coffee.

"How was Lukachuki?"

Sam studied the tall Indian for any sign of surprise at seeing him alive. He need not have worried; Charlie was just as he seemed, road weary and glad to be home.

"Lukachuki was fine. It turns out that the stolen sheep and the missing brother were related." He smiled at his pun, and added, "I found them both near a cabin up by Round Rock. Seems he and his sister have been feuding for years and this was just the latest incident in their squabbling over the family fortune."

"Any trouble?" Sam couldn't help but grin at the way Charlie told a story.

"Naw, I just sat them both down and told them if they didn't learn to get along I was going to handcuff them together, and put them in a jail cell and throw away the key. Anything going on with you?"

"Oh, a little bit."

Charlie Redman put his feet on his desk and looked at Sam.

"What?"

Sam set his coffee down and started to sort out the mess on his desk. He hadn't answered Charlie's question, and his partner started to pester him.

"So tell me. Don't just say 'a little bit' and then shut up."

Charlie never got the hang of the Navajo way of waiting politely for someone to get ready to speak. His impatience was more like the way of the white man.

"Sam, don't make me have to drag it out of you," Redman said, yawning.

Sam took a sip of coffee and saw that Charlie was about to lose his patience.

"Somebody tried to kill me."

Redman was lifting his own cup; he set it back down and looked at Sam.

"Charlie," Sam asked with a level stare, "have you talked to Jim Avery or any of the Albuquerque crowd this week?"

"Nope: not for a couple of weeks. I've been too busy climbing over rocks and dodging rattlesnakes, chasing down a herd of smelly damn sheep! Why?"

Sam gulped the last of his coffee. "It was Jim Avery that ordered it done."

Charlie Redman was wide-awake now. He pestered his partner for more information, until Sam relented and told him everything, beginning with his investigation of the missing native families.

"Avery set up a meeting out by Prewitt, and I was met instead, by two airplanes with guns, and some men in a wrecker who pushed my truck off a cliff."

"Your new truck got pushed off a cliff?"

"Yeah after being shot up by the airplanes. I managed to dive out and hide before it went over. It caught fire and burned at the bottom of the arroyo."

"Caught fire and burned?"

Redman was quiet for a moment, and then he burst out laughing.

"*He, he, he!* Your brand new shiny gov-ment truck all smashed and burn up? *Oh, ho, ho*, you almost had me going there Sam. Did you really wreck your truck? *Ho, ho*, don't tell me you had to make up this whole big story just as an excuse for wrecking it?"

Redman wiped at the tears of laughter in his eyes, and then he noticed Sam's serious look and quickly sobered up.

"Ho-ly shit. It's all true?"

"Get your hat. I'm going to take you to meet the pilot who was shot down so you can hear his story first hand."

Ten minutes later, the two men were speeding east on their way to McGaffee. In a half hour, they drove into the Johnson yard and were met by Bob and Vicki and invited inside.

"Is your nephew Kip, around?"

"He's out at Chaco Canyon I expect," said Bob.

"Yes," added Vicki, "he flew out Saturday morning in Bob's old plane. Why?"

"Nothing much, I just had a couple of other things I wanted to ask him. He went back to see the girl eh?"

"Well there was something else." Bob seemed reluctant to say it. "The morning he left, he was chasing a big dirigible that flew overhead just before daylight."

Ten minutes later, the two law officers were back in the Judge's old Ford, winding their way south to the main road back to Gallup. They were halfway to town before Charlie said anything.

"You didn't tell me anything about a dirigible Sam."

"Nope, and I didn't tell you about the monster that's been running around killing people, either."

After a long pause Charlie replied, "Oh."

CHAPTER 52

Kip woke abruptly from a dream of choking and drowning, and when he recovered from a fit of coughing, he realized that his whole body ached. His tried to focus his eyes in the darkness, but all he could see was a small campfire burning nearby. He attempted to move and found himself wrapped tightly in a blanket. A weathered Indian face appeared in front of him, watched him for a moment, and then spoke.

"Careful, you're not in good enough shape to move around. Just be still. I'll bring you something to drink."

Kip watched the man moving about in an odd stilted way. He looked old, but then you could never tell with the desert Indians; the hot sun wrinkled their skin prematurely, and the blowing sand made it as tough as leather.

"Where am I?" he asked in a weak voice."

The Indian remained silent and soon brought water.

"I will tell you what you want to know, but drink first."

Kip sipped the cool water and then lay back.

"You dropped from the sky in your airplane, and you fell out and became wedged in the roots of a dead tree. When the floodwaters came down the wash, I pulled you out and thought you had gone to the spirit world. You were still alive though, so I brought you here and made a fire and cooked some food. You can eat now if you feel well enough, and then I will listen to your story."

Kip went to sleep right after finishing a small bowl of soup. When he awoke again, daylight was shining into a wide sheltered space carved out of the rock like an amphitheater. He could see the tall Indian approaching from outside of the high rock ceiling.

He brought water, and Kip swallowed the liquid gratefully. In the light, he saw that the man appeared only slightly older than he was. He had a large nose and a lined, tanned face with dark eyes. The Indian built up the fire, and started to cook some beans and a few strips of bacon. He spoke to Kip without looking up.

"I am Dan Yazzie."

Kip moved to get up and hissed between clenched teeth as he experienced a sharp pain in his side and leg. He lay back down.

"My name is Kip Combs. Where are we?" When the Indian didn't answer, he said, "I was shot at by some other aircraft. I had a hand gun and got off a few shots back at them before I crashed."

Kip thought of the de Havilland. "Damn! Bob and I just got that old plane running again, and now it's gone!"

Dan considered the injured man's story.

Kip sipped some water from the cup at his side and then examined his injuries. He lifted the blanket and saw the wrappings on his leg and chest. He found his head also wrapped. He touched his forehead and felt a dull ache. His chest hurt when he tried to move, but he managed to sit up and lift the bandage on his leg. The wound wasn't as bad as he feared, though his leg was extensively bruised. There was a long cut from above the knee down to his calf, but it wasn't deep.

"Is my plane still out there?"

"I don't think so," Dan replied. "The old man led me to you when the flood waters came."

"Is he here?"

"No, he is a spirit."

Kip thought about what he said as the smell of food began to revive him. He accepted a plate of beans and bacon and ate gratefully.

"I don't know much about spirits, but I'd like to thank him and you for saving my life."

He regarded the Indian as he finished his plate. "You said your name is Dan Yazzie? What are we doing in this cave? Do you live out here?"

Dan finished his own plate and leaned back against his saddle.

"I'm hunting a monster."

"A monster? What kind of monster?"

"It is a monster called Ye'iitsoh. He is very old. He is also a spirit."

"Just what is a spirit?" Kip wasn't sure he understood what the man was talking about.

Dan got up and walked into the sunlight in front of their shelter. He stood there for a moment in deep thought. When he came back, he sat by the fire again and began to speak of the old legends.

"Many ages ago monsters ran all over the Earth. They were killing all of the People, so the Hero Twins set out to rid the world of the evil. They were two boys; the youngest was called Born for Water, and the older was called Monster Slayer."

The Indian tossed a few more small sticks into the fire before he continued.

"They went to see their father, who was the Sun. He told them that they were brothers of the monster they came to slay. However, he said if that was no longer so, he would help them by making them immune to injury. The Sun then told them to go to Mt. Taylor where the monster Ye'iitsoh lived."

Kip listened quietly, watching the man as he told his story.

"When the twins arrived, they hid and waited for the monster God to come to the spring to drink, as he did every day. When he came, they jumped out and fought him. Monster Slayer shot lightning at the God, and the monster bled a great deal and died. Born for Water used his club to divert the monster's blood as it flowed from his body. The blood then changed to lava, and it lies around Mt. Taylor today."

"But now the monster is back, and I am going to slay him."

Kip didn't know what to say, and he didn't want to antagonize the man.

"Well, if the monster is a God, how do you expect to kill it?"

"I don't know."

"Well, I know a few monsters that I'd like to kill; those pilots who shot me down! Wait 'till I get the cops after them."

"When you feel better, I'll take you to see Sam Begay. He's a Federal Indian Policeman and a good friend. He told me about the monster, and how it killed my daughter and grandfather."

"Sam Begay? Hey, I met him when I was at Chaco Canyon a few weeks ago. He gave me a ride home when I crashed my other plane. I was shot down then too, by the same guys. What makes you so sure he can help?"

"He is a brave man, and he is my friend. He watched over me when I was younger, and he looked after my family while I was in prison."

"Oh." Kip couldn't think of anything else to say.

Dan sensed that he had made the white man uncomfortable, and he added, "I used to drink, and there was an automobile accident. I was convicted of manslaughter."

Dan turned his head toward the opening of the cave and pursed his lips in the Navajo way of pointing direction.

"Where are you from?"

"Albuquerque," Kip said, "for the past three years anyway; The Navy before then. I grew up in Michigan in the north near Lake Huron."

"Is that a big lake?"

"Oh yeah, almost like an ocean; you can't see across it. There are big ships that sail on it too. My parents ran a lighthouse."

Kip looked at Dan to see if he understood what that was.

"That's a tower with a big light on top to guide the ships at night, isn't it?" Dan asked.

"Yes, that's right."

Dan added, "I read about them once in a newspaper."

"We lived there until my father died…" Kip paused to explain. "He drowned trying to save me. I went out on the ice one day to see the ships better, and I walked all the way out near the open water. He told me not to; he said it was too dangerous. He was right. The ice broke off and I couldn't get back to shore. He ran out and tried to jump to the patch of ice where I was, but he didn't make it…dumb huh?" Kip took a deep breath

"I hated him because we lived so far away from anybody, and all he could think to do when I disobeyed him was to risk his life trying to save me. It was all so quick, and before I could even do anything, he drowned a few feet in front of me."

Kip hung his head and closed his eyes. The silence lay heavy for several minutes, and then Dan spoke.

"My father was a drinker. He froze to death walking home from a bar one night. My mother disappeared a year later. I was still young then, and I went to live with my grandfather not too far from here. I spent most of my life around this area, except for the three years I was in prison in Santa Fe. I was married once, and we had a little daughter."

"I used to drink too, and when I wrecked my truck and killed my wife, I was sent to prison. I just came home a month ago and found out that my daughter and my grandfather were both killed by the monster."

"Geez," said Kip.

"Sam Begay is the only friend I have now. It's funny, he kept telling me I should live better and follow the Navajo way. He's the one that arrested me after the accident, and also the one that looked in on my daughter and grandfather while I was away. He also came to see me in Santa Fe from time to time, and tell me how they were getting along."

"He met me when I got off the bus from prison last month. That's when he took me out to the old hogan where they died, and he showed me the monster's tracks."

"Sam knew I had nothing to live for. I told him I had to make myself worthy of something, so he got me outfitted to go out and kill Ye'iitsoh. I've been searching for the monster ever since, and I've seen signs of it around this area. In fact, Sam and I stayed here a short while ago and the monster came in the night and killed one of our horses."

Dan paused and looked directly at Kip before continuing. "There are other strange things happening in this desert, too. I saw a 'star eater' in the sky one night, and Sam told me it was something else. He said he saw it in a movie; it was a big ship like a long tapered ball, and it was filled with air."

Kip blurted out, "A dirigible? I heard one passing overhead the other night, and that's what I was chasing when the Sparrowhawks got me!"

Dan pondered what Kip said, and then left to get more water. Kip lay back to rest. He felt a kind of kinship with this man. They were from different cultures and different parts of the country, but he could identify with what Dan said about having to become worthy of something.

As Kip lay there, he thought of how badly he'd felt about Doo breaking his ankle when he pulled him from his wrecked plane a few years ago. His thoughts turned to Lisa Ann, and he realized that he really did care for her, but she had some baggage too, and lately they never seemed to be able to stay civil with each other for more than a few minutes at a time.

Then he thought of Vicki and Bob. She had taken him under her wing after his mother died. She'd sure be proud of him now; wrecking another airplane.

When Dan returned, Kip said, "You say you saw evidence of the monster around this area? Did you really mean it when you said you had nothing else to live for than to kill this monster?"

Dan nodded his head, "I will either kill it, or it will kill me. It will be a good fight though, don't you think?"

"Yes," Kip said with a growing conviction, and then he added slyly, "I guess that would make you the 'Monster Slayer' like in the legends, huh?"

"Perhaps."

Kip smiled, "Then maybe I'm 'Born for Water.' Don't you see? I should have died out there; more than once. I survived the crash and the flood waters, and if that doesn't make me feel born from the water, I don't know what else to call it."

Dan pondered Kips words before he spoke, "Then that would make us the 'Hero Twins.'"

"Yes!" exclaimed the pilot. "And right now I don't have anything else remotely worthwhile to do, other than to help you kill that damn monster. What do you think?"

What Dan thought, was a mystery to Kip, because the tall Indian left the cave again. He returned some time later with a handful of cactus buttons and some other plants. Kip had a feeling that something was up. Dan boiled some of the leaves in water while he chopped up the rest.

"We must have a ceremony," he said. "You will not be able to join me on my journey unless your mind and body have been purified first. I am going to tell you more about this monster, and then you will be tested. If you are worthy, we will hunt together."

Dan carved a small wooden flute and fashioned some sticks for drumming. He built up the fire as evening fell, and he and Kip inhaled some of the burning herbs and drank down a bitter broth made from the cactus buds.

Dan showed Kip how to beat a rhythm with the sticks and how to chant the right words. With the proper mood set, he told the story of the Hero Twins and their battle with the monster again, but this time in more detail. He also described the tracking lore he used to find the monster, and what he knew of its habits, and what it might look like.

Kip was mesmerized by the stories and by the ritual. He began to hallucinate as darkness gradually hid the world outside of the fire circle. Kip had been drunk before, but he never felt anything like how he felt right now.

He could see the words as Dan spoke them, and the story came to life in his mind's eye. He saw the top of the rainbow where father Sun had his house. He saw the flint garments and weapons that the boys had to protect themselves. He saw the zigzag lightning arrows they would use to kill the monster.

Sometime later, Dan shook him awake, and spoke. Kip woke sluggishly to daylight, and when he could focus his eyes, he saw Dan stooped before him.

"Are you ready?" he asked.

Kip answered by throwing up.

CHAPTER 53

Kip struggled to stand, and then he walked stiffly in the chill morning air. Dan saw the miserable look on his face.

"Feeling any better?"

"Yeah, I—I'm sorry I puked, but I feel better now."

"Here's some water so you can clean up."

"I don't know what happened," Kip said.

"That's okay, it's supposed to be that way."

"What?"

"Everybody reacts the same way the first time. It's called peyote. The Great Spirit gave it to the People to help us appreciate the invisible world. Besides, you needed to get rid of the bad spirits you held inside you. You wear the signs now that that has happened."

"Do you mean to tell me you gave me that stuff, all the time knowing it would make me throw up?"

Dan nodded and grinned. Kip frowned, but then couldn't help but smile lopsidedly. Dan laughed, and Kip said, "I should have barfed on you too."

Dan placed a finger along one nostril and blew his nose. He caught most of it on his thumb and wrist, and Kip pointed at him and laughed. Soon they were both laughing so hard Kip had to bend over to keep his side from aching.

When they recovered from their mirth, Dan said, "Now that you've seen the visions, I have some important words to tell you. I will tell you of the two wolves that live inside us. One is good, but the other is evil, and they fight a terrible battle. The evil one is greed and anger, resentment, and lies. However, the other is kindness, truth, hope, and peace. Do you know what determines which one wins?"

"No."

"The one that wins is determined by which one we feed. I think that you and I are a lot alike. We blame ourselves for some very fierce things in our past; but I also think that the good wolf in us is stronger than the evil one.

Kip thought about this as Dan saddled the horse.

"Over there," Dan said sticking out his lip toward the green shoulder of Mt. Taylor "is where the monster lives."

They rode double, traveling south for five miles across the high desert. Though they were already a mile above sea level, it didn't detract from the majesty of the 12,000 foot peak of Mt. Taylor.

"The People call it the Turquoise Mountain," Dan said, "because it looks blue in the distance."

The landscape changed with the increasing elevation. The vegetation was more abundant and grew taller and greener. They came across a small stream and followed it up into the foothills. The water was cool, and they saw a few small fish. Eventually, they stopped and ate a cold breakfast of jerky before continuing their ride to the pine covered ridges above the river.

A blanket of fallen needles muffled the noise of their horse's footfalls. Dan halted the animal as they entered an area full of tall pines and whispered to Kip, "Listen."

Kip could hear a rushing sound coming from ahead where the river disappeared around a shoulder of rock.

"I think it is a waterfall. We'll tie the horse and walk up and see if we can find anything moving around."

They walked stealthily past the fringe of pine and crept up a jagged incline to peer over the edge. There was an open canyon fifty feet below them, and at one end was a pool at the bottom of a small waterfall. They could hear the water splashing over the rocks and dead wood; tall grass and cattails defined the edges of the pool.

Dan motioned again with his jutting chin. Below them to the right, a large brown bear moved into sight near the edge of the water. It stepped into the stream hunting for a meal. It was less than a minute before it moved a mighty forepaw and hurled a fish onto the shore. The bear walked into the grass, stopping to shake the water off its body.

Dan told Kip it was a big female, and it must weigh well over a thousand pounds. He was glad they approached downwind, not wanting to tangle with a bear her size. They watched quietly as the animal began to eat its catch.

"Is that the monster?" Kip whispered.

Dan was silent. He'd been asking himself the same question. It was big enough, but it just didn't seem right. It didn't fit the tracks and the other clues, but it was here where he figured the monster would be. He just didn't know. The animal was big, and it would take many well-placed shots to kill it. Then he realized that the bear was twice as heavy as the creature he sought. It couldn't be the monster.

He was just about to answer Kip's question when the bear suddenly reared up on its hind legs. It looked huge and fierce as it roared a challenge at something across the river, hidden from sight below the men. As they watched, it dropped down on all fours and dashed flank-down across the stream into the brush below them. Its savage roars soon mixed with horrid shrieks of rage as the bushes shook violently.

The battle lasted no more than a minute, and then everything was still. A loud crunching sound like the breaking of bones came to them from below, and then a large round object the size of a medicine ball rolled into the open and down to the edge of the river. The two men held their breath as their eyes took in the evidence before them. The dark object was the fearsome, blood-matted head of the bear.

Kip felt his body tingling with fear. Dan lifted a finger to his lips for silence, and they both began to move slowly backward from their vantage point. When they reached the horse, they mounted and rode back down the path along the ridge. Neither said a word until they were a mile away and stopped to stretch their legs.

Kip just had to say something. "What the hell was that? Did I see something rip the head off that huge bear? What kind of animal could do such a thing? Look Dan, I don't know about you, but I don't think we have enough firepower to take on whatever that thing is."

Dan smiled slyly at Kip. "I agree, we don't—at least not here. But I know where we can get it."

When the two men approached their rock shelter, Dan dismounted a hundred yards in front of it and walked over to a pile of rocks. He began to remove them one by one to reveal a stout wooden box hidden underneath.

The box had two words stamped across the top and sides: 'Explosive' and 'Dynamite'.

"It's time we found a better place to stay that we can defend: some place where we can prepare for our battle with the monster. I know where a small cliff ruin is, and it's not too far from the waterfall."

The men loaded their supplies on the horse, and they walked the animal toward the ruins.

"Hey," Kip said as they passed an abandoned hogan, "why don't we set ourselves up here? The logs seem to be in good shape and the door looks like it still works."

Dan remembered his grandfather's hogan. He looked at the dirt roof and turned to Kip, "It's not safe."

"Are you sure?" Kip eyed the stout logs.

"Pretty sure." Dan told him how the monster dug through the dirt roof of his Grandfather's place.

CHAPTER 54

They reached the ruins well before sundown and moved their supplies inside the broken, stone walls. There was room for the horse in a separate area alongside the space they chose for themselves.

"We need to draw the creature out of its hiding place and get a good look at it," Dan said. "We have to see what kind of animal it is if we're going to find a way to kill it."

"Are you saying you're going to walk up that little stream to the waterfall and call it out?" Kip asked. "Are you crazy? You saw what it did to that bear. I say we dynamite the cliff above it and bury it."

"No, we have to see what it is first. I have to make sure it's the monster, and then we can kill it."

Dan started a fire while Kip walked around the jagged walls. What were the men and women like who once lived here? Were they some of Dan's distant ancestors from eight hundred years ago? He wondered what kind of dangers people faced back then when these small rooms were first built; monsters? No, probably not. It was more likely, undesirable neighbors.

Kip turned his attention to the problem of how to coax the creature out of hiding without putting their lives in danger. He took a stick and started drawing on the dirt floor.

"I've got it," he said finally. "The problem is how to draw the monster out of hiding without being eaten, right?"

Dan grunted, "Preferably."

"So, what would make it curious? A noise? Perhaps something moving?"

The Indian nodded.

"Look, I know about airplanes and what makes them stable enough to fly. I've been making gliders of one kind or another since I was six years old. I used to build them and take them to the top of the lighthouse and throw them into the wind."

"When I got older, I'd even set them on fire first and pretend that I shot down a German Albatross. I'd watch them glide away and crash and burn. It used to drive my mother nuts, but I did it anyway."

"I bet I could build a glider from some of the stuff we've got around here. As for noise, how about one of those flute things you made last night when we were at the cave? We could attach it to the glider and the wind would make it whistle as it flew."

"Heck, we could toss it from up on the ridge and the thing would never see us. I'll bet it would come out to find out what it was, though. What do you think?"

Dan thought it was such a good idea, that he began to figure out a way to deliver the dynamite to the creature when it came out to investigate.

The next morning both men got busy with their projects. Kip tried out different designs, but finally decided on an arrow-shaped, canvas wing supported by thin wooden struts. He cut some branches from nearby trees, and after he shaped them to the proper size, he worked on finding the right position and weight of the fuselage. He wanted the glider to sail into the wind, and it took him two days to complete and test it. His final model was five feet long from nose to tail with a canvas wing that filled with air like a kite.

Dan was busy too. He made a bow with a strong pull and fashioned some specially designed arrows to use with it. He cut the shafts from the trees near the stream, modifying the ends to support a stick of dynamite tied to it. He practiced with different lengths, substituting a piece of rock for the weight of the explosive. When he got it right, he carved ten shafts and practiced with them until he could place his shots with accuracy. In three days, they were ready.

They decided to approach the waterfall from the other side of the ravine and were careful to stay downwind of the open space. They got into position late in the morning, crawled to the ledge, and peered down. They were in a perfect position over the waterfall and pool. They could see the bushes where the bear had attacked the other creature. There was a dark crevice beyond the vegetation, and Dan thought it might be the monster's lair.

Kip tested the breeze for speed and direction, and he told Dan they should wait for the wind to change before trying their gambit. They both hunkered down for a few hours until Kip signaled that the time was right.

They moved into position, and Kip checked the glider to make sure it was ready for flight. Dan had his bow in his hand with the special arrows at his side; five of them already fitted with a stick of dynamite. He was taking no chances.

Kip looked at Dan, Dan nodded, and he let the glider fly. It darted straight, then dipped, and then lifted with the wind. All the while, a weird hollow note moaned softly from the music pipe attached to the fuselage.

They watched the glider circle above the open area, canvas flapping as it lifted and fell with the thermals near the cliffs. Dan crouched, holding the bow with an arrow nocked. Kip held a match ready to light the dynamite at Dan's signal.

They both feared to breathe as they eyed the bushes across the way. The glider finished its flight, and it rolled over and nosed into the stream with a splash. Nothing moved; the busy sound of the waterfall made the moment seem surreal. The birds were silent and the cicadas stopped their shrill buzzing.

Kip's heart sounded loud in his ears, and his hand shook as it held the match. He glanced at Dan, and then saw a quick motion out of the corner of his eye. The creature was almost too fast to see clearly. It had a weird shape; tall as a horse with long stiff hair along its back. It had an odd two-legged gait, and its arms seemed to windmill as it dashed out and pounced upon the broken glider.

Dan whispered urgently, "Light me."

Kip lit the fuse, and Dan took aim and released the deadly arrow. Ducking down, they watched the sputtering shaft arch toward the creature. The thing looked up at the last minute and reacted by leaping away. The explosion came before the arrow hit the ground, and the concussion bowled the animal over. Dust sifted down and small rocks began to fall along the side of the stream and in the water.

Dan notched another arrow and nodded for Kip to light it. He let loose again, and though he overshot the target, the explosion loosened some rocks from the cliff. More debris fell where the monster's body lay obscured by dust and dirt. Again, there was an eerie silence. The men waited, but the large, partially covered shape didn't move.

"Let's go see what it is," Dan said, standing and grabbing his remaining arrows. They hiked a short distance along the ridge and climbed down a jagged cleft to the river. They walked cautiously upstream to the pool and the waterfall. Reaching the open area, they both looked across the water for the creature's body. Dan motioned to stop.

"I don't see it," he said.

"Neither do I." Kip began to look around nervously. "How could it just walk away after that? What about that cut over there behind the bushes? That's where it came from; do you think it went back in to hide?"

Fearing an attack from a wounded creature, Dan fitted another explosive arrow to his bow.

"Light me again."

Kip touched a match to the fuse, and Dan drew back and let the shaft fly into the dark space beyond the foliage. The following explosion loosened the wall of rock above it and the cliff cascaded down, filling the opening, and burying the thick screen of greenery in front of it.

"Woo-hoo," shouted Kip. "We got it! Scratch one monster."

Dan stood silently as Kip did a victory dance. "You took down the whole rock wall and killed it dead."

"Maybe," Dan said, a frown displaying his uncertainty. Both men searched the area for any evidence the creature may have left behind.

"What kind of animal was it?" Kip asked. "It ran on two legs, didn't it? It seemed to have some kind of weird arms or something; they waved around when it ran. At least I thought they did."

Dan stopped, staring down at his feet, and then picked up a hairy quill. It was about ten inches long, and he showed it to Kip. It looked identical to the specimen he found in the desert some weeks ago.

Kip found one also, leaving them both to guess what kind of animal it came from. There were no tracks due to the debris from the explosions. They knew what they saw, but they still didn't know what it was.

The men returned to their horse and rode silently back to the ruins. Kip was in a buoyant mood, and he hummed merrily as he danced around the camp.

"We are the Hero Twins," he chanted. "Did you see how that whole cliff came down? I'll bet that thing was squashed flat and left noting but a big hairy grease spot."

Kip noticed that Dan kept silent and didn't share in his elation.

"Why are you so glum? You don't have to play the stoic Indian. Be happy. We did what we set out to do. You're the Monster Slayer aren't you?"

"I just don't know," Dan said softly. "I just don't know."

Dan wasn't being talkative, and Kip soon caught his solemn mood. When night fell, they built a small fire inside the walls and ate their dinner in silence.

In the morning, with coffee warming on the coals of last night's fire, Dan spoke to Kip about what had bothered him yesterday.

"It was too easy," he said. "If it was Ye'iitsoh, and I don't know what else it could have been, then it can't be dead."

"Can't be dead?" Kip exclaimed. "But the dynamite...we saw it on the ground."

"Yet the monster was gone from where the blast knocked it down."

"But the cave, and the cliff coming down on top of it..."

"Who says that's where the creature went to hide. Who says it can't dig its way out if it wants? We just don't know. Besides, I can still sense its evil in my mind. I don't think we killed it."

"Well it was pretty big," Kip said. "Almost the size of a horse; and it did tear the head off that bear. What kind of fur was on those quills we found? Were those long spines really its hair?"

"I don't know. Neither of us got a good look at it; it moved too fast. With the dust from the explosions, we never did get to see it any clearer. There is one thing I am sure of though, it was Ye'iitsoh. I have to know that it is dead."

"I've been thinking Kip, maybe it's time for you to go back to your people. I must stay and make sure in my own mind that my family has been avenged. You can take the horse today and return home."

"Now wait a minute," Kip said. "I'm not going to leave you out here alone without any way to get around. Heck, maybe it is still alive, who knows. The point is; I'm not the kind of guy that runs out on a friend when there's trouble."

"I know you're not. You have a brave heart, and you and I have taken a journey as brothers. I ask you now as a brother to leave me to continue my own journey. Our test is through, but I feel mine still has some distance to go. I will not need the horse. When I'm finished, I can walk to where I need to go. This is my home, and I know where I am."

"That's good, because I don't," Kip admitted, looking over the ruins and off to the horizon. "Okay Dan, I'll go, and I'll find Sam Begay and tell him what we've done and where to find you. There are just two things though."

  "What are they?"

  "You look me up when you're done with your journey."

  Dan nodded smiling, "I will, and the other thing?"

  "Tell me where the hell Chaco Canyon is from here."

CHAPTER 55

Doo heard a horn beep outside the hanger. He put down an engine part he was cleaning and walked to the front. A young man in a Western Union hat came into the office.

"Can I help you?"

"Telegram for Mr. Robert Doobridge," the messenger had a hopeful look.

"That's me."

Doo was mystified. He signed the receipt and opened the envelope as the man's car accelerated down the service road.

Lisa Ann came running in, "Did you just get a telegram?"

"Aw, give a guy a chance to read it in private will you."

He turned away from the girl and walked back into the shop. He read the message at least six times.

Lisa had the sense to let the boy alone. She could see he seemed shaken by something he read in the telegram. Her curiosity would not let her leave the building, however, without knowing what it said. She busied herself straightening up the clutter in the office and then got a rag and began to dust, glancing occasionally toward the back at Doo.

Doo stood in the same place for ten minutes. He read the words repeatedly until he looked up and saw Lisa Ann still in the office. He folded the paper and stuffed it in his pocket.

Lisa watched him expectantly as he walked toward her. She saw the troubled expression on his face.

"Doo, I'm sorry, I didn't mean to pry. Is it...is it bad?"

The young man took a moment before he answered.

"Yeah; don't worry though. I'm sorry I snapped at you."

Lisa came closer and hugged him, and Doo took a deep ragged breath.

"It's okay; just family. I've already cried all the tears I'll ever cry. Look, I'm going to have to go away for a while; maybe a month. Tell Kip when he gets back, that I won't be too long. Everything is pretty much caught up here anyway."

"Can you tell me what happened?" Concern showed on Lisa's face.

"Not now. When I get back I'll tell everybody, but right now I have to go. I have a few things to put away and pack. Can you take me to the bus station in about a half hour? I guess we can take the Harley."

"Sure. I love to drive that thing anyway. I'll put on some slacks and meet you back here."

Lisa drove him to the Greyhound Station downtown. Doo stepped out of the sidecar and gave her a quick kiss on the cheek. He smiled shyly, and then took his bag and walked into the building.

A dusty bus snorted into the parking lot as Lisa started up the Harley and drove back to the airfield. Her thoughts were in turmoil.

When she pulled up to the hanger and shut off the engine, she could hear the phone ringing inside.

Lisa caught her breath and said, "Hello?"

"Hello, is Kip there? This is his aunt, Vicki Johnson."

"Oh, hi Aunt Vicki, this is Lisa Ann. Kip's not here. I thought he was with you and Bob."

"Oh he was dear, but he took off four days ago to fly to Chaco Canyon. He said he'd be gone for a few days, but he hasn't returned yet. I thought he might have flown back to Albuquerque. Have you seen him?"

"No I haven't," Lisa said, starting to worry.

"Well is Doo there? Maybe he's seen him."

"No Aunt Vicki, Doo had to leave on a trip today, and he won't be back for a month. Honest, Kip hasn't been back. Do you think he's in some kind of trouble?"

Lisa Ann was very worried now. This wasn't like Kip.

"Aunt Vicki, what can I do? Do we need to start a search?"

"Oh no, I don't think so honey. Kip can take care of himself, and he knows how to fly. It's just that Bob and I expected him back by now, and well, Bob had to go into town, so I came with him to use the phone. I'm sure he's okay, dear."

"But it's not like him to be gone like that. Oh, Vicki I'm worried!"

"Now, now, honey, I'm sorry I got you all upset. Really, I'm sure he'll be back before long, and I'll make sure he goes right into town to call you first thing. Is that all right? That way he can tell you all about what he's been up to."

"Oh, would you do that please? I don't know why, but I worry about that man. He's such a child sometimes."

"Yes he is dear, they all are." Vicki laughed trying to reassure her. "I'll have him call you as soon as he gets here. I have to go now, bye."

"Bye, Aunt Vicki."

Lisa Ann hung up the receiver. She was anything but reassured; in fact, she was steaming.

"That bastard," she hissed. "He's gone off to Chaco Canyon to see that black-haired archeologist. Oh, I'll fix him!"

Lisa fumed and muttered until another thought came to her. What if Kip' plane crashed again? She remembered bullying Doo into telling her all about how Kip crashed his old Jenny after someone shot at him. What if it happened again?

She paced back and forth in the small office and then stormed out the door to her Uncle Jack's machine shop. She found him tinkering on one of his projects.

"Jack," she shouted. "I'm taking Kip's motorcycle out to Gallup, and I won't be back for a week. I hope you can do without me, because you don't have a choice."

She was out the door before Jack could voice any objection. Besides, he knew he couldn't stop her when she was like this. He sighed deeply and returned to his work.

Lisa packed a bag with food and water and some extra clothes, and threw it in the sidecar. Then she wheeled the Harley to the gas pump. When the tank was full, she put on her goggles and roared off.

CHAPTER 56

Kip saw the line of high mesas that Dan described in his directions to Chaco Canyon. It was late afternoon, and he was saddle weary and tired of the monotonous creak of leather. The warm water in his canteen tasted of age and dust, and he was sure that the sun would make his face burn and peel. His body rocked loosely to the rolling gait of the horse as it stepped sure-footedly through the rocks. He saw a bank of clouds spread out across the horizon, and below it something else; a thin cloud of dust billowing from a vehicle making its way north along the primitive road toward Chaco Canyon.

He thought of Diana Witherspoon and her old Ford and stopped to look through his binoculars. He could see that it wasn't an automobile, but a motorcycle. Disappointed, he coaxed the horse to move on.

His thoughts turned to Dan Yazzie, and he wondered if the man was truly sane. He liked the tall Indian, but he didn't know how to take all of his talk about spirits. Dan was right about the monster though, or whatever that thing was. It all seemed so strange; maybe he was still under the influence of peyote.

He did admire Dan's calm manner and confident attitude about life. He was obviously at home in the desert. Kip shook his head and wondered if he would ever see him again.

The horse picked its own path as the air shimmered like a moving curtain in the distance. When he saw the plume of dust from the motorcycle again, it was coming diagonally towards him and was close enough to see it better. It was light colored and it had a sidecar. It looked almost like his Harley.

He stopped the horse and grabbed the binoculars again. He could see the shape of the rider and saw blonde hair flowing behind in a ponytail…a girl? Then the motorcycle disappeared from sight.

It was *his* Harley, and it had to be Lisa Ann riding it! Only she would do such a crazy thing! Somehow, she must have learned he was out here, and it was just like her to take his motorcycle and try to find him. He kicked the horse's ribs, and the beast leapt ahead.

Lisa knew Kip could take care of himself, just like he knew she could do the same. Still, it didn't stop him from going after her when her uncle told him she was late from a ride with her boyfriend. Yes, they were more alike than Kip cared to admit.

Lisa Ann powered the Harley down the rough trail. The goggles kept the wind and dust from her eyes, but flour-like caliche dust covered the rest of her. She was tired and sore from riding, and the closer she got to her destination, the more her concern for Kip turned to anger. She wasn't thinking logically and was past being fearful for his safety. Instead, she envisioned a dozen versions of that dark-haired bitch, Diana seducing Kip. She could see him nuzzling her as they lay in each other's arms. She ground her teeth in frustration, her eyes blurry with tears.

Sure, she'd taunted him with her flirtations and dates with other men, but that was just to make him jealous enough to stand up and tell her that she was his girl. She loved him desperately, and she hated him at the same time. Why wouldn't he just tell her that he loved her; was that too much to ask?

Val was just returning to Fajada Butte. He heard the deep snarl of the Harley and saw the motorcycle and the female rider speeding down the canyon toward the camp. He remembered the two men from the mine waiting there for visitors. Val spat an oath and ran to follow her. She might be a crony of the two men, but he doubted it. This rider was probably a tourist, and he feared that trouble was waiting for her. Just then, Val had to duck for cover as a horse and rider galloped by, following the motorcycle.

Lisa Ann arrived at the Chaco camp and saw a man standing in the road waiting for her. Carl and Nicholas, upon hearing the motorcycle approaching, decided that Nick would stand in plain view while Carl hid off to the side. Lisa stopped the bike, shut off the engine, and waited for the dust to settle before she removed her goggles.

The big man's face broke into a wide smile of appreciation as she shook the dust from her long hair. A line of dust around her eyes made her look a little comical, but he was more interested in her shapely figure. She may be dirty, he thought, but she looks like my kind of girl.

"I'm looking for a man," Lisa said as Nicholas walked up. "He's a pilot, and he's supposed to be somewhere around here. Have you seen him?"

"Well sister," Nick said with a smirk, "If you're looking for a man, then you've found one. And it just so happens I'm also a pilot."

"Not you, you moron, I'm looking for Kip Combs. Do you know him? Has he been here?"

"Kip Combs?" Nick repeated the name as a thoughtful look crossed his face. "I used to know a Kip Combs in the Navy a few years ago."

"Oh yeah? Small world; have you seen him?"

Nick's expression changed to a wary frown. "You say he's around here somewhere?"

Her patience gone, Lisa Ann exploded. "Yes you big idiot, I'm asking you if you've seen him? Do you have trouble understanding English, or do I have to bounce a rock off your skull to get your ears to work?"

"Hold it sister," Nick said, "I don't like your smart-ass talk. In fact I think old Nicholas is going to have to teach you some manners."

Lisa was never one to back down; she'd handled overconfident jerks before, when she lived in the city.

"Yeah, well maybe you'd like to try, but in the meantime get your chunky ass out of my way. I've got my own hormones to deal with, and I'm not going to back down to someone just because he's pumped up on testosterone, unless I feel like it!"

"Okay, that'll be quite enough," Carl said, stepping out from his hiding place. He held his pistol on the girl. "Miss, please just step off the bike and keep your sweet mouth shut."

For ten long seconds, Lisa Ann thought over her chances of kick starting the Harley and getting away.

"Uh, uh," Carl said, and Lisa slowly stepped off the bike.

Nick moved in front of the girl. "I'm going to have to search you miss; for your own safety, of course. When Carl pulls his gun out, he gets so jittery that he's liable to shoot if he sees your titties jiggle. Just let me see if you've got anything hidden on you."

Nicholas enjoyed rubbing his hands across her chest and hips. She smiled at him lazily, and then stepped closer and jerked her knee up with such force that she lifted Nick to his toes. He fell to the ground on his side and moaned like a sick dog. Lisa stared at Carl, daring him to shoot.

Carl blandly rolled his eyes. "You're just going to make it harder on yourself when he gets back up."

"So what's all this about?" she said. "I came out here looking for my friend, and you two gorillas jump out from under a rock and act downright unfriendly. What's the matter; your momma's never teach you how to treat a lady?"

Nick groaned, and gingerly got to his hands and knees. He struggled painfully to stand, and when he did, he puffed up ready to leap at the girl. Carl shouted him down.

"Stay put Nicholas! Let's talk to her first. We don't want to hurt her just because she's feeling a bit peevish from her dusty ride, do we?"

"Why no," Nick agreed, and abruptly swung a hammy fist across her chin, knocking her sprawling in the dirt. "No, I sure don't want to hurt her, at least not yet." His words dripped with menace and matched the evil look in his eyes.

As Kip rode closer, he saw Nicholas knock Lisa down, and he charged directly at him. Nick jumped back just in time, and Kip wheeled the horse around and charged the other man holding the gun. When a bullet snapped over his head, he quickly reined the animal back and jumped from the saddle. He ran to Lisa's side. She was moving now, and as he stooped down to help her, Nicholas struck him from behind, knocking him unconscious.

Val warily approached the camp and saw the two thugs talking to the rider and the girl. They tied the new arrivals to chairs under the canopy of the mess tent. Occasionally the stocky man lashed out with his fist at the bound man.

Kip saw red, as he tasted his own blood. He would have to endure this beating for now, but he hoped to confront this simian bastard soon, on his own terms.

Nicholas smirked in triumph. "Kip Combs, I never expected to see your sorry face again in this life! Hey Carl, do you know who this is? Do you remember me telling you about that jerk pilot, back when I was in the Navy? You know the one I set up to take the blame for some shenanigans I pulled."

"Only a million times Nicholas."

Carl wasn't interested in hearing Nick repeat his sordid story; he was more concerned about what these two visitors might mean for the safety of the mission.

Nick was oblivious to Carl's sarcasm, and he puffed up ready to brag about his underhanded victory over the man in the chair. He glanced at Lisa Ann and smiled at the bruise on her chin.

"Girlie, do you know this guy?" Lisa ignored his question. "Well I guess you do, but do you know what I did to him back in San Diego a few years ago? It'll make you laugh 'till you cry. You see, we were both test pilots on an aircraft carrier out there."

"Yeah," Kip said through bloody lips, "you framed me for your thieving and sabotage and caused another pilot to crash and lose his life."

"*He, he,*" laughed Nick, remembering his cleverness.

Kip said, "Why don't you tell her about when they found the poor pilot's body." He turned to Lisa Ann and said, "His uh…member was missing, and they never did find it. Most of us figured it out, and we started calling this guy 'Nick the biter'. Now you know how he got his name."

Lisa, always quick to catch on, looked at Nicholas with surprise and said, "Oh my, it's so nice to meet a man who knows what to do with his mouth."

"Aaarrrghh!" Nick screamed and ran at Kip, picking him up, chair and all, and threw him backward to the ground.

"Enough," shouted Carl.

Nick got his anger under control, and his expression soon became thoughtful.

"Say Kip old buddy, you wouldn't be the crazy pilot that's been nosing around out here for the past month, would you?" A look of certainty spread across his face. "You were the guy in that Jenny I threw lead at last month, weren't you! And you were the same fool in the de Havilland that got shot down last week!"

Thinking quickly, Carl said, "If he's that pilot, I think Bloundt will want to talk to him. I'm going to saddle a horse right now and take him back to the compound." Carl didn't mention that this was the excuse he was looking for to leave Nicholas behind at the camp.

"You stay with the girl," he said suggestively. "I'll be back tomorrow, and you can tell me all about what you found out from her."

Carl knew what Nicholas would find out, and how he'd go about doing it.

Nick quickly agreed. He licked his meaty lips and glared at the bound girl.

Val Tannin watched impatiently from his hiding place as Carl saddled a horse. Carl then untied the man from his chair and lifted him to his own horse. He tied Kip's hands to the pommel and looped a rope under the animal to tie the man's feet together.

"Anything I can bring back for you after Bloundt gets done with this guy?" Carl asked, playing his ruse.

"Yeah," Nicholas glanced suggestively at Lisa Ann. "Bring me some champagne. I'm going to feel like celebrating."

CHAPTER 57

Kip was uncomfortable and helpless, but all he could think about was Lisa Ann.

He'd botched his attempt to rescue her by being brash and just plain stupid, and now she was a captive of the vilest person he'd ever known. No wonder he thought he'd recognized the names of the men who beat up Doo at the hanger, it was Nicholas Ells and one of his buddies. Nick was a sadistic killer. He had no remorse for the pain he brought upon others; and now he was alone with Lisa. Kip knew that she'd grown up to a hard life and could take care of herself, but Nick was a brutal deviant in a class of his own.

He said to Carl, "You know he's going to hurt her real bad. What kind of jerk are you to leave her alone with him?"

"Shut up," Carl said, "just be happy she's not going along with us to see who you're going to see. He makes Nicholas look like a school boy."

Carl was a professional spy; he hated Thomas Bloundt, but he also feared him. He knew the man cared nothing for the misery and deaths of the captives who worked in the mine. Not that Carl was any better or worse a person, but Bloundt was just too full of himself to feel remorse for any of his actions. It was the man's lack of appreciation for Carl's work however, that galled him. He would like to kill the bastard, but that wouldn't help the mission.

He thought of the silver and turquoise jewelry the Commandant had taken from the captives and kept for himself. No, Carl wouldn't kill him; he would just do what he'd thought about for some time; steal the jewelry and escape into the desert to start a new life somewhere else. He didn't need to return to Germany; he had no stomach for the fascists, anyway.

He thought he wouldn't mind staying in the United States, but he knew the government would stop at nothing to find him. Better that he escaped north to Canada and disappeared with the stolen loot. Perhaps he could sell his talents to others with enough money to purchase his loyalty.

Val Tannin didn't like what he saw after the two men left on horseback. It was obvious that the stocky man was planning to hurt the woman. He backed away from his cover and circled around the camp, coming up to the mess tent on the side with a canvas flap staked to the ground. The girl was less than four feet away on the other side, still tied to her chair, and Val heard the man talking to her.

"Well girly, it looks like it's just you and me for the next day or so. I think we might as well get to know each other right away, don't you?"

"Buster, I already know you. I've known dozens of jerks just like you; big talk to hide their small minds and insignificant lives. I'd suspect everything about you is small."

"You foul-mouthed little bitch, that's where you're wrong." Nick lowered his voice. "You might say I have a certain gift for impressing the ladies."

"So why don't you impress me by sticking your head up your ass and suffocating?"

She stared at him defiantly as Nick raised his hand to slap her. "No, I think I'll start out easy and not damage you too much at first. I'll be back in a little bit, and we can get started."

He turned and whistled an off-key tune as he walked out of sight down a path behind some tents.

Lisa Ann sobbed quietly for a moment, and then she began frantically testing her ropes for any weakness.

"Psst, be quiet," whispered a voice from behind the tarp.

She was startled, "Hey, get me out of here. Who are you?"

"Just sit still, I'll crawl behind you and cut you free. Watch out for the gorilla in case he comes back."

Val was behind her now, cutting the ropes that bound her hands.

"Who are you," she said as her arms fell free of the bindings. She turned to say thanks, but then noticed Nicholas coming back around the tents.

"Hurry up, hide," she hissed. "He's coming."

"Can you distract him so I can tackle him from behind?"

"Sure, sure, just go. Quick."

Lisa kept her hands behind her acting as if the rope was still in place.

"Miss me?" Nicholas asked when he returned grinning.

Lisa Ann muttered something very quietly, feigning fear.

"What's that? I couldn't hear you." Nick moved closer.

Val crouched behind the canvas waiting for a chance to surprise him.

Lisa mumbled softly again, eyes downcast in submission.

Say that again sister?" Nick bent over, hands on his knees with his face in front of hers. "Were you saying that you're sorry?"

Lisa whipped her arms from behind the chair; palms open, and slapped them hard over his ears. She heard a popping noise, and Nick reared backward screaming in pain. He fell, writhing on his back holding his head.

Val was there in an instant. He leapt upon the man, trying to grip his throat to cut off the flow of air. Nicholas grasped Val's arms, and both men struggled, sweat beading from their faces with exertion.

Slowly Nicholas pried Val's hands from his neck. He got a knee between them and flipped Val over his head. He fell hard, his head hit the corner of a wooden chest, and he went limp.

Lisa frantically worked to untie her legs and finally succeeded. She jumped up to run, but Nicholas was quicker. He tackled her, and pinned her down with the weight of his body. She struggled, but to no avail. He marched her back, and made her tie the arms of the unconscious man, while he kept a big hand gripped around her neck. When she finished, he picked her up and carried her across the camp.

He pushed her roughly into a tent, and she landed on a pile of wrinkled and smelly blankets. She glared at the man as he came in and stood over her. Lisa reached into a pocket, hidden from Nicks view, and palmed the jackknife she took from Val when she tied his hands. Nick got down on his knees and gripped the top of her slacks.

"Wait," she said, "don't rip them. Please, just let me take them off."

The man sat back on his heels and leered as she removed her shoes and unbuckled her belt and slipped her pants down.

Great, she thought, I would have to wear this fancy underwear today.

The man's eyes lit up when he saw her lacy undergarments. "Aw, did you wear those just for me?"

He stared at her white skin as he removed his own boots. Then he undid his trousers, and dropped them to his ankles and crawled roughly on top of her. She lay quietly, and worked the hidden blade open with one hand.

As he prepared to take her, she reached purposefully to his genitals, and then made a quick, vicious slash that all but severed them.

Nick reared back, bellowing like a bull, astonished at the volume of blood flowing down his legs. He tried to stand and tripped on his own pants and fell, and then desperately tried to crawl away.

Lisa was up with her knife. She sliced at the back of his ankles as he crawled awkwardly out of the tent.

Lisa dressed quickly. She could hear Nicholas sobbing and swearing as he dragged himself further away. She ran out of the tent to Val, and cut his ropes and helped him to his feet.

"What's all the noise about? Where's the big guy?"

"Bleeding to death I hope. Let's get out of here and see if we can help Kip."

Val quickly searched the area, looking for weapons, while Lisa Ann went back to see Nicholas. He was in bad shape.

"You bitch," he spat, as he lay on the ground with blood pooling underneath him. "I'll kill you for this."

"You're an evil old spud aren't you," she said calmly, "You were going to kill me."

"Sure you little slut, but now I'm going to split you like a melon when I do."

"You know, I could almost forgive you for thinking like that. An animal like you doesn't really know any better. However, I can't forgive you for trying to kill Kip. He's the only thing good that ever happened to me, and I won't let you or anyone else hurt him."

"Just wait 'till get my hands on you." Nick spat blood. "You're dead, do you hear me. And Kip Combs is dead too."

"No Nicholas," Lisa said coldly, "you're dead—or at least you will be before long."

She was a realist. A hundred years earlier, she would have been the kind of self-sufficient woman who would bravely defend her home and family from rustlers and Indians. She felt no remorse in killing this rabid animal.

"I've got some rifles and ammo and a couple of canteens," Val said as he came up. When he noticed Nicholas, he was taken aback to see all the blood and what Lisa had done to him.

"He didn't know the proper way to treat a lady," she explained as she gave Val his knife back. "I had to show him what 'no' means. We'll need to take the Harley if we're going to catch up with Kip. I'll drive."

Val was just squeezing into the sidecar with the rifles and canteens, when Lisa Ann jumped on the starter and opened the throttle. She spun the bike around, nearly throwing him out, as they headed down the canyon trail. She kept the throttle open as wide as she could and took chances as they bounced and careened down the rutted road.

Later, when they could see the entrance of the mine some distance ahead, she stopped the Harley and watched as Carl and Kip rode through the gate and disappeared inside.

She shut the engine off and removed her goggles; tears of frustration dripped down her cheeks. "What do we do now?"

Val stepped gingerly out of the sidecar and stretched his sore legs. He looked at the distant gate.

"I think we need to get some help. Let's see if we can find a Sheriff or some other lawman."

A while later, Lisa and Val arrived at the Thoreau Trading Post. The small bell above the screen door tinkled a cheery note as they entered the building.

"Howdy," said a croaky voice behind the counter to their right.

Lisa and Val told the gnarled old man that there had been some trouble, and something suspicious was going on at the mine. They asked who they could talk to about it.

"Sam Begay," answered old Jake confidently.

"Where can we find him?"

Jake looked up through the flyspecked front window. "Well, I'm no magician, but in a minute he's going to walk right through that door behind you."

The bell tinkled again and two men entered.

"Officer Begay," Jake said, "these people want to talk to you about something you might be interested in hearing."

CHAPTER 58

Sam Begay and Charlie Redman listened carefully to Lisa and Val's story about their altercation at Chaco Canyon. Val also added his suspicions about the disappearance of the university students.

"We've got to get back to the mine and help them." Lisa was frantic with worry and wanted to do something immediately.

Sam shook his head sadly. "Our government has stupid laws that prohibit me from interfering in non-Indian matters. I simply don't have authority to enter the place."

"Well what about the FBI? We can't just sit here."

Sam said, "I know, we have to do something, and we will, but I have reason to believe that there may be people in that organization that are involved with the Blacksparrow Mine. Besides, without a large armed force, it would be foolish to try to take control of the place."

Sam looked at Charlie. "The first thing we're going to do is go back to Chaco and look for the man called Nicholas. If he is injured, he won't get far, and we should be able to find him."

When they reached the ruins, they searched the surrounding area but couldn't find the injured man. Lisa and Val described all the details of their altercation as they walked through the camp and pointed out where the events happened. Sam and Charlie found a large blood trail, but then lost it in the rocks.

"It looks like he got on a horse and rode away," Charlie said. "The tracks were headed south."

"He's going back to the mine," Val said.

Sam looked at the blond man, remembering his own confrontation at the gates. "What do you know about the mine?"

"I know there are strange things going on inside it," he said, and began to tell Sam and Charlie what he saw while spying from the cliffs above the compound.

"They have some aircraft too, and I think they use captive Indian slaves for labor." The two officers exchanged a quick glance while Val continued.

"One of their guards was killed a while back. His body was torn apart, and it looked like he'd been partially eaten by some kind of animal."

Like a jigsaw puzzle, they began to fill in the gaps of an evil and incredibly ugly picture.

"I hate to say it, but this is all starting to make some sense." Sam said. "But I still don't see why they took such extreme steps to keep their coal mining a secret. Why abduct the workers? Why not just hire them?"

"The coal that they're mining," Val said, "is just a front to hide what they're really digging out of the ground."

"What's that?" Sam eyed the man suspiciously. "And how do you know so much about this mining operation?"

"I've been inside the compound at night, and I managed to get a good look around the place. They're collecting yellowcake ore; uranium."

"This just keeps getting better," Charlie said as he added to his notes. "Is there anything else?"

"Yes, two things. They have a dirigible hidden in a cavern inside the rocks of the compound."

Sam blew out a breath of air. "And what's the second thing?"

"I think they are Germans: Nazi's. I saw a flag draped on a wall in one of the buildings."

Silence followed Val's statement. Sam said gravely, "I need you both to keep quiet about this. I'm going to deputize you. You'll stay with Charlie and I while we work out some kind of plan to rescue the captives and bring these men to justice."

"I'm in; no matter what," Lisa said.

"I'm with you too," said Val.

They all tried to suppress the anxiety and turmoil that ran through their minds as they got into Sam's car and drove back to Gallup.

The sun was setting, and as it dipped below the horizon, it left a sky full of blue-grey cloud islands and shorelines in a pale, yellow sea.

CHAPTER 59

Carl brought Kip through the compound to the stables. A few men followed them, curious about the bound man on horseback. When Carl dismounted and untied his captive's hobbled feet, Kip kicked at him, but Carl, expecting such a response, deftly ducked away.

"Help me get him down boys, and someone tell Bloundt that I've brought him a present."

Carl filled a dipper with water and brought it to Kip. "You might as well drink. It'll be the last you'll get for a while."

A man ran up, "The Commandant says he'll see you and your present right now."

Inside his office, Thomas Bloundt splashed water on his face. He dragged his fingers through his thin hair before toweling off. At last, Carl may have found a worthwhile clue to what's been going on around here. The shooting down of one of his pilots, the Navajo cop calling at the gates, and the mutilated body of the guard had all stretched Bloundt's nerves to the breaking point. With less than a week to go, he feared his whole plan might unravel before they could get out of this cursed place.

Kip noticed the look of the men around him; although they all wore civilian clothes, he could see the signs of military discipline. He stumbled as he walked, and wondered how the military could be involved in all this.

Kip was marched into Bloundt's office and told where to stand. Bloundt came in from another room, glanced at Kip, and sat down. He leaned forward, hands flat on his desk.

"What have you got for me Carl, another worker? He looks in poor shape. Why have you brought him here?"

"Take a look at our mystery pilot." Carl put a hand on Kip's shoulder, and Kip jerked away.

The Commandant leaned back in his chair. "So this is the annoying little bird who has been giving my pilots fits."

He looked at the disheveled young man and saw the marks on his face.

"Why did you shoot down one of my planes?"

Kip observed the thin man behind the desk. There were dark circles under his eyes that made his bony face look skull-like.

"One of your pilots started it," he said. "He fired at me a month ago."

"Oh yes, I know all about that. I was so angry when I found out; I had the man punished." His smile suddenly became fierce, "His orders were to shoot to kill." Bloundt glared at the man. "I would have shot him instead, but I remembered he possessed some skills I felt I might have use for later."

Bloundt stood from his chair, his face red with menace. "You have destroyed one of my planes, and you have killed my pilot. You have also severely wounded another pilot. Now, you will tell me your name and why you are here!"

Kip wanted to spit accusations back at the man, but he figured it would only make it harder on himself.

"Well, now that you put it that way," Kip smiled as if relieved. "I'm here because this fellow tied me to a horse and brought me. As for the pilots, I couldn't help it. It was easy to pick them off; and after all, they were being so annoying, flying around and shooting at me."

"All this bravado and swagger from someone who has been shot from the air twice by my pilots? Humph; and your name is...?"

"K. J. Combs, what's yours?"

"Mr. Combs, why have you been flying around in the vicinity of this mine?"

"Air's free isn't it?"

"Not around here it isn't. Who gave you orders to spy on us?"

Kip dropped his smile. "Look chief, I don't take orders from anyone unless they're a paying customer; and only then if I like them. I'm not spying on you. What's the big idea of your men attacking innocent people at Chaco Canyon?"

Carl spoke up. "He rode in to Chaco and tried to rescue a girl who drove into camp earlier on a motorcycle."

"And where is she?" the Commandant asked, guessing she was probably alone with Nicholas.

Carl glanced at Kip, then back to Bloundt, "Still back there, probably dead by now."

Kip spun around with a yell and tried to head-butt Carl, who deftly rolled aside and let the man fall to the floor against the wall.

"Nicholas insisted on keeping her company while I rode back here with this guy."

Carl saw that his meaning was not lost on Bloundt.

"Yes I see. Take him to the cages. Let him work off the trouble he's caused us. Perhaps he may feel more like talking later. When you are done Carl, please come back here. We have some things to talk over."

CHAPTER 60

Carl marched Kip across the compound toward the mineshaft. On the way, Kip noticed a Sparrowhawk in one of the open hangers.

He turned to Carl, "Whatever you're doing here, you're going to get caught, and it's not going to go easy for any of you. What is this, some kind of military operation? What about the planes?"

Carl ignored Kip's questions. As they stepped into the mineshaft, Kip noticed the electric lights placed along the roof of the tunnel. They continued down the gravel-strewn floor beside some railway tracks, and then turned right down a smaller tunnel. Kip could smell the sweat of unwashed bodies as the shaft opened into a large chamber lined with cages.

Dozens of wretched looking people peered at him from the shadows behind the iron bars. Their eyes were dim beacons of despair. As he marched along, the smell nearly overpowered him. In one cell, he saw a woman stand up and move to the front. She gripped the bars with her dirty fingers, and pressed her face in between them.

He heard her say, "Kip, not you too," and she began to cry.

When he realized who it was, he tore himself away and rushed to place his face next to hers.

"Diana he whispered. What have they done to you?"

She sobbed quietly as tears ran down her face.

Pulled roughly away, Kip felt adrenalin rush through his body. With his hands still tied behind his back, he struggled and kicked, and managed to knock Carl's legs out from under him. He kicked savagely at the man until a guard clubbed him down from behind. They dragged his unconscious body into a cell and dropped him unceremoniously on the floor.

Carl stood outside the bars wiping the dust from his clothes. "I guess you owed me one; too bad it'll be the last free act you'll ever make."

Carl turned and walked quickly out of the chamber, glancing briefly at Diana as he passed.

"You inhuman bastard," she hissed at his back.

Carl stepped into the brightness of the yard, and made his way back to Bloundt's office. His mind was made up; it was time to distance himself from this rotten undertaking. Unlike Bloundt, he didn't care for the glory of returning to Germany with a cargo of uranium. The leaders back home were sick buffoons who used racial superiority as a salve to treat the festering sores of their own hate and greed. Bloundt was one of them, and the rest of the men here were no better.

Carl was different. He was an opportunist; cruel in his own ways, but he respected his adversaries. He acknowledged their strengths, took advantage of their weaknesses, and felt a sense of pride in his ability to outwit and overpower them. Now was the time for him to act.

He strode across the yard preparing to face Bloundt. As close as it was to the end of the mission, he knew he could escape with the Commandant's loot and not fear an extended effort to find him. In a few days, the men would be too busy with their own escape plans to waste their time looking for him. Their thoughts would be full of their accolades in the halls of their leaders in Berlin; and after that, drinks in the noisy beer shops and fondling the soft powdered skin of the women.

Carl announced himself at the door and entered. He gazed quickly at the locked chest partially hidden in an alcove off to the side. Bloundt sat at his desk looking at a map. He spoke without lifting his head.

"Ah Carl, we are near the end, eh? Have a seat. I have some things I wish to discuss with you."

Carl sat in an upholstered chair in front of the desk. Bloundt looked up from his map, and then rose to his feet with a gun pointed at Carl's chest. Carl did not act surprised. He had expected treachery.

"You," Bloundt said, "have mistakenly thought that I would tolerate your insubordination and condescending attitude toward my authority. I have weighed your value to the mission, and at this time I find it to be of no consequence."

He waited for Carl to say some words of rebuttal, but the seated man kept silent and even smiled.

"Oh, in the early days you did provide some utility. You scouted this site; you sought out the contacts that have served us well during the mission, but in the final analysis, I find your insolence and disparaging attitude has negated any residual value you may have."

Carl leaned back with his hands cupped behind his neck, still appearing relaxed.

"So Carl, I can only offer you one thing to compensate you for your past efforts; a quick death."

He steadied the gun as he said these words and began to put pressure on the trigger.

Carl's arm moved with the speed of a striking rattlesnake. The sharp, weighted blade bit deeply into Bloundt's arm, and made him drop the gun. He fell back into his chair clutching his wound. Carl was at his side in an instant. He scooped up the fallen weapon and cruelly slashed the heavy butt across Bloundt's forehead. Bloundt slumped unconscious in his chair.

Carl retrieved his throwing dagger from the bloodied right arm and wiped the blade on the man's sleeve. He dragged the limp body to the bedroom, where he gagged the man and tied his arms and legs. Carl then placed the unconscious body on the floor behind the bed.

Returning to the desk, Carl took a key from one of the drawers and opened the chest. He chose the most valuable pieces of jewelry, placing them on a blanket, and rolling it up as he went so that it would fit in a duffel bag. It wasn't too heavy, and the metal didn't clink together as he lifted it to his shoulder.

When he stepped out of the building, he waived a man over.

"The Commandant say's to get a sack of grub for Nick and me. I'll get the horses ready, and then I'm off to Chaco again."

Carl saddled one horse and had the other outfitted to carry a pack. He waited on the Commandant's front porch, and when the man returned with the food, he cinched the bag down alongside the duffel.

"We'll be back in a few days before you leave. Oh, the old man says not to bother him until he calls for dinner. No exceptions."

The man nodded his understanding and went back to his post.

Carl mounted and left the compound heading north into the desert. When he was out of sight, he turned east toward the uplifted ridges of the Continental Divide and vanished into the rugged hills.

CHAPTER 61

Kip held Diana's hand through the bars of the cage. At his urging, she told him how Carl and some other men had abducted her and the students, and how a dirigible brought them back to this place in the night.

"Where are we?" she asked, "Do you know?"

"I'm afraid I do. We are at the mine. I rode a horse to Chaco and was beaten and tied up by Carl and a sick toad named Nicholas. There was another girl..." He stopped as he felt his throat tighten. "He was...going to kill her."

Kip let go of her hand and sat down with his head against the bars.

Diana, sensing there was more to the story, gently placed her hand on his shoulder.

"Did you know her?"

"Yes."

There were nearly four dozen captives in the cells. Some were sick, and there was a constant background of coughing and sobbing. Diana told him that their job consisted of loading ore into small rail cars, and that they were forced to work long hours with little food or sleep.

Kip remembered something Carl and Nicholas talked about, and he felt a cold knot of dread in his stomach.

"I heard someone say that the mission was nearly over. Diana, we have to find some way to escape soon. If we don't, we'll all be dead."

That evening they found Bloundt tied up in his room. He roared vehement oaths as his wounded arm was treated. He ordered men to ride out, and for planes to take to the skies in search of the traitorous Carl.

At dusk, when the riders and planes returned, they told him that no one had found any sign of the man. The riders that went to Chaco couldn't find Nicholas either.

CHAPTER 62

Nicholas knew he was in trouble. He had lost a lot of blood before he managed to secure a bandage of sorts between his legs. He'd used all of his energy to saddle the horse and had nearly given up, but his anger at the woman and what she'd done eventually gave him enough strength to lift the saddle and cinch it. He had to use a chair to climb on the horse, and he nearly passed out from pain when he did. His left foot was bloody and useless. The Achilles tendon was severed, and he'd painfully stuffed it into his boot to protect it. He felt light-headed, and he feared that he would die before he found any help.

When the horse started walking, he'd screamed in pain with every jostling movement the animal made. He'd sobbed like a baby, and salty ribbons of tears streamed down his face into his dusty beard.

Nicholas somehow managed to stay on the horse, drifting in and out of consciousness while the sturdy animal picked its way through the desert. When it stumbled badly on some loose shale, Nicholas fell from the saddle and lay still on the ground. The saddle was loose, and as the horse walked toward the mine, it eventually fell off.

The animal reached the gates as darkness fell, and one of the men immediately notified Bloundt. In the lights, he was pleased to see a large amount of dried blood smeared across the animal's flank. They called the guard who assisted Carl with provisions earlier in the day to identify the animal. He was noticeably nervous.

"Is this his horse?" Bloundt demanded angrily.

"No sir. He rode a bay." The man's eyes refused to meet his superior's stare. "It looks like Nicholas' horse."

Bloundt stood silent for a moment. "Just as well then; the treacherous bastard was probably in it with Carl. It served him right."

From the amount of blood on the horse, it was doubtful that the man had survived his wounds.

"Send some riders out in the morning to look for buzzards circling a dead man. If for some unlikely reason he is found alive, bring him to me; otherwise bury him."

Nicholas woke and found himself alone. His horse was gone, and he thought it would return to the mine and someone would surely come looking for him. He tried to stand, and he screamed and fell. He slowly came to the realization of what awaited him. Unless someone found him soon, he would die in this damned desert.

He squinted up at the sky and knew he had to find shade and shelter. Crawling and dragging his body along, he eventually came upon a low overhang of shale. He used a stick to displace an ugly, fat lizard, and it hissed at him as it scurried away to find another place to hide. Nicholas removed his holster and tossed it into the shaded space, and then he crawled in after it. He positioned his body to where he felt the least amount of pain and placed the pistol where he could reach it. He felt marginally satisfied that he could protect himself from marauding animals at night.

Bloundt's riders might have found Nicholas the next morning if it hadn't been for the small deer killed nearby and partially eaten by wolves. The vultures ignored the men who investigated the carcass from a distance with their binoculars.

Nicholas woke to pain throbbing in his head. It hurt so badly, that it felt like clubs were beating his skull like a drum. In the heat of the new day, he realized if he didn't find water, he would be dead by nightfall. Sharp pinpricks of pain soon spread across his back, and when he reached behind him, he retrieved his hand and found it covered with ants.

His screams were ghastly as he flopped and dragged himself out of the hole. His ragged exertions brought on more pain and blood, and he simpered and cried like the dying animal he was. He rolled in the dust trying to rid himself of his small tormentors, and he finally ended up stripping off his clothing and removing the insects one by one.

After struggling to put his clothes back on, he fought off a wave of dizziness as he surveyed the vista of rock and sand around him. He got up and slowly limped away.

As the day wore on, he found tracks and realized he had come across the route his horse had taken after his fall yesterday. He found a stout stick that he could place some weight on and use as a crutch, and he hobbled along following the sign. Nicholas rested every few minutes and eventually realized his efforts were futile. The sun was already moving westward. As it sank lower, he gratefully took advantage of the pools of shadow. He rested and woke again at dusk.

Nicholas started walking again, seeking a shelter, and he noticed something in the path between two shoulders of rock. He stumbled ahead and found his saddle. Through grateful tears, he realized he must have cinched it poorly, and he thanked dumb luck that the horse had shed it and left him his canteen and a saddle blanket.

Nicholas drank gratefully and felt for the first time that he might get out of this desert alive. It was cooler now, and he found a sheltered spot to sit and wait for nightfall.

CHAPTER 63

Dan Yazzie sat within the broken walls of the Anasazi ruin and tended a small fire. A rattlesnake crawled through the door opening earlier in the day, and its flesh now cooked over his meager fire. The meat was tasty, and his spirits were renewed.

Dan felt that he had approached a crossroad in his life; a new life since leaving the smothering confines of prison. His quest for the monster had given him purpose, and the vastness of the open desert, instead of making him feel small and insignificant, had let his spirit soar without limits.

There were many times in his concrete cell, that he'd felt like he was suffocating. He would pass out only to awake later and repeat the cycle. He had hoped that he would die. He didn't remember exactly when he first began to experience the flight of his spirit from the jail cell while he slept. He did know, however, that it had kept him alive.

Now that he was free, what free man does not have something to live for? Dan lived to kill the beast that had taken his family from him.

He'd sent the white pilot away two days ago, and since then, he'd scouted the area for sign of the monster. He'd returned to the river near the pool and the waterfall looking for tracks, but had found nothing. Dan was beginning to doubt the reality of his quest. Just like when he'd traveled in his dreams, and when he'd seen the spirit of the old man and his dog. He wondered if the creature existed at all.

If it existed, did he not kill it with his dynamite arrows? There was no body, but there was some evidence. He pulled out the odd feathered quill he'd found near the pool and laid it alongside the one found earlier in the desert. They were identical.

Dan realized he was losing his focus, and he decided to build a sweat lodge and purify himself. He cut and placed pine branches in the ground to create a small circular space, and then he bent and tied the branches at the top. He laced other boughs through the branches and created an enclosed area where he could sit and have his ceremony. He hauled water and gathered some fist sized stones to heat. When darkness fell, he entered his steam-filled shelter to prepare himself for his final battle with Ye'iitsoh.

In the hot, pine scented darkness; Dan spent the night in a dreamy sub-consciousness. He made a potion from some herbs, and in his sweat lodge, he sought to see visions and find answers. Before the first blush of dawn, the dog appeared, and soon after, the old man materialized and spoke to him.

"Ye'iitsoh is very angry, and he is injured. He is coming to kill you. His thirst for vengeance is terrible, and I have other things I must tell you now. Hear me; the monster is more ancient than you can even think possible; much more ancient than the First Man and First Woman. He is older than the very rocks and sand beneath your feet."

The old man paused, and Dan thought about what he said. He was about to ask a question when the old man spoke again.

"Go back to the river, but this time further upstream. There is a spring and another small waterfall. You will find it beyond a wall of lava rock. This is where the beast has its lair. It is where you must go to kill it."

Dan finally slept, and on the mesa above the ruins, a malevolent evil stalked. It lifted its snout to drag it through the scent of the man far below; one red eye peering into the night, the other one clouded and half closed, oozing pus. Its mind was full of seething hate—and something else, something smaller and not so intense, but still real. Fear.

CHAPTER 64

The four riders arrived before dawn. They tethered their horses in a deep arroyo before crawling stealthily to the walls of the large mesa. Charlie Redman kept watch as Sam Begay and Val Tannin scaled the rugged cliff. He passed his binoculars to Lisa Ann, and then gazed around their place of concealment.

"They're out of sight now," she said, letting the glasses hang around her neck by the strap.

Charlie squinted at the orange sun just rising above the hills; it would be another hot day. He had to admit that Val gave them good information about the route up the escarpment and about the layout of the compound inside. The fact that he came about all this information alone and undetected was encouraging. He trusted him, but Sam still wanted to know more about the secretive man before he formed his bond of trust.

Charlie glanced at Lisa Ann, and she met his eyes directly. The straps of the heavy binoculars defined her breasts, and he felt his face warming under her frank stare.

Lisa Ann's stomach was in knots with worry about Kip. Her fatigue from the night's journey on horseback was the only thing that kept her from pacing.

"You don't think anyone will see them up there, do you?"

Charlie saw her concern. "Don't worry, Sam's an Indian; he was born sneaky, and I think this guy Val might know what he's doing too. If not, Sam will keep him out of trouble."

"Thanks for letting me come along," she said. "I know I insisted, but… well, just thanks."

Charlie snorted. "As I recall you were pretty graphic about what you'd do to us if we left you behind. I wasn't aware we had any other choice." He grinned lopsidedly, "I don't think even an Apache could have invented such cruel tortures as you promised us."

Lisa gave Charlie a shy smile. "Yeah, well I just wanted to be here to help Kip. I sort of owe him."

Even Charlie could see that there was more than that between Lisa and Kip.

Two men crawled over the weathered rocks on the mesa top and crouched for a moment behind a growth of gnarled juniper. Deep lines cut into the smooth, weathered rocks, and the place look like the scarred face of time itself. Val noted that Sam climbed well in spite of his size. Without a sound, the two men continued working their way across the rocks toward the inner wall of the compound. Val soon motioned to Sam to duck for cover, and they crawled behind a low ridge and cautiously peered around it to see a guard standing with his back to them. Taking advantage of his unawareness, they snuck around toward the inner cliff a few hundred yards away.

When they reached the edge, both men hunkered down and took in the open area below. Not much had changed since Val was here last. There were a few more rail cars, most appearing to be loaded with drums. They brought an engine in, and it sat on the tracks in front of cars.

"I guess you were right," Sam whispered, "it looks like they're getting ready to go somewhere pretty soon."

Val pointed out the hangers and the disguised cliff wall that hid the cavern where the dirigible was stored. Over the course of an hour, they counted three dozen men moving about. From time to time, a few ragged looking natives were seen carrying loads from the buildings. They were often beaten and treated with cruelty. Val pointed out the barracks and the house where the boss stayed.

Sam's eyes traveled along the inside perimeter and stopped at the stables where he saw a dozen horses in a corral. He lifted his binoculars to get a better look. When he took them down, Val noticed his expression had become very grim.

"What?" he whispered.

"One of the horses down there belongs to me. I gave it to a friend to use a month ago."

Sam's heart was cold as he thought of Dan Yazzie; was he a captive here too?

"I've seen enough," he said. "Let's get back down and find some men who can shoot and aren't afraid to get bloody. I think that once they hear about what we've seen, we'll have no trouble finding all the help we need."

They retraced their way across the mesa, avoiding the guard again, and came down the cliff to rejoin Lisa Ann and Charlie.

Sam said, "We've got to find some good men we can trust, and then get some firepower; and we had better do it fast."

They moved stealthily back to their horses and rode back to Judge Reilly's place.

CHAPTER 65

The morning sun had already warmed the desert when Dan Yazzie left the ruins and set out east towards Mt. Taylor. The People called it 'Tsoodzil', the turquoise mountain, the home of the Monster God.

He had slept after his ceremony in the sweat lodge, and woke with his mind and senses sharp. He'd savored the sounds of the world, and appreciated the bouquet of the new day. He had also smelled death; faint at times, but closer and stronger at others. Sometimes he sensed it behind him, sometimes ahead. It was the beast, and it had followed him.

"Come," he said to the wind so the beast would eventually hear him. "Follow me. See the warrior I am. I do not fear you. I have come to kill you. You can hide, but I will find you."

Soon, Dan was hiking up the wooded folds of the mountain. Much of the ground was a rough blanket of porous lava rock, blown out of the fiery belly of the volcano it once was. The hot sun brought the sweat from his skin, and when a cool breeze touched him, he savored the feeling.

He estimated he was about eight thousand feet above sea level when he reached the ridge where he and Kip first saw the large bear. He headed further along the slope and then climbed down and cut over to the other side and walked along the stream. Sometimes he had to step through water to get past obstructions in the narrow canyon.

The water burbled innocently as he negotiated downed trees and falls of rock, that obscured his way. The water knew he was here, the trees knew; he could hear them whispering.

Throughout the day, Dan wondered what the old man meant when he said the monster was older than the rocks, older than the First People; could it also be older than the other Gods?

The cool wind came again, and Dan noticed the sky turning darker. It was going to rain. August always brought some much-needed moisture, but for many weeks, it only teased the desert with sheets of falling water that evaporated before reaching the ground.

A large droplet hit him, followed by a half dozen others, and then a wall of pounding rain. He quickly looked for a route that would take him to the top of the ravine. The rain would soon wash away dirt, rocks, and even trees from further upstream, and it would create a grinding wall of debris as it rolled downhill. His foot slipped in the mud, and he jammed his knee against a rock. Limping slightly, Dan knew the pain would remind him of the danger he was in.

He neared the top and pulled himself over the lip by grabbing a small tree growing out of the bank. As he stood there catching his breath, the world suddenly exploded around him in a blinding flash of lightning.

When he came to, Dan was on his back; his bow was broken, and his pack scorched and in shreds. His shirt was a blackened rag. He stripped the wet remnants from his shoulders. Dan's arms didn't have much hair on them to start with, but what he had was now curled and burnt. He brushed the ashes from his arms and felt the short, remaining stubble. He lifted his head and hungrily lapped at the falling rain, and then he laughed loudly.

"I have found zigzag lightning," he roared drunkenly to the trees, "and I still live."

He left his damaged belongings and walked stiltedly across the top of the ridge until he found cover under a small overhang. He waited, shivering, for the rain to pass. A half hour later, the downpour stopped and the sun appeared again. Steam rose from the wet rocks. Dan continued his trek along the slope, and he could see the faded blue of the higher peak in the distance between the shaggy brows of pinon pine.

The ground became less rocky as it rose gently uphill. He walked through a narrow meadow where he found a game trail that cut between two shoulders of rock. Another small meadow continued beyond it, downward a short distance to a wall of lava by the edge of the stream.

He figured this to be the place the old man spoke of. The water appeared to seep from behind the lava, and when he climbed the rocks, he found a cool, dark grotto with a pond fed by a trickle of water from a higher ledge. A dark cave waited there, partly hidden by some bushes.

Dan sat down to catch his breath. His knife and his resolve were the only useful weapons he had left. He gazed along the ledge near the cave, looking for movement. When a small flock of birds landed near it, their lack of alarm buoyed his spirits, and he began to creep forward.

He came up to the cave and noticed a sluice of water falling over the rocks on one side forming the uncanny outline of a large, grinning skull. It was an omen. Dan shuddered and grasped the medicine pouch hanging from his neck. He picked up a rock and tossed it into the dark opening, and when nothing reacted, he entered.

The hollow area echoed with the sound of dripping water. Dan lit a match and found the space littered with debris and shattered bones. The room narrowed at the back and seemed to lead to another one. As he moved ahead through the opening, he noticed rivulets of water seeping across the floor. At the back of the smaller room, in shadow, he found a rounded, shoulder-wide hole in the wall. He struck another match, and peered into a narrow tube sloping upward five feet, with another dark opening at the end. Dan withdrew and returned to the first room.

Still cautious, he knelt to study the large chipped pelvis of a bear. As he lifted it, a loud, eerie scream came from the ledge outside the cave. The monster was here, and he had nowhere to run! Dan dashed into the second room and crawled desperately into the small hole at the back.

A loud roar reverberated behind him as he clawed his way to the top of the tube into a small black space. The beast roared its rage at the intruder, and it dug frantically at the small opening. Dan was no more than six feet away from the thing, and the air was bitter from its animal stench; its foul breath stung his eyes.

In a short while, the scratching and the smell of it was gone. His heart was still pounding so hard that he feared it would explode from his chest. When he reached for his matches, he noticed his hands were shaking uncontrollably.

He finally managed to stop shaking and light a match, and in the flickering light, he surveyed the small area. It resembled the inside of a clamshell, four feet high, and about eight feet in diameter. The floor was smooth, and he saw a small pool of water at one end. Dan guessed that seeping moisture had formed this place.

He lay quietly for several minutes, and then crept to the edge of the tube. Dan made only a slight sound as he moved, but the dim reflected daylight suddenly was blocked, and he recoiled again from the deafening bellow of the creature. The stench of the beast filled the small space again, and Dan crawled to the far end and lay silent in the darkness. Fatigue soon took him, and he fell asleep and dreamed.

He saw himself inside his cold prison cell again, and he felt the close walls suffocating him like a heavy blanket.

Outside, on the ledge above the stream, the creature howled its hate and frustration to the world.

CHAPTER 66

Sam and Charlie gathered supplies and maps as they contacted men they trusted, and who could take care of themselves in a fight. A general meeting was set at the Judge's house to brief everyone about the abductions and other things going on at the Blacksparrow Mine.

At the meeting, Sam talked to the group and laid out his evidence. Afterward, he gave everyone the chance to go home and forget about everything he said, with no questions asked, or to join him and Charlie in an assault on the mine. Everyone stayed. They sat quietly with fierce expressions on their faces.

Sam laid out his plans, and a group of men took five trucks to a local welding shop to begin working on them with torches. They attached metal beams to the front ends to act as battering rams, and welded thick sheets of steel over the doors and windows to protect the riders from gunfire. They also strengthened the suspensions to handle the extra weight.

Charlie took an advance group of scouts on horseback to set up a clandestine perimeter around the mine. They would keep watch under concealment until Sam and the rest of the men finished modifying the trucks and collected the last of the supplies they would need.

Sam went to his office with Val to get the weapons that were stored in a large gun safe. In addition to rifles and boxes of ammunition, Sam handed out five Thompson submachine guns. He held one in his hands and admired it.

"Model 1921; .45 caliber, 100 round magazines. A little over eight pounds empty. I love these ugly things."

"Are they accurate?" Val asked.

"Who cares; at 700 rounds a minute, the guy you're shooting at will crap himself to death just hearing it go off."

"I hope we can get close enough to use them. Me, I'll take one of these rifles. Should we take the hand guns too?"

"Yes, I'm taking everything I can find, including my skinning knife."

The trucks were finished late the next day. While the men loaded the supplies and weapons that evening, Sam returned to his office and called James Avery at home.

The FBI man had just fallen asleep after emptying the last of a bottle of gin. He had been drinking heavily for weeks since setting up Sam's ambush by the planes. He had taken money from Bloundt for too long to hope to put it behind him. In addition to his duplicity, he had also recruited Donaldson and Jacobs, two of his agents with mediocre records and convenient moral flexibility, to help him. Unfortunately, he'd found it necessary to arrange for Donaldson's killing too. The bastard had gotten greedy, and his partner Jacobs had cheerfully volunteered to do the actual killing, making it look like the work of a local gang. That left just the two of them to split the money coming in every month from the mine.

The phone rang a second time, and he woke up and reached groggily across the bed for the handset.

"Hello," he rasped. The line was silent. Annoyed, he said, "Hello," in a louder voice.

"Hello James," lisped a familiar Indian voice that Avery's brain refused to recognize. "Oh it's me alright, your old buddy Sam Begay. Surprised to hear from me?"

Avery scrambled to sit up, his eyes wide with horror.

"But…" The man stuttered as his mind tried to make sense of this impossible thing. "Sam is that you?" He was fully awake now. "Where are you? When you didn't show up for our meeting a few weeks ago, I tried to reach you at home and at the office. I sent men out to look for you. Where have you been?"

Sam chuckled, "Good try Jim. I just called to let you know that I'm alright, and I'm looking forward to seeing you again in person. You won't be leaving town anytime soon, will you? Because I'd like that. I'd like to track you down and see the fear in your eyes when I finally catch you with your back against some cold wall. No, on second thought, your smartest move is to stay home and just wait for me. You'll be more comfortable, don't you think? You needn't bother stocking up on extra food though, you probably won't have time to eat it."

"Now look you bastard…"

Sam interrupted, "Well Jim, it was sure nice talking to you and catching up on things. We'll see each other soon."

Sam slowly hung up the phone.

"Sam, I…" Avery heard the click of the broken connection.

Sam's expression was savage. If Avery could have seen him, his blood would have turned to ice, and his heart would have stopped.

Instead, Jim Avery dropped the phone and ran to the bathroom.

CHAPTER 67

One of the junior officers came to Bloundt's quarters, catching him in an ill-tempered mood as he was going over some maps. Bloundt gave him an annoyed glance before nodding for him to speak.

"Shall we send out the men again sir?"

Bloundt turned back to his work, dismissing the man, "No Kirk, tell the men to stay here and finish their other duties. We no longer have the luxury of time to search for Carl and Nicholas."

When Kirk didn't leave, Bloundt raised his eyes to the uncomfortable looking man.

"What is it Kirk? Is there something else?"

"It's…some of the men sir."

"Oh damn it man, what is it this time?" The Commandant's face became red as he anticipated hearing some absurd nonsense.

"It's just that, when we blow up the mine sir, just before we leave; some of the men would like to use their guns on the prisoners first."

Bloundt couldn't hide his surprise at hearing such a thing; even from the misfits in his crew. He stared at the man and pondered the unusual request.

"It is a bit unnecessary, but then I guess we can afford to allow the men to let off some steam. We have plenty of ammunition to spare. All right Kirk, tell them I'll allow it, but only after I give the order. We can't let the bastards get too trigger happy, can we?"

The Commandant watched the man leave, and leaned back in his chair with a disgusted look on his face. Then, as if deciding something, he stood up, buckled on his side arm, and walked out of the building. He called over two guards and had them follow him across the yard to the underground cages. Bloundt pointed out the prisoner he wanted brought back to his quarters, and then left.

When the guards arrived with Diana Witherspoon, Bloundt frowned at her disheveled condition. Her hair was dirty and tangled. Her shirt and pants were torn and filthy. Diana made it a point to stand as straight and proud as she could, and only fatigue keep her from crying.

"Miss Witherspoon, I'm sorry that our facilities aren't what you're used to. It can't be helped, but I'd like to offer you the use of my washroom to clean up. Someone will bring you some water and fresh clothing. When you're finished, I have a proposition to discuss with you."

He waited for her response, and when she didn't speak, he told his men, "Put her in the guest room so she can use the private bath. One of you will stay and guard the door while the other brings the water and clothing. Take your time Miss Witherspoon; wash away the last few weeks. We'll talk again when you're more presentable."

Diana stood numbly in the bathroom. She looked at her dirty face in the mirror and began to cry softly. After a short wait, there was a knock on the door in the other room. A guard stepped in, and brought her a large container of water and a bundle of clothing.

When he left the room, she noticed that there was no lock on the door. Her heart began to beat faster; a possible means of escape? No, she heard Bloundt speak to the guard standing on the other side of the door.

"See that she is given all the time she needs to make herself presentable."

The guard give a clipped, "Yes sir," and Bloundt walked away to answer a ringing phone. She listened at the door and heard him speak, but she could only make out a few words. It sounded like he was frustrated or angry with someone.

"Look Avery," his words were spiked with menace, "you are not to come here under any circumstances. That was part of our arrangement."

At the other end of the line, Avery's face contorted with rage. "Not any more it isn't Bloundt! Because of your men bumbling Sam Begay's death, I've been invited to a shootout with the crazy bastard himself at my own house! I'm getting out of here and you're taking me with you."

Bloundt didn't say anything.

"Did you hear me?" roared Avery.

"Are you telling me that Begay is still alive?"

"Yes he's still alive!" Avery screamed. "Don't ask me how; and he's threatening to kill me! You have to get me out of here, now!"

Bloundt responded calmly. "Alright James, but you can't come here. Tomorrow before dawn, be waiting in the *Valles Caldera* at the Via Grande east of Las Alamos. Keep your car lights on, and when you hear us overhead, be ready to climb a rope ladder. If you must bring any belongings with you, be sure that you can carry them by yourself or they're not coming aboard. Is that clear?"

"Yes, yes," the red-faced Avery agreed. He was obviously relieved. "I'll be there; just be sure you are."

"Very well James."

Bloundt hung up the phone. If Begay was alive, the call to Avery meant that something was about to happen.

Bloundt turned to the guard across the room, "Gerald I'm moving up our departure schedule again. We will be leaving after midnight tonight. Tell Fisk to meet me at the dirigible hanger in twenty minutes, and then come back here to guard the girl."

When Gerald returned, Bloundt left and walked across the compound. Word was already getting out about the new departure time. Fisk was waiting for him. The man had checklists to complete prior to flight. He assured his leader that they could accommodate his new schedule.

Because of Bloundt's planning, and insistence on speed over recent weeks, most of the work was already finished. There was the final matter of prepping the dirigible, which would begin now. Bloundt's other team would inspect the locomotive and start it at the proper time for a dawn departure. Of course, the horses would stay; let them eat their fill today and turn them loose before dawn.

There was the matter of the captives. The charges would need to be set. Bloundt called off the promised 'gun practice,' stating that the men had more important things to focus on.

Kip was sick with worry over Diana. He returned from the morning's work and couldn't find her. He asked some of the other men and women about her, and he was told that the Commandant had come earlier with two guards, and took her away.

As Kip sat on the floor with his face in his hands, he heard a commotion from the cages down the line. The sound of shouting and wailing became louder, and Kip stood and went to the front of the cell to try to see what was going on. He saw a team of guards working on something, moving slowly down the corridor toward his end.

"I don't like the look of this," he muttered.

Then he saw what they were doing. They were stringing dynamite along the walls and ceiling throughout the entire section. He looked around and realized that if the charges were set off, the entire cavern would collapse and bury them all.

Bloundt motioned to the guard to step away from the guest room door.

"Miss Witherspoon, I know I told you to take all the time you wanted, but things have changed. I must insist you finish what you are doing in the next twenty minutes."

He heard a small noise from beyond the door, and then the soft pad of feet across the floor. Abruptly, the door flung open, and the woman ran directly at him with a pair of scissors held high in her right hand. He managed to get his own hands up, and then he fell over backwards, gripping her wrist and dislodging the weapon.

The guard quickly grabbed her from behind and held her as the Commandant regained his feet. He stood up, obviously shaken, and smoothed his hair back and regarded her calmly.

"I'm afraid we don't have much time to talk, so let's agree to be civil with each other. Here is my proposal. You will come willingly, aboard the dirigible when we leave tomorrow, and I will release all of the prisoners when we depart. I am sure there are some in your group that you would gladly make a sacrifice in order to save their lives. I have told the men not to shoot any captives. If you do this, you will be treated with respect, and you will not be put in chains."

Bloundt smiled inwardly at his ironic promise not to shoot the prisoners. Shooting would not be necessary; there would be no one left alive.

Back in the cages, Kip continued to worry about Diana; was she safe? No, she would never be safe in the hands of that evil butcher. Kip's heart was heavy, and his face, a mask of agony. In his mind, he replayed his botched rescue attempt of Lisa Ann at Chaco Canyon. Now he had another failure to torment his soul. He had to do something. Perhaps he would die, but at least he would die trying.

His reeling mind brought up images of his father Bertram on the day he'd walked out on the ice at the lighthouse. Was this how his dad had felt when he saw him on the ice floe? Kip had been horrified to see a long crack form; separating him from the beach. He'd run to the edge of the ice, just as his dad saw him and dashed from the lighthouse to help.

Had his father felt the same way as Kip did now? His father knew he might die, but he would rather die trying to save his son, than not act at all. Kip had always believed it was his fault that his father had drowned, but it was his father who had thought more for his son than he did for anything else, even his own life.

Kip understood it all now, and he felt the warm fire of his decision. He would find his chance, and by the look of things, it had better be soon.

CHAPTER 68

Dan Yazzie awoke hearing shuffling sounds from the chamber below. The sound eventually stopped, and the faint glow of sunlight reflected in from the entrance of the cave.

Dan decided to take action now. He was the strongest and the most capable he would ever be in this place. It was time to act before hunger and cold sapped his strength and his resolve. He preferred to live, but his vow of vengeance on the creature did not require that he survive the ordeal.

He gathered his thoughts for a moment, and then he gripped his knife in his teeth and slithered quietly down the tube headfirst with arms outstretched in front of him. If the monster were waiting for him, he would surely die. The fiend might just be playing a trick. It could be hiding somewhere, listening to the tiny scraping sounds of his movements.

Dan smirked and thought of the often-quoted line; 'it is a good day to die.' This was not a good day to die, unless his knife would first slit the throat, and take the life of Ye'iitsoh.

His fingers touched the bottom lip of the tube with his feet still hooked on the edge above. Dan was about to let himself fall out of the opening, when a heavy thrashing noise sounded directly in front of him. A shadow suddenly blocked the light.

Dan wriggled backward like a salamander as he struggled to reach safety. His arms and elbows scraped desperately against the gritty rock. Out of the blackness, a sharp, swift claw shot out and raked deeply down his forearm. He jerked his arm free, and with his hips now above the upper lip, he pulled himself backward, hitting his head on the low ceiling. Dan lay there in the blackness as his heart thrashed inside his chest and bright stars swirled in front of his eyes.

His forearm bled freely from the deep gash. It felt as if the wound was on fire. He used most of his matches to enable him to see, while he brought his ripped skin together and wrapped it with cloth torn from his trousers. The bleeding eventually stopped, but his arm still burned as if a branding iron were pressing against his skin. He wondered if the creature's claws were poisonous.

Dan rested, lying back in the small space, and thought of the times he'd been weighed and tested in his life. He had to admit to failure more often than not. He had learned from each test, however, and he knew what it told him about himself. He had made poor decisions; but when he failed, he made changes and corrections, and he grew as a man each time. He would wear the scars of what he'd done forever, like a brand on the inside of his skin where only he could see it. It would define him in his own eyes. The actions he chose to take because of his lessons learned; the course changes he made would instead, show on the outside and define him to the rest of the world. Dan chose to seek honor, and to attempt to redeem himself and bring peace to his spirit. A person could not go back, but he could walk a new path forward.

His thoughts returned to his current dilemma. Some hero I am, stuck in a dark, rock grave. I can die here like a fearful rabbit and never be found, or I can take this fight to the monster.

A light tingling rippled over his skin, and it was probably hunger, more than his resolve, that made him declare aloud; "I am a man! I am a warrior!"

He screamed the words at the top of his lungs, and lay back, stunned, as the sound echoed and faded. He listened intently, nothing, not even a small scuffling noise from below. It took him a moment to grasp the significance of this. He slid over, and put his knife in his teeth again and crawled down the tube. He heard only the small noises of water and the rushing of the wind.

Dan slid out the hole and fell to the wet floor. He crouched, holding his knife in the dim light. The creature was gone, but it would surely come back. Dan looked around desperately for some other weapon to help him fight the demon. He found nothing useful, but he stumbled upon a wide crack along the back wall of the cave, hidden in shadow. It looked big enough to accommodate his narrow frame. He knelt down, stuck his head into the dark crevice, and heard water dripping far away. He felt a cool, wet breeze against his face.

A loud eerie screech sounded close behind him. The beast had returned. Without thought, Dan dove headfirst into the cleft. There was no sense worrying about how he might end up. He fell blindly in the darkness for several seconds.

CHAPTER 69

Sam Begay stood in the lot outside the blacksmith shop watching the sun touch the western mesas. The building sat on a small piece of flat ground in the hilly, north side of town. A thick pinon shaded a corner of the lot while a ragged line of olive bushes marched down one side, growing through a broken wooden fence.

When the last truck backed out of the building, Sam gazed at the handiwork of his men. The five vehicles looked like jury-rigged military trucks. Battering rams jutted from the front ends, and thick metal plates with narrow viewing slits covered the windows. Each truck was soon loaded with guns and explosives, water, food, and medical supplies. Some of the trucks would pull horse trailers. Sam's would carry Kip's Harley. Their mission would be dangerous, and he desperately hoped they would all come out of it alive. His biggest worry, however, was that they might not be in time to rescue the captives.

It was getting dark, and Sam looked at his pocket watch. The men gathered around him as he went through a final briefing. They talked quietly among themselves afterward, waiting next to their trucks for the signal to be on their way. Sam put away his watch when it was time to go. He whistled, and lifted his arm in a circular motion.

"Time to head out," he shouted.

Val and Lisa Ann rode with him. The odd-looking armored trucks revved their engines, and they all drove single file out of the parking lot, down to Railroad Avenue. They turned left, traveling through Gallup, and then east toward Rehoboth. They turned off the highway a few miles beyond that, and took the primitive road north through the desert toward Standing Rock. The grim-faced passengers rode without speaking. The trucks slowed as darkness fell, and they eventually reached the staging area two miles from the large mesa.

They parked the vehicles out of sight along the banks in a wide wash, and some of the men saddled the horses and rode to where the forward scouts were waiting. When they arrived, they sent a rider back with news from the surveillance. They reviewed the information, and made a few minor changes to their plans. The riders then returned and informed the scouts.

The assault would begin at dawn, preceded by two men dropping into the compound under cover of darkness. Their mission would be to locate and release the prisoners, and attempt to keep them safe during the attack. Before dawn, a group of advance scouts would position themselves on the upper rim to provide sniper fire, and to lob sticks of dynamite into the compound to create confusion and aid in the assault. This would signal the five trucks to race to the front gates and batter their way in. Other men with guns would follow them through the opening.

Each truck held two men, the passenger carrying a Thompson submachine gun. It was a crude plan, but with surprise, and an attack coming from multiple directions, Sam hoped the confusion would overcome much of the resistance. In the cold, silent darkness, he asked their ancestral spirits to watch over them.

Sam joined up with Val, Lisa, and Charlie, and they hiked stealthily to the edge of the tall mesa. The dark wall rose above them, reaching to the glittering blanket of stars. Val and Charlie left Sam and Lisa behind, and began to climb. They made it only thirty yards before Charlie tripped, twisting his ankle, and suffering a deep cut to his hand.

"Shit," he said with dismay as he lay on the ground.

"What it is it?" Val asked, creeping back to his side.

"My hand...aagh, I jammed it on something and cut it wide open. I twisted my ankle too."

Val helped Charlie back to where Sam and Lisa waited.

"Someone else will have to climb and go inside with Val," Charlie said, clutching his bloody hand, and gritting his teeth in pain. "There's no way I can climb like this."

"I'll go in alone," Val said.

"No you won't," said a stern, female voice. "I'll go in with you, and don't any of you say different, or we're going to fight it out right here." Lisa's voice was full of determination. "Look, I used to be a gymnast in school. Kip Combs and I were part of a barnstorming show, and I was the wing walker. I know more about high places and climbing, than anyone else here."

Sam looked at Charlie and said, "I'm really not that good at rope climbing." Charlie glanced at Val.

"Like she said, Lisa and I will climb the mesa and drop inside and release the prisoners. We'll have them safe and secure when the attack begins."

Charlie gave Lisa his gear, and she and Val begin their climb. Sam and Charlie watched from cover as the two inched their way upward. When they could no longer see them, Charlie turned to Sam.

"I'm really not that good at rope climbing?"

"I'm getting old," Sam explained.

"Ok grandpa."

"Besides," Sam said, "do you think we could have stopped her from going?"

"Hell no," Charlie said. "She would have kicked both our asses if we tried. Good thinking on your part."

CHAPTER 70

Thomas Bloundt stood on his porch and surveyed the men working in the compound. The sun was setting, and the generators began to run, providing a background din as night fell. He drove his men hard, even though the loading and readying of the dirigible and train would be finished hours before their departure. He wanted to be out of this filthy place. Bloundt would leave in the dirigible well before dawn and meet Jim Avery at the Via Grande.

His body still felt the effects of the adrenaline that coursed through him, and he admitted to himself that something else also caused his blood to race: the girl, Diana Witherspoon. She was a dark-haired beauty, but she would be just one of the prizes he would take with him from this mission.

He would show them all back home, that he had succeeded against the odds and brought back a vital supply of uranium; and not only that, a captured military dirigible, and a mysterious, futuristic aircraft.

As for as the woman, he would tell them nothing—let them look at her and wonder how he, the son of the inept and disgraced, General Frederick Bloundt, could manage to complete such a mission and do it with such flair.

His mother had arranged to have him chosen for this assignment in the first place; courting favor from the Generals with her powdered breasts and willing lips. Bloundt didn't care what she used; he would heap wealth upon her, and she could hold her head high for the rest of her days. It was a fitting reward for her shrewd efforts to win him the chance to prove himself.

He smiled and pictured their foolish looks of surprise and disbelief. His pitiful father was the flawed one, not the son.

CHAPTER 71

Lisa proved that she was a strong athlete by easily keeping up with Val as they climbed the walls of the mesa. Now, they both rested and drank from their canteens as they sat hidden in a narrow cleft above the compound, keeping their eyes on the activity below.

"You were right about climbing, not many women could do what you did."

Lisa looked at Val with a raised eyebrow. "You'd be surprised at what we women can do when we set our minds to it."

She held Val's eyes with her challenge until he blinked.

"This girl, Diana Witherspoon; she's really something eh?"

Surprised by her question, Val said, "Oh she's alright. Are you in love this guy, Kip?"

It was Lisa's turn to grimace, but then her expression softened. "Yeah I am, but don't you ever tell him I said so. He can make me as mad as a bear, but then he'll do something sweet and…oh heck, I guess I love him, but that doesn't matter, he doesn't love me."

Val contemplated Lisa's words and said, "He rode a horse into those men's guns at Chaco to rescue you. I'd say he cares quite a bit for you."

"Yeah, well he was probably more worried about his Harley than me."

"Oh I see; you, not needing any help because of how you women can do so much when you set your minds to it. He probably knew you had everything under control, so he just focused on the safety of the motorcycle."

Lisa's eyes flashed, and she was ready to flay him with her words. She stopped when she saw his knowing smile, and stuck out her tongue, instead.

"Okay, I'll leave you alone about Diana if you'll do the same for me with Kip."

"Deal," Val said quickly, and noticed the shadow of something moving above them. He brought his finger to his lips for silence, and slowly drew his knife. They heard the scuffing of boots followed by a sigh of relief and the sound of water dripping. When it stopped, the sentry broke wind, and the shadow and the scuffing boots moved away.

The generators buzzed, and the lights made bright pools around the buildings. Val chose the path they would take after they dropped into the compound. Just as they were making ready to scurry down their rope, a large portion of the cliff wall below lit up as if someone opened a gigantic stage curtain. The opening grew into a huge, bright rectangle, and then they saw men appear from the opening, pulling a web of threads attached to something big. As they brought more of it out, Val and Lisa could see the shape of the black dirigible. It was as big as an ocean liner.

They shared amazed looks as the massive thing emerged.

"My gawd," she said under her breath.

"Quick let's go," Val whispered, "their attention will be focused on the airship."

CHAPTER 72

Diana Witherspoon reluctantly agreed to Bloundt's proposal. Fear and desperation had coiled inside her like a tightening knot, but now, she chose to turn it into anger and purpose. The horrid man's offer of freedom and safety for the others, in return for her agreement to be his consort, was at best, a lie and a nightmare. She was determined to rid the world of Thomas Bloundt at her first opportunity. She suspected that he was the one who ordered the death of her father, and she swore that she would die happy if she could take him with her.

The attempt with the scissors had been a mistake. She saw now, that a properly obedient and submissive female would eventually find an opportunity to end his life. Whether escape was to be a part of her plan, she would just have to see.

Diana was back in the guest room under guard, while Bloundt left the building. She opened her eyes from a nap and woke to the sound of rain starting to splatter on the roof. Soon the sound filled the room with its din. She decided to try to open a window and let in some cooler air, and thought briefly of escape. She shrugged it off; there was nowhere to go or to hide. Her face reflected back in the darkened glass, and she was startled to see her features morph into another face. Val?

Val stood in the darkness behind the building with Lisa Ann. Both were soaked to the bone. When Diana realized the apparition in the window was real, she lifted the sash, and with a look of joyous disbelief on her face, she reached out and touched his face. He started to speak, but she motioned for silence. She squeezed out the small window as Val pulled her into his embrace. She held on to him, covering him with kisses.

"I've heard of a girl acting forward, but this is a bit much," Lisa Ann said with a smirk.

"Who is that?" Diana was surprised and felt a touch of jealousy.

"I'm Lisa; now shut up, we've got work to do." She couldn't help feeling a small twinge of jealousy herself.

"She's right," said Val. "We've got some people to save."

The three of them made their way slowly down the dark alley behind the buildings. The rain came down even harder now, pelting them with large, cold droplets as they made their way toward the mineshaft.

In the center of the compound, standing under the envelope of the dirigible, Bloundt viewed the loading of the supplies and the incredible winged aircraft. They left the Sparrowhawks behind to make room, and to cut down on weight. The crew wheeled the machine past him, to a crane that lifted it into the bay above. Even with the rain, Bloundt's spirits were high. The sight of the flying wing always filled him with joy, and he smiled as he watched it secured in its berth.

He mentally went over his remaining tasks. He would check on the locomotive and the five loaded cars next. Then he would inspect the preparations made to destroy the mine and the human evidence inside. He thought of Diana again and called one of the men over.

"Gunter, as soon as you finish here, go to my quarters and bring the girl to the ship. Lock her in my cabin and see that she is comfortable. We'll be leaving in just a few more hours."

When Gunter arrived at the Commandant's quarters, he told the guard that he was to take the girl to the dirigible. They both entered Diana's room and found it vacant. Then they saw the open window.

"Fool," spat Gunter. "If you've let her escape…" He let his statement trail off, leaving the guard's own imagination to complete it. "You stay here and search the quarters in case she's hidden herself. I'll go out and look for her."

He ran out into the rain and circled around the building. He set off down the alley, and thought he saw a blurred shape moving ahead of him.

"Shit," Val whispered from their quick cover. "There's someone coming. "You two go ahead; I'll try to stop him."

Diana and Lisa both looked worried. Val waved them away and crouched ready to ambush the intruder. As Gunter came closer, Lisa Ann suddenly jumped out with her jacket held over her head, and walked toward him.

"Well it looks like you got me," she said. "This rain is sure something, isn't it? I didn't count on getting so wet. Say, how about you just take me back to my room, and we can forget all about this."

Gunter couldn't see the girl's features very well in the darkness, other than that she was wet and shapely. He led her back to the building, and shouted to the guard that he found her and was taking her to the airship.

Val and Diana watched in dismay as the man led Lisa away.

"Why did she do that?" Diana asked. "They wanted me."

"I think she realized that you know more about the slave pens than we do. You'll give us a better chance of saving the captives."

"But we've got to save her too."

"No time right now. We've got some work to do and not much time to do it in."

CHAPTER 73

Bloundt returned to his quarters after he inspected the train, and the radioactive ore stored in the steel drums. Each had a painted label identifying the contents as salt. His best crew would occupy the train and make sure it found its way across Texas, over the Mississippi River, and through Florida. At a certain southern harbor, another crew would load it onto a freighter. The ship would make its way to northern Europe and arrive in Germany two weeks after Bloundt and his men landed in the dirigible.

The purloined airship would cause a sensation, and the futuristic aircraft, a scientific furor, but the arrival of the uranium ore would be like the cherry on the strudel. Thomas Bloundt would complete his revenge on his enemies and detractors. He would feed crow to the lot of them, and hold his head high as he stepped down the marble halls of the Chancellor's Palace with his beautiful, dark-haired consort on his arm.

He thought of all this as he lay back in his quarters, relaxing until it was time to take to the sky. Diana would be waiting for him in his cabin. He wondered if she would be compliant, knowing that no escape was possible, or if she would react like a jungle cat backed into a corner. She was full of surprises. He was smiling when he dozed off.

Outside, along the edge of the compound, Val and Diana stealthily evaded the men around the periphery. When they neared the mine entrance, they almost ran into a group of workers who were complaining about Bloundt deciding not to let them have their gun practice on the captives. The pair hid behind a small shed, and soon realized that they would have to wait for the time being. Another work crew joined the group, and they all milled about finishing the loading of the airship.

Val breathed his frustration as Diana snuggled closer. They held each other to keep from shivering while they waited for the men to leave. Val used this time to brief her on the plans for the dawn attack. He told her what they needed to do to insure the safety of the captives.

CHAPTER 74

An hour after Val and Lisa Ann began climbing the mesa, Sam watched the clouds begin to cover the darkened sky, blotting out the stars. As he waited, he heard the first rumble of thunder, and then rain began to pelt the dry ground. The droplets quickly increased to a downpour, and he ran in the mud to where the men waited with their trucks. He waived his arms and whistled for their attention. The rain meant danger; the rain meant flood, and the trucks and all the men were standing in a wash.

They quickly got the idea and rushed to throw their gear into the vehicles and race for the higher embankment. A few put on their lights, and Sam gritted his teeth, hoping no one would notice. He was right to worry. The sentries notified Bloundt, and he gave the order to board the dirigible immediately and prepare for liftoff.

Relieved that he had decided to launch a day early, Bloundt gathered the last of his things and crossed the courtyard to the tethered airship. It was still raining, and he gratefully stepped under the protection of the vast envelope bobbing above him. He called to his officers, and told them of the sighting. The lights could only be evidence of men in the desert. Because of the nearness to the mine, and in light of Jim Avery's frantic call, it could only mean one thing; that they were here to attack.

The dirigible would be ready to leave in fifteen minutes. Those who were not boarding, would escape on the train, and would likely face some armed resistance when they left. He ordered his men to set off the charges in the mine just before they were ready to start down the tracks. They must leave no evidence of the captives behind. The train would move out a little before dawn to give the men some darkness to help cover their escape.

The *Nighthawk* lifted from the compound a few minutes after 3:00 a.m. Sam stood near the trucks, and he and his men watched the dark ship rise above the mesa. Lights from the compound reflected dully off its lower surface, allowing them all to see the size and shape of the craft.

"Will you look at that," Charlie Redman said reverently.

"What is it?" asked one of the men, looking around to the others with concern.

"It's a dirigible," Sam said, sensing fear of the unknown in the men. "It's a white man's boat for sailing in the air."

When the muted moaning of the ship's engines reached the men, Sam added, "Listen, you can hear the motors that make it fly."

They all watched the long cigar shape turn to the east. Sam was worried. Were they too late? They needed to get inside the mine now.

"Alright," he bellowed, "you men who are snipers and explosive handlers, get moving to the top of the mesa. You have one hour to be in position and start throwing lead and dynamite. We can't afford to wait any longer. You men with the trucks will leave for your staging point in fifteen minutes; and keep your lights off. We have to start our assault early, and hope that our people make it to the captives in time. You men on the mesa, I want you to begin lobbing your dynamite as soon as you get in position; if you can pick off any of the mining crew, do it. The trucks will begin their run at the gates as soon as they hear the first charges go off. Is everybody clear on this?"

Words of acknowledgement followed, and the group quickly dispersed.

"Sam, you sound a little worried," Charlie said, joining him by the truck.

"Not worried; scared shitless that we may be too late to save anyone."

Five miles north of the mesa, a dark form groaned and shifted painfully underneath a small ledge. Nicholas was cold, and he shivered uncontrollably, even though his feverish brain was burning up.

He had come to the point that he wished for death to take him and relieve his suffering. Infection raged through his loins, and he had begun to bleed again. His foot was swollen and cemented into his boot by the crusted blood he'd lost due to the slash of the girl's knife, severing his Achilles tendon.

Through the drumbeat of his overworked heart and the pounding rain, he heard the moaning of the *Nighthawk's* eight diesel engines. It took him some time to register the meaning of this, and then he screamed and tried to rise from his prone position. Alas, his body would not obey. Left behind, and no doubt presumed dead, he fell back crying. With his last hope for rescue gone, Nicholas closed his eyes and accepted his fate. A blessed numbness washed over his body, and he slept.

CHAPTER 75

From their hiding place, Val and Diana watched the dirigible rise above the mesa walls. When the remaining men dispersed to attend to their other tasks, the two made their way to the entrance of the mine. The rain was letting off as they walked inside and followed the iron tracks. Diana showed him where the tunnel to the prisoners cages split off, and Val noticed wires along the floor. As they crept along in the dim light, they could smell the stench of sweat and the sounds of wailing and crying.

When they could see the cages, they also saw where the wires connected to the wrapped bundles of dynamite placed throughout the chamber.

"Those inhuman bastards," she said. "They meant to kill every one of them."

"Not anymore," corrected Val. "We'll make sure of that."

Just then, he heard a sound coming from the tunnel, and he quickly pulled Diana behind cover.

"But I know I saw someone come down here," complained a voice echoing from the opening.

"You just saw a reflection from some quartz rock, you fool," chided another.

Two shadows approached the entrance of the chamber.

"I get to shoot first. I remember an Indian squaw that bit me when I was trying to make nice, and I'm going to teach her. Who are you going to shoot first?"

"Never mind you buffoon. We both have two guns with six shots each. Let's just see who can get the most. Just be careful not to shoot anywhere near the explosives."

"Yeah, ka-boom!" the first man giggled.

"Shut up, here we are."

"You don't think anyone in the yard will hear the shots, do you?"

"Nah; good thing too, the Commandant ordered us not to shoot the prisoners, but what he don't know won't hurt him. Besides, he's already miles away on the *Nighthawk* by now."

Once they saw what was about to happen, the captives began to shout. They pleaded with the two men, but to no avail. The gunmen gloated, brandishing their pistols, and they never heard the man and woman approach from the shadows behind them. Both carried a large rock above their heads, ready to strike. At an exchanged glance, each brought their rock down on their man's skull. The gunmen dropped like shapeless bags of flesh. Diana and Val quickly grabbed the pistols and ran to the cages.

She saw Kip pointing frantically at the other side of the wall.

"The keys!" he said, "The keys are over there!"

Within ten minutes, they freed all the captives. Some men were disconnecting the dynamite from the wires, while others made sure the two gunmen were dead. They were safe for now. Kip saw how Diana looked at Val as he explained to everyone what was going on outside.

"Kip I've got some bad news," she said. "We think Lisa Ann was taken aboard the dirigible when it left a little while ago."

"Lisa Ann? You mean she's alive? She was with that Neanderthal, Nick Ells, at Chaco Canyon the last time I saw her. Are you sure she's alright?"

"Yes," Val said, "but just for the time being. I was there at Chaco, and saw what was going on when you were taken to the mine. I rescued her; and then she ended up rescuing me."

"You did? I mean, she did? Then how did she get caught again, and put on the dirigible?"

Val looked at Diana, and then back at Kip. "Well, it's sort of a convoluted story"

"Say no more," Kip held up his hands. "Anything to do with Lisa Ann is always convoluted. Save it for later; let's get out of here."

CHAPTER 76

The *Nighthawk* climbed as it headed east. Their course would take them over the peaks surrounding the Via Grande. They traveled slowly to save fuel, and to arrive to meet James Avery just before dawn. At this height, the eastern horizon already showed the faint blush of the new day.

Satisfied that the ship was running smoothly, Bloundt took his leave of the control car and made for his cabin. He would check on Diana and assure her that her greatest adventure had just begun. His ego wouldn't let him consider that she wouldn't be a willing partner when they became the new sensation of German high society.

He reached the cabin and rapped on the door before inserting his key. He remembered the surprise she gave him with the scissors. Would she be demure, or would she charge him like a wild animal? The question intrigued him, and frightened him at the same time. He would be ready for whatever role she wished to play. He opened the door slowly and peered inside.

She lay facing the wall on the built-in cot across the room, possibly asleep. He noticed something different about her. Her hair color was lighter; it fact, it looked blonde. How did she manage that? My, she was a surprising woman. His blood warmed at the thought of the months they would have together, and how he would learn the secrets and pleasures of her body. She would learn too, though she may not find it as sublime an experience.

It would not last forever, probably a year, or even less, before he would discard her to pursue some other conquest. He closed the door and walked to a cabinet to remove a bottle of schnapps. He filled two glasses, and then spoke softly to the girl.

"My dear, we are finally off on our adventure. Would you like a drink to celebrate?" He saw her move slightly. "All I have is this Schnapps, but I think you will find it pleasant."

He lifted both glasses, as Lisa Ann sat up and faced him. His jaw dropped, and he spilled some of the liquid.

"Who the hell are you?"

"Well, who the hell are you, too?" she replied. She got up and snatched one of the glasses from his numb hands. Lisa quickly tossed it down. "You're going to have to give me more than that to get me in a talking mood."

It took a moment for the man to regain his composure. He tossed back his own drink.

"Please make yourself comfortable. I have an errand to run, and when I return, we can continue our conversation."

Bloundt left the room and locked the door. He returned quickly to the control car. His face was red by the time he arrived, and he roared at the first officer.

"Where is he? Where is that motherless, shit-stick, Gunter?"

The men in the car turned their heads at his outburst. The first officer stammered, "He's on the aircraft deck sir, checking on the tethers of your flying wing."

Bloundt stormed out of the room, up the ramp, and back to the aircraft deck. When Gunter saw the Commandant approaching, he clicked his heels and saluted.

"Your aircraft is traveling well sir."

Bloundt feigned nonchalance. "Ah, yes that's good. Gunter, I just realized I didn't ask if you had any difficulty bringing the young lady to my cabin before we left."

Gunter brightened up and began to tell the story of how he'd discovered that the girl had escaped through the back window of her room.

"I suspected that she had only recently gone missing," he said, "so I ordered the guard to thoroughly search her rooms while I ran outside behind the building. I saw her escaping in the rain and captured her. I then brought her back to the ship and locked her in your quarters, as you ordered, sir."

Bloundt scratched his nose. "So you found her behind my quarters and brought her to the ship?"

"Yes Commandant."

"And you saw no others? No other girl?"

Gunter appeared mystified. "Why, no sir. She was the only one there."

"I see. By the way, did you check the lashings underneath the wings here?" He pointed to a part of the aircraft that hung over the open space, beyond the trapeze retractors.

"No sir. I couldn't get down that far to observe the connections."

Bloundt stepped back and pointed to a support beam. "I believe you can get a proper view by leaning out over this section. I'll support you while you observe the lashings."

Gunter moved quickly to perform the task. He honestly felt that he had found new favor in his leader's eyes. He felt that the special attention he was receiving could possibly bring him some preferential treatment, or a promotion one day. He eagerly crawled out across the perforated aluminum beam while the officer grasped his ankles. The man hung down and stretched to view the underside of the wing.

"By the way Gunter, did you get a look at the girl when I first had her brought from the cages to my quarters?"

"Oh yes sir. She was a bit dirty, but quite a looker."

"And what did you think of her blonde hair?"

"Gunter squirmed slightly as the other man held his legs. "Blonde hair, sir? But her hair was black."

"Ah, yes it is."

Gunter felt uneasy now. He inspected the wing lashings and waited for the other man to pull him up. He glanced fearfully at the open bay below him, and the darkness beyond it.

"Imagine my surprise when I went to my cabin and found that the girl had changed her hair color to blonde."

"B-blonde, sir? But..."

"Well, no matter. Her hair is probably still black, seeing as how the woman in my cabin is a different girl altogether. How do you explain that?" Bloundt asked reasonably.

Gunter, suspended in air above a black hole to oblivion, felt his face flush, and his skin tingle with fear.

He stammered weakly, "A-a-are you joking sir?"

"Yes, yes I am," Bloundt chuckled. "And the joke is on you!"

He released the luckless man and watched him fall through the hole and quickly disappear. He savored the sudden scream that faded away just as quickly.

Bloundt returned to the control car. He informed the men that Gunter had suffered an unfortunate accident, and had fallen out of the ship.

He offered no other details, and none of the others dared ask. They exchanged a few furtive glances and quietly resumed their duties.

CHAPTER 77

The rain finally let up, and with dawn fast approaching, the men with the train were nearly ready to set off the dynamite charges and start their overland journey. The junior officer couldn't find two of the men. When he asked about them, a fearful looking guard admitted that he'd seen them sneak off into the mine.

"Each had two guns, and they said they were going to kill a few Indians."

"When was this?" shouted the officer, his anger directed at the not-so-innocent messenger.

"It was less than an hour ago."

The officer turned to a sturdy man on his left. "Take four others and go into the tunnel and bring them back. Try not to be too gentle with them." His eyes were full of fury.

The five men took their weapons and hurried into the tunnel. They stopped at the junction leading to the cages and listened, but they heard nothing. The group walked ahead, guns ready. When they reached the chamber, the dim lights revealed something they were not expecting; all of the cages were empty except for one that held the bodies of the two guards.

Before they could react, four guns blazed at their backs, and they died without firing their rifles. The emboldened captives now had five rifles and three more pistols. The strongest and healthiest took up the weapons and crept to the main tunnel.

The leader of the train crew was losing his patience. On top of that, he was becoming more and more nervous about an attack from the unknown force in the desert. He looked at his watch for the third time in five minutes, and made up his mind. If the team hadn't come back by now, that was their problem. His job was the safety of the train and the men on it.

"Set off the charges," he ordered. When the soldier standing next to him didn't react, he screamed at him. "Set off the charges now!"

The startled man hurried to connect the wires. He pushed the plunger, but nothing happened. He reconnected the wires and tried it again, and again. He looked at the officer with a shrug, just as a stick of dynamite exploded a few feet away, killing them both.

The rest of the crew with the train ran for cover as rifles began sniping at them from the walls above. Another explosion went off near the tracks, and two more detonated right after that. The men kept their heads down as thick dust and smoke filled the air. Those near the front of the train soon heard the roar of vehicles outside the gates. As a barrage of buzzing shells ricocheted off the engine, the lights of the trucks came on, and the gates burst open. The strange looking vehicles roared into the compound unleashing pandemonium with their machine gun fire.

The men on the train sought cover. Some jumped off and ran to the mine entrance, and encountered the murderous guns of the men they once held as slaves. There were many deaths to avenge, and the Germans who fell before them were just a start.

Somehow, the men remaining on the train were able to reach the engine controls. With a hissing belch of steam, the engine, and the cars loaded with radioactive ore, began to move along the track. The powerful engine pushed through the trucks at the gate and picked up speed as it charged into the desert. None of the men they left behind survived.

When the dust settled, Sam's crew rejoiced in finding none of their men killed. When the captives joined them in the yard, they received medical attention and food.

Val looked at the dark shape of the rapidly departing train, and he remembered the motorcycle in the back of Sam's truck. He had an idea. He quickly went looking for Kip and found him in a hanger, working on one of the planes.

"Kip, let's take your motorcycle and catch up with the train. I'll try to board it and stop it somehow."

Kip said, "I can't, I've got to get up in the air and chase down that dirigible. Lisa's on it and that bastard Bloundt has her."

Sam walked into the hanger just then, and Val turned to him. "Do you know how to drive a motorcycle?"

"Sure, I used to ride years ago."

"Good," Val said, "I'm going after the train, and you can drive me."

Kip was almost finished prepping the plane, when Diana came running in with a handful of charts.

"Kip I think I found something." She set the rolled papers on a nearby workbench. "Here," she said, "this is where we are. See all the lines coming from this spot; one going south off the page, and the others shorter and all in black. Now look at this one. It's in pencil, and it goes east to somewhere not too far away, and then turns northeast off the page."

"Where exactly does it make its turn to the northeast?" Kip asked.

"Right at the Via Grande, just west of Bandelier."

"That's where the airship is going. Someone said it headed east when it left. Hurry; help me get some men to wheel this plane out. I hope there's enough clear space so I can take off."

Fifteen minutes later, the Sparrowhawk roared down the runway and took to the air like a vengeful bird. Kip saw a pale plume of dust rising from the desert, and he knew it was the two men pursuing the train in his Harley.

CHAPTER 78

Kip gained altitude as he headed east in a pale dawn world of sky and earth. The Sparrowhawk performed flawlessly. It felt good to feel the powerful, well-built plane under his seat. How the men at the mine ever got ahold of the planes and the dirigible, was beyond him.

He let the cold air blow away the memories of his brief captivity, until the only thing he had on his mind was Lisa Ann. Funny how he could barely stand to be around her sometimes, and now all he wanted to do was find her and rescue her from the assholes that held her prisoner.

He urged the biplane for more speed, and he desperately hoped he could find the airship in the vast vault of the sky. The dirigible was a big needle, but the sky above New Mexico was a far bigger haystack. He had one clue; the course change at the huge volcano crater marked on the map. It could be a meeting place for something, before heading out toward their real destination.

Dawn brought out the details of the Jemez Mountains as the *Nighthawk* flew above the vast, grassy meadows where James Avery was waiting. They saw his car lights and slowly descended, maneuvering the eight hundred foot craft near to his location. Avery drove his car closer to meet them, and then he waited outside until he saw the long rope ladder dropped for him.

Bloundt stood at the open hatch with a few of his men, and they watched Avery heft a pack to his shoulders.

"Climb up," Bloundt yelled. "We have no time to stop."

As soon as Avery began his climb, the ships propellers swiveled and pulled the craft higher. The man struggled with the weight of his pack as he slowly made it up the ladder. He lost his footing near the top and clung desperately to the rungs with only his hands.

"Help me you bastards," he screamed. He was out of breath and clearly not in shape to be climbing with the weight strapped on his back.

"I told you to only bring on board what you could carry," Bloundt shouted. "If your pack is too heavy, you'll have to leave it."

"But…I can't." Avery was sobbing. "I can't leave it."

"Make up your mind. The ship will be at her cruising altitude before long, and you won't be able to hang on when the wind speed increases."

Avery sobbed again, and then struggled with his pack and let it slip from his shoulders. With the weight gone, he managed to regain his footing, and he soon crawled breathlessly over the top rung and into the cabin.

"You pompous ass!" he screamed at Bloundt. "There was almost two hundred thousand dollars in cash and gold in that pack."

Bloundt regarded Avery with a bored frown that drove the exhausted man to fury. Avery reached out to grab Bloundt, but the man moved quicker. He placed a foot behind Avery's ankle and shoved. Jim Avery staggered backwards trying to regain his balance. He teetered on the edge of the open hatch for a few seconds, his face a mask of hopeless terror. His scream was lost in an instant as he fell to his death.

"There, another loose end taken care of. Speaking of that, there is a young woman in my cabin who, undoubtedly, has information that I would like to be privy to. I may be occupied for some time. Captain, you may return to the controls and take us on the next leg of our journey."

With that, they closed the hatch, and the men left for their stations.

CHAPTER 79

Sam had a tight grip on the handlebars of the Harley. With Val wedged in the sidecar, they bounced and skidded down the narrow, rutted trail alongside the railroad spur. It was difficult to pick out the smoother parts of the road, and they almost flipped twice; saved only by the stabilizing effect of the sidecar. Sam had yet to glimpse the train, but black smoke hung low in the sky over the hills ahead of them.

Val clung to the edge of the sidecar for dear life, and he began to doubt the wisdom of their headlong flight after the train. Sam was gutsy, but he didn't have the same skill in handling the powerful machine that Lisa Ann did. He wanted to say something, but it was no use trying to shout over the noise of the deep-throated engine.

Val closed his eyes and immediately opened them again as they became airborne. They hit the ground twenty feet beyond a dip in the trail. He glared at Sam, who ignored him and concentrated on the rough road ahead. The car suddenly kicked upward, and Val found himself looking down at Sam while gravity and centrifugal force fought over his Earthly fate. Sam desperately jerked at the handlebars as the speeding machine spun drunkenly. They landed, still heading, more or less, in the same direction as before.

Val flayed the crazy Indian with his eyes. This time Sam noticed and answered with a sheepish grin. Val scrunched uncomfortably in his seat and stopped thinking of the danger that waited for him on the train—he wouldn't survive the ride getting there.

Sam braked, skidded sideways, and darted to the left down another set of ruts. They picked up speed again. Val wondered why the turn, but figured at this point, the best thing he could do was just hang on. The trail headed toward some hills. They slowed as they climbed, and eventually Sam stopped on a ridge. He jumped stiffly off the bike and jogged to the edge. When Val joined him, Sam pointed down the slope to the railroad tracks.

"Listen, I can hear the train coming closer. That means we might be able to get down to the tracks before it gets here. C'mon."

Sam found a trail, and they jostled and bounced downhill. At the bottom, he shut off the bike, and the two men crept closer to the tracks.

"We've only got a few minutes."

Val nodded at Sam's assessment, and said, "One of us has to go back and alert law enforcement about this."

Sam was thinking the same thing. He looked around and said, "Yeah. Stay safe on that train. I'll make sure to call out an army of men to help you." Pausing for a moment, he added, "And be sure to come back, I have some questions I want to ask you."

The chuffing of the train became louder as it negotiated a curve, climbing the mild slope.

Val clasped Sam's hand. "Don't kill yourself driving back like a fool with his ass on fire."

Both men grinned, and Val left to climb an overhang near the tracks. He would be in position to jump onto of one of the cars as it passed.

"I'll be back, Sam. Tell Diana, I'll be back."

"I'll tell her."

The train came up the track, and as it passed the ledge, Val made his jump safely. Sam watched the last car wind around a curve, and then he returned to the bike and kicked it back to life.

Gutsy guy, he thought, as he let out the clutch. He didn't know much about him, but he knew he would be glad to have him watch his back anytime.

CHAPTER 80

As Kip Combs flew over the vast bowl of the Via Grande, he saw a lone car parked in the middle of the expanse of grass. He overflew the vehicle and saw something on the ground nearby. He decided to risk a landing to find out what clues the scene might give him.

With the Sparrowhawk idling fifty feet from the car, he walked over and picked up a canvas pack. It was heavy, and when he looked inside, he could see why; it contained a large stack of wrapped bills and bags of gold coins. He dropped the pack and walked to the car. It was empty, but the engine was still slightly warm. He removed the keys and opened the trunk, but found nothing out of the ordinary.

Looking back at the plane, he took his bearings with the car and walked away in a straight line for a few hundred feet. As he got near what he had seen from the air, he ran up to the lifeless, broken body.

Thank goodness, it wasn't Lisa Ann. It appeared to be a middle-aged man wearing good clothes. His limbs were bent askew like those of a rag doll, and his body was sunken in the soft earth and flattened as if he'd fallen, or maybe was thrown from the dirigible. Kip ran back to the sputtering biplane, stopping at the heavy pack. He thought for a moment, then removed the stack of wrapped bills and left the rest. He stuffed the package into a bag in the cockpit and bounced through the grass until he picked up enough speed to become airborne.

The sun was up now. The pencil line on the chart Diana had found pointed northeast from the valley. Kip figured northeast would eventually cross the lower corner of Colorado, and then part of Kansas, Nebraska, and then Iowa; but no need to consider that, he would be out of gas long before then.

Many miles away, high above the Earth, Bloundt quietly unlocked the door of his cabin; no sense tempting a lethal surprise in case the girl was rash enough to try something. He opened the door slowly and saw her sitting on the bunk with a cigarette.

"I see you smoke; go ahead and finish it. We can talk when you're done."

"What do you want to talk about?" Lisa Ann exhaled.

"First; why don't you tell me who you are, and then you can tell me how you got here."

She took another drag and stubbed the butt in the ashtray. "That's easy, I'm Lisa Abbot, and one of your stupid guards brought me here."

Bloundt sighed and fought to control his temper; no sense souring the relationship so early. He smiled thinly.

"Well Lisa, tell me just how, exactly, did my guard come to bring you to my cabin, when I instructed him to bring someone else entirely?"

"I don't know; you'll have to ask him. As a matter of fact, I'd like to know too."

The Commandant pictured Gunter falling through the open hatch.

"That won't be possible, I'm afraid."

He reached nonchalantly toward his cigarette box near the girl and swiftly backhanded her. Lisa fell over, but she quickly leapt from the bunk and bore the man to the floor. She reached for his throat, but Bloundt reacted quickly and threw her across the room. He stood up, touched his neck, and looked at the smudge of blood on his fingers.

"I'd hoped to be civil," he said, "but I see you don't have the breeding to appreciate that."

He went to his desk, opened a drawer, and fumbled under some papers. He soon pulled out an ornate letter opener that resembled a dagger. Bloundt twirled the blade absently, and noted that the point dug a small hole in his thumb.

His meaning was not lost on Lisa.

"Like I said," she quickly piped up, "the guard was looking for someone else behind the houses. It was dark, and the rain was coming down hard. I jumped out from hiding with my jacket over my head. He grabbed me and brought me over to the airship."

"Ah," Bloundt replied, "now we're making progress." He paused to wipe the spot of blood from his thumb.

"And how did you come to be in the compound behind the houses in the first place; after dark, in the rain, by yourself...or perhaps not by yourself, eh?"

"It's probably all over with anyway, so it won't hurt to tell you. Two of us dropped into the compound to release the prisoners, while the rest of the men planned to hit the gates when there was enough light."

"How many men were in the group?"

"Between twenty and thirty, I guess."

"So, you say there were around two dozen of you altogether?"

Bloundt watched as Lisa Ann nodded. Her demeanor was much more compliant now.

"I don't believe such a small force could subdue all of my men. And even if they could, they still wouldn't be able to stop the train. No, I think your friends have already been dealt with, no doubt suffering the same fate as the captives."

"Oh yeah? Your men aren't so tough. Take that big goon of yours I took care of at Chaco Canyon."

"Do you mean Nicholas?"

"Yeah, the one who calls himself Nick the biter. What a joke."

"What do you know of Nicholas? He and Carl Walker were missing when we left the mine."

Bloundt eyes were narrow slits as he stared at the girl, remembering Carl's betrayal and thievery. He was sure the two men had plotted all along to rob him.

"I don't know anything about the Walker guy, but I had to take a knife to the other jerk."

"You killed him?" Bloundt face showed amazement.

"Maybe. I don't know for sure, but he took off on a horse with his balls almost cut off."

A slow smile formed on the man's face, and then he laughed.

"Then that's why his horse returned without him, and why its back was covered with blood."

Bloundt laughed again, and appraised the girl with a newfound respect. She had more spunk that he had given her credit for. It would be best to avoid antagonizing her unnecessarily, and certainly, keep her under lock and key.

The man yawned. "It seems I have no further need for information from you. You are somewhat pleasing to look at, however, and a man does appreciate having a woman like you around. I'll put you in another cabin—locked of course, and I may look in on you from time to time, just in case I have…more questions."

His sly look told her something altogether different.

CHAPTER 81

With the sun rising at his back, and a brisk, morning breeze blowing sand in his face, Sam retraced his path back to the mine.

When he drove into the compound, he found out that while he was gone, the men had seen to the immediate medical needs of the captives. By now, most had eaten and cleaned themselves up. A group of men had moved the bodies of the gunmen to the side, while others began searching the buildings for evidence. They interviewed the captives, but none could shed a light on the motives behind those who forced them to work so mercilessly.

They had wounded one of his men. He would go to the Indian Hospital in Gallup, along with the captives, for further treatment and evaluation.

A while later, Charlie Redman said, "We've looked everywhere, but we can't find any information about the destination of the train. We found burned papers, and the phone is disabled. Someone did come across an old road map of Florida, but it didn't have any special markings on it."

"Good work. I'll stay here with some of the men to secure the site, while you take the rest back to Gallup. You can bring the trucks up to carry those unable to ride a horse. As soon as you can, get to a phone and call the FBI in Albuquerque. Tell them about the train and the dirigible, and tell them what we have done here. Let them know that we have a man on the train, and that there are some dangerous people on it as well. Tell them the cargo is extremely dangerous: probably uranium. The train may not have passed through Albuquerque yet, but by the time you call, it could be part of a larger train, so have them check all recent traffic."

Sam thought for a moment, "And be sure to have them pay special attention to anything headed toward Florida."

Charlie nodded. "Do you want me to tell Avery anything, if I speak to him?"

Sam glared meaningfully, "Yeah, tell him I'll be giving my statement to the Secretary Director in Washington."

After the trucks and riders left, Sam and the remaining men secured the compound. He would have a mountain of reports to complete in a few days, so he started collecting his thoughts about the events of the past five weeks.

The freed captives, and those who died before them, had suffered most. He couldn't help thinking that it wasn't much different than the treatment his people had been subjected to, many times over the past hundred years, by other white men.

He and Charlie would speak to the tribal authorities in Window Rock, and their leaders would be quick to make their concerns known to the BIA. As for the captive Anglo students, they would have their own families to speak for them.

Sam toured the compound and listened to the stories about the battle. When he approached the aircraft hangers, he saw three bi-wing planes just like the one Kip had taken. What were the odds of him catching up with the dirigible? How could he even hope to find it; and how would he board it if he did? His was a fool's errand, just like Val's train ride. Hell, maybe they were all fools.

Funny how the odds meant nothing to someone who felt he had to take some kind of action, regardless of the risk. He hoped Val would survive the dangers on the train, and then return. He wanted to have a long talk with him. What little he knew about the man, only made him itch to know more.

Near the end of his tour, he thought of Dan Yazzie. He had feared for the safety of his friend when he sighted his horse in the stable, but Kip had told him that he'd taken the animal to Chaco Canyon after he and Dan confronted the monster with explosives. They hadn't found the body of the creature, and Dan told Kip he felt the monster was still alive.

Sam couldn't fathom the kind of danger Dan might be in, but he'd seen the determined look in his eyes, and he understood his savage resolve to seek revenge for the killing of his daughter and grandfather. Perhaps Dan was the only one who wasn't a fool.

Sam wanted to finish his reports as quickly as possible. Then, he wanted to ride into the desert to find his friend...to find out if he still lived.

CHAPTER 82

Dan Yazzie awoke and sensed a cool breeze on his face. It was dark, and he saw a few stars overhead through the branches of a twisted tree. His clothing was damp. Startled, he sat up and felt the cold rocks beneath him. Where was he? His mind had no answer, and he wondered if he was dreaming. A gust of wind whistled by, and he realized he was no longer underground. He felt the rough bandage on his arm and then remembered.

The creature had found him. He remembered the hot, hissing breath and the snapping jaws, as it tried to reach him. It sank its teeth into the sole of one of his boots, gnawing the bottom completely off as Dan escaped. He felt his bare foot sticking out of his right boot.

Dan remembered falling, and then seeing a rope dangling above him. He had climbed frantically, as a voice called to him and pulled him to safety. He remembered seeing the scar on the forearm of the leathery old Indian. Dan touched his own arm where his crude bandage covered the wound the creature had given him. It was on the same arm, and in the same place as the healed scar on the old man.

How could this be? What did it mean? Logic told him that this was all a dream, but he was no longer in the underground grotto; he was resting on the rocks of a low hill. Overhead, a cloudy veil was drifting away from the glittering whorls of stars.

An Indian is fearful when the spirits give too much attention to a mortal. Much is expected in return, and it is usually paid in blood. Dan knew he had a large debt to repay. He lifted his head to the sparkling night and shouted his willingness to give that payment. As his words vanished, he heard the moaning of the spirits. The eerie sound came closer, and then Dan saw the star eater. He still thought of the huge shape in those terms, rather than Sam's, gas filled airship. It was more fitting of a spirit. Dan lay on his back and he slept deeply and dreamed. In his dream, he heard another moaning high above him. It was raspier, and it sounded more urgent.

He awoke at dawn and worked out the stiffness in his limbs. His right boot was worthless, but he decided not to discard it. Instead, he tore more cloth from his pant legs and wrapped it around some moss and grass. He held the bundle under his bare foot like a pad and tied it to the remaining boot top. Crude but serviceable, he thought.

Dan was grateful he still had his knife, and with that simple tool, he prepared some traps to snare a meal. Later, he set out to find some wood to make a lance and a war club. By the end of the day, he had his weapons. He also fashioned a stout pole that might be useful as a lever or a blunt ram. He found shelter and slept fitfully through the night. At dawn, he set out for the badlands. He knew the monster would follow him, and he planned to choose the place he would make his stand.

Dan walked all morning, and when it became too hot, he found shade and set his snares. By evening, he had a hapless rabbit and a small dove for his supper, and then he slept again.

Late the next morning, Dan reached the place he planned to stage his ambush. In a weird landscape of eroded, sandstone pillars, and balancing cap rocks, he saw the massive arch that stood high over rough ground. The span was nearly 100 feet long, and it arched solidly, 150 feet above the scattered rocks below. The smooth upper surface varied between ten and twenty feet wide and it overlooked a tall, stone needle. The needle stood fifteen feet away from the arch, its flat top, slightly lower. This would be the killing field.

He spent the rest of the day planning his trap, and as the sun passed westward, he called to the spirits to come and watch.

CHAPTER 83

The roar of the powerful Wright engine hammered at Kip Combs' ears as he sped his way over the Sangre de Christo Mountains. The engine noise would have given most people a headache, but to Kip, it was music. As the sun rose, he flew over lower Colorado and then towards the upper corner of Kansas. His face was a mask of grim resolve. Kip watched his fuel gauge, grateful that the Sparrowhawk carried an extra teardrop fuel tank—quite useful for trying to catch a fast dirigible over the open prairie.

He saw a few small towns and a small airstrip every so often, but for the most part, it was just flat grassland below. Sweeping the numbers on the clock, he looked for the dirigible as he cruised at five thousand feet. He knew it was the maximum altitude for a lighter-than-air craft. The sun was overhead now, giving his eyes a rest from the glare. He knew fatigue would become a factor as the day wore on, and he hoped luck would bring the airship in sight before dark.

Hours later, Kip caught himself daydreaming, worrying about Lisa Ann. He glanced at the fuel gauge, and saw it was time to find a place to land and refuel. There was a town ahead; perhaps it had an airfield.

Kip found one past the far edge of the settlement. He touched down on smooth grass and taxied to the larger of two weathered hangers. A boy came running out to meet him, grinning in awe at the rare plane.

"Sparrowhawk isn't it?" he asked, knowing it was, trying to show off his knowledge of airplanes.

Kip jumped stiffly to the ground and stretched his knotted legs and back. He couldn't help but smile at the boy who appeared to be no older than twelve, but he sure knew his airplanes.

"A genuine F9C-2, ain't that so mister?"

"You got it right Kid. Say, is there a place here where a guy can get some coffee and a sandwich?"

"Yeah sure," he pointed to the building he had just come from. "There's a small restaurant inside; they can get you something."

"What's your name boy?"

"Jeet; everybody calls me that."

"Okay Jeet, there's fifty cents for you if you can find someone to get me refueled by the time I wash my face and grab some chow."

The boy assured Kip that he could get the tank filled quickly, and he dashed off with a 'whoop'.

"And don't forget, a Sparrowhawk like this has an extra teardrop tank to fill."

"Aw mister, I know that. I'll tell him you need it filled in fifteen minutes."

"If you can get it done that quickly, I'll give you an extra fifty cents."

The kid ran away with a big grin as Kip dropped his own. He could feel the heavy weight of fatigue bearing down on him. Sleep would have to wait: now he needed food.

He found the plane fueled and waiting for him, and Kip paid for the gas and made a quick, walk around inspection. The boy followed him quietly, until he couldn't keep silent any longer.

"Are you in a race mister? Is that why you're in such a hurry?"

Kip ruffled the boy's hair. "Yeah, I need to get someplace fast. Here, you did a good job." He handed the boy a dollar. "Oh, by the way, has anyone seen any unusual aircraft passing by earlier today?"

"Oh you bet, but it wasn't a plane, it was a dirigible; a big one too. Me and my friend Mickey saw it from the other side of the airfield, over that way. It was before noon, and it was flying high, so we couldn't tell what kind it was. It looked big though."

"Could you tell what direction it was traveling?"

"Well… I'd have to say northeast; maybe more east."

A few minutes later, Kip was back in the air climbing to five thousand feet again. The short break and the coffee and sandwiches made him feel much more alert. A wolfish grin replaced the grim expression he wore earlier.

Hours later, the landscape was dotted with houses and barns. Roads crisscrossed more of the ground and an occasional railroad track stretched into the distance. The towns still looked small, but there were more of them. People would be coming home from work by now; kitchens would be full of the smells of cooking and baking. His mind treated him to a vivid memory of hot stew and fresh bread, and his stomach growled as he thought of how long ago he had eaten his egg sandwiches at the airfield.

Dusk was falling, and Kip's eyes felt grainy. His fuel situation was a problem again. Worse yet, he could see a wide expanse of water and a large city on the horizon. He knew he had to land and refuel before attempting to cross, what he presumed was, Lake Michigan. Kip was scanning the horizon for an airfield, when he caught a glimpse of something in the distance, high over the water. Was it a dirigible? It had to be!

He glanced at his fuel gauge and then back to the speck above the horizon; he decided to risk the chance of running empty. He throttled back slightly to conserve his remaining fuel and slowly overtook the dirigible well over the water.

He had no other option but to find some way to enter the ship. As he approached it, he took a chance that no one was at the observation windows in the tail. He maneuvered around the long, lower fin, and then directly underneath the envelope. He was surprised to see that the design was reminiscent of the lost *Akron* and *Macon*. He ignored the observation windows in the front of the fin and heard the deep buzzing of the twin rows of propellers. When he saw what appeared to be the hanger bay, he noted with dismay the closed doors.

Of course, they were closed; so how was he going to get on board? Kip glanced fearfully at his fuel gauge and saw even worse news. If he didn't find a way to get in within the next few minutes, he would experience what grim pilots called a "water landing."

Could he fly over the top of the airship and jump? If he ditched the plane, would he survive the fall and not slide off? Or instead, would he follow the biplane into the waves below? It was risky but he was desperate. Why didn't he think this through before?

Well you did it now buddy; this is probably the end for you. You can't get aboard, and you can't go back.

"Shit," was all he could think to say. It was the most common remark uttered by a pilot making a fatal error. He said it again. "Shit."

He was about to try his desperate gambit, when he spied a small "U" shaped hoop hanging beneath the ship. Relief flooded over him. It was as if a hand was reaching down to save him.

Since a dirigible could lift only one plane at a time into the hanger deck, they constructed a small, fixed yoke for waiting planes to essentially "park" while they waited their turn.

Adrenalin sharpened his senses, and Kip maneuvered to the perch and caught it with the skyhook on his upper wing. He immediately killed the engine and collapsed back in his seat with relief.

CHAPTER 84

Kip eyed the rear of the control car 200 feet ahead of his plane. There were observation windows in the back where the gangway was located, and someone would see him eventually. It was getting darker now, and he hoped a casual onlooker would not notice him. Come morning, however, someone would see the plane. He had to find some way to get aboard and find Lisa, and then get back to the Sparrowhawk before dawn.

Kip looked at the vast expanse of varnished cotton skin above him. A stout knife could penetrate it, but he didn't carry one. He looked around the sides of the cockpit and behind his seat, and he found a metal box with a first aid emblem and the word 'survival' lettered on it. Opening it, he pulled out gauze and scissors, and then found a very sturdy and serviceable knife. It even had special saw teeth on one edge of the blade. Kip attacked the fabric above his head, and he was able to cut back a large flap.

As he crawled from the cockpit into the darkened belly of the dirigible, he heard the rumbling sound of the inboard diesels. Having logged a modest amount of time aboard the Navy dirigible *Akron* three years ago, he knew that inboard engines meant the ship used nonflammable helium for lift.

Kip looked around to get his bearings. If Lisa Ann were a captive in here, it would be in one of the cabins up front. Kip reached a narrow catwalk and moved forward cautiously beneath the huge, pillow-like gas cells.

He felt an odd sense of familiarity. It was hard to explain, but if it weren't impossible, he would swear that this ship felt like the *Akron*. True, it didn't have the white cotton skin; this one was painted black, but the girder design and layout seemed familiar. He knew a place where the name of the ship might be displayed on a plaque, but that was in the control car. It would be too risky to try to get in there to see it.

Entertaining an odd thought, he remembered, three years ago, scratching a design on one of the girders of the *Akron* out of the way of foot traffic. It was located in a corner on the port side near where the enlisted men bunked. If his etched image was there, then he had a real mystery on his hands. His heart skipped as he thought of the impossible likelihood of something this inexplicable being true, for the *Akron* sank in the Atlantic in 1933 with a loss of seventy-three men.

Kip hid twice to let crew members pass by, and he finally came to the spot he was looking for. It was an outer support girder, and he reached around the side and felt faint marks with his fingers. He needed more light to see.

Kip reached into his pocket for a match and peered at the back of the duralumin girder in the flickering light. His face went pale when he saw a scratched outline of a biplane. He blew out the match and turned to leave, when three men grabbed him and quickly subdued him and bound his hands.

Kip refused to answer any questions. Bloundt frowned; he was determined to find out how this man was able to breach security and get aboard. He had an idea and ordered the other captive brought to him. The only place he could have boarded was at the mine; perhaps these two knew each other.

Men brought Lisa Ann into the room while Kip stood sullenly with a guard at each arm.

"Kip," she blurted, and then regretted her outburst.

Kip smiled briefly and said, "It's okay Lisa, I was just coming for you. They saved me the time of finding you, is all."

"Yes, yes," said Bloundt, with a satisfied smile, "you do know each other. I would like you both to save me some time too, eh? You will tell me what I wish to know or…I can resort to other means of eliciting your cooperation."

He glared at the girl, and then at the man for emphasis. Kip tried to coax a bit of information from their captor, while appearing to cooperate.

"I'll tell you whatever you want to know, but first, tell me how you came to be in possession of the *Akron*?"

Bloundt, impressed by the young man's uncanny deduction, said proudly, "Yes, yes, but first, how did you get on this ship? The last I saw you, you were in one of the cells at the mine."

"I escaped and stole aboard." This was true, and Kip hoped the German would think that this occurred at the mine, rather than just recently.

"Very well," Bloundt said, "and I will tell you that some of my men were aboard the *Akron*, and they took control of the airship while it was over the Atlantic. They killed the other crewmembers of course, and some of my men were coached to carry out the ruse that they survived the sinking and were rescued in the water. They told the authorities a fictional story of a fierce storm breaking the airship to pieces. The crew, however, tethered the *Akron* to a mooring tower on a freighter waiting for it at the scene. Its cargo hold was full of debris, supposedly from the wreck, and it was scattered into the sea."

"But that's impossible," Kip said with a sneer. "There's no way that you could fake the special framing design of the *Akron*. They sent divers down and saw it."

"Oh yes, but come now, think of who made the ship: The Goodyear Zeppelin Corporation. And who do you think designed the craft in the first place?"

"A team of German engineers," Kip said, grudgingly.

"Yes, so you see it is not so mysterious; just innovative. Now be so kind as to tell me what connection you have to this girl?"

"Her uncle owns an airfield in Albuquerque. She works in the office, and I run a flying service in one of the hangers."

Lisa Ann had her own question. "So where are you taking us?"

Bloundt thought for a moment before answering. "Possibly nowhere; at least that would apply to your friend here. You, on the other hand, may have some options, but that's enough talk for now. Tie them both and place them in her room. Have the door locked and keep a twenty-four hour guard outside in the hall"

CHAPTER 85

Bloundt woke before dawn and went to the control car. The airship had traveled through the night over the broad expanse of Lake Michigan; truly more like an inland sea than a lake.

Nearing the thick forests of Michigan's northern peninsula, Bloundt had the captain slow their forward speed. After a quick check of the airship's position, he had the *Akron* brought down to four hundred feet above the cold, churning water.

"Keep the course due north at fifteen knots. I have some duties elsewhere, and when I return, you can take her up again."

He climbed the stairway and made his way to where the two captives were. The guard saw him enter the passageway and stood at attention.

"That's alright Horst; I came to see the prisoners. Were there any disturbances or problems?"

"No sir. They've been quiet"

"Fine, let me in. I'll be out in a few moments with the girl. I'll signal you when I'm ready."

Kip and Lisa Ann heard the two men talking, and rushed to replace their gags. They got down on the floor and rearranged the ropes across their ankles.

It had taken them hours to untie their hands and feet and remove the gags. While they were free, they had discussed how they would overpower the guard and slip away to the Sparrowhawk. Bloundt's arrival caught them before they were ready, and it presented a new challenge to their escape plan.

They waited for the door to open with their hands behind their backs as if still tied. Bloundt entered the room and the door locked behind him.

He addressed Kip first. "I'll be taking the girl while you remain here. I have a proposition to discuss with her." With that, he bent down and removed Lisa's gag.

"Yeah, well maybe *the girl* doesn't want to go," she snarled.

"I can assure you that what I have to discuss will be of great interest, not only to you, but also to your companion. I regret having to bind you. Here, let me untie your feet."

Bloundt went down on a knee and reached for her ankles, realizing too late that the rope was loose. Lisa swung a roundhouse punch that connected solidly with his jaw and knocked him backwards on top of Kip. Kip had his gag off, and he twisted it tightly around the man's neck while Lisa lay across Bloundt's legs to keep him from kicking and alerting the guard.

"Is he dead yet," she hissed.

"I sure hope so. Okay, you go over to the other side of the room and distract the guard when he comes in. I'll jump him from behind. Are you ready?"

"Wait," she whispered, and opened her shirt, baring enough skin to distract a dead man. She nodded, and Kip rolled his eyes. He muffled his voice and called to the guard.

"Okay, open up."

They heard the man get up from his chair, and then the rattle of the key in the lock. Just as they had choreographed it, the guard opened the door and stepped in with his eyes bugging out at Lisa. Kip hit him on the back of the neck, and the man crumpled to the floor like a rag. They tied and gagged him, and then peered out along the corridor.

"What do we do now?"

"We get to my plane; follow me." Kip didn't want to tell her that it was nearly out of gas and had room for only one person in the cockpit.

Watching out for the crew, they stayed behind cover as much as possible and took a roundabout route through the hanger deck. Kip stopped suddenly in the dim light as his eyes took in the lines of the strange aircraft secured there. His mouth hung open, and he made little gasping noises. Lisa Ann roughly grabbed the front of his shirt.

"Jeez, let's go. Do you think we're on some kind of sightseeing tour?" She dragged him away from the unusual flying wing, and they continued toward the back of the dirigible.

"Wait a minute," Kip said. "I've got to do something first." He answered Lisa's impatient look of inquiry. "I can't let them take this ship."

He went through a tool bin and found what he was looking for: a sharp crow bar. He began to rip open each massive helium bladder as they passed beneath it.

"Try not to breathe the gas."

The alarms soon went off, and after slicing open another bag, Kip took Lisa toward the place where the Sparrowhawk hung outside the ship. Already the dirigible was tilting and beginning to move sluggishly.

A yell from behind made him turn around and he faced the charging, wild-eyed, Thomas Bloundt. The man tore at Kip with his nails and beat him with flailing fists. Kip was down, sprawled across a girder as Bloundt tried to break his back. Kip struggled to gain room to throw a punch, when he heard a meaty *smack* and saw the sole of a boot appear like magic between Bloundt's legs. The man made a high, helium altered squeal as he grabbed his crotch and collapsed between two beams.

"Will you hurry up," Lisa said impatiently, "It looked like you two were going to start dancing."

Kip grinned broadly, "Saved again by Lisa and the boot of doom." He pulled her to him roughly and kissed her on the lips. "That's for being mad at him and not at me."

He led the way, crawling across the girders to the open flap. When Kip stuck his head out, he could see the surface of the lake a few hundred feet below the plane. They were losing altitude, and the sound of water ballast jettisoned, and the revving of the engines added to the chaos erupting all around them. He slid feet first through the hole into the cockpit and yelled for Lisa to follow.

"I forgot to tell you, there's nowhere for you to sit."

"Great," she said, as she slid into his lap. She crawled forward onto the upper wing between the braces of the skyhook. "I've walked on crazier wings than this before, let's go!"

With a quick, appreciative glance at her bottom, Kip started the engine. It fired, just as the insanely enraged Bloundt dropped headfirst into the cockpit. The two men struggled desperately, while Lisa turned and tried to kick the flailing attacker. She missed and caught Kip in the mouth.

He glared at her for a second before he yelled; "Hold on."

Kip reached for the release lever on the skyhook and pulled it. The Sparrowhawk dropped like a rock, and Bloundt's body became airborne as he and the plane parted. Kip knew they were very near the water; he also knew the dirigible was going to crash. He opened the throttle and banked away from the airship, barely leveling out a few feet above the waves.

Lisa pointed, "I see the shoreline."

Sure enough, in the dim light of dawn, Kip saw the outline of a wooded landmass. Just then, the engine sputtered. It caught, then sputtered again and fell silent.

"What are you doing?" she screamed.

"No more gas honey, we're going swimming."

The plane was a very poor glider, but Kip managed to keep the craft level until the wheels touched the water. The plane nosed in, flipped, and quickly began to settle. Lisa's head was the first to pop out of the water. She looked around desperately for Kip, and he finally surfaced nearby holding a flotation vest and a canvas sack.

They both watched with solemn reverence, as the *Akron* touched the waves bow first. She settled with gasbags exploding through her skin. The airframe groaned and twisted as it slowly disappeared beneath the boiling sea. A last burst of helium escaped the ship with a flatulent roar, and she sank as if in apology.

CHAPTER 86

By the time Kip and Lisa managed to reach the shore, there was no evidence left of the *Akron*. They staggered onto the beach, lay in the soft sand, and slept, both grateful for the warm rays of the sun.

When Kip awoke, he looked at Lisa. She sat with her arms around her knees and gazed across the water with a faraway look.

"You came to rescue me," she said.

"Yeah, I did." Kip lay back with his hands behind his head.

"We made a pretty good team back there, didn't we?" She toyed with a strand of matted blonde hair. "We worked pretty well together, huh?"

"Yeah, I guess."

She finally got to the real question she wanted to ask. She knew there was unhappy baggage between them; they had both done their best to push each other's buttons for almost a year.

"So why did you do it?"

"Why did I do what?" He peered at her with one eye closed, squinting from the glare of the sun.

Lisa jumped over and straddled him. She grabbed two handfuls of shirt and stuck her face into his.

"Listen you flying clown, I'm just telling you that I'm grateful, that's all."

Kip quickly rolled over and trapped her beneath him. She tried to push him away, then stopped, confused by the serious look on his face.

"Lisa, I don't care what you think; I'm just going to tell you straight."

She held her breath, fearing his next words.

290 Thomas Alan Ebelt

Kip's expression softened. "I love you. In spite of everything, maybe because of everything; I just can't help it, I love you."

Lisa was lost in his eyes, and she raised her hands to his face, fingers trembling. With a little sob, she crushed her lips to his and clung to him fiercely. They kissed again, and again, each time more tenderly.

Soon their bodies responded. She tugged at his belt, and he shakily worked at the buttons on her shirt.

Later, they lay naked on the beach. A soft breeze cooled their skin, warmed by their exertions and the sun. After their mellow aura faded, they walked together to the water and dove into the cool waves to wash away the sand.

When their bodies were dry, they shook out their clothes and dressed.

"Do you have any idea where we are?" she said, rolling up her pant legs and picking up her shoes.

"Somewhere in Michigan; the northern peninsula I think."

He rolled up his pant legs too, and picked up the bag he had brought to shore.

"I'm hungry," she said. "You don't happen to have a sandwich in there do you? I don't even care if it's wet."

"Nope, no sandwich, but I've got something we can buy a few million of them with."

She watched Kip pull the tightly wrapped bundle of money from the canvas sack.

"I took it from a pack lying near a dead guy at the Via Grande. He probably fell out of the dirigible. There was a bunch of gold too, but I left that behind."

Lisa looked at the money. "Do you think anybody will miss it?"

"Nope, I don't think dead guys need it for anything."

They walked a mile down the beach, and when they saw some houses beyond the trees, they put on their shoes and hiked through a narrow strip of woods. They came upon a small settlement of weather-distressed houses. The buildings appeared abandoned for years. They followed an overgrown pathway to an open area with larger buildings grouped around a small, sheltered harbor. The clear, blue water protected from the weather by a long arm of limestone capped with a green carpet of trees.

"What is this place?" she said. "It's so pretty; and it's a ghost town. That looks like an old factory over there; see the dock area?"

"Yeah," Kip said, "just stumps and pilings now. I don't think we'll find any food here. Maybe the trail will take us to a town, or at least a farm house."

As they walked away, they both felt warmed by the glow of this beautiful, silent place. They eventually found a farm and inquired about something to eat. The people were friendly and fed them. They were glad to have company to brighten up the boredom of living so far from town.

They learned the name of the abandoned community was Fayette, and Kip and Lisa Ann vowed to return someday. The place would be forever special to them.

CHAPTER 87

Two thousand miles south of Fayette, a small tropical disturbance formed east of Florida near the Bahamas. As it drifted westward, it strengthened. By the time it entered the Gulf Stream, the United States Weather Service classified it as a weak Category 1 hurricane.

It moved slowly away from Andros Island in the Bahamas toward the upper Florida Keys, rapidly increasing in intensity. By September 2, around 9:00 p.m., it made landfall at Craig Key and was the fiercest Class 5 hurricane to hit the U. S. in the twentieth century.

With wind speeds of over 185 mph, and a storm surge of 20 feet, the hurricane struck near Islamorada in the upper keys and destroyed nearly every building in the area. It was called the Labor Day Hurricane. The total loss of life was in excess of 400 people.

The Florida East Coast Railroad was the main transportation link from mainland Florida and the Keys, and the storm destroyed or severely damaged major portions of it. On Upper Matecumbe Key, an engine and ten cars lay washed off the track caught in the storm surge and high winds. Only the engine remained standing.

On Tuesday morning September 4, Sam Begay was working at his desk in Gallup when he got a call from the Temporary Acting Station Chief at the FBI office in Albuquerque. Sam and Charlie Redman were awaiting news of the missing James Avery, and of the attempts to locate and stop the missing train.

"Begay, this is Acting Chief Jack Whorten. We are still getting some last minute details about the train, but I have some news for you about former Chief Avery. First, the car and the body found outside of Las Alamos last weekend are his. He suffered multiple broken bones, consistent with a fall from over 200 feet. How that could happen in the middle of that big meadow hasn't yet been determined, although he may have been killed elsewhere and dumped.

We found something else that doesn't seem to fit. There was a backpack full of gold coins found near the car, and we can't figure why an assailant would leave that kind of loot behind.

It seems your report of a dirigible at the mine, and Avery's collusion with these men, may provide us with an answer; if indeed his body was dropped from the air."

Sam thought of the possibility and said, "He knew I was on to him, and he may have been trying to run; but why he would be thrown from the dirigible is a mystery to me. Not that I'm unhappy to hear about it. Do you have any other information on the plane that was chasing it?"

"No, nothing yet—a few flying saucer sightings from Kansas and Nebraska, but nothing confirmed."

"I did get one report on the train. It seems the hurricane really messed up their operation. Damn sad thing; all the people dying, and the property loss, but the news is that we managed to secure the material we were after. Seems there were a bunch of Veterans nearby that helped us out—all on a classified basis of course. It's sad that so many never made it through the storm."

"Any reports of a white male matching the description I gave you?"

"You mean the guy who calls himself...let me find it here...ah, Val Tannin?"

"Yeah, that's him."

"No, no word about him. A little hard to pick out one blond, white man with a tan, out of a crowd in Florida, I guess."

"Yeah I guess," Sam agreed.

"Sam I'll need to have your full report this week. The people at the top in Washington want me to bring it in person, and they want it yesterday."

"Okay. Charlie can watch things here. I'll set out for Albuquerque within the hour."

"Thanks Sam, I'll see you this afternoon. And Sam, I just want you to know that I think you did a damn fine job with this; for whatever it's worth."

"Yeah, thanks." Sam hung up and saw Charlie Redman's inquisitive look. He told him what Whorten had said.

CHAPTER 88

Dan gazed across the stunning forest of weird, eroded rock. The rising sun turned shadows into grotesque creatures hiding amid the strange tableau. He watched a few bright flashes of lightning shoot through the dark clouds on the horizon. He believed this to be the land where spirits lived.

Dan felt the presence of the beast somewhere, just beyond the whisper of the wind. He knew this would be the day. They would both enter the killing field, and one of them would die.

Dan sat on a low, adobe wall that was once an ancient kiva, and he began to chant his warrior's song. He told the monster that he would kill it today.

After a quick breakfast of jerky and water, he picked up his weapons and made his way to the top of the mesa near the natural bridge. He repeated his song. He wanted the creature to know exactly where he was, and to know that he was talking to him.

He came to the arch and walked halfway across to where the needle of rock stood a short fifteen feet away. Measuring the distance with his eyes again, he imagined how he would use the pole; placing the end against a lip of rock near his feet and vaulting through the air.

Dan retraced his steps to the shoulder of the mesa and walked the route he would use to lead Ye'iitsoh to his doom. He hefted his spear and admired the pointed obsidian tip bound to the end. It was a well-balanced weapon. Dan knew he could put some strength behind it, and it would fly true. He would use this first, but unless he was very lucky, the creature would still come for him. He would wait with his war club. It was a wooden shaft about two feet long with a short leather rope attached to one end, a rounded, fist-sized rock tied securely to the other end of the rope. Fighting men back into dim history had used this type of weapon. He hoped to stun the creature with it, and maybe, damage it.

With the beast injured, he would taunt it and run, leading it across the bridge. He would use the stout pole to vault to safety on top of the needle, and draw the monster to fall to its death on the rocks below. It could work.

Dan made a face. He was glad to be away from the dark cave and the damp underground grotto, even though the experience seemed to have cured him of his fear of small, closed spaces. Perhaps fear no longer had a place in his life. He no longer feared the monster.

He had been close to it and had felt its sharp talon. His nostrils had burned from the stench of its breath, and its rank, feathered body, but he did not fear it; instead, he hated it.

He went to a place where he could see the creature when it approached, and he began his vigil. It was a shame he had no more dynamite. He shrugged. Dan guessed the creature's running speed would be close to his own. If he could just slow it down a little, he should be able to stay ahead long enough to lead it to its deserved end.

The sun was high overhead when the monster finally came. It was swift and silent; waves of heat distorted its shape as it charged. Dan barely had time to stand and heft the spear before it was upon him. He released the shaft and dodged out of the way, as the creature passed. He saw the stone point imbedded in one of its legs when it stumbled briefly to the ground. The body was tan and brown in color; blue quill feathers jutted from its head and down its back. The heavy tail had a feathered knot at the end, and it stuck straight out as it ran.

The beast's mouth was full of finger-sized teeth that snapped noisily in its pain and anger. When it got up, it dislodged the spear, and Dan saw that its elongated forelegs supported a feathered membrane attached to its body.

The fiend hissed its rage and charged again. Dan whirled the war club over his head and lashed out as it passed. He bounced the tethered rock off its head, narrowly escaping the long talons again. When Ye'iitsoh staggered and turned, he could see that one forelimb hung at an odd angle, and one of its deep-socketed eyes was a bloody mess.

Dan felt the hair rise on his neck as the creature made a horrible, wailing cry. This was when an animal was the most dangerous; when injury and frustration transcended pain and turned it into a thing of mindless fury.

"Come catch me weak one," he shouted and threw his club at it. He picked up the long shaft. "If you can catch me, I will let you kill me."

He ran toward the rock arch with the creature in fast pursuit. A flood of adrenaline shot through Dan as he willed his feet to go faster. Soon, he heard the monster's heavy pad and rasping breath close behind him.

He chanced a backward glance and was distracted for a second. He stumbled on a loose stone and felt something pull in his ankle. A blossom of heat radiated up his leg, but there was no pain. By the force of his will, he continued at an even greater pace.

Dan was on the arch now. He had no feeling in his legs. He sensed he was speeding along drunkenly as he came to the spot where he must place the pole. A mistake here would mean a bloody end to his life.

Dan could smell the scent of the beast nearly upon him. In one fluid motion, he placed the end of the shaft in the crevice and leapt, pulling himself upward and ahead. He gave a desperate cry of exertion as he vaulted over the wide gap and landed on his back atop the sandstone needle. The rough rock tore at his skin, and he narrowly avoided sliding off the far edge.

Dan rolled over and saw the monster in the air, gliding awkwardly toward him. Without thinking, he reached for the pole and pointed one end at the animal's chest; the other end lay propped against a shallow lip of rock. When the creature struck the pole, its momentum carried it upward and over the edge of the needle. The wooden shaft spun end over end as it followed Ye'iitsoh to the rocks below.

Dan lay on his back and laughed. He shrieked his victory, long and loud. Exhausted, he started to feel waves of pain, each one washing harder against his senses. He crawled to the edge of the rock and gazed down at the broken, feathered body. A cool wind whistled past his lofty perch, and Dan closed his eyes and slept.

When he awoke, he had no idea how much time had passed. Heavy raindrops stung his skin as he gingerly rolled over to look at the body on the rocks below. He collapsed where he lay and began to sob with anguish and disbelief as the downpour came. The creature was gone.

CHAPTER 89

Sam Begay sat in Jack Whorten's office in Albuquerque. He sipped the bitter coffee handed to him a half-hour ago by a secretary in the lobby. It was cold now.

Sam sized up the man behind the desk. He was nondescript, average height and build, facial features as neutral as his brown hair. Most people wouldn't notice him on the street unless they saw his eyes; they were the most piercing grey he'd ever seen.

The man read the preliminary report about the attack at the mine. When Whorten set the file down and looked up, Sam resisted his Navajo upbringing to avert his eyes, and he stared back.

I want to hear it all in your own words now. I'm going to have my secretary write it down and type it for your signature before you go home.

Sam related the story again; about the missing persons and the students from Chaco Canyon held captive. He described the dirigible, the Sparrowhawk fighter planes, and the train. He gave the names of the people involved and the roles they played.

Sam said, "There are a few loose ends: The whereabouts of the spies who escaped on the dirigible with Lisa Abbot as their prisoner, her boyfriend Kip Combs who took a plane and flew after her, and Val Tannin who is presumed missing or dead in Florida."

"What about your Indian friend?" Whorten flipped through the folder, "Dan Yazzie. You said his grandfather and daughter were killed in the same general area by an animal."

"Yes, he's missing too. The agency has information on the incident."

Whorten asked for the report filed by the two agents a month and a half ago and Sam waited for him to read it.

"It says here that a large animal, probably a mountain lion or a bear, attacked them at their cabin north of Crownpoint, mauling them both to death. And you say your friend Dan Yazzie went into the desert to hunt it down and kill it?"

"Well, that's not exactly the whole story," Sam said, fidgeting in his chair. He was becoming more uncomfortable by the minute.

"Oh, how so?"

Sam downed the last of the cold coffee and quickly chewed and swallowed the residue of grounds that came with it.

"It wasn't a mountain lion or a bear that killed them."

"Well it says right here in the report by agents..."

"They're both idiots," Sam said, betraying his frustration by interrupting his superior. "Neither one knows his butt from a bear's nose. There were clues that were misinterpreted and ignored. I wasn't given a chance to add my descriptions of the evidence. Ask them."

"Err, well, it seems that both of the officers are unavailable: one killed in the line of duty recently, and the other on an extended leave. Why don't you just tell me what you saw, and we'll add it to the record."

Now Sam had done it. He had opened his big mouth, and he was going to have to tell the outrageous story to a white man from Washington. Sam closed his eyes and envisioned the events, still clear in his mind.

"First of all, the bodies were chewed and partially eaten."

"I don't see how that differs from the report," Whorten said.

"It would if they had included the evidence of the creature's tracks and the size of the bite marks on the bodies."

"How so?" The man was interested now.

"First, there were no tracks or signs of a mountain lion *or* a bear anywhere in the area. Second, I showed them some large, unidentifiable tracks nearby that they completely ignored. Third, though there wasn't much left of the child's body, the old man's was whole and showed the marks of a crushing bite across his torso. The bite marks were from a jaw nearly eighteen inches long and eight inches wide."

"Well...what do you think made them?"

Here was the question Sam dreaded answering. He spoke slowly and clearly.

"The tracks I found were bird-like, but very large and broad. They were fourteen inches long and about ten inches wide with three long toes and a large spur. By the depth of them, I estimated the weight of the thing to be around 500 pounds. The teeth marks on the old man's chest resembled those of a…crocodile." There, he said it.

Whorten regarded the Indian with his piercing eyes and a frown. He picked up the report and flipped through a few pages.

"I see no mention of that here."

"Exactly," Sam said. "Dan Yazzie, the girl's father, went out to hunt for the creature. He found me some weeks later when some men pushed my truck into a canyon, just after I was shot at by two airplanes and left for dead."

Whorten said, "That's when you first suspected Jim Avery of being in league with the Blacksparrow group. Is that right?"

"Yes. Dan Yazzie took me to his camp, and we were attacked that night by the same creature. It killed one of our horses and dragged away the hindquarters. We found a few partial tracks the next day that resembled those I found at his grandfather's hogan."

"This wasn't in your report about the mine," Whorten scolded.

"No sir, I couldn't see how it tied in with the Blacksparrow events, except for being in the same general area. Maybe it does, I don't know."

Whorten chewed on his lower lip. "Well it sounds to me like another matter entirely. We'll leave your statement about the mine as it stands. If you wish, you can send me your version of the killings at the hogan, and I'll attach it to these records.

After lunch, Sam returned to the FBI office and signed his statement in front of the Acting Chief.

"Officer Begay, I want to thank you for the work you've done and for cooperating with your reports. Keep an eye out for the pilot and the girl. The other man—well, we will just have to see. Perhaps he was a casualty of the storm."

Whorten stood and stuck out his hand. Sam hated this ritual of the white man. He felt the man's assertive grip on his own limp hand. Whorten retracted his arm and acted mildly repelled. Cultural differences, thought Sam.

"Don't forget, we'll have a full hearing on the entire matter as soon as we get all the statements. If you locate any of the others, report to me at once. You're dismissed Officer Begay."

Sam left the building and drove east on Central Avenue to the University of New Mexico campus. He left his vehicle in a no parking zone and walked into the Administration building. A bored secretary sat behind a counter with a tall stack of papers on her desk. She ignored him long enough for him to understand the proper place of students and visitors.

When she finally looked up, she asked in an impatient voice, "Can I help you?" She clearly meant that she would rather not.

"I'm sure you can miss." Sam spoke politely with a broad smile. "I'm Officer Begay, Federal Indian Police. I need to locate someone in your Archeology department; one of your best people I'm told, for some help with an urgent matter."

"Mmm?" The stocky Hispanic girl did not leave her desk.

Sam thought she could be pretty if she just combed her hair, but apparently, she was too busy for that too.

"Just who is it you're looking for?"

"A young Anglo woman named Diana Witherspoon. I understand she is a professor. Would she be available?"

"Let me check."

The girl pulled a thin notebook from the stack on her desk. She found a tab and flipped a few pages.

"Yes, she's here today." She looked at the clock on the far wall. "She doesn't have her next class for two hours."

"Does that mean I can see her or not?"

The secretary regarded him with narrowed eyes, trying to determine if he was being sarcastic. Sam grinned lazily and leaned on the counter.

"That means she is here in her office and is probably preparing for her next class or counseling a student." She said it icily.

"Great," he said, "now could you tell me where I can find her office."

"Down the hall, last door on the right; and you'd better knock first." She turned, dismissing him, and went back to her precarious stack of papers without another word or glance.

Sam knocked on an old varnished door with a pebble glass window. A sign above it said Archeology.

"Yes, come in."

Sam recognized the voice. He opened the door and walked into a warm, cluttered office. There were books on shelves and stacks of them against the walls. On the far wall, a long cabinet with glass doors was full of artifacts and more books.

"Officer Begay," the woman said eagerly.

She stood with a wide smile and stepped around her desk to meet him, offering her hand.

Sam reluctantly clutched it and asked, "Do you have a few moments to talk?"

"Of course." She gestured to a chair. "Can I get you some coffee? I'm afraid it's all I have, and it's probably cold by now."

They both exchanged grins, and Sam declined.

"Miss Witherspoon, I just came here to cover a few things from the statement you gave me, and also to ask a few more questions."

"Sure, sure, ask away."

"First, how are you and your students doing now that you're all back in Albuquerque?"

Diana made a face, and then her expression softened.

"It's a shame, but half of the students left after we returned from Chaco. It's not the kind of experience that most people are prepared to deal with. The other half; they're doing alright I guess."

"And you?"

"Me? I'm okay. Yeah, I'm doing fine. I'm busy, even though I have fewer students now. Within a few semesters we'll have a full class load again."

She turned her head and raised a hand to her eyes before turning back to Sam.

"No word from Val?" he asked, noticing a number of photographs pinned to a large corkboard on the wall to his left.

"No." Her eyes were turning moist again.

Sam's voice became softer. "Diana, Val seemed to be a pretty resourceful guy. I'm sure he's alright. Remember, he said he would be back. I'm expecting him to show up any day, and I need to talk to him. Until he does, I wonder if you could tell me what you know about him."

"Like what?" She sat back and crossed her arms.

"Where did you first meet him?"

"It was at Chaco Canyon, actually east of the valley at Fajada Butte, in a small cave some of my students found. He was camped there, and I was concerned about the wall drawings we found inside."

"Did he say why he was there?"

"No, not that I recall."

Sam saw blood color the girl's face and he wondered what that might mean.

"Did he talk about anything in particular?"

"Yes, it was the oddest thing." She leaned forward. "The drawings were in a small area in the back of the cave, and they were like nothing I've ever seen before. The style was vaguely reminiscent of some of the South American cultures, but also like some of the ancient Mediterranean civilizations too. He seemed to know all about them. He said that they depicted a story that some people in Eastern Europe still tell their children."

"Did he say he was from Eastern Europe?"

"Not exactly; he was kind of vague about that, and he said he'd been at a small university back east before coming to New Mexico. He never did say where. There was one other thing though; he showed me a small crystal globe about two inches in diameter. He said he found it buried in the cave. At first it just looked pitted and dirty, but then I saw that it was a tiny globe of the Earth with all the continents etched on it."

"That sounds odd."

"Yes, especially considering the potential age of the artifact, and what he told me about the children's story from the wall drawings. He said it told of a family that traveled a long distance to a pretty blue planet."

Sam had no idea what to make of that, but he knew his own culture, and many others, had unusual tales about how the creation of the world came about, and how people came to be there. He shrugged the thought aside and thanked her for her time.

"If he should show up here to see you; and I can't see how he could possibly stay away," he grinned, "please have him get in touch with me right away. It's important."

He took her hand and placed his card in it. "Will you promise me you'll do that?"

"Yes of course." She said it with a grateful grin, and wiped at her eyes again. "But the first fifteen minutes, he's all mine, okay?" she giggled conspiratorially.

"Deal," said Sam, grinning broadly. As he stood, he glanced at the photos on the corkboard again.

"May I take a look at those pictures?"

"Sure; they're mostly of Chaco Canyon, but there are a few from other places nearby. My father took most of them."

Sam glanced at the pictures and stopped at the ones that first caught his attention.

"Is this the small mesa north of the mine?"

"Yes."

"Are there any old ruins around there?"

"Not really, just the outline of a small shelter, a fire pit, and some petroglyphs. My father used to spend quite a bit of time there. I'm not sure why, though. He kept a notebook about the things he found, and it had some drawings and maps."

"Do you still have it?"

"No, it was missing after he was found dead from a fall."

"Who found him?" Sam's investigative instincts tuned in.

"Carl Walker, our site foreman. That was before we found out he was involved with the gang at the mine. I think he was the one who killed him. He may have taken the journal."

"Possible," Sam said absently as his eyes stopped on one photo. He felt an itch crawl across his scalp.

"What's this one?"

Diana joined him. "That's one of the petroglyphs dad found."

"What do you think it is?" Sam pointed to the hammered outline of a figure on black lava rock.

"If I had to guess, I'd say it was some ceremonial, costumed figure. It looks like a man walking bent over, wearing a mask and a long tail. The arms look funny too. I don't recognize the deity—some god with big teeth maybe."

"Can I have it?"

When Sam walked past the girl behind the counter, he was grinning even more broadly. He touched the photo in his shirt pocket and waved her a cheerful good-bye.

CHAPTER 90

Sam walked to his new Plymouth truck. It came from the motor pool, and was the same vintage as his other one. He took off his Stetson and sat in the cab, noticing again, the coffee stain on the passenger side. He would see about having it cleaned tomorrow in Gallup.

He was feeling weary from the long day—first the trip to Albuquerque, and then the hours of repeating the details of his statement for the Acting Chief. Whorten wasn't a regular FBI official; he was more of a trouble shooter who reported to higher-ups in the Government. When this whole Blacksparrow thing was over, a new permanent Station Chief would take his place.

It was a long drive back to Gallup, and Sam topped off the gas tank before he left. There was still more work to do at the mine. He wanted to be done with it so he could go out and look for Dan Yazzie.

The next morning, he arrived at the Gallup office late. He noticed Charlie had already been there and gone. The note he left said he was driving to Chinle to look into a suspected murder. The note also said that Kip Combs had phoned from Michigan that morning, and he left a number to reach him.

Sam quickly set his gear down and poured a cup of coffee. He sipped it to test the temperature, made a face, and then carried it to his desk and called the number. It rang three times before an older woman answered and called Kip to the phone.

"Sam, is that you?"

"Yes, I was beginning to think you were dead. Did you catch up with the dirigible? Did you find your girl?

Kip laughed, "Yes to both questions."

"Good. I'm going to need a full statement from both of you when you get back; but before that, tell me briefly what went on."

Kip gave him a sketchy run-down of his chase, capture, and escape with Lisa.

"When will you be coming back to New Mexico? The new Acting FBI Chief wants your formal statements A.S.A.P."

"Well, we're staying here in Bay City with my grandparents for a few days, but we're planning to catch a train back on Thursday. That should put us in Albuquerque early next week some time. Lisa will want to check in with her Uncle Jack first, but we can both come out to Gallup after that. I'll call you when we hit town and make arrangements to meet you. How is everything else going?"

"Too much to cover on the phone, I'm afraid. It can wait. It's good to hear from you and know that you're both safe. I'll see you when you get here."

Sam hung up the receiver. He pulled the picture Diana had given him, from his shirt pocket and tapped the edge on his desk. He thought for a moment, then put it back in his pocket and left the office and drove to Blacksparrow.

CHAPTER 91

The train carrying Kip and Lisa Ann arrived in Albuquerque before noon on Sunday. Lisa called her uncle and arranged for a cab to take them to the airfield. Captain Jack hugged his niece fiercely, and then he helped take her things into the house. He wanted to hear all about their journey.

Kip went to the hanger and retrieved a pile of mail. Dust covered every surface in the office. He looked at the sunlight streaming through the high windows in the back, lighting up the floating dust motes.

In the silence, with the smell of grease and oil triggering memories, he thought of Doo. It just wasn't the same without his buddy griping about something or dropping a wrench.

Kip's thoughts began to depress him, and he opened the windows in the office. He remembered Lisa Ann telling him how Doo had received a telegram and then packed and asked her to take him to the Bus Station. She said he never told her why he was leaving.

Kip brushed the dust off a chair and began sorting through the mail. He found nothing of great importance: a few bills and some advertising. Between two fliers, he found a letter—from Doo! Kip tore the envelope open and pulled out the folded pages.

> *Dear Kip,*
>
> *I am sorry that I had to leave so quickly while you were out of town, but I got a telegram from my father. He said the doctors told him that he had less than a month to live. I know I was always evasive whenever you asked about my family, but I*

can tell you now that I haven't been close to my dad since my mother died two years ago. I guess she was the only thing that the two of us had in common, and without her around, I had no reason to stay. He didn't care anyway. So, that's how I came to be hitchhiking in New Mexico and found you mashing up that first Jenny you used to have. I never regretted pulling you from the plane, even though I messed up my ankle doing it. Our friendship has been worth it.

Anyway, he wrote that there were some things he needed to tell me in person, and that he missed me fierce, so I dropped everything and went. To make a long story short, when I got there, he sat me down and told me about how he struggled to pay for the doctors for mom and how business was bad back then. In the past year, things had changed. His machine shop got some big deals, and he expanded to four times the size. He was pulling in more money now than he ever could spend.

He said that it didn't mean anything to him though, without mom and without me, and that now the doctors told him he would be gone soon. He said he wanted me here to say goodbye and to turn over the shop to me if I wanted it. He said he hoped I did, because it would be the last thing he could ever give me: that, and his love.

I couldn't say no to that, so I left. I hope I didn't cause any problems for you when I did, but I want you to know that I was able to get to know him better in the last month than I ever did when I lived at home. He's gone now, and I've finally got the gumption to write to you and tell you that things are alright here. I have taken over the business and have some good supervisors to help me run it. We have a lot of government contracts and it looks like more coming every day.

I don't know if I'll be coming back to Albuquerque. I guess that's what I wanted to tell you. You've been a great pal, even if you're a real pain in the ass pilot! Ha, ha, but you know that already. So keep the wheels down, and be sure to give Lisa Ann some hugs and kisses for me. She really loves you, you know, even though most of the time you can't tell.

So, it's goodbye for now. Here's my address and phone number in case you want to write or call me sometime. You've been the best buddy I could ever have.

Your friend always,
Doo

CHAPTER 92

It was Monday when Kip and Lisa Ann met Sam at the train station in Gallup. They got in his truck and drove to the Blacksparrow Mine where Sam had a temporary office while he finished the investigation.

He parked his Plymouth in front of Bloundt's old quarters. Kip's Harley stood at the end of the building, covered with dust. Sam noticed him cringe when he saw it, and after he took Lisa and Kip inside, he called to a passing agent to wash the bike and fill the gas tank.

When the three of them took a chair at his desk, Sam wheeled some paper into a black typewriter and started asking questions. He stopped often for clarification as he typed his report.

After an hour, Sam paused to put a third sheet of paper in the machine. "Let's go back to the body you found at the Valle Grande. A pack was found nearby full of gold coins. Do you know anything about that?"

Kip looked uncomfortably at Lisa, and then back a Sam. "Well, I found the bag and saw the gold, and well, there was also some folding money with it. I took it to buy fuel for the plane."

"How much was it?" asked Sam.

"A lot."

"A lot? How much?" repeated Sam.

"A lot." Kip swallowed hard while Sam stared him down. "Over seventy thousand dollars."

Sam stared at Kip.

"But I still have most of it, I had to buy fuel, and then we gave some to the people who helped us. We had to pay for some clothes and transportation…"

"You're dreaming kid. There wasn't room in that bag for anything but the gold. It's a good thing you had some cash on you before you left the mine. Is that clear?" Sam stared at Kip until he nodded.

"That goes for you too, young lady."

Lisa also nodded, and she and Kip exchanged wide-eyed looks.

Sam cleared his throat and said, "Okay, let's finish this up. Are you sure there were no survivors from the sinking of the dirigible?"

"Well, it's hard to be sure. All I can say is that it sank very quickly. The only person we saw outside the ship, besides ourselves, was Bloundt, and we were about 200 feet in the air at the time. He fell when we took off in the plane."

"He fell from 200 feet up? Could someone survive a fall that high into the water?"

Lisa said, "I suppose an experienced cliff diver might do it, but he would risk broken bones and drowning, that is if he survived the fall in the first place."

"Did you see any bodies in the water at all?"

"No, not any."

Kip and Lisa completed the rest of their story up to meeting with Sam today.

When they were finished, it was early afternoon, and Sam told them he had some other work to do before he could take them back into town. He stood and put his typed pages in a folder.

Kip said, "What about Diana and Val; and did Dan ever show up?"

"Diana is back at the university. She's fine. Val hasn't been heard from since he boarded the train. The hurricane wrecked the train down in Florida over Labor Day. Hundreds of people died; I don't know if he was one of them or not. As for Dan; as soon as I can finish up my work here, I'm going to pack a couple of horses and ride into the desert and try to find him."

"Sam, I'll go with you…"

"Thanks Kip, but he's my responsibility. I'll go it alone. There's no more to say about it."

While Sam finished what he had to do, Kip and Lisa went to get something to eat and then go for a hike on top of the mesa.

CHAPTER 93

A soft, dry wind made the afternoon pleasant for hiking. Kip led the way up the mesa on a wide path starting inside the front gates. They easily hiked to the top and were soon hundreds of feet above the desert floor. The air was cooler here.

They stood on a flat spot near the edge as the wind whispered through the stunted junipers growing from the fractures in the rocks. They both breathed deeply as they looked out across the horizon.

Lisa Ann turned and raised her lips for a kiss.

"How about we find someplace we can undress each other," she said.

"Up here in the open?" Kip looked around, pretending modesty. He didn't tell her he'd been thinking of the same thing for an hour.

"You weren't so reluctant back on the beach in Michigan. In fact I remember you tore two buttons off my blouse because you couldn't wait for me to take it off."

"That was a week ago," he said, pushing her hands away from his belt. "I'm just getting my strength back."

"Okay, if you're so frail." She turned to walk away, knowing he wouldn't let her get far.

"Just a minute now, who says I'm frail?" He caught her arm and pulled her back for a long kiss.

The breeze dried their damp skin as they lay naked together "I didn't tell you about getting a letter from Doo," Kip said, tracing the soft curve of her hip and waist and gently cupping the roundness of her breast.

"Hmm?" she murmured as she opened her eyes.

"There was a letter from him in the mail back at the hanger. He said he's doing fine. It seems his father died and left him a factory, and he's doing a lot of government business and making good money. He said he won't be coming back to New Mexico."

"Aww, did he say anything else?" Lisa rolled to her side and propped her head on her arm.

"Well he said I'm a 'pain in the ass pilot,' and he said to tell you 'hi.' Actually, he told me to give you some hugs and kisses."

"Well, I think you've done more than that," she teased.

"The rest of it was my idea."

"It better be," she giggled.

Kip remembered Doo also wrote that he knew Lisa loved him, and Kip smiled because he knew it too.

"We'd better get going," he said. The sun is getting lower and Sam said he would be ready to leave before dusk.

"Can we take a different trail back and have a better look around? It's so pretty up here." she said.

"Sure, we've still got some time."

After they dressed, Kip led the way across the uneven rocks, and they jumped carefully over the cracks in the weathered surface. Halfway back, they stopped for a break near a tall pile of boulders and saw something move from the shadows behind it. They were startled to see a large form step from hiding and stand for a moment before approaching them in a clumsily, threatening manner.

The man was big and dirty. His matted dark hair and beard were filthy, and his clothes torn to shreds. As he came nearer, they could see dark, dried stains on his pants and shirt. His face appeared swollen out of shape, and he slurred as he tried to talk. Kip was shocked when he finally recognized him. "Nicholas!"

Lisa Ann was horrified, but she quickly put on her game face.

"Damn, isn't that just like some men; never there when you need them but always showing up when they're not wanted."

Kip didn't hide the hatred he felt toward his old nemesis. He noticed the revolver stuffed in the man's pants, and he looked around for something to help defend them.

"Combs!" the disheveled creature bellowed. "I'm going to kill you and your bitch; but she's going to go hard. I've cursed the devil to let me live long enough to get back at her for what she did to me."

Nicholas pulled the gun and held it by the barrel. "Oh, don't worry, it isn't loaded, but it'll make a good club to split your skulls with. I'll eat your brains before I die."

He came at them in a stumbling gait, and they could see that something was wrong with one of his legs. Kip pushed Lisa away and stepped forward to draw Nick's attention.

He picked up a twisted branch and jabbed it at the man's face. Nicholas backed away and circled crab-like. When he rushed in and tried to swat the branch aside, Kip could see how bad the man's condition really was. Nicholas, severely hampered by his injuries, was still quick. Kip saw the sweat dripping freely from his swollen face, and he kept wiping at his eyes. He must be half-insane, Kip thought, from fever and infection.

Kip stepped back, picked up a flat rock, and hurled it at the man. Nick dodged and came at Kip with his head low. When Kip stepped to the side, he caught his heel on a rock and fell. Nicholas was on him in an instant. Kip gripped his thick wrists while the animal stench and fetid breath of the man made him want to gag. Nicholas bared his dirty teeth and tried to snap at Kip's throat.

The next instant, there was the sound of a solid *wonk*, and the big man's head jerked sideways. Kip rolled away and saw Lisa holding a stout piece of wood like a club. He yelled, "Run back to the compound, I'll slow him down!"

"Nothing doing hero, either we both go, or I'm staying here with you."

"Fine," he said, and quickly grabbed her hand. They both ran across the rocks.

Nicholas staggered to his feet and growled like an enraged animal. He shook his head to clear his senses, and with an incoherent howl, he began to lope drunkenly after them.

Kip glanced back to see Nick keeping pace. He was catching up by increments as he took shortcuts over the rocks. Apparently, his unsteady gait was not a hindrance to him covering ground. As Nick worked his way closer, Kip feared that if he or Lisa fell, the man would be upon them.

He saw a wide gap in the rocks ahead—a long opening about eight feet across.

"Lisa, we've got to make this jump."

The two of them sprinted toward the crevice, and Nicholas bayed like a rabid animal as he saw the two of them leap and fall to ground on the other side. Nick was approaching the crevice now, mouthing his rage as he took to the air.

Kip and Lisa drew back in horror as a large, swift shape erupted from the chasm and snatched the big man's body. Nicholas came to an abrupt halt in mid-leap as huge jaws clamped onto his loins. He screamed horribly as the thing bit down and crushed his pelvis. With the sound of splintering bones, the creature made mewling noises as it viciously shook the bloody body. It clawed savagely with long talons, tearing the man's clothing and skin to shreds. The sound of Nicholas' screams were cut short.

Kip and Lisa were terrified. He recognized the creature as the same one he and Dan Yazzie saw near the river on Mt. Taylor. They slowly backed away and were ready to run when the beast turned its gore-covered head and looked at them.

It seemed to lose interest in the shredded body, and it tilted its head as if recognizing something. It stared directly at Kip, and lifted its head and screamed like a demon.

Kip pushed Lisa behind him and said, "If it moves to attack, run as fast as you can and get help."

"No Kip, I…"

"Lisa, just do it!"

Ye'iitsoh looked at Kip, and without taking its eyes from him, it attempted to leap and crawl from the chasm. It couldn't jump high enough, and Kip noticed that one of its forelimbs was broken and useless.

He glanced around looking for a large rock to throw, thinking only of buying some time for Lisa to get away. He could hear running behind him, and then a surprised female yelp. Kip took his eyes from monster for a second and saw a near-naked man run past him toward the beast.

Ye'iitsoh now became insanely enraged, and it succeeded in reaching the top of the crevice. It screamed horribly as a tall, ragged man ran directly up to it holding a long spear. Kip couldn't believe his eyes; it was Dan Yazzie.

Kip lifted a heavy rock, and as Dan's spear jabbed at the creature's eyes, Kip threw the projectile at the beast and heard the snap of broken bone.

Roars of anger and pain came from the monster as Dan stabbed repeatedly. The sharp spear drew more and more blood from Ye'iitsoh, and the beast soon slipped back into the crevice. Kip found another heavy rock and hurled it at its skull. He heard a satisfying *crunch*. After he found and threw a third rock, he stopped to catch his breath and watched as Dan cut out the last flicker of life from the creature.

"Dan?" he said, trying to catch his breath. "Dan, how did you find us?"

Dan was also out of breath. He dropped his spear and fell to the ground, panting. Lisa Ann was stunned as she watched from a few yards away.

"How did I find you?" he said between gasps for air. "Who said I was looking for you?" He smiled briefly. "I tracked this damn thing all over the desert to find you taking it on all by yourself. We're the 'Hero Twins' remember? I told you it would take the two of us to kill it."

"Jeez, you're both big, damn hero's as far as this girl's concerned. Who is this guy, Kip?"

"Lisa," Kip said, still catching his breath, "I want you to meet Dan Yazzie; the orneriest, bull headed, craziest, Indian friend a man ever had. Dan, this is Lisa Ann. You'll have to pardon her shy ways and sweet talk; she's my girl."

"Pleased to meet you," Dan said, still gasping. He looked at Kip, "I could tell she was a girl because she looks so much better than you do."

CHAPTER 94

Sam Begay brought his FBI team to the top of the mesa. They wrapped the pieces of Nicholas' body in a tarp and took it down to the compound. They gave more attention to the creature's body lying in the crevice. They retrieved it with difficulty, because of its size and weight, and placed it on ice as quickly as possible. Sam called Jack Whorten who insisted that he keep everyone away from the animal's carcass from this point on.

"I'll bring out a team of specialists tomorrow," Whorten said. "How are you doing on the statements?"

I just finished up with the girl and the pilot, and I have Dan Yazzie here now. I'll have his done by the end of the day."

"Good, keep everyone at the mine until I get there. I'll be out in the morning to debrief everyone."

Sam hung up the phone and shook his head; nothing made sense anymore. From the very start, this whole thing had been one crazy turn after another. He walked outside and looked for Dan. He found him talking to Kip and Lisa outside one of the hangers. Sam caught part of their conversation as he walked up.

Kip said, "I think it's pretty ironic that Nick the biter ended up getting bit back, don't you? Oh, I hated that jerk! The way he died almost makes up for all the grief he's caused."

"Nothing ironic about it," Sam said, "it was just poetic justice. I've seen it time and time again. You see, a criminal unbalances himself by his actions. This causes other forces to compensate and bring it back to him."

Kip said, "You mean like some kind of spiritual thing?"

Sam thought for a moment, "No, more like a rubber band."

He looked at Dan. "Do you feel up to giving me your statement now? The Acting Chief is driving out tomorrow morning, and he wants everyone to stay here until he gets a chance to talk to you. I'm sorry, but you'll all have to stay the night."

As Sam took Dan back to the office, he remarked about the ragged condition of his clothes.

"We'd better get you a new shirt and a pair pants and some boots. The stuff you're wearing looks like it's ready to fall off you."

Dan gave him a detailed accounting of the days he'd spent tracking Ye'iitsoh. Sam typed as he listened to his telling of Kip's rescue after the planes from the mine had shot him down; it matched the statement Kip had already given.

His story of shooting dynamite at the beast was also the same, but Sam wanted to hear the rest of the story, after the two men parted, and Dan continued his pursuit of the creature.

Dan Yazzie told a tale that sounded almost mystical. He described the old Indian and the dog, and he explained how he knew they were spirits and not real beings. He told of how he tracked the beast to a cave and escaped through an underground grotto. He showed Sam the partially healed wound on his arm from the slash of the monster's claw, and he told him how the old man had the same scar on his arm. He voiced his suspicions that the old man might be a spirit form of himself, only older.

As Dan continued, Sam was impressed by the trap he'd set to kill Ye'iitsoh. He knew of the natural arch and the needle of rock, and he was astounded that the creature had survived the fall.

"I finally tracked it here and spent hours trying to find out where it was holed up. The rest you know. Kip and I killed it together just like the Hero Twins. He is a brave man, and we are brothers now."

When Dan was finished, Sam sat back in his chair and took a deep breath. He was proud of what his friend had done. The man was truly a warrior.

After Dan left, Sam finished typing his statement. He put the papers away and decided that Dan was strong enough now to make something good of the rest of his life.

CHAPTER 95

Sam splashed water in his face and went to meet the others at breakfast. He didn't sleep well because he kept thinking about Dan's statement. After reading the account several times, he feared Whorten would think the Indian was delusional. The part about the spirits of the old man and the dog would be hard for a white man like him to understand. Fortunately, the body of the creature was here, packed in ice, or he wouldn't believe anything about Ye'iitsoh either.

The agency men were almost done sanitizing the area when Whorten arrived by car. Sam introduced him to the others.

Jack Whorten read the statements. He took his time to taste the words and gain as much insight as possible into the person giving the information, as well as the officer putting it on paper. When he finished, he pulled a cigar from his pocket and lit it with a kitchen match.

"Do you have anything else you want to add, Sam?"

"No sir, I took the information down just as it was given."

Whorten moved the cigar from one corner of his mouth to the other as he chewed on his thoughts.

"You know we'll have to bury all of this, don't you? It's for the good of the country."

Sam nodded, "Sure, but there are a lot of people who've been badly hurt."

"Right, right, I'll have the new Station Chief attend to that. He'll be on the job Monday, his name's Decker. I don't know the guy, but they say he's a company man. I'll leave him a note with my recommendations. I wouldn't be surprised if you get a commendation for this. Good work from what I can see. It'll show the water cooler types than the Indian Officers are sharp and capable. Oh, any word on this guy, Val Tannin?"

"No, I spoke to the Witherspoon woman the day I saw you. I told her to contact me when he shows up."

"You mean *if* he shows up?"

"Nope, there's something about him that tells me he's pretty resourceful. I don't believe he'd let himself be taken out by a hurricane."

Whorten chuckled, "Well maybe not. Let's see your friends again and convince them that the quicker they develop amnesia about all of this, the better off they'll be. Sort of put the fear of the almighty Government into them, eh?"

Jack Whorten smiled, but Sam saw only the capable man he was; they were the same qualities he saw in Val Tannin. The men were two of a kind.

Whorten gave his speech to everyone, swearing them to secrecy. Soon after, a small convoy of vans showed up to take possession of the large carcass for further study by top scientists.

"You can tell your friends that they can go now. Tell them their Government thanks them and appreciates their silence in the matter."

He stuck out his hand. Sam gripped it loosely and let the man pump his arm.

"You're a good man Begay. If you ever need anything, or if you think of doing something else besides police work, look me up. Here's my card, and Sam, work on that hand shake. You've got to show people that they need to take you seriously."

Everyone watched Whorten's car leave ahead of the vans. While the others were preparing to go, Sam took Dan aside. His friend was truly alone now. His family was dead, and the creature responsible, also dead by his own hand. What did he have left?

"You did a brave thing Dan. You make your clan proud." Sam let out his breath, not knowing what else to say. "I'll be here if you need me."

As he said it, Sam realized how hollow the words sounded. He had no idea what Dan needed.

Dan Yazzie nodded. "I've been thinking for some time about what to do with myself; even before I fought the monster. Now that he's dead, what do I fight? What can I do that has some meaning?"

Sam understood completely.

Dan continued, "I think I will go away to where I can be alone. When I find that place, I will make a medicine bag and spread out my blanket. I will call to the Great Spirit and tell him he can have me. If he chooses to take me, I will be with my family again. If he chooses to talk instead, maybe he will tell me what to do."

"I'll give you a horse and rifle and some provisions."

Dan nodded his thanks.

"When you find out what you're going to do, come back and see me. Maybe I need some advice to help me find the same answers for myself."

CHAPTER 96

The Saturday morning breeze carried the smell of flowers and the twitter of songbirds across the University of New Mexico campus. Diana Witherspoon walked up the sidewalk through the doors of the Administration building. She strode past the front offices and down the hall to her room and set her papers on her desk.

She remembered what Sam Begay had said about being sure Val would come back; but she feared the opposite. She felt as if her life had become unraveled. Val had left when he should have stayed with her. She also carried a burden in her heart of the experiences she and her students had encountered at the mine. None had lost their lives, but she doubted the emotional scars would ever heal completely.

She sat down, and as she gazed absently out the window thinking of Val, the sound of footsteps coming down the hall interrupted her daydreaming. It was a man's step. Her heart lifted and her eyes turned to the open door. If she could only hope...

Jeffrey Taylor, the Assistant Dean, walked into the room with a stern look on his face. "Dean Thomas will see you in his office now."

Diana's shoulders sagged with disappointment. She stood and followed Jeffrey down the hall.

"Miss Witherspoon, please take a seat. That will be all Jeffrey. Thank you for coming in today Diana. Would you like some water?"

She shook her head and whispered, "No."

Dean Thomas, a tall man with a receding hairline, cleared his throat and got right to the point.

"I have met with the board concerning the unfortunate incidents involving the students at Chaco Canyon. The overwhelming opinion is that you failed, in your mentorship capacity, to keep the young men and women safe on the University's field project. I must say, some of the parents were so outraged it was all we could do to convince them not to sue the institution."

Diana was astonished to hear the Dean's words.

"The men held us up with guns! What could I have done? They threatened to kill us if we resisted!"

Dean Thomas raised his hand to halt her passionate outburst. "That being said, we do know that your inexperience with such matters is partly to blame. Now, now, let me finish. Your father was a good friend of mine. He was instrumental in building our Archeology department and none can deny the efforts and sacrifices he made for this University."

The man paused to let his words sink in.

"That is why we are not formally censuring you. However, saying that, we cannot allow you to continue as the head of the department. Mr. Sommes will take over your position when classes begin on Monday. I know that there are some important things that need to be completed at the Chaco site, and I'm sure Mr. Sommes would prefer to take over your position here without your presence to confuse the students."

The man drew a deep breath before finishing. "If you wish to continue employment with this University, Miss Witherspoon, you will make plans to be on site at the Chaco dig by the middle of the week. You will report directly to Sommes from this point on. Do you have any questions?"

Diana was numb; the blood drained from her face, and she felt cold sweat on her hands. She tried to speak, but her mouth was too dry.

She finally managed to croak out, "What about provisions; communication?"

"The department will have a staff person meet with you on Monday to arrange for all that. A courier will take you to Chaco and will bring your supplies and any ongoing communications every two weeks. Are there any other questions?"

"No, I guess not," she said, heartbroken.

"Diana," the Dean's voice was softer now, "your father was my friend. I miss him. You have a chance now to continue his work, and yours, without any distractions. You should consider using this opportunity to make your discoveries speak for you. You can make something good come from this."

Diana looked at him and nodded vaguely and left.

CHAPTER 97

Sam Begay met Charlie Redman Monday morning at their office in Gallup. The noise from a train a few blocks away made the air pulse with its heavy, coal-fired breath. The tracks cut the town of Gallup in half, and Sam felt his own life separated in the same way by the summer's events.

He had been thinking about what Jack Whorten had said. "Good work from what I can see. I wouldn't be surprised if you get a commendation for this. I'll leave a note with my recommendations."

Sam always took pride in his work, and he wanted recognition for it. He wanted to prove something to himself, to his people, to everyone. Isn't something done well its own reward? No, that was not enough; he wanted to prove something to the other agents in Albuquerque. He wanted to show them that a Federal Indian Officer is no more, and no less, than any other Federal Officer.

The new Station Chief would be at his desk this week. He would take some time to get to know his men there first. He would read their records and perhaps have a personal conversation with each of them. He would probably get around to calling Charlie later in the week before talking to Sam. Even though the young half-breed was just a junior officer, he was still regular FBI, rather than the offshoot Federal Indian Officer that Sam was.

The week came and went. Charlie was in charge of closing up the Blacksparrow Mine. He returned to his office duties on Wednesday, but as far as Sam knew, no call came for him either.

There were reports to complete, and by the time Friday was nearly gone, he spoke to Charlie.

"Our new Director must be busy with things in the city. I expected him to call this week."

"Oh, he did," Charlie said, and then understood why Sam had asked. "He called me Thursday while you were at lunch. Didn't you get a call?"

"No."

"Well, I'm sure he just got sidetracked. He'll probably call Monday."

"What did he say to you?"

Charlie thought for a moment, "He said I did a good job and gave me the usual; 'we're proud to have you,' talk."

"Didn't he mention me at all?"

"No, I thought he would call you with the same kind of rah, rah."

Sam considered this as he put his things away in his desk and got up to leave.

"He'll probably call Monday, like you said."

Next week came, and Charlie was starting to feel uncomfortable. Sam became more irritable as each day passed. There was still no call from the new Chief.

Finally, on Friday afternoon, Charlie answered the phone and turned smiling to Sam, "It's for you; it's Chief Decker."

"Officer Begay," Sam answered, clearing his throat first.

"Officer Begay, this is Thaddeus Decker in Albuquerque. I understand you were the Indian Officer on the Blacksparrow case. I wanted to make sure I had all the background before I called you."

Sam decided he could understand that. There were many offshoots to the investigation. He listened as Decker continued.

"I also have a note about you from the Temporary Acting Chief. Frankly, when I got all the reports checked out, I have to say it was a good thing Agent Redman was there to keep the Bureau's nose clean."

Sam's face dropped so noticeably that Charlie's own expression changed from relief to concern.

"Nose clean, sir?"

"Yes, and I know all about the people you were working with, too."

"I don't understand."

"Look here Begay; first you got involved with an Indian ex-con, and then you got tied up with some rogue pilot who was drummed out of the Navy. And his girlfriend, she was once a prostitute! Oh, the other girl, the archeologist from the university, it says here, she was disciplined and relieved of her teaching duties."

"But sir…"

"Don't 'but sir' me Begay. The last one just takes the cake. This guy named Val Tannin who disappeared and can't be found. It seems no one has ever heard of him before. He was probably working for the other side all the time, and you helped him escape. You did all of this without any authorization from former Director Avery. There wasn't a single note on file approving your actions. What do you have to say for yourself, Begay?"

Sam face was as red as a chili pepper. Charlie watched with horror as his friend's puzzled expression turned to fierce anger. Sam slammed the phone down, and without speaking, put his hat on and walked out the door. Charlie got up and started to go after him, but stopped when the phone began to ring.

CHAPTER 98

In a comfortable, dimly lit office in Washington, Jack Whorten laid a file on the desk of another nondescript man. Their appearances were similar, except for the thinning, dark hair and heavier look of the man behind the desk.

"Jack, you said you had some news?"

"Yes, take a look at the file. You'll find bio's on some people I ran across who we may be able to use."

"Well, you know we're always looking for new talent; attrition being what it is in our rarefied business. Just give me the highlights for now, would you."

"Very well, we have a young man that can fly a plane, and he's pretty good at taking care of himself. He seems to have a knack for survivability."

The thin-haired man nodded his head, "Go on."

"He's got a girlfriend, and she's as cool headed and dangerous as they come. She's street-wise, afraid of nothing, and scrappy as hell."

"Next, is a capable Indian lawman who wants to do the right thing. He's the kind of man you can count on to get something done. He's smart, tenacious, and very pissed off at the FBI."

"The last one is another Indian. He's an ex-con, and he thinks he sees and talks to the spirits."

"Hmm? And why him?"

"Well for starters, he took on a 500 pound dinosaur that had teeth as long as your fingers; and he did it with just a club and a knife—and he survived."

"That sounds promising." The man shifted in his big leather chair. "Tell me more about the Indian Officer who's pissed off at the FBI."

Jack told him.

"And you say this new Station Chief, Thaddeus Decker, dressed him down, and questioned his professionalism? I heard Decker was a pencil pushing piss ant, but not a complete idiot."

The man behind the desk appeared thoughtful. "I take it you have a reason for bringing all this up right now?"

"Yes," admitted Whorten. "Sam Begay is angry enough to leave the Bureau and create a big stink. He's mad, and he's got the balls and brains to back it up."

"Well, we can't have him doing a thing like that and still be a potential resource for us. Come Jack, you've handled worse before; you must have a reason to bring all of this to my attention."

Jack smiled and crossed his legs, getting more comfortable. "Of course I do. I talked to him on the phone this afternoon. He wants something. He'll forget Decker's crap if I give him title to the Blacksparrow Mine. He wants it all; lock, stock, and barrel."

"Then give it to him. Oh, and make sure Decker knows that I am concerned about his lack of finesse in dealing with a seasoned Federal Indian Officer. Jack, why do I feel you had a hand in this little row taking place?"

Jack smiled hugely, "Well, I learned from the best, sir."

The man behind the desk, smirked, and adjusted himself in his chair. He frowned at the wheel chair standing to his side.

"See to it that the title to the mine is deeded over to Begay. After all, it's only the taxpayer's money. You know what I always say."

"Yes sir, 'If it can be solved with money, then it isn't a problem.' "

CHAPTER 99

The clang of a dropped wrench followed by a faint, "Damn it," broke the silence of the afternoon inside Kip's hanger at Mathews Airfield. Kip Combs was nearing the end of his well-known, short supply of patience. He lay on his back on a bench under the nose of a small plane; arms inside the cowling. He dropped his wrench again. It bounced off the edge of the bench and hit the floor with another *clang-itty-clang.*

"Damn," he hissed in frustration.

"Well what do you want me to do?" Lisa Ann said, betraying her own stress and frustration. She was trying to help Kip, but everything she did was wrong.

"Here," Kip said, "come up here. Now lean over me and reach up by my hand. Hold the wrench steady while I get the pliers up there. No, move your hand over there, now get back so I can see what I'm..."

Clang-clang-ata-clang-clang went the wrench and the pliers.

"I'm sorry," Lisa said, "I tried to hold it, but you pinched me with the pliers and it slipped."

"Oh for crying out loud. Okay, get off me; let me see if I can do it by myself."

Lisa crawled back down to the floor, "Look, I know I'm not Doo, but he isn't here, and I am, and I want to help."

"Oh yeah? Well Doo wouldn't get his tits in my face and nearly smother me."

"*Oh yeah?* Well you like it, and you know it." She said it with some heat.

"Pffftt!" Kip made a dismissive noise.

327

"If that's how you feel, then I'm going back to Uncle Jack's office."

"Aww c'mon Lisa," Kip crawled off the bench as she walked away. "I'm sorry."

Lisa stopped at the front of the hanger and looked back with a frown. She reached to her waist and lifted her blouse; she wore nothing underneath.

"They're called BOOBS, not TITS, and this is to show you what you're going to be missing from now on."

"What?" Kip said. "Why you little..."

He jumped away from the bench and started walking toward her.

Lisa let out a squeal and ran. She got halfway to the office and darted behind a shed.

When Kip found her, she was leaning against the wall, waiting for him with her blouse unbuttoned.

"What took you sailor?" she smiled.

CHAPTER 100

Carl Walker slouched in his chair in a log cabin at the end of a two-track deep in the woods of northeastern Maine. His disposition mirrored the weather. The October afternoon came with an icy, drizzling rain, and the sky took on the dull grey color of an old aluminum pot. He was working on the last of a fifth of cheap gin. The trees bobbed and sagged from the wind and rain, and a dead branch rattled sporadically against the side of the cabin.

He'd used the last of his money on another month's worth of groceries, and he hoped to get word soon from his contact that he could head back to Germany. He'd been drinking heavily for a month, and he grudgingly realized that his supply of gin would run out sooner than the food would.

He coughed from a cold that he couldn't seem to shake and never heard the man at the back door until it was kicked open. Carl jumped, reaching for his gun, and a voice threatened to blow his head off if he moved again. The voice was chillingly familiar. Carl looked to confirm his suspicion.

"Yes Carl, it's me."

"Bloundt?" he said, not believing his eyes.

"Ah, ever the resourceful Carl; nothing gets past your notice, does it? At least my little hoard of silver and turquoise jewelry didn't."

Carl sobered fast and gauged his chances of turning the tables on the man.

"It's all gone. This gin and some food is all I have left."

"No matter, I didn't come here to kill you. I'll even put my gun away if you promise to listen to what I have to say."

"Sure, let's talk," Carl agreed, still cautious.

Bloundt sat down at the small kitchen table and took off his hat. He wiped a hand over his damp face.

"The mission was a failure," he said.

"A failure, how could that be?"

"The dirigible is on the bottom of Lake Michigan, sabotaged by that same damn pilot you brought over from Chaco. The train reached Florida, but it was derailed by a hurricane and never made it to the docks."

"Phew," Carl whistled. "Did you lose that fancy aircraft of yours too?"

"Yes dammit! It's all gone, and we'll be dead if we show our faces in Germany." He dragged a hand through his hair. "It's all over."

After a moment, Carl said, "Do you want some gin?"

Bloundt nodded. Carl got up and retrieved another bottle and a glass from the cupboard. Bloundt tossed down half of his drink and exhaled noisily through his teeth.

"I don't know what to do," he said. "Oh, at first, all I wanted to do was to kill you and make my way back home. However, as I heard the news from Florida, I realized that going home would mean certain death. I started making contact with some of our safe houses and finally ran across your trail. I thought we might put our heads together and figure out some kind of solution to our problem."

Carl considered the man's words as he swallowed the last of his drink. He refilled both glasses.

"Perhaps we could come up with a new mission plan," suggested Bloundt.

"A new mission?" Carl put the bottle down as a shrewd look crossed his face. What was there left to do if he couldn't go back in Germany?

Carl sat down at the table across from his old nemesis and tipped his glass back. When he set it down, he cleared his throat and said, "I might have a couple of ideas. I have an old journal we could try to decipher."

CHAPTER 101

Diana Witherspoon returned to her camp at the eastern side of the small mesa. Grateful for the warmth of the rising sun, she lit the camp stove and positioned the pot of coffee on the burner.

She had gotten up earlier and took a walk in the chill of the new day; the jays scolding her as the wind brought the first hint of the changing season.

She realized that Dean Thomas had been right; getting out in the field alone without distractions was proving to have the same effect on her as a healing elixir. Already the events of the past months were beginning to fade from her mind.

She'd come here two weeks ago with thoughts of trying to discover what had interested her father so much about this place. Other than the university courier, she'd seen only one other person; that was Sam Begay. He had come to her camp on horseback one day and told her some unusual news. He said he had quit law enforcement, and he managed to take over the ownership of the Blacksparrow Mine. He told her that it encompassed the surrounding area, including the small mesa, and he said he wanted to find some good purpose for the facility.

Sam told her not to worry about trespassing; she was free to explore the area as she pleased. He said he was taking up residence in the old compound, and he invited her to visit whenever she felt the need to talk to another human being. He even brought her a horse to use as long as she was out here. A nice man, she thought. She was grateful to have him for a friend.

When he'd asked if she'd heard from Val, she could only shake her head no.

Diana didn't want to dwell on the bad experiences anymore; instead, she wanted to find some new mystery, some new discovery to occupy her mind. She sighed; it was time to put Val's memory behind her. She went to her tent to change her shirt before making breakfast, and as she fumbled through a suitcase, she noticed something on the edge of the small table next to her cot. It was round, smaller than a baseball, and…it was the crystal globe from the Fajada Cave!

Diana ran from the tent and looked frantically about, and then she heard Val Tannin's voice behind her.

"Diana."

She ran into his arms, nearly smothering him with her kisses. Then she began to cry and tried to push away. She hit his chest with her fists, but he held her tightly.

"I'm sorry Diana, I'm sorry," he said, as she shook with tears.

From a distance away, Sam Begay watched the couple embrace. After a moment, he flicked his reins and rode back to the mine. He would come back tomorrow. There would be plenty of time then to talk to Val.

As he picked his way back, he thought of the questions he wanted to ask the man.

He wanted to ask what he knew about the unusual aircraft Kip had described nestled in the hold of the dirigible. He wanted to hear what he could tell him about the creature that the government scientists had taken to study.

And then, he wanted to ask him what secrets were still hidden in the small mesa.

—but that's another story.

ABOUT THE AUTHOR

Thomas Alan Ebelt is a retired banker and member of Mid-Michigan Writers Inc. While living in in New Mexico for several years, he became enchanted by the ancient Pueblo cultures of the region and uses those images as backdrop for his mystery writing. He lives with his wife in West Branch, Michigan.